Martine Oborne lives in North London. She has spent most of her working life in the City where she was a director of Rothschilds. She has two daughters and two sons.

Also by Martine Oborne:

Mother Love

Children's Books

Princess Lullaby & the Magic Word
Juice the Pig
I Love You More

baby love

Martine Oborne

PIATKUS

For more information on other books
published by Piatkus, visit our website at
www.piatkus.co.uk

Copyright © 2001 by Martine Oborne

First published in Great Britain in 2001 by
Judy Piatkus (Publishers) Ltd of
5 Windmill Street, London W1T 2JA
email: info@piatkus.co.uk

The moral right of the author has been asserted

A catalogue record for this book is available from the British Library

ISBN 0 7499 3235 X

Typeset in Palatino by Palimpsest Book Production Limited,
Polmont, Stirlingshire

Printed and bound in Great Britain by
Mackays of Chatham plc, Chatham, Kent

To Catherine, George,
William and Matilda

'Madre Santissima. Madre Santissima, protegeme.'

The time had nearly come. Dolores clenched her fists and prayed and knew that she would soon need to wake her mother.

Dolores' mother had once been a big woman but, since the death of her husband, she seemed to have shrunk and was now hardly bigger than Dolores herself. Between the two women slept Dolores' three sisters – Lola, who was eight, Pilar, five, and little Carmencita, who was only two. In the other bed slept the boys – thirteen year old Juan, and Jorge, who was ten. The boys both had school the next day, thought Dolores, so they needed their sleep.

'Madre Santissima, Madre Santissima.'

Dolores shuddered as the pain racked her young bones. Her mother had always joked that she had called her first child Dolores, the Spanish word for suffering, because her labour had been so bad. It seemed that Dolores would now suffer in the same way too.

'Mama, Mama,' Dolores whispered in the darkness. There was no reply, just the heavy rhythm of sleep all around.

Dolores rolled off the side of the bed and got down on all fours like an animal. It was easier that way when the pain was bad.

If only she had never set eyes on Mario, she thought. Her mother had warned her to be careful but now it was too late.

This time last year, she had had it all. She had left school and immediately got a job working for a young couple in San Isidro, one of the wealthiest districts in Lima. Andres and Mercedes Campana had been newly married and were both working in the city. Dolores' job as their maid was a breeze. She just had to look after the house, do the cleaning and cook in the evenings. There was lots of time to spare. Perhaps that was why it had all been so easy to fall for Mario, a driver who worked for a family in the apartment block next door. Dolores shuddered as she thought back to those illicit afternoons. She and Mario had made love in every room of the Campanas' apartment – once even in her employers' bed.

She had been paid a good salary for her age, over US$100 per month. Mercedes always made sure there was plenty of food in the apartment and it was good to eat well. One day soon, thought Dolores, Mercedes would be having her baby and Dolores had hoped to help her look after the child.

But now she would be looking after her own child. She had lost the job. It was understandable that her employers would not want a maid with a baby. Why should they? There were plenty of other women, better women, ready to step into her shoes.

2

And now she would soon have no shoes and her brothers and sisters would continue to have no shoes. Her mother would go on doing her cleaning job at the Museo Larco Herrera and the boys had to carry on at school. Lola would, of course, no longer have to look after Pilar and Carmencita all day; Dolores could do that. But, without Dolores' income and with yet another mouth to feed, Lola would have to find some work. She would join the *ambulantes*, selling torches, magazines, fruit – whatever there was – at the side of the road, scrounging leftovers from people leaving smart restaurants after lunch and dinner. Her sister would be little more than a beggar.

'*Madre Santissima,*' Dolores cried out as the pain came again. This time her mother heard her cry and, although it was too dark to see a thing, Dolores felt the reassuring movement of her mother as she rolled across the bed to reach her.

The angry words had now been spoken. Times had been hard since Dolores' father had been killed and the family had moved down from the mountains into the *barriadas*. Dolores knew how pleased her mother had been when she had found the job with the Campanas and how disappointed she was when Dolores told her about the baby. She had called her selfish and a whore and worse. But now, Dolores felt only the warmth of her mother's arms around her and her voice, soft and calm.

'*Coraje, mi chiquita. Coraje.*'

They could not afford to pay a midwife, of course, but Dolores' mother knew what to do. Not only had she had six children herself but she had helped with the delivery of many other babies. Dolores knew that she could not be in safer hands.

'*Madre Santissima, Madre Santissima.*'

The two women prayed on through the night and until the child was born.

Chapter One

Thousands of miles away, on the other side of the globe, a phone began to ring. It rang so long that it entered Richard's dream and became the striking of a gong, the gong his father had used to summon the family to dinner. The gong that he and his brothers had hated but now, of course, it would sound no more, thought Richard, as he picked up the phone.

'Hello,' he croaked, as he struggled back to consciousness. He squinted at his watch. It was four a.m.

'Hello darling,' he heard his wife's bright, familiar voice. 'Sorry to wake you up but I've just had the most amazing dream and simply had to tell you about it.'

It was Caroline, of course, thought Richard. It had to be Caroline and, although he had had less than three hours' sleep, Richard could not help smiling warmly when he heard her speak.

'A dream?' he said. 'You've woken me up just to tell me a dream? Can't it wait until later?' Richard heaved himself up onto one elbow and switched on the light. Caroline had been away less than twenty-four hours but already the house looked a tip. He really missed her when she went away and not just for her housekeeping skills.

Richard's clothes were piled together on the floor with his laptop, briefcase and papers dumped on top of them. He had been modelling Centro Utilities' bid for a water supply and sewerage concession in Eastern Europe and the work had taken much longer than he had hoped. By the time he had finished, he was too exhausted to tidy up. He would have to wear another suit in the morning.

'Oh sorry, darling,' said Caroline. 'But, well, it's really important. I couldn't wait to tell you about it.'

Richard yawned and rubbed his eyes. 'Really,' he said wryly. It must be about seven a.m. in Mombasa, he calculated, and Caroline would just be getting up. She had obviously just called for a chat.

'Well, when I explain everything, you'll understand,' said Caroline. 'But, first, you must promise to meet my flight when it arrives at Heathrow this afternoon. It's really urgent.'

'Meet you?' Richard laughed and ran his hand through his thick black hair. 'You know, darling, I'd really love to but it's impossible. Tazz is flying to Jo'burg today to check out that shit plant we're thinking of bidding for. I've promised to hold the fort at the office.'

'I'm sorry, darling,' said Caroline. 'But, please meet me. I really need you and no one else will do.'

'I really need you too,' said Richard, closing his eyes and resting his head back on the pillow. 'And no one else will do.'

Caroline laughed. 'Exactly,' she said. 'But you don't understand – *I can't wait*.'

'Let's do it by phone then,' said Richard, sinking further below the blankets. 'Tell me what you're wearing.'

'Oh, if only you were here now,' continued Caroline. 'You see, I just did that traffic light thing and it's gone green – I seem to have had the most enormous LH surge during the night.'

Richard frowned and then realised what she was talking about. 'Really?'

'Yes,' cried Caroline. 'The green line was very strong and so, you see, we really need to get together as soon as possible. Any more than twelve hours and it might be too late.'

Richard sat up again. He remembered Caroline showing him this urine-testing kit she had bought which was supposed to tell them precisely when she was ovulating.

'Fantastic,' he said. 'But are you sure we can't wait a bit longer? I mean, until the moment you get in the door – I can be ready and waiting.'

'No, I'm absolutely certain,' said Caroline. 'I've read the instruction leaflet three times. And the line is definitely green. You know, I'm a bit colour blind and I kept holding it under different lights and wondering if I wasn't seeing things. But I got the room-service girl to check. She speaks quite good English and she said that it was "green as the grasses". And then she asked me if I wanted to see a doctor.'

'She must have thought you were crazy,' laughed Richard.

'Yes. I said I hoped very much to see a doctor – but only after I'd been shagged stupid by my husband.'

'Caroline!'

'I don't think her English was *that* good.'

'So where does the dream come in?' asked Richard.

'Oh the dream! I nearly forgot,' cried Caroline. 'It's the dream I really wanted to tell you about. The dream makes me feel certain that this is the month.'

'Tell me about it,' said Richard. He was now wide awake and scrabbling about for a cigarette. Since Caroline had given up smoking over a year ago, he only smoked when she was not around.

'Well, I dreamt that I was pregnant . . .' said Caroline. Richard lit his cigarette, lay back on the pillow and slowly exhaled as his wife began to describe her dream. It sounded quite erotic, he thought, and he was glad that it was only twelve hours before he would hold Caroline again in his arms. Tazz need never even find out; his boss had a lunch out of the office and would be going straight to the airport after that. Richard's colleague, Jeremiah, had only just joined them from Wharton but a Master of Business Administration could surely cope with taking telephone messages for a few hours, thought Richard, and he could take his mobile with him.

'OK. I'll meet you,' he said, picking up a pen from the bedside table when Caroline had finished speaking. 'If you really must have me then I suppose I must submit.' The pen turned out to be Caroline's mascara wand and he wrote *1510, Terminal 4* with the tip of it on the back of his hand.

'Thank you, darling. And remember – I'm a desperate woman,' laughed Caroline. 'So don't be late.'

I shan't be, thought Richard, as he said goodbye and put down the phone. He switched out the light, smiled, and pulled the pillow over his head. It was only seconds before he was back to sleep and suffused in erotic dreams of his own.

Great, thought Caroline, as she put down the phone and hugged her knees like an excited schoolgirl. Richard really was the kindest, sweetest man in the whole world. She had been a bit worried that he might refuse to meet her because she knew how hard he was working, how much he wanted to impress his new American boss. But now she chastised herself for having doubted him.

Caroline suddenly felt hungry and got up to inspect the breakfast tray which the room service girl had left on the table. There was something mushy in a bowl that smelt encouragingly of banana but tasted like hot wet sand. She picked up a slice of rather salty bread and a cup of coffee and went back to bed.

Caroline lay back against the pillows and sipped her coffee. It had said Nescafé on the breakfast menu but the coffee tasted more like warm yoghurt, she thought, as she put down her cup and picked up the bottle of mineral water that stood by the phone.

It was already getting hot and, after a few minutes, she got up again and brushed her hair. She had to use the inadequate complimentary comb she had been given by British Airways on the plane, since she had forgotten to pack her hairbrush. But still her red-gold hair gleamed healthily as she tucked it neatly behind her ears.

The Masai Simbara was the best hotel that Mombasa had to offer but still there was a rather oppressive broodiness about the place. Somewhere outside a drum was beating, a beating that seemed to have been going on when Caroline and her party had arrived the night before, that seemed to have been going on all night. The hotel was obviously used as a hunting lodge for people on safari and Caroline half expected a wildebeest or a rhinoceros to peer in through the open window.

But all was calm. Only a fistful of bright purple butterflies clouded the horizon as she looked out across the lush, landscaped gardens to the dark, slumbering mountains in the distance.

It really was a beautiful country, thought Caroline. It was her first visit to Africa. When one of her clients had suggested arranging a charity fashion show to raise money for the Third World, Caroline had come up with the idea of doing the show in a aeroplane as it cruised over the continent. The Mile High Fashion Show had been born and it had been a spectacular success. They had raised lots of money and her firm's clients had had a brilliant time, but Caroline now regretted the idea. She could not help feeling the event had been a bit vulgar.

All that wealth and extravagance and indulgence. All that fashion and frippery. It had been in a good cause but, as they had looked down from the aircraft to the plains beneath them, looked down on the invisible people below, it had seemed wrong.

They flew over Uganda, across Lake Victoria and down to Mombasa on the coast and they had come down through the shadow of great Mount Kilimanjaro itself. Caroline felt very humbled by the proud energy of this land. She had been glad to get her noisy entourage quickly through the airport and into the shiny fleet of cars that had been waiting for them and took them, in no more than fifteen minutes, on the bumpy but air-conditioned drive down Mama Ngumbi Boulevard to the hotel.

Caroline went over to a small table near the door and scanned the itinerary she had left out on the table the night before. It was written on Good Lord Productions headed paper.

There was a brief farewell performance by the Mambo Jambo Tropical Band at nine a.m. and then they would all go straight back to the airport.

The event had gone smoothly and Johnny was very pleased with her. There had hardly been a discernible hitch. Everyone thought she was so efficient, so organised, mused Caroline. It was a pity that she could not be so prescriptive, so perfect, in her personal life, she thought – in getting pregnant.

Caroline sat on the bed and flicked through the copy of *New Mother* magazine that she had bought at the airport and had quickly hidden in her bag.

She and Richard had been trying for over a year now and she calculated fifteen unwanted periods had come and gone.

But this month, things would be different.

Caroline had followed the BabyPlan Ovulation Kit instructions meticulously and, if only the plane arrived on time and Richard was there waiting for her, she felt sure it would happen.

The dream was, of course, what made her really confident. If it had not been for the dream, she might not have asked Richard to meet her. She might have taken the chance of waiting a few more hours.

But the dream had been so real, so powerful, that immediately upon waking Caroline knew that she

11

needed to call her husband. She felt sure that the dream was some kind of premonition.

She shoved the magazine into her bag and then lay on the bed and closed her eyes, trying to picture the dream again in her head.

She was standing naked before him as he took her head in his strong hands and began to kiss her. He passed his hands down over her neck, her shoulders, her breasts and at last to her huge swollen belly where he kissed and caressed her. She arched her back and felt his hands all over her, all over her and her enormous pregnant belly. 'I love you,' he said. 'Madonna.'

Madonna. Yes, she was sure that he had said Madonna. It just had to be an omen, thought Caroline, as she stood up and got her things together. Before she left the room she picked up a box of hotel matches and popped them into her bag. If she *did* get pregnant, she thought, it would be nice to have some memento of this place, this fertile African place where she would always feel the conception had really begun.

Then she quickly rubbed a wet flannel over her shoes – she had forgotten to bring any shoe cleaning things and her new Emma Hope shoes, were coated in thick red dust – picked up her bags and opened the door.

The drum was still beating as Caroline glanced at her watch and, realising she was now five minutes late, she broke into a run.

She was glad that she had told Richard about the dream although she knew, as a scientist, he would be sceptical about attaching too much significance to it. She was sceptical herself, on the whole, but perhaps just feeling positive would do the trick. It did not matter how or why she became pregnant, she thought, only so long as she did. Nothing mattered except that she and Richard should at last have a baby.

And so, as Caroline hurried down the stairs and into the noisy lobby, it did not seem important to her that the man in her dream, the man who had caressed her naked body, had not been her husband, Richard, but a total stranger.

Why should it matter, she said to herself. It was just a dream but, nonetheless, she realised that it was a detail she had deliberately omitted mentioning to Richard.

Chapter Two

Richard rifled in his pockets for some change.

'God rest ye merry gentlemen, let nothing you dismay . . .' It was far too early for carols, he thought, but he was wrong. There were only two weeks to go before Christmas and the Convent of Providence of the Immaculate Conception had cornered the Arrivals gate at Terminal Four. Richard had already freeloaded through 'Good King Wenceslas' and 'Little Donkey' and, given both the convent's name and his recent conversation with Caroline, it seemed only appropriate to pay up.

A very young nun with baby blue eyes stood at his elbow rattling her collection tin and Richard put in a pound coin.

'Thank you, sir,' smiled the nun, cheekily looking Richard up and down with her virgin eyes and taking in his new cashmere overcoat.

Richard grunted and scrabbled around in his coat pockets. There were only a few coppers and so in exasperation he eventually pulled out a wad of notes and wedged twenty quid into the tin.

'Thank you very much,' said the nun. But Richard had already edged away and his gaze was refixed on the automatic double doors that opened and closed every few seconds disgorging more and more arriving passengers.

'Where on earth is she?' he thought. It was nearly four o'clock and, checking again on the screen, Richard confirmed that the plane had landed on time. He fished out his mobile and called his office. Jeremiah had popped out an hour ago, said his secretary, and was still not back. 'Tazz will go mad if he calls and finds no one there,' he thought, flicking off the phone. Even if Caroline arrived that very second, it would take fifteen minutes to get to the airport hotel and then, Christ, he had to *perform*. He had been more than ready and willing to do the business when Caroline had called in the middle of the night but now he felt less confident.

'Whatever you need, I can do it,' said Laurence Percival as he heaved Caroline's briefcase out of the overhead locker. The plane was still taxi-ing into its slot but, despite instructions to remain seated and belted up, people were already getting ready to go.

They had been discussing cosmetic surgery and Laurence, who ran a highly successful practice in St John's Wood, had been explaining what one of his new blepharoplasties could do for a woman's self-image.

'I think you've done a brilliant job with Anabel,' said Johnny, as he brushed down his black leather jacket and swept his hands over his bald head. 'I hardly recognised her when I last saw her . . . I quite fancied her again. Fantastic boobs.'

Laurence laughed and jabbed Johnny in the stomach. He had met Anabel through Johnny; she had been

15

Johnny's fourth wife. But Johnny was already seeing Gaby, the future Wife Number Five, so it had been no problem for Laurence to step into his friend's shoes.

Johnny Lord was nearly fifty. He wore three tiny gold earrings in one ear and, a few months ago, he had had all his hair shaved off. Everyone assured Johnny that the bald head made him look cool but Caroline thought it made him look at least ten years older.

'Anyway, a blepharoplasty is an eyelid job,' said Caroline.

They clanked down the steel staircase to the waiting buses and Caroline looked at her watch. It was three thirty p.m. and she felt a strange fluttering feeling inside as she thought of Richard waiting for her.

'Squeeze in here,' Johnny said, shifting along a seat on the bus to make room for his colleague. All their clients, giggling, reeking of booze and hiding their potential eyelid-jobs behind wrap-around sunglasses, had been piled onto the first bus but it was quite sober and quiet on the second. Laurence, thought Caroline, had been the only one to say thank you when they all said goodbye.

She felt tired and was glad to sit down next to her boss. She looked at her watch again and rummaged around in her bag for some lipstick. There were only a few people on the second bus and, most noticeably, there was no driver.

'I hope we're not stuck here for long,' she said, as Johnny jogged her arm and she smeared lipstick all over her teeth. She closed her make-up bag and glanced at her watch again. She calculated that there were only twenty-six minutes before she was past her peak.

'Just relax,' said Johnny. 'And stop looking at your watch all the time. You remind me of my ex-wife when we were trying to time her contractions.'

If only, said Caroline to herself. Johnny and she had worked together for so long that he could almost read her mind.

She had met him through her sister, Sasha, who had worked for Johnny when he had run a model agency. The agency had been a big success and Johnny had made lots of well-connected friends. Eventually he went into PR and set up his own company. Good Lord Productions was in its tenth year and Caroline had originally been recruited to run the accounts but now she was Johnny's right-hand woman, about as indispensable as one could get. Far more indispensable than Johnny's wives had proved to be, thought Caroline. He was now on the fifth, the youngest and most glamorous yet. She was expecting Johnny's sixth child at the end of January.

'How's Gaby?' asked Caroline.

Johnny grinned. 'Bigger and more beautiful every day,' he said. He thought for a moment and then added, 'When you think about it – I've got a job that's a rave and a woman I can't get enough of. You can't deny that I am one lucky bastard.'

'No,' laughed Caroline. 'But I think you've made your own luck, Johnny. You've had difficult times and you've worked hard too.'

'It's just luck where you end up,' said Johnny. 'Or destiny, perhaps.'

'I'm not sure I believe in destiny,' said Caroline. 'I

think if you want something bad enough, you have to make it happen,' and that would be nigh on impossible, she added to herself, if she did not get together with Richard soon.

She scanned the deserted tarmac for the missing driver and looked at her watch again. It was getting dark and there were now only nineteen minutes until her lutenising hormone would be on the wane for another twenty-eight days. She thought of her precious virgin egg whooshing down her fallopian tube, expecting to find zillions of eager little tadpole suitors lying in wait, their little tails wiggling with anticipation . . . and finding nothing.

'Sorry about that, folks,' said a big uniformed woman, lumbering aboard with a huge knob of hair balanced on her head like a ball on a sea lion's nose. She closed the bus doors then hoisted herself into the driver's seat, started the engine and, as if trying to make up for lost time, zoomed off towards the terminal building – the way all those sperm are supposed to shoot off in search of an egg, thought Caroline, still absorbed with thoughts of her womb.

The bus lurched and bounced violently over the tarmac and Caroline now found herself wishing that the driver would slow down. She could not help worrying that the bumpy journey might shake her precious egg clean out of her body. She reclined in her chair, to the extent she could, crossed her legs tight and – hoping Johnny could not tell – she did something she had only ever done before while she was having sex. She pulled her pelvic floor so tight it would have even made even a eunuch come, she thought to herself.

*   *   *

When Caroline eventually emerged through the Arrivals doors, Richard did not recognise her at first. She came hobbling out, taking tiny steps and was almost bent double.

He rushed up to greet her and put his arm around her. 'What's happened? Are you all right?' he asked.

'She's desperate for the loo,' explained Johnny.

Caroline winked meaningfully at Richard but Richard stared blankly in return.

'Wasn't there a loo in there?' he asked, nodding towards the doors that Johnny and Caroline had just come through.

'She insisted on waiting,' said Johnny. 'Didn't want to keep you hanging around.'

Caroline winked again and tried to smile but Richard still did not understand.

'I'll wait for you here,' he said to Caroline. 'The ladies' is just over there.'

'Yes, go on, Caroline. Richard and I can have a quick drink while we wait for you,' said Johnny, pointing Caroline in the right direction. But Caroline just crossed her legs tighter still, shook her head and continued to wink furiously at Richard. Both Richard and Johnny were now looking bemused.

'No, I'm all right. I don't need to go any more,' said Caroline. 'But Richard and I are in a bit of a rush. I'll see you tomorrow, Johnny. Thanks.'

Johnny shrugged and backed away and Richard put his arm around Caroline's waist.

'Are you sure you're OK?' he asked.

'Yes, I'm fine,' said Caroline. Then she suddenly doubled up again, as though in agony. 'Oh God, I think I can feel it leaking out.'

'I thought you said you didn't need to go any more,' said Richard.

'No – the egg,' whispered Caroline. 'We have to hurry.'

Richard gasped, at last seeming to understand. 'OK, don't panic,' he said, picking up Caroline's bag and shuffling her away. 'I've got it all sorted. We'll take a cab – the hotel's only down the road but it will be quicker.'

'No, Richard – wait,' cried Caroline. 'I don't think we have time. We have to do it at once – I can't hold on any longer.'

'But what's the alternative?' asked Richard, wishing that he had had the chance to take Johnny up on his offer of a drink.

'Over there,' said Caroline. 'Quick, I'll go in first and you follow.'

Richard was horrified to see that Caroline was hobbling straight towards the Mothers' Breastfeeding Room.

'Look, it's really nice,' said Caroline, as she hauled him in through the door. There was a low armchair, a table and wallpaper covered in huge, leering teddy bears.

'But we'd better get on with it straight away,' she added, as Richard looked anxiously around him.

'Are you sure? It doesn't seem quite right,' said Richard, running his hands through his hair and feeling desperate for a cigarette. But Caroline pulled him towards her and kissed him.

Suddenly Richard overcame his hesitancy and confusion as he returned his wife's kiss. 'God, it feels good to hold you again,' he said, covering her face and hair in kisses, as he undid the buttons of her shirt.

'You don't need to bother with all that,' said Caroline, as Richard lifted her bra over her breasts. 'Can't we just get going at the other end?'

'No,' said Richard. 'I'm not a bloody sperm-dispensing machine – I can't do a thing without having a go at those beautiful breasts first. So Junior will just have to wait.'

Caroline laughed. 'Sorry,' she said, as Richard set to work again. It was strangely erotic to be making love in the middle of the airport.

'I love you,' she said.

'I love you too,' mumbled Richard, as he held one nipple and bent down to suck at the other.

But suddenly, to his horror, there was the loud unmistakable clunk of the door opening, followed by a sharp intake of breath. Someone had come into the room.

Richard clamped his bare-breasted wife to his chest and they both stared at the door as it slammed shut again.

'I thought you locked it?' Caroline said.

'I thought *you* did,' said Richard, leaping across the room and quickly bolting the door as though a mad axeman were on the other side.

He was sweating and, if he had needed that drink and cigarette earlier, he certainly needed them now.

'Oh God,' said Caroline, trying hard not to giggle, but Richard had gone white with shock.

They got back together and kissed again but Richard felt very tense. After several minutes of determined fumbling, he pulled Caroline's hand out of his trousers and turned away. 'I'm sorry, Caroline,' he said. 'It's no use. I can't get an erection after that.'

Caroline said nothing and Richard watched his wife as she readjusted her bra and began to button up her shirt. He loved her with all his heart and could not bear to disappoint her. Her cheeks were almost as red as her hair, he noticed, and her eyes were filled with tears.

'Don't worry,' said Caroline. 'It was a crazy idea anyway.'

Richard shook his head. He knew that he would have to do something. 'Stay there,' he said. 'I'll be back in a minute – I've got an idea.'

He went to the door, took a deep breath and un-bolted it.

Sure enough, the unwelcome intruder was still waiting on the other side. She was a big woman in uniform, with a huge ball of hair balanced on her head. For a horrible moment Richard thought she was going to arrest him but her face suddenly broke into an enormous grin.

'You's a very big baby, luvvie,' she said pointing to the Breastfeeding sign. 'Did you get enough?'

Richard felt his face fill with blood until it must have been as bright as fire. He said nothing and bolted off towards the news stand.

As he went, he breathed deeply and told himself to keep calm. Surely nothing worse could happen now, he thought.

But, as he quickly skimmed through a magazine from the top shelf, Richard realised to his horror that it could.

The tap on his shoulder was unmistakable and, as he turned his head, he came face to face with the young blue-eyed nun, accompanied by a rather plump and fearsome colleague.

'Sister Maria and I just wanted to say thank you properly—' started the young nun and stopped suddenly as she registered the photograph of a mammoth-breasted woman that Richard hugged to his chest.

'Ah, yes,' stammered Richard, quickly crumpling up the magazine and stuffing it awkwardly into his pocket.

'I, er, was telling Sister Maria how generous you had been,' finished the nun, staring at Richard's bulging pocket and then looking down at her feet.

'You don't understand,' protested Richard, grabbing the nun's arm and feeling desperate to explain, but Sister Maria already understood perfectly.

'God have pity on your soul!' she cried, glancing pointedly at Richard's wedding ring and steering her young colleague back towards the safety of the other nuns who were still singing by the Arrivals gate. Then Sister Maria turned back to Richard and said in a loud voice, 'A married man reading pornographic magazines. May God have pity on your poor wife too.'

Richard's poor wife, who had just at that moment appeared on the scene, could not fail to hear the last few words.

'What on earth are you up to, Richard?' she asked.

The angry nun glared at Richard and flounced away, shaking her head sympathetically at Caroline as she went.

'Sorry,' said Richard. 'There was a slight misunderstanding with a couple of nuns – you know, how these things happen—'

'Well, not really,' said Caroline. 'But I *do* know I've

been sitting in the Breastfeeding Room with that bus driver for ages while you're out here upsetting nuns.'

'I'm sorry,' said Richard resignedly. He was too exhausted to even try to explain.

'Never mind,' said Caroline, taking Richard's hand. 'Let's go and have a cup of tea and then we'll go to that hotel you suggested. A few more minutes won't make much difference and, if we carry on like this, we'll end up getting arrested.'

Quite unwittingly, Caroline could not have said a more prophetic thing. But Richard was oblivious of this as he meekly let his wife lead him away. Short of Johnny Lord's offer of a quick drink, a cup of tea seemed the best thing anyone had suggested all day.

Once again, however, respite was to prove short-lived and Richard froze as he felt another ominous tap on his shoulder. He turned around and this time came face to face with a security guard.

'I'm sorry, sir. But I saw you put that magazine in your pocket,' said the grey-faced man.

'What?' cried Richard. 'What magazine?'

The security guard smiled and said, in an unnecessarily loud voice, 'The copy of – what was it? *Bottoms Up* or *Grreedy Girrls*? I didn't quite catch the title when I saw you select it and then conceal it in your coat, sir.'

Richard clasped his hand to his pocket and felt his stomach roll inside him. He had entirely forgotten about the magazine.

'I don't want it. I didn't want to buy it,' he said, pulling out the crumpled papers and rather pathetically trying to smooth them out.

'Ah yes. *Bottoms Up*. That's what they all say,' said

the experienced grey-faced man, as he took a firm hold of Richard's elbow. 'Now, sir, if you would just come with me.'

'Just come with me,' repeated Caroline to herself. That was all *she* had wanted, she thought. But all hope of that was now extinguished.

'I'm sorry,' said Richard. 'Go home. I'll catch up with you as soon as I can.'

Caroline wanted to stay and help her husband but the security guard said it would take some time to sort things out and Richard said there was nothing she could do.

Caroline watched as the guard led away the father of her unborn, unconceived child – then she left the terminal and wearily put her heavy bag down in the taxi queue outside. It was cold and pouring with rain and she did not have a coat. The heavy warm African plain seemed a million miles away, as though it might be on another planet. She was back in London, she thought, and back to reality.

The taxi queue crawled miserably forward. No one wanted to do anything in this weather, thought Caroline, except to get home and get home quickly. She felt defeated and, although she had given up smoking ages ago when they had first started trying for a baby, she would have loved a cigarette.

When, at last, she reached the head of the taxi queue, her mobile started to ring.

She scrabbled in her bag to find the phone as she heaved her bag into the hot fuggy cab. Richard and Caroline lived on the ground and lower floors of a large Georgian house in Islington. Caroline gave familiar directions to Barnsbury Street and then put the phone to her ear. 'Hello,' she said, as the taxi sped away from the kerb. 'Hello baby, it's Mum,' came the cheerful reply.

Mum, mum, baby, mum, Caroline could take it no more. She burst into tears.

Chapter Three

But just over twenty-four hours later, Caroline was on her way home again and this time she felt elated. She had had a good day at work and had left early to prepare a romantic supper for Richard and herself.

Dear Richard, she thought. Caroline realised she had put her poor husband through hell the day before and desperately wanted to make it up to him. The security guard, after making him wait in an interview room for *five* hours, had given him a stern warning and let him go.

Richard had been exhausted when he eventually got home but, nonetheless, he had taken Caroline straight to bed even though she had said that it could wait until the following morning.

Richard had ignored this suggestion, which was as well, thought Caroline, since Tazz called at six o'clock the following morning and poor Richard had to get up at once and go into work. Caroline, however, had stayed in bed almost half the day. Even though it was twelve hours since she and Richard had had sex, she was still worried that, if she got up too soon, then everything might leak out.

She lay in bed with her legs propped up vertically

against the wall and called Johnny to say she would be in late. Johnny was still basking in the success of the Mile High Fashion Show and asked no questions. So long as the work got done somehow or other, he said, and the clients were happy, then he was happy too.

By the time Caroline got into the office it was lunchtime but she did not feel hungry. Was it her imagination or was she really starting to feel rather nauseous? She sat at her desk imagining her precious embryo busily dividing into a larger and larger bundle of cells and wafting about in search of a suitable spot to implant itself in her womb. She could almost feel her hormone levels shooting up and she had to keep going to the lavatory which was a sure sign that something was going on, wasn't it? Or was it just the vast quantity of herbal tea she had developed a sudden craving for and had been drinking all day?

'I think my breasts are getting bigger,' she whispered to Richard on the phone.

'That sounds good,' said Richard, puzzling over the negative internal rate of return that his model had come up with.

'Are you suggesting they're too small then?' said Caroline petulantly.

'No, not at all,' laughed Richard. 'But, I suppose breasts are like profits – they can never be *too* big, can they?'

'Can't they?' replied Caroline.

'Oh damn,' said Richard and Caroline could hear him furiously tapping at his computer. 'I'm having so much trouble with this model. I'll have to get it straight before Tazz gets back tomorrow or he'll really go ballistic.'

'I was hoping you'd get home early tonight,' said Caroline.

'I'll try,' said Richard.

'Forget it,' said Jeremiah. 'You've been working on the damn thing for hours and must need a break.'

It was seven thirty in the evening and Richard did feel exhausted.

'Leave it until the morning,' said Jeremiah, uncrossing his long, thin legs that he had stretched across his desk. He sat up and chucked Richard a cigarette.

'Thanks. Tazz will eat me alive if it's not finished the minute he walks in the bloody door,' said Richard. 'He's already seriously pissed off about yesterday.'

'Sorry about that,' said Jeremiah, hooking his jacket off the back of his chair. 'There seemed to be nothing going on here – I only meant to pop out for a minute.'

Richard shrugged and frowned at his screen. 'It wasn't entirely your fault,' he said. 'It was just unfortunate that the old bastard chose to ring then and my secretary told him I'd gone home early to meet my wife.'

'At least my horse won,' mused Jeremiah. 'Noble Stranger came in at twenty-five to one. The least I can do is buy you a beer.'

A beer, thought Richard, exhaling cigarette smoke and licking his lips. The suggestion was irresistible.

'OK,' he said, quickly downloading the model onto a floppy and tossing it into his briefcase. 'Just a quick one.'

Richard worked so hard, thought Caroline, as she shoved the garlic and shallots into the roasting pan and looked at her watch. She had decided to roast a chicken since it was virtually impossible to overcook and so it would not matter if Richard was a bit late getting home.

She went downstairs to the bathroom and tossed handfuls of lilac bath salts into the running water.

Richard's company, which had been a very dull regulated water and sewerage business, had recently been taken over by Centro Utilities from the US, and since then her husband's career had been transformed. A bright engineer, with an Oxford degree, he had been quickly spotted and moved to the Projects Division. Water and sewerage were big growth international sectors, according to his boss, and Centro wanted to be up to their necks in it.

Richard now spent his time racing around the world bidding for concessions and contracts and his salary had doubled. But it was a very competitive business. The French and the other US utilities firms were all working as hard as Centro. If Tazz and Richard brought in a big deal, Richard knew that this would not go unnoticed. Some of the guys in the States were earning ten times what he got, so there was everything to go for, his boss said.

But it was a pity that she and Richard were starting to see so much less of each other, thought Caroline, as she pulled her sweater over her head and turned off the taps. She unhooked her bra and examined her breasts in the mirror.

Small, yes, she had to admit as she viewed them from the side. But surely at least a cup size bigger?

She slipped off her trousers and pants and ran her hands over her stomach. It was still wonderfully flat but she arched her back so that it stuck out a bit and re-examined her profile in the mirror. She thought back to her dream in Mombasa and smiled to herself.

Through the wall, a doleful singing broke across her thoughts. It was Pearl, the woman who lived next door – she always played her music at top volume and it was always 'music to commit suicide to', as Richard put it. Poor Pearl was only in her forties and yet she behaved as though she were twenty years older. Caroline had never seen anyone come to visit her and she rarely went out except to the local shops. Since the accident a few years ago when her face had been badly scarred, she said she felt more comfortable at home on her own.

Caroline felt sorry for Pearl but she did not want to let anything disturb her mood so she switched on the radio and stepped into the bath. It was wonderful to be home alone, she thought, and have time, at last, to relax and reflect on the new life that might be beginning inside her. She gently lowered herself into the warm water but immediately, of course, the doorbell rang.

At first she was irritated that Richard must have forgotten his key. But then she felt excited at the idea of opening the door to her husband, naked except for a thin veil of bubbles.

She could see the shape of Richard's broad shoulders through the opaque glass of the front door.

'Come in – quick,' she said, shielding herself from public view with the door and opening it a few inches.

A big man pushed his way into the hall, rubbing his hands and muttering about the cold weather. When he looked up, he was shocked to see his daughter standing in front of him, stark naked.

Caroline immediately blushed and fled downstairs. 'Sorry Dad,' she called behind her. 'I thought you were Richard.'

'I might have been anyone,' said her father. 'A Jehovah's Witness, a sex-crazed lunatic – or both.'

'Sorry,' called Caroline again.

'I can't imagine why that husband of yours gets home so late if that's the welcome he usually gets,' continued Graham Roth, taking off his coat and hanging it on the banister. He went into the drawing room and made straight for the cupboard with the whisky in it.

'Make yourself at home,' yelled Caroline. 'Have a Scotch,' she added, as Graham took his half-filled glass into the kitchen in search of water.

'Thanks,' he said.

He took a slug of whisky and waited for Caroline in the kitchen. Something good was cooking in the oven and Graham started to feel hungry.

'Have something to eat,' said Caroline when she eventually reappeared.

Graham watched his beautiful daughter as she stretched up to the top shelf of a kitchen cupboard and brought out a packet of mixed nuts. She was even more beautiful with her clothes on, he thought. She wore a soft purple jersey and tight black jeans and her red hair was bundled loosely into a clip.

'Where's Mum?' asked Caroline as she filled a bowl with the nuts and placed it on the table in front of Graham.

'She's coming in a taxi.'

'What? Did you have a row or something?' Caroline

could hardly think of a time when she had seen her mum and dad argue. Dad was far too laid back for that – he let Mum get away with murder.

'No,' laughed Graham. 'It's just that she wanted to bring over your Christmas present and I couldn't fit it in the car.'

'Sounds exciting,' said Caroline, pouring herself a glass of fizzy water and joining her father at the table.

Graham smiled. In his eyes, Caroline was still the little girl who could not wait for Christmas Day to come. He and Belinda had been blessed with their two beautiful daughters even though he felt, at times, that he did not deserve them.

'Where's Richard?' asked Graham as the doorbell rang again.

'Oh, this is probably him now,' said Caroline, leaping to her feet.

But it was not Richard this time either. It was Caroline's mother.

'Hello baby, how *are* you?' Belinda burst through the door and embraced her daughter expansively.

Before Caroline had the chance to answer, however, her mother had disappeared outside again.

'In here, in here,' she could hear her mother directing someone.

Suddenly a huge rectangular shape appeared with two stocky legs buckled up beneath it and thick fingers at the edges.

'It's bloody heavy, missus,' came a gruff voice from the shape. 'I hope I'm going to get a big tip for this.' The shape staggered up the steps and deposited itself in the hall. Then the taxi driver appeared from behind it and looked expectantly at Belinda.

'Graham! Graham!' called Belinda and dutifully her husband appeared. 'Sorry, darling – no money. Sort this chappie out for me, will you please?' She bustled Caroline back into the warm and left Graham to pay off the driver.

'So tell me, baby. How *are* you?' Belinda repeated meaningfully. Caroline looked quizzically at her mother for a moment and then remembered her outburst in the taxi the day before.

'Oh, sorry about all that blubbing,' she said. 'I must have scared the life out of you, but you just happened to call when I'd had a really dreadful afternoon.'

'If it hadn't been for Margaret's exhibition – I had to go – you know how Margaret is. If it hadn't been for that, I'd have come over last night,' said Belinda.

'Don't worry,' said Caroline. 'I'm feeling much better. Really.' She opened a bottle of wine, poured her mother a glass and took her through to the drawing room. 'I was just feeling a bit tired and sorry for myself,' she explained as Belinda rearranged Caroline's cushions and made herself comfortable on the sofa.

'You work too hard,' said Belinda. 'If I'd had a husband who made as much money as yours does, I would never have worked another day in my life – oh, thank you darling, come and sit here,' she added, patting the seat beside her, as Graham came back into the room. 'I mean, do you really *need* to work so hard?'

'I enjoy it,' said Caroline sitting down in front of her parents. 'I mean, I'd go crazy mooching about here all day with nothing to do. Who knows what trouble I'd get into?' Graham put his arm around Belinda's shoulder. It was amazing how close they still were, thought Caroline.

'Baby!' laughed Belinda. 'You've always been the most sensible one out of the whole family. I can't imagine you *ever* getting yourself into trouble.'

Caroline frowned at the rug. It was oddly irritating when her mother teased her for being too sensible.

'Perhaps we should let Caroline open her present,' said Graham.

'No,' said Caroline. 'Let's wait for Richard.'

So they waited for Richard and waited and waited. Caroline had filled the bowl of nuts twice and was on the point of opening a second bottle of wine.

'Perhaps we should eat?' she said.

'Let's wait a bit longer,' said Graham who, with the smell of the roast wafting from the kitchen, felt he could eat a horse.

Caroline tried calling Richard on his mobile but it was switched off.

'No,' she said. 'It's nine thirty. I'm going to serve up the chicken.'

Belinda helped Caroline with the food and they sat down to eat.

'It's delicious,' said Graham, tucking in heartily.

'Absolutely, baby,' said Belinda. 'What a pity Rich—'

'He's really busy at work,' said Caroline beginning to feel upset that her husband was so late. It wasn't meant to have been like this, she thought. Supper with her mum and dad. She loved them dearly, of course, but she had meant it to be a romantic dinner for her and Richard. A celebration dinner.

They ate chocolate profiteroles for pudding.

'They're only from M&S,' said Caroline as her father prepared, after the first mouthful, to effuse with praise.

'Very good, very good,' he said nonetheless.

Caroline looked at her watch. It was nearly ten o'clock and she was finding it hard to concentrate on her parents' conversation. Belinda was chatting on about the art course she was doing in the spring. She was going to South America for a month to paint.

'Of course, it would be impossible to do my trips if I didn't teach at the same time,' she said.

Caroline said nothing.

'There are still a few spaces on the course,' added Belinda. 'So if you know anyone interested in painting . . . It's very reasonable once you've paid for the flights.'

'I think it's time we were off,' said Graham as Caroline got up to take the plates.

'Perhaps we should just wait until Richard gets back,' said Belinda, getting up to help Caroline.

Caroline was just about to tell her parents not to worry when, thank heavens, at last there was the sound of the front door opening.

Caroline rushed into the hall to welcome her husband. All thoughts of his lateness were forgotten as her spirits soared again. If she was pregnant, if she and Richard really were to have the child they wanted so much, how could she be angry?

But she could not help noticing that Richard had been drinking, as she watched him stumble into the house and crash straight into the brown-papered rectangle that leant against the wall.

'Belinda! Graham!' cried Richard, rubbing his leg. 'How nice to see you. Come and have a drink.'

Belinda smiled at her son-in-law and, for a moment, Caroline thought she was going to accept his offer but Graham took his wife swiftly by the arm.

'Sorry Richard,' he said. 'We were just leaving.'

Belinda and Graham kissed Caroline goodbye and left. Richard watched as Graham stroked his daughter's cheek and whispered something in her ear, something that brought a beautiful smile to her lips.

'Sorry I'm late, darling,' said Richard, following his wife through to the kitchen. 'You didn't say your mum and dad were coming round.'

'I didn't know they were,' said Caroline, filling up the kettle. 'Do you want some coffee?' she asked.

'Yes please, black,' said Richard slumping into a chair. 'I was so exhausted I couldn't resist going for a drink with Jerry. I'm really sorry – I shouldn't have gone . . .'

'Never mind,' said Caroline as Richard pulled her onto his lap. 'I don't blame you, after the torture I put you through yesterday.'

Richard laughed. 'I can't believe I saw those two nuns again – just as the security guard was marching me away to his office.'

'Poor you.'

'No,' said Richard. 'If I hadn't been so pathetic in the Breastfeeding Room—'

'You made up for it when you got home,' said Caroline, kissing Richard and getting up to make the coffee. 'Mum brought round our Christmas present,' she went on.

'Oh. Was that what I bumped into in the hall?' asked Richard, rubbing his leg again as he recalled the encounter.

'Yes. Shall we open it?'

'Let's leave it until tomorrow,' said Richard. 'I feel completely out of it.'

Caroline put two cups of coffee on the table. 'Shall we drink it in bed?' she said, standing behind her husband and putting her arms around him so that the back of his head rested between her breasts. 'I want you to have a look at my breasts, tell me if you really think they're getting bigger.'

'Sorry?' said Richard, swivelling round to stare at Caroline. It took a moment for him to recall their earlier conversation. 'Oh sorry, darling, of course. They look superb. Enormous.'

Caroline laughed as Richard nestled his face in her chest. 'Come to bed, you idiot,' she said.

'I'm coming,' said Richard. 'I've just got to spend five minutes doing something for work and then I'll be down.'

'OK,' said Caroline, picking up her coffee and leaving the room. 'Don't be long.'

Richard picked up his coffee too and followed his wife. But rather than going down to the bedroom, he went into the hall, collected his briefcase and then went into his study.

He plopped the disk into the computer and squinted at the tiny numbers on the screen. They seemed to make no sense at all and so it was over an hour later when he eventually switched off his PC and got up to join his wife.

Caroline was by then fast asleep. Richard gently removed the magazine that was lying under her face. It was one of those baby magazines, he noticed, and it had left a small mark on her pale cheek. Richard thought of that moment earlier in the hall when Graham had stroked Caroline's face. He wondered what his father-in-law had whispered in her ear that had made her smile so beautifully. It always amazed him, the intimacy that Caroline seemed to share with her parents, particularly with her father.

Richard had loved his own father more than he had ever realised. And now, of course, it was too late. His father's death had come so suddenly, so brutally, that Richard had never had the chance to say the things he should have. One moment they had been walking in the spring sunshine, his mother had said, and the next moment poor Dad had been lying in the mud. An aortic aneurysm – it can strike you down like lightning, a doctor told his mother at the time.

Richard looked across at Caroline and switched out the light. He had wanted to say things to Caroline. He wanted to tell her how much he loved her and to talk about the baby and ask how she felt and tell her how big and beautiful her breasts were. But it was too late now.

'I'll make it up to you tomorrow,' he whispered and switched off the light.

Chapter Four

Sasha had had sex twice in the last twenty-four hours, once with Max and once with Brown. The thought made her giggle. She looked around the smart Covent Garden café at other mothers, out to lunch with their children like her, and wondered what they would think if they could read her mind.

But there was nothing for her to feel ashamed about. Both men loved her, of course, and she loved them: they were the fathers of her two children.

As Sasha contemplated the panini that the waiter had just put in front of her, she could not help feeling like the ham inside the sandwich.

The waiter returned to ask whether there was anything more she wanted.

Sasha shook her head and pushed the plate away from her. She was twenty-nine, very tall and slim and very pretty. She was used to heads turning wherever she went. She was used to more than her fair share of attention.

'Sorry I'm late,' said Caroline rushing in, kissing Sasha, then kissing her nephew, Toby, who was asleep in his buggy, and sitting down at the table.

'It's OK sweetheart,' said Sasha. 'I've already ordered

but I don't feel hungry any more. Do you want this?' She pushed the plate across to her sister.

'Thanks,' said Caroline. 'I'm starving.' Caroline's appetite had certainly increased over the last few days and she could not help wondering whether this was also a sign of pregnancy.

Sasha inspected her long blue fingernails as Caroline took a huge bite out of her sandwich.

'I brought a sample,' said Caroline. Sasha looked up. The word sample reminded her of days at the antenatal clinic. Although she loved her two-year-old son dearly, she had to admit that Toby had been a mistake – as her daughter, Siena, had also been ten years earlier.

Caroline produced a square of paper covered in pale squiggly blue and pink stripes and interspersed with what looked like little white bunnies. 'What do you think?'

'It's for your guest room?' asked Sasha.

'Yes, It's so pretty, don't you think?'

'I think it would be better for a kid's room,' said Sasha waving for the waiter, who was now chatting on the phone.

There was silence as Caroline returned to her sandwich. The waiter ran up to their table and Sasha ordered a cappuccino with lots of chocolate on the top.

'How's Siena?' asked Caroline.

'Oh, same as usual,' said Sasha. 'She wants to get her navel pierced. What do you think?'

'No,' said Caroline emphatically.

Sasha laughed. 'You're so straight, sweetheart. Why not?'

Caroline reddened slightly. Her sister was right.

41

As her mother had said the other night, Caroline had always been the sensible one, anxious to do the right thing. Sasha, on the other hand, hurled herself through life with breathtaking recklessness, but she always seemed to land on her feet, no matter what she did.

'I sometimes feel you miss out on life,' continued Sasha. 'You're so organised and nice and, well, *reliable* all the time. People will end up taking you for granted, Caroline. Take my advice – you have to do something crazy once in a while, something irresponsible.'

Caroline opened her mouth to answer and a loud wail arose from the buggy. Toby had woken up. Sasha groped around the side of the buggy for his dummy, gave it a quick wipe with a napkin, and put it in the child's mouth. Toby sucked noisily for a bit and then fell back to sleep.

Suddenly Sasha's mobile rang. 'Sorry sweetheart, it's Max – do you mind?' said Sasha, covering the phone. Caroline shook her head and got on with her lunch, as her sister lit a cigarette and settled back in her chair to chat with Partner Number One.

Sasha had always been more of a worry to her parents than Caroline had but, nonetheless, she had been the baby and undoubtedly was her mother's favourite.

'It's the artist in her,' Belinda would say. 'I know how she feels – she can't help herself.' And so Sasha had been allowed to drop out of school at sixteen when she had signed up at Johnny Lord's model agency.

She was soon earning huge amounts of money and constantly in the gossip columns being escorted to fashionable parties by rich and famous men.

Max Cowley had been a photographer in those days and, when Sasha found herself pregnant with his child at the age of eighteen, Max suggested that she should move in with him.

And she and Max had lived together ever since but, as Sasha put it, they also led their separate lives. Max had moved from photography into design work and had had considerable success with a birthing chair that he had patented a few years ago. As a result, Max and Sasha had moved from their flat in Hackney to a huge Victorian house on Highbury Hill.

They had needed the extra space, not only for Max's studio but also because Sasha was pregnant again and the father of her second child wanted to move in with them.

Sasha had been seeing Brown Alma for some time and Max knew all about their relationship. Brown was one of the hippest street DJs on the scene in London and it was hard for anyone to dislike him, even Max.

So they all moved into the new house over two years ago and were still together. It was an unusual arrangement and Richard said it would end in tears but Sasha was happy and the children seemed relaxed about having two dads.

'Don't worry, Max,' said Sasha into the phone. 'Brown is picking me up. We're going shopping together, but thanks anyway.'

Caroline had finished her sandwich and sat watching Toby as he made a second attempt at waking up.

The dummy had slipped from his lips and his mouth was half open. His eyelids were flickering open and shut, open and shut, and he rubbed his eyes hard with the backs of his plump little fists.

Caroline stood up and went over to the buggy and undid his straps. She heaved the big sleepy baby into her arms.

'Don't worry, I'll take him,' said Sasha, sticking her cigarette in her mouth, wedging the phone against her ear with her shoulder, and waving her hands at Caroline. 'Must go,' she said to Max and put the phone down on the table.

'It's OK,' said Caroline, sitting back down again with Toby in her lap. 'He's so sweet.' Perhaps interpreting his aunt's remark as a challenge, Toby immediately buried his head in Caroline's neck and bit her hard on the shoulder.

'Sorry,' said Sasha as Caroline screamed. 'He's into biting at the moment. I think it means he likes you.'

Caroline prised Toby away from her neck and gave him some bread. 'Get your teeth stuck into that,' she said, as she rubbed her shoulder and then stroked the child's sticky curls.

'You really love kids, don't you?' said Sasha, as though the idea had never struck her before.

'I adore them,' said Caroline.

'Take this little monster then,' said a voice behind her. It was Brown, who had slipped into the café and appeared at the table. Brown grinned broadly as he lifted his son out of Caroline's arms and threw him up in the air.

'Only joking,' he said as Toby squealed with delight. 'We wouldn't swap you for the world.'

'Hideous,' cried Richard. 'It's absolutely hideous.'

'Do you really think so?' asked Caroline. She had had an exhausting day – after going out for lunch with Sasha, she had needed to stay late at the office to finish her work. She was preparing a report for Organo-gasm, a new organic restaurant that was opening soon, and although she knew that Johnny would be relaxed if the report was one day late, she hated to let him down. Perhaps Sasha was right, she thought, as she went into the drawing room and collapsed onto the sofa. She was just too responsible for her own good.

'What's it supposed to *be*?' asked Richard, coming into the room from the hall.

They had just opened Belinda's present. It was a huge canvas covered in tiny blue, pink and white splodges.

'I don't know,' said Caroline. 'But I think the colours are rather pretty.'

'Mm, but the pattern,' said Richard. 'It looks like a giant piece of really naff loo paper.'

'Richard!' laughed Caroline.

'And it's huge,' Richard went on, laughing as well. 'A big enough piece of poncey loo paper for Tyrannosaurus Rex to wipe his backside on. Where on earth are we going to put it? The bathroom is already crammed full of her previous efforts – there's no room for this one.'

'I like it,' said Caroline, sipping her fizzy water. 'It's rather like some wallpaper I was thinking of buying. Perhaps, we could put it in the baby's room—'

'Put it where?' said Richard.

'Oops,' said Caroline. 'I meant the guest room.'

Richard smiled and put his arm around Caroline.

'The baby's room? Do you really think so?' Caroline smiled. She looked so beautiful, thought Richard. There was a sort of glow, a radiance about her – perhaps she *was* pregnant after all.

They soon moved downstairs to the bedroom and were on the point of making love when the phone rang. It was Tazz. Just after Richard had left the office, a fax had come through from Lima, he said. They had been invited to pitch for one of the biggest water supply concessions in the world.

'Couldn't this wait until tomorrow?' asked Richard, still lying on top of Caroline and stroking her face. But it couldn't, said Tazz. He was so excited, he said, that he had been playing his trumpet all evening to calm his nerves but it was no use; he really needed to talk about it with someone.

Richard sighed and rolled onto his side to listen.

'This is the biggest one yet, Richard,' said Tazz. 'I want you to give this one your mind, body and soul. OK?'

'OK,' said Richard, stroking Caroline's stomach.

'No really,' said Tazz. 'If we win this, it will mean promotion. How does Director of Centro Utilities International, Projects Division, sound?'

Of course, literally, thought Richard, it sounded very much like his current title – Director of Centro Utilities Projects, International – but, in reality, he knew it would be a big step up. The Board of CUI was far superior to that of CUP.

'Great,' said Richard.

'Exactly,' said Tazz and went on to explain in detail his strategy for winning the bid. After at least half an hour, he let Richard go.

'I'll see you in the morning then,' he said.

'Yes, thanks for letting me know,' said Richard, putting down the phone.

He leant back on the pillow and thought through his conversation with Tazz. If he got this promotion, Richard said to himself, his salary would probably double again. It would be fantastic. It would mean that Caroline would be able to chuck in her job at GLP, if she wanted, and stay at home and be a full-time mum when she had the baby, the way his own mother had been. He touched Caroline on the shoulder to talk to her about it but she just murmured in her sleep.

Richard sighed and switched off the light but, as he did so, Caroline turned and took him in her arms.

'I thought you were asleep,' said Richard.

'Just faking,' said Caroline.

They made love and there was no faking the intensity of their passion for each other. Caroline sometimes loved her husband so much that she almost felt physically part of him. It was a different love to the love she had first felt for him. They had been married now nearly seven years but it was a stronger, deeper, fuller love than ever, thought Caroline, as Richard kissed her tenderly when they had finished and turned over to sleep. She had read once about a woman whose husband had desperately needed a kidney transplant but a matching donor could not be found. In the end, the wife insisted that the doctors tried transplanting one of her own kidneys although the medics said it would end in certain failure. Miraculously, the husband's body accepted the wife's kidney without problem. Caroline could imagine doing something like that for

Richard. They had now become such a part of each other's lives that they were almost one being rather than two separate entities. She could not imagine that anything could ever pull them apart.

Chapter Five

Ten days passed as quickly as they do at that time of year. It was Christmas Eve and there were a thousand things to do. Caroline had promised to do the stuffings for her mother and only now realised that she had not bought enough chestnuts. She still had not wrapped any of her presents and she had forgotten to pick up the computer game Richard had asked for from PC World.

Nonetheless, as Caroline refixed the mistletoe that had fallen on her head the moment she had stepped through the door, she had only one thing on her mind.

Why on earth had she not bought it already, she asked herself. It was ridiculous. There had been rows and rows of them at the supermarket in their shiny blue packaging and it would have been so easy to have slipped one into the trolley.

It wasn't as though it was too early to buy one. After all, these tests claimed to be accurate from the day your period was due – there was no need to wait until it was late. And Caroline's period was three days late already; well, three days late if you were working on her usual twenty-eight-day cycle.

She hardly ever went as long as thirty-one days and it was now Day Thirty-one. She picked up the diary by the phone and frowned. She realised that, because of the Christmas holidays, if she did not buy a test that day then she would not be able to do a test until the following Wednesday which would be Day Thirty-six. That would be unbearable, she thought to herself.

Caroline put down the diary and looked at her watch. It was four o'clock. She already had to go out again for the things she had forgotten and it would take no time to make a quick stop at the chemist. She stuffed her supermarket shopping into the fridge and freezer and grabbed her coat.

It was already dark and the Christmas lights of the local shops twinkled prettily as Caroline squeezed into the only free parking space in one of the loading bays on Upper Street. She crossed the road and jogged up to the chemist. It was icy cold. Her white breath streamed out behind her as she ran and there was a light, slushy rain which might, she thought, turn to proper snow in the night. She was nearly thirty-five years old but was still young enough at heart to be excited at the prospect of a white Christmas. As she pushed open the chemist door, there was a merry old-fashioned ding to alert the shop assistant to her presence and Caroline felt suddenly flushed with goodwill, that everything was conspiring to make this a truly magical Christmas.

The assistant in the chemist beamed at Caroline, recognising her at once. Ah, the woman who came in last month to buy a BabyPlan Ovulation Kit, you could see her thinking, thought Caroline, but fortunately she said nothing. The shop was crowded with people waiting for their last-minute prescriptions to see them over the long holiday weekend. As well as goodwill, Caroline suddenly felt flushed with embarrassment too.

The staff had obviously been celebrating. The assistant's plump red cheeks looked plumper and redder than ever and she had entwined silver tinsel around the headband of the personal discman that she was wearing.

'Do you have, er, a pregnancy kit?' whispered Caroline, stretching as far as she could across the counter.

'A pregnancy kit!' boomed the assistant. Then, registering Caroline's embarrassment, she whipped off her tinselled headset and said, 'Sorry, I always find myself shouting when I'm listening to my CDs.'

'Don't worry,' said Caroline, glancing around and feeling as though everyone in the shop was staring at her.

'It's not pop music or anything,' said the woman, gesturing to her discman. 'I'm learning Turkish, you know.'

'Good,' said Caroline. 'So can I have the kit, please?'

'Ah yes, one or two?'

Caroline looked confused – surely one kit was enough.

'Take two love,' advised the hideously familiar woman. 'After all, if you do the test too soon it might come out negative. And the two-packs are almost the same price as the one-packs.'

'OK,' said Caroline. 'Thanks.' She paid and quickly grasped the packet from the assistant's hand.

'Do you want me to put it in a bag for you?' yelled the assistant as Caroline turned to go. 'After all, it can be a bit embarrassing holding one of those pregnancy kits. You don't want to sound the trumpets and let the whole world know yet, eh?'

But that was precisely what Tazz Fletcher intended to do. He had been driving Richard and Jeremiah crazy about the Lima bid for the past ten days.

'This timetable is ridiculous, a sacrilege. Isn't Peru a Catholic country any more?' moaned Jeremiah, who was responsible for producing the documentation on Centro's credentials for the job.

'The deadline for submitting our Application to Bid is twelve thirty p.m. Lima time on thirty-first December,' said Tazz, putting down his trumpet and peering over Richard's shoulder at the tiny letters on his computer screen. 'We really need to say more about our sources of finance,' he added.

It was six thirty p.m. London time on the twenty-fourth of December, thought Richard, and it was clear that he was going to be at his desk for several hours longer if he was to avoid coming in the following week. He had promised his mother that he and Caroline would go up to Edinburgh on Monday and stay with her until the New Year. His brothers, Mark and Freddie, were both out of the country for the whole holiday period and, since it was the first Christmas without Dad, it was the least he could do for her.

'I'm sorry,' said Richard wearily, as he wedged the phone between his ear and his shoulder, lit a cigarette and carried on typing and squinting at the screen.

'Poor you,' said Caroline. 'I was hoping you'd get back early – there's something, well, I wanted to *do* with you . . .'

Richard laughed and told her not to worry – he would not be too late for that.

'No,' said Caroline. 'You don't understand. I'm desperate.' She sighed and put the pregnancy testing kit down on her bedside table. 'Be as quick as you can or I may have to do it by myself.'

Richard laughed again and said goodbye.

Caroline was, of course, tempted just to go straight ahead and do the test, since she had read the instructions over and over again. It was very simple but she wanted Richard to be with her to read the result. It was a special moment and she wanted them to watch that heraldic thin blue line appear *together*.

The doorbell rang and Caroline went upstairs and let her mother into the house.

'I brought round some of Margaret's mince pies,' said Belinda, going through to the kitchen and putting down a tin and three large plastic bags full of lavishly wrapped Christmas presents. 'She always puts far too much rum in with the mincemeat but that's Margaret for you.'

'Thanks,' said Caroline. Both she and Richard hated mince pies – with or without too much rum – but she was glad to have them. It was always nice to produce mince pies when people dropped in for a drink over Christmas. Caroline liked to do the right thing.

'Where's Dad?' she asked. Her father always seemed to follow her mother wherever she went. It was unusual for Belinda to be on her own.

'Poor darling, he's laid up in bed with a dreadful cold. He insisted I came round though. I think he thought that you would be *so* disappointed if you woke up on Christmas morning and did not have all your presents.'

'Dear Dad,' said Caroline, taking her mother's rain-soaked coat. The slushy snow had now turned to a heavy driving rain. 'He's right though. I don't suppose Richard will have had time to get me a present yet. He has been working night and day for the last fortnight – his boss is driving him mad.'

Belinda went to the fridge and took out a bottle of Australian Chardonnay that was already half empty. She held it up to Caroline, who nodded her head.

'Please, go ahead,' she said. 'And pour me a small one too.'

'I thought you only drank fizzy water these days,' said Belinda, taking two glasses out of the cupboard.

'I do,' said Caroline. 'But I'll have a tiny drop to keep you company.' She sat down at the kitchen table and put out her hand to indicate that Belinda had already poured enough into her glass.

'I need to be careful – just in case,' she said.

'Just in case what?' asked Belinda mischievously.

'Oh, you know,' said Caroline blushing a little and looking away. She took a sip of her wine. Richard would not be home for hours and she just had to talk to someone about it.

'I think I might be pregnant,' she said.

'Oh Caroline, baby, how wonderful,' cried Belinda leaping to her feet.

'Well, I haven't done a test yet, but I'm three days late and, well, I feel funny. I felt quite faint and nauseous at the supermarket this afternoon.'

'Not an unusual feeling when you're shopping at

this time of the year,' remarked Belinda. 'But why didn't you get one of those test things?'

Caroline said nothing.

'Of course, they didn't have them in my day. I had to pee into an old aspirin bottle or something. Can you imagine? And then you had to take it into the chemist and slip it over the counter without anyone seeing. You young people today don't realise how embarrassing things used to be.'

Caroline smiled. 'I did buy a test actually. But I'm waiting until Richard gets in to use it,' she said.

'Richard,' cried Belinda, as though for the first time she had realised he was not around. 'Where is he? After all, it is Christmas Eve – surely, no one works on Christmas Eve?'

'Well, Richard does. And most of his colleagues seem to too. When I rang half an hour ago, I could hear his boss playing that infernal trumpet of his. I know that Richard is earning a lot more money now than he used to, and we've been able to move into this really nice maisonette . . . But I sometimes wish things were how they were when we first got married, when we didn't have so much.'

'Oh dear,' said Belinda, taking a big slug of wine. 'You do sound a sad old bag.'

They both laughed.

'Sorry,' said Caroline. 'Would you like one of Margaret's mince pies?'

Belinda put the oven on and sat down again. 'Husbands,' she said with an exaggerated sigh. 'They're all the same.'

'Oh, come on,' said Caroline. 'Dad's devoted to you. Besotted. Always has been and always will be.'

'Yes,' said Belinda. 'But since he stopped working, since he stopped teaching, he's changed, you know.'

'How?' Caroline got some fizzy water and topped up her glass.

'I suppose it's having more time to spare, more time to think about things. He's become rather, well, morose.'

'Morose?' said Caroline. 'He always seems cheerful enough when I see him.'

'Well, that's when *you* see him,' said Belinda. 'When he's home alone he's quite another person.'

'You make him sound like Dr Jekyll,' laughed Caroline, getting up to put the mince pies in the oven.

'I think he's depressed about something. I think something's worrying him but he won't tell me what it is. You know what men are like,' said Belinda.

'Perhaps he's just bored.'

'Thanks,' said Belinda.

Caroline laughed. 'No, I mean missing his work or something,' she said.

'He's started this genealogy thing,' said Belinda. 'You know, tracing back his family tree. He's hoping to get back to Alfred the Great. He spends hours at the computer working on it, he says, but sometimes, when I pop in, he's just staring into the distance, in a sort of trance.'

'Poor Dad,' said Caroline.

'No, don't worry. It's probably just his age,' laughed Belinda. 'Anyway he's really looking forward to having you over for Christmas lunch tomorrow. Max and Brown can't make it this year but Sasha and the children will be there.'

'Great. I'm really looking forward to it – I haven't seen Siena for ages,' said Caroline.

'Well, you're in for a shock then,' said Belinda. 'She's suddenly grown up over the last few months. She's got bigger tits than you have.'

Caroline laughed and got up to get the mince pies out of the oven but she could not help feeling irritated by Belinda's personal remark. Her breasts weren't in the Page Three league, that was for sure, but they were a perfectly respectable B cup, she thought to herself.

'Do you think Dad will be all right on his own?' said Caroline as her mother drained the bottle of Chardonnay into her glass.

'Oh, he'll be asleep by now. I'll hang on here until Richard gets back if you like,' said Belinda.

'Thanks,' said Caroline. It was nice to have some company, she thought, even if it was just her mum.

Caroline opened another bottle of wine for Belinda and then she and her mother went into the drawing room and watched some TV together. After the news, Belinda got up and made some cheese on toast for them both, with lots of Worcester sauce the way she knew Caroline liked it.

Then mother and daughter curled up on the sofa and watched *Notting Hill* on the video together. Caroline felt like a little girl again with her head resting in her mother's lap.

When it got to the bit at the very end of the film, where Julia Roberts is lying on the park bench, clearly pregnant, Caroline sat up and her mother flicked off the TV.

'Come on,' cried Belinda, looking at the clock. 'We've waited long enough. Let's have some fun – let's do it.'

Caroline stared at her mother and looked confused. 'Do what?'

'The pregnancy test, of course,' said Belinda.

Why not, thought Caroline. It was half past eleven – nearly Christmas Day – and Richard was still not back. It was not the way it was meant to be but her mother had been so sweet to her . . .

'Sorry darling.' Richard had crashed into bed and Caroline immediately woke up.

'What time is it?' she asked, rubbing her eyes.

'Christ knows,' replied Richard. 'But bloody late. I'm really sorry.'

'Don't worry. Mum came round.'

'That was nice,' said Richard, turning his wife over and getting himself comfortable.

'Yes,' said Caroline.

But things were not nice, thought Caroline, as Richard switched out the light. They were far from nice. They were horrible and poor Richard was so tired that he was asleep before she could even talk to him.

'Perhaps it was all that fizzy water you drank,' her mother had said. 'You're supposed to do these tests first thing in the morning – you know, when your urine is at its most, well, concentrated.'

Caroline had tried to put on a brave face. 'Yes,' she had said. 'There were two tests. I'll do the second one in the morning.'

Chapter Six

But there was no need to do the second test in the morning as, by that time, Caroline's period had already started.

'Happy Christmas, darling,' said Richard the moment he woke up.

Caroline said nothing.

'I'm so sorry about last night,' continued Richard, 'But, at least, I shan't have to even *think* about work for over a week. We can have a really nice break over Christmas.'

Caroline still said nothing. She just wanted to curl up under the duvet and go back to sleep. And the last thing she wanted to do was to see her mother and Sasha for lunch. They would both be so sympathetic and encouraging. Someone was bound to say, 'Don't worry – you can always try again next month.' It was unbearable.

Richard had switched on the radio and was sitting up in bed. 'I'm sorry I haven't got you a proper present yet,' he said. 'But I saw this in a shop yesterday and couldn't resist it.' He reached down beside the bed and produced a small parcel.

Caroline was still hiding under the bedclothes. Her

head was just peeping out but, as Richard leant over to give her his present, he noticed her tear-stained cheeks.

'What's the matter?' he asked.

Caroline sniffed, wiped her eyes and wriggled up in bed. 'Nothing,' she said. 'Thanks.' She took the present and unwrapped it. When she saw what it was she burst into tears.

'It's just for fun,' said Richard. 'I'll get you a proper present next week.'

Caroline shook her head as she stared at the little furry kangaroo that Richard had bought her. It had a little joey in its pouch.

'It's sweet,' she said through her tears.

'What's wrong?' asked Richard.

'Nothing,' said Caroline. 'It's just you forgot – the thing I wanted to do last night.'

Richard moved closer and took Caroline in his arms. 'I'm sorry,' he said, kissing her neck.

'No, I don't mean that,' said Caroline, pulling herself away.

'What then?' asked Richard, looking confused.

'I bought a pregnancy test.'

'Oh, right, of course,' said Richard. 'Great. Let's do it now.'

'No need. I started my period this morning,' said Caroline.

'Oh darling, I'm sorry,' said Richard, stroking her head as Caroline dissolved into tears once again.

'I really felt different this time,' she sobbed. 'I felt so sure that I was pregnant, after the dream and everything . . .'

'Don't worry,' said Richard. 'We can always try again next month.'

The words seemed to make Caroline cry even harder.

'Please Caroline, don't,' he said, pulling his wife into his arms. 'It would have been nice but it's not exactly the end of the world, is it? We've still got each other and there are things to enjoy in life other than babies.'

'Oh Richard.' Caroline wriggled free and sat up on the side of the bed. 'You don't understand at all. It really does feel like the end of the world to me, the thought that we might never have a baby.'

Richard was silent and stared up at the ceiling.

Caroline wondered whether he was thinking what she thought he was thinking. But, as usual, neither of them wanted to talk about it.

Caroline could hardly even bear to think about it. The truth was that she had got pregnant soon after she and Richard had been married. She had still been in her twenties and wasn't ready to have a baby. They had agreed that it was only sensible to wait until they were properly settled, financially more secure. But Richard had said it was ultimately up to her and now, of course, she regretted the decision with all her heart.

'It's all my fault,' said Caroline.

'Don't Caroline,' said Richard. 'It's not your fault.'

'I feel like it's divine retribution,' sobbed Caroline.

'Nonsense. It's just bad luck. But, if you think something is wrong, just go to the doctor and let's see if we can find out what it is. Perhaps it can be easily sorted out.'

Richard, as usual, was right, thought Caroline. But she had already been to see her doctor, of course. She knew – but could not bear to tell Richard – that having an abortion sometimes, very occasionally, makes a woman infertile. Dr Gorgoyne had offered to refer her to the hospital for a salpingogram which would determine once and for all whether an infection at the time of the abortion had blocked her tubes. But Caroline could not bear to do this. If her tubes were badly blocked then the only alternative was to try IVF. But Richard was not keen to discuss IVF.

'Let's take it one step at a time,' he said.

'I'm just terrified we will leave it too late,' said Caroline, getting out of bed and pulling on her dressing gown.

'Don't worry,' said Richard.

But he was talking to himself as Caroline had already left the room. He lay back in bed and sighed. He could not bear to see Caroline so upset. She might think that he did not care whether they had a baby or not and, in some ways, that was just what he wanted her to think. He did not want to put any further pressure on her. But the truth was he cared very much indeed. Richard wanted to be a father more than anything in the world.

'Merry Christmas,' said a small voice, as Caroline and Richard loaded up the car with presents for Caroline's family.

Caroline looked up and came face to face with Pearl, the woman who lived next door and played non-stop Leonard Cohen at full volume. Pearl's face was often downcast and drawn but that morning, unusually, she was smiling. Caroline could scarcely see the scar that used to cut, deep and raw, across her left cheek.

'Merry Christmas, Pearl,' said Caroline. 'You're looking well.'

'Thank you,' said Pearl.

There was an awkward pause and it suddenly occurred to Caroline that her neighbour might be spending the day all alone. As the thought crossed her mind, she had to admit again that Richard was right. Perhaps, she *should* count her blessings. At least Caroline had a nice, caring family – she would not be spending Christmas Day on her own.

'We're having lunch at my mum's. I'm sure there will plenty for one more,' said Caroline. 'Would you like to join us?'

'Oh no, thank you. I'm fine,' said Pearl.

Caroline looked concerned but Pearl continued to smile.

'Are you sure?' Caroline asked.

'Completely,' said Pearl. 'I'm quite happy on my own. I enjoy playing my music.'

Richard, who had finished packing all the presents into the back of the car and now waited beside Caroline, could not help snorting at this remark.

'See you later then,' said Caroline, as Richard opened the door and she got into her seat.

'Poor Pearl,' she said, when Richard eventually started the engine and pulled away from the kerb.

'What?' asked Richard. It was already one o'clock and he was looking forward to his first glass of champagne.

'Pearl. She's so lonely. I've never seen anyone visit her – I don't think that she has any friends or family.'

'She must have,' said Richard. 'I'm sure someone will rally round and come to see her over the holiday.

I mean we all make a special effort at Christmas, don't we?'

Caroline laughed. 'Are you implying that Christmas lunch with my family is more duty than pleasure?'

'Not at all,' said Richard. 'I was just thinking of my own mum.'

'No need to feel guilty there,' said Caroline. 'You've been a brilliant support to her since your father died and we're staying up there for five days.'

'Yes,' said Richard. 'But I wish I'd not left it so late. I was looking at my old diaries the other day and I think I only went up to see Mum and Dad for *one* day during the whole year before Dad died. I regret that.'

'You weren't to know,' said Caroline. 'No one could have guessed what would happen. Your father always seemed so fit and well.'

'Yes, I suppose so. It just goes to show how dangerous it is to take people for granted.'

'The most generous man in the world,' sighed Caroline as she came into the kitchen weighed down with a huge bunch of flowers.

Richard looked up. It was nearly ten thirty and he had assumed that Caroline had been talking to the taxi driver at the door.

'Is the taxi still not here?' he asked.

'No,' said Caroline. 'I was looking down the street for it when I came face to face with Laurence Percival.'

'The boobs man?'

'He's a plastic surgeon,' laughed Caroline. 'He does other things than just boobs.' She put the flowers on the table and got a vase. 'I couldn't believe it,' she said. 'He'd brought me these beautiful flowers as a 'thank-you for all the work I've done for him this year but wouldn't even come in for a drink.'

'Just as well,' said Richard. 'We're already running late.'

'He said he didn't have much to do and so he decided to deliver them himself. Such a sweet man.'

Richard looked at his watch and stood up. 'I'll have to walk down to Upper Street and get one,' he said, having a last sip of his coffee.

'Aren't you even a little bit jealous?' teased Caroline.

'Do I need to be?' smiled Richard.

'No,' said Caroline, kissing her husband and then slapping him gently in the face with a white tulip. 'But you might just pretend to be.'

Richard smiled. 'Come on. I think you're trying to make us miss our flight so you can stay here with Mr Boobs.'

'You go and find a taxi,' said Caroline. 'I'll quickly get these in water and join you.'

'There hardly seems any point,' said Richard, picking up a couple of bags and leaving the room. 'They'll be dead by the time we get back from Mum's.'

Richard was right, thought Caroline, as she arranged the flowers in the vase. She wondered who might like them and immediately thought of Pearl. She felt guilty. It was now the Wednesday after Christmas and she still had not gone next door to check that her neighbour was OK.

Caroline pulled on her coat, picked up the vase of flowers and went along to Pearl's flat. There was no answer and Richard was calling from across the wall. 'Hurry up. The cab's arrived at last.'

Caroline knocked again and shivered as she waited

for a response. After a few minutes, she began to wonder whether she should just leave the flowers outside the door, when suddenly she heard a faint sound.

'Caroline. Hurry up,' cried Richard.

'Coming,' said Pearl.

'It was such a relief,' said Caroline later, when she was in the cab with Richard. 'I worry sometimes that she might die in there all on her own and no one would know.'

'You worry too much,' said Richard, looking at his watch and crossing his legs.

'I suppose so,' said Caroline. Pearl had seemed reluctant to open the door at first but her face lit up when Caroline gave her the flowers. Women are never too old for flowers, thought Caroline, and she could not remember the last time that Richard had bought her some.

They had eaten a big dinner and played charades and yet there were still two hours to go before it was midnight and the New Year began.

Richard felt exhausted. All the extra work he had been doing on the Lima project had built up and he would have loved to have an early night but his mother sat beside him and he knew he could not let her down. Hogmanay was a big thing in Scotland.

'Have some brandy,' said Jane Carnforth, tucking up her wispy blonde hair.

'I thought you only got offered Scotch in this house,' laughed Richard's uncle, Robert. His brother, Archie Carnforth, had married the wealthy Glencairn whisky heiress but Archie had more than pulled his weight in the business. He had always been very loyal to the firm.

Jane echoed Robert's laugh. 'That was certainly the way things were, when your brother was alive. Dear Archie would never have allowed any spirits in the house other than Glencairn. But things are different now,' she added softly. 'I've acquired rather a taste for brandy – it's good to have a change.'

Richard smiled and patted his mother on the arm. 'You must miss Dad so much,' he said.

Caroline sipped her wine and watched her husband hang on every word that his mother said. He obviously loved her intensely and, although she knew that it was stupid, she could not help feeling a little bit jealous.

'She's a sad, lonely woman,' laughed Richard. 'I thought you were into feeling sorry for sad, lonely women.'

'I know. I am,' cried Caroline. 'But I do think on the stroke of midnight you might have kissed me first.'

'Oh, Caroline, you are being ridiculous,' chided Richard, taking Caroline into his arms and kissing her. 'And keep your voice down! She's only in the room next door.'

'Sorry,' said Caroline petulantly.

Richard got into bed. 'You are silly sometimes,' he said, pulling back the crisp linen sheets on Caroline's side for her to get in. 'I do so much prefer sheets and blankets to duvets, don't you?' he added.

Caroline sighed. Sometimes she felt that Richard wanted her to be just like his mother, the perfect homemaker and mother. Jane Carnforth had married when she was only a teenager and she still looked very beautiful. It was not surprising that Richard seemed to adore her.

'Why don't we have another go at making that baby?' whispered Richard as Caroline turned out the light and climbed into bed beside him.

They made love and it was good, really good, thought Caroline, and extingushed all the tension between them.

'I'm sorry I was so stupid earlier,' she said when they had finished.

'No, I'm the one who should apologise,' said Richard. 'I've been neglecting you.'

'It doesn't feel that way now,' said Caroline.

'Good. Happy New Year. I feel this year is going to be very special for us.'

'Me too,' said Caroline. 'Happy New Year, darling.' She kissed her husband and snuggled up in his arms and, in return, he stroked her hair and nuzzled her cheek.

It was the little things that counted for so much. Richard could be so affectionate, she thought as she drifted off to sleep, and it was at those times that she realised how much she loved him.

Chapter Seven

'I can't believe it,' cried Caroline, holding up a copy of the *Independent*.

Richard grunted and buried his head in his own newspaper. He was regretting drinking so much brandy the night before, followed by several glasses of champagne.

'Look,' insisted Caroline. She thrust the paper under her husband's nose. There were the usual stories and pictures of the first new babies of the year. Richard grunted.

'Very nice,' he said, forcing a smile and passing the paper back to his wife. He assumed that Caroline was feeling broody about babies again.

'No, look. Read it,' said Caroline. 'It's Johnny. It's Johnny Lord's baby.'

'I didn't know Johnny was having a baby,' said Richard.

'Oh Richard,' sighed Caroline. 'You never listen to a word I say.' She passed the paper to her mother-in-law who had just come into the room and set down a tray of coffee.

'Mm, wonderful,' cried Richard, sitting up and putting his paper down. 'So much better than that dreadful instant stuff we survive on at home.'

Caroline ignored her husband's unintended snub and took a mug of coffee from the tray.

'Look Jane,' she said. 'My boss's wife has had the first new baby of the year. The baby wasn't due for another month but he arrived early – seconds after midnight.'

'Knowing Johnny, he probably had his poor wife specially induced,' said Richard. 'Anything for a bit of free publicity.'

'Richard,' laughed Caroline. 'Don't be so cynical.'

She hugged her hot mug of coffee and studied the photograph of the proud mum and dad and the swaddled wrinkly little infant.

'I know what you mean though,' she said. 'Johnny is very lucky; things do always seem to turn out well for him.'

Caroline tore the page out of the paper, folded it up and put it in her bag. Later, when she was alone in her room, she took it out again and studied it.

Johnny really was a lucky bastard, she reflected. He loved kids, he said, but he had never been that fussed about having his own. This New Year baby was his sixth, although it was his new wife's first. The baby looked so beautiful, thought Caroline, huddled up in his blankets in his mother's arms. It made her ache with desire for a baby of her own but it also focused her resolve. There was nothing for it, she told herself, folding up the cutting and putting it away again. She would not leave things to luck or destiny – she would have to go back to the Gorgon.

But seeing the Gorgon was always an intimidating

experience. Even sitting in Dr Gorgoyne's waiting room, Caroline began to have misgivings.

The room was, as usual, crammed full with people. A little boy of about five was clambering about the place while his mother sat close to the television, munching crisps and watching a chat show.

The boy was soon bored and struck up a conversation with one of the waiting patients, a young black girl. 'My mum's got spots,' he said.

The young girl smiled and nodded.

'What have you got?' asked the boy.

The girl looked surprised but laughed. The mother was so intent on the TV programme that she was watching, she was oblivious of her son's conversation.

'I have to have some stitches out,' said the young girl, pointing to a cut on her head.

The boy was impressed and examined the wound carefully before moving on to the next person, a big man in jeans and a dirty sweater covering his huge belly. 'My mum's got another baby in her tummy,' he said. 'Have you?'

The man laughed and patted the boy on the head. 'I've got a nasty cough,' said the man and coughed loudly to make the point.

The boy tried coughing louder and the two had quite a competition before the child moved on to the next person.

The boy slowly worked his way around the room. Everyone, it seemed, had some quite acceptable minor aliment, thought Caroline, beginning to panic as she saw that her turn was next. The boy's mother was still busily munching away and engrossed in the TV and so there seemed no escape.

71

'My mum's got big tits. She wants the doctor to make them smaller,' said the boy to Caroline. 'What have you got?'

Caroline, although prepared for the question, flushed bright red. 'I'm sorry, I don't want to talk about it,' she said in a quiet but firm voice. The other patients in the room, who had all been watching the boy and smiling, suddenly coughed politely and looked away.

'Is it your tits too?' asked the boy, putting his head on one side sympathetically. 'You know, the doctor can make them bigger as well . . .'

'Of course,' said Dr Gorgoyne emphatically. She wrinkled her brow so that her hairy eyebrows crept about her forehead like caterpillars and scratched vigorously under her arm. It was not surprising that most of her patients had nicknamed her the Gorgon. 'Of course, it's perfectly understandable to start worrying about what is going on inside, my dear,' continued the doctor, scratching the back of her head with her stethoscope.

'But we've been trying for over a year now,' said Caroline. 'That's enough for something to happen, surely?'

'Well it depends,' laughed the Gorgon, opening wide her scarlet painted lips and throwing back her head. 'It depends on whether you are *getting* enough, enough sex, of course.'

'I think we're OK in that department,' mumbled Caroline, blushing slightly. She might have been a patient of the Gorgon for years, she thought, but it was really unprofessional for a doctor to laugh while she was discussing something as intimate and, well, sensitive as her patient's fertility.

Dr Gorgoyne, reading Caroline's face, immediately apologised. 'I'm sorry,' she said. 'But we *have* discussed the options a number of times. Have you decided what you would like me to do to help you?'

'I thought maybe we could check Richard's sperm count,' said Caroline.

'Is he happy to do that?' asked Dr Gorgoyne.

'Well, not happy exactly, but he said he *would* do it, if it's really necessary,' said Caroline. 'We had a bit of a chat over the holidays. He told me that he had had mumps when he was a teenager, so perhaps—'

'Perhaps,' interrupted the Gorgon, shaking her head. 'But, I doubt that it is *his* problem.'

Caroline looked up, somewhat startled at this remark. 'What about the mumps—' she said, but the Gorgon again interrupted.

'Look my dear, there's no point beating about the bush,' she said, lolling her head to one side and pushing back her wiry grey hair. 'You *have* been pregnant before. So long as no one else was involved at that time, then it's unlikely that Richard's sperm is a problem.'

Caroline looked down at her thin white hands in her lap and fiddled with her wedding ring. 'No, of course, there was no one else. But we might just have been lucky that time. Or he might have *developed* a low count since,' she persisted.

'It could be,' said the Gorgon, heaving a great elastic-stockinged leg onto the side of her desk. 'But, really, I think we should check you out first. If you had an infection at the time of the ab— termination, then your tubes might be blocked. We really need to do that salpingogram.'

'OK, yes,' said Caroline meekly. 'But it will be so

awful if I have wrecked our chances of having a baby. I wish to God that I'd never had that abortion.' Caroline put her hands over her face and began to sob.

The Gorgon passed her a tissue, patted her arm and smiled. 'Come on,' she said. 'Try not to worry. If you prefer, we can check Richard out first but, in the meantime, you must relax and take things a bit easier.'

Caroline was trying to stop crying but the tears continued to flood down her cheeks. The Gorgon passed her the whole box of tissues.

'You seem overstressed,' said the doctor. 'Are you still working?'

Caroline nodded.

'It might be an idea to take a bit of time off work,' said the Gorgon. 'Sometimes too much running about can make it hard to conceive. Have you been travelling much?'

Caroline nodded again and the doctor nodded in return.

'If you *really* want this baby, I think you should take some time away from your job – if you can afford to,' she said. 'Relax and indulge yourself and, well, see what happens.'

'You? Indulge?' laughed Sasha, shifting a pile of clothes from a chair to the floor so that Caroline could sit down at the kitchen table.

Sasha's house, as usual, was in a state of utter chaos. It was amazing that Sasha, nonetheless, was always immaculately turned out. She was wearing a pink cashmere twinset, short skirt, fishnet tights and long black leather boots. From the waist up, she looked like the archetypal girl-next-door but from the waist down she looked more like a hooker.

'Doctor's orders,' said Caroline. 'I've got to take things easy and indulge myself.'

'How much does your doctor get paid?' asked Sasha, opening a bottle of red wine. 'I could have told you that myself for free – it's the way I've been living my life ever since I can remember.'

Caroline got up and found the only two wine glasses in the cupboard. The rest were littered about the kitchen, and probably the rest of the house too, waiting to be washed up.

'I don't know what Johnny will say if I ask for a few months off,' said Caroline.

'There you go again,' said Sasha. 'Worrying about other people. Relax. Johnny is fine – he's got everything he wants in life and certainly more than he deserves.'

'I wish I could be more like you,' said Caroline, taking the glass of wine from her sister's hand. It had been a busy day. After seeing Dr Gorgoyne, she had rushed into work and then she had left early to meet Sasha. They had done some late-night shopping in Oxford Street. Sasha had wanted to buy clothes, of course, for some party she was going to but Caroline had wanted to buy something for Richard's birthday which was the following Sunday.

'Hi gorgeous,' said Max, coming into the kitchen and kissing Sasha. 'Good shopping?' he added, looking at the huge pile of carrier bags that Sasha had dumped by the door.

Sasha grinned. 'Stupendously expensive,' she said.

'Please make sure you're sitting down when you open the next Visa bill.'

'At least, it wasn't me who had to traipse around after you,' smiled Max, looking across at Caroline. 'It's worth a lot of money to have someone else take this woman shopping.'

'I managed to get what I wanted too,' said Caroline gesturing to the small WH Smith bag on the counter. 'It's the latest Lara Croft. Richard really wants it for his birthday.'

'Lara?' cried Brown as he sauntered into the kitchen to join them. He had a wide smile on his face, as usual, and carried a rather sleepy-looking Toby on his shoulders. He gave Sasha a long kiss and then went over to Caroline and kissed her briefly on both cheeks.

'Do you mind if I have a look?' asked Brown, putting Toby down on the floor and picking up the bag. 'When Max is hogging my bird, I have to resort to Lara too,' he said.

The two men studied the box.

'They've made her boobs even bigger than ever,' said Max.

'Men!' laughed Sasha, grabbing the computer game and handing it back to her sister. 'Now piss off and put Toby to bed, will you please? Caroline and I want a proper girlie chat, OK?'

'OK,' said Brown, grabbing a handful of popcorn from a bag on the side. 'But Max and I are just going to have a quick game of table footie first,' he added. Brown plonked Toby down on the floor and the two men left the room.

'You really have an amazing set-up here, Sash,' said

Caroline. 'But it seems to work OK. You all seem happy.' She looked around for some paper for Toby, who had found a felt-tip pen and was busy scribbling on the floor.

'We are,' said Sasha. 'If we are nothing else, then we are all happy. We never do anything we don't want to.' She waved at Caroline to sit down. 'Don't worry,' she said. 'He always draws on the floor – it comes off.'

Caroline sat back down in her chair and sipped her wine. 'I took a taxi over to Oxford Street to meet you,' she said. 'I think the driver tried to chat me up.'

'Why, what did he say?' asked Sasha, sitting down opposite her sister at the cluttered kitchen table.

'He asked me whether I was meeting a boyfriend and when I said no, he said he really liked women with red hair.'

'So what did you say?' asked Sasha, opening a bag of crisps and offering them to Caroline.

Caroline shook her head. 'Oh, I didn't say anything. I just ignored it.' There was silence for a moment, apart from the sound of Sasha munching her crisps, and then Caroline added, 'What would you have said?'

'I don't know,' Sasha replied, giving the half-eaten bag of crisps to her son under the table. 'What did he look like?'

'I don't know,' laughed Caroline. 'Does that make a difference?'

'Of course, it makes a difference,' said Sasha. 'I mean if he was really cute – or, as Siena would say, if he was really *fit*, then maybe—'

'Sash, you really are impossible. I'm a married woman. If I just let myself be led by my hormones all the time, I'd be in a terrible mess,' said Caroline.

'My poor big sis, you really a sad case,' laughed Sasha.

Although Caroline laughed, the words echoed in her ears. Wasn't that what her mother had said only a few days earlier?

'Mum, can I play with your Barbie dolls?' called Siena, her head suddenly appearing round the door.

'No,' said Sasha and then she reconsidered. 'I thought you hated them,' she added.

'I do,' said Siena. Her face was so made up, thought Caroline, that she looked easily sixteen. 'I just heard you calling Aunt Caroline sad and wanted to remind you that anyone who still plays with Barbie at thirty is sadder than hell.'

The head disappeared as suddenly as it had appeared and Sasha laughed. 'That girl is impossible,' she said. 'Of course, she's wrong.'

'About what?' asked Caroline. 'You don't still play with your Barbie dolls, do you?'

'Of course, I do. I love them. But she's wrong about me being thirty – I've still got six months left of being twentysomething.'

'Lucky you,' said Caroline, who had been thinking recently how frighteningly close she was getting to forty.

'What?' cried Johnny, when Caroline returned with the Cokes and told him she needed some time off.

'Come on,' said Caroline. 'You'll be fine without me for a few months.'

'Well, at least, we'll have a bit of a breather from crazy stunts like this,' said Johnny, waving his hand at the man in the window. 'Just make sure you hold the book over your penis,' he yelled and turned back to Caroline. 'Are you sure we can't be arrested for this?' he asked.

Caroline laughed and shook her head. 'I don't think so.'

They were helping with the launch of a new book at a Piccadilly bookshop. It had been Caroline's idea to hire a male model to pose naked in the shop window holding a copy of *The Naked Guru*. If done properly, she said, it could look very tasteful.

Caroline climbed into the window to adjust the book.

'But I can't read it, if I hold it right down there,' said the model.

'It doesn't matter,' said Caroline.

Johnny took a big slug of ice-cold Coke. 'Can't you just take things a bit easier?' he asked, climbing up into the window to give Caroline a hand.

'No,' said Caroline. 'My doctor says I've got to take this relaxing thing *seriously*.'

'OK,' smiled Johnny. 'But I've never heard relaxing described as serious before.'

'I have to sit at home and just *think* myself pregnant,' said Caroline.

Johnny laughed. 'Ah well. That might be where you are going wrong. I mean, Richard does have to do *something*, you know.'

'Oh piss off,' said Caroline, giving Johnny a shove. As she did so, Johnny stumbled and the ice-cold Coke shot out all over the naked man's body. There was a shriek as the model leapt into the air and dropped the book.

There was a gasp of horror from the crowd of spectators who had been watching in the street outside. When Johnny and Caroline looked where the crowd was looking, they saw that the model had suddenly developed an enormous erection.

'Sorry,' he said. 'It'll only take a few minutes to go down.'

Chapter Eight

She had been out of her job for many weeks and things were not easy. Dolores loved her baby son, Diego, but it was hard work looking after him and her three sisters – much harder than it had been looking after the Campanas' apartment.

She passed much of the day sitting outside the hovel that her mother called *la casa*, with Diego at her breast. It was always sunny so, at least, she could thank God for that.

When Dolores first saw the stranger, she had been struck by the cold set of his face. He seemed a man who rarely smiled, who had important business to get on with, as he strode past in his grey suit. He was clearly quite affluent and so it was a mystery to Dolores what business he could possibly have in the *barriadas*.

Dolores had never seen him at the mission house, so it seemed unlikely that he was connected to the Church, unlikely that he was there to dispense charity. And yet, each time that he passed her by, he would stop for a second and nod his head respectfully.

One day he stopped and spoke. '*Hola chiquilla,*' he said, his eyes fixed firmly on the back of Diego's head as the baby nuzzled inside his mother's shirt. Dolores pulled her rough shawl around her shoulders to conceal her breast from the stranger's prying eyes and said nothing. Her three sisters were out selling toothbrushes on the roadside.

The stranger moved closer to Dolores and glanced around him. '*Que lindo bebe que tienes*,' he said. Dolores looked down at Diego's black head. The stranger, of course, could not see her baby's face but he was right. Diego was a very beautiful baby.

She smiled, like any proud mother would do when hearing her child praised.

The stranger came again the following day and came every day until, of course, he was no longer a stranger but Dolores knew him as Don José.

Some time passed before Dolores realised what Don José was after. It was not her, as she had initially suspected. It was not the sight of her heavy, milk-laden breasts that had interested him, but her child. He wanted Diego.

He could find the child a good home, he told her, good parents, and her son would want for nothing.

Dolores had shaken her head and hugged her baby close. But the image of Diego being brought up in a smart apartment like the Campanas' home in San Isidro, where she had worked, where he might have loving parents, like Don Andres and Doña Mercedes, would not go away. Perhaps little Diego could escape from the filth and squalor of the cesspit that she and her family were forced to live in.

But Diego was now nearly three months old and his face shone with joy when he laughed. It would be unbearable to lose him.

'*Tres mil dólares,*' José whispered again.

Three thousand dollars, thought Dolores. That would keep her family fed and clothed for years, at least until the boys had finished school. The girls would be able to go to school too.

Diego chuckled and stretched up to stroke his mother's cheek.

'*¡Vete!*' she said angrily and obediently Don José got to his feet.

'*Hasta mañana,*' he said.

And the following day he came again. Caroline could hardly believe her eyes.

She had been to the newsagent to buy a magazine and had come face to face with him walking down Barnsbury Street towards her house. 'Laurence!' she cried. 'What on earth are you doing here?'

The eminent surgeon looked confused and even embarrassed. 'Er, I had an appointment with a patient nearby and thought I'd pop by and drop some papers off for you.'

'How sweet,' said Caroline. 'But you know, I'm not working for *GLP* at the moment.'

'Oh, it's not wholly work-related,' said Laurence, fumbling with his briefcase.

'Come in and have some coffee,' said Caroline. 'Since I stopped work, I'm starting to feel really bored being stuck at home all the time.'

'Sorry,' said Laurence, finally producing some papers out of his case. 'I can't stop. I was just going to post these through your door.'

Caroline took the papers and stared at Laurence's flushed face.

'It's a new brochure I've just had done,' he said. 'Not, of course, that you really need any treatment but I thought you might be interested.' His face was redder still and, although it was a cold day, a thin trickle of sweat ran down the side of his face.

'Thanks,' said Caroline. 'Are you sure you won't—'

But Laurence was sure. He forced a smile, kissed Caroline clumsily on each cheek, then turned and hurried away.

It wasn't until Caroline was back inside the house that she looked at the brochure. It was headed *BIG – Breast Increase Guaranteed*. Caroline's first reaction was to toss the papers into the bin but, a few minutes later, she fished them out again, glanced through them and then put them in a drawer of her desk.

She made herself some coffee and sat down to read her magazine. The first article she turned to was about a film star who claimed that she had had a child, after years and years of trying, by borrowing someone's baby for the day. It was apparently an ancient African therapy. If a woman could not conceive, another woman would lend her a baby for the day and then, hey presto, the infertile woman would get pregnant.

It seemed too simple to be true but Caroline felt prepared to try anything. She had been off work for six weeks and there was no sign as yet that her enforced relaxation was having any effect. Mooching about the house all day with nothing to do but read magazines and watch daytime TV was beginning to make her feel more desperate and obsessive about the whole baby thing than she had ever done before. At least work had been a distraction.

After a while, she decided to go out and buy a few things for supper. She strolled along Upper Street, her head tucked into her scarf to protect herself from the icy wind. She stopped at the stationer's next door to the King's Head pub to buy a card. The window was full of huge red hearts and the shop was crowded with men. All their wives and girlfriends would have bought their cards long before.

It was 14 February and she and Richard always exchanged cards over supper on Valentine's Day. She wondered whether Richard would remember this year. He had been working flat out recently on the Lima project and had been home late every night. She had called earlier in the day to chat but he had been too busy and said he would call her back.

Suddenly the mobile phone in her bag started to ring and Caroline wondered whether that was him. 'Hello,' she said, absent-mindedly scanning the rows and rows of Valentine cards in front of her.

'Oh darling, it's me.'

Right words, thought Caroline, but the wrong voice. It was her sister, Sasha.

'What are you up to?' asked Sasha.

'I'm just looking at a huge display of willies,' said Caroline.

'Sounds as though you really are taking this self-indulgence thing seriously.'

'Only smutty Valentines, I'm afraid,' laughed Caroline. 'I'm in Ryman's.'

'Oh great,' said Sasha. 'Look, darling, I wouldn't ask you if I wasn't *desperate* but Max and Brown are taking me to a new restaurant tomorrow night – the Organo-gasm.'

'Oh, the one GLP helped to launch last month,' said Caroline. 'How romantic.'

'No. The romantic bit's tonight. We're having a quiet supper at home, just the three of us.'

'Sounds fun,' said Caroline, flicking through the cards and being quite shocked by some of them.

'Yes, it should be. But I was really calling about tomorrow night.'

'Do you want me to babysit?' asked Caroline.

'Oh no, my daily is doing it – the kids are fine with her. But, the thing is, darling, I've got simply nothing to wear and the restaurant is, well, rather the in place at the moment. You couldn't be an absolute angel and come up and look after Toby for me for an hour or so while I go shopping? Toby is already a typical man. He hates shopping and, whenever I take him with me, he ends up having a massive freak-out.'

Caroline looked at her watch. It was only two o'clock. Richard probably would not be home until late and she had nothing planned for all the time in between.

'OK. It would be a pleasure,' agreed Caroline, finding a beautiful old-fashioned card with cupids and roses that was far nicer than the one she had already bought. 'When do you want me?'

'Well, as soon as poss really,' said Sasha predictably.

So Caroline said goodbye, took her card to the counter and paid. It was six years to the day that she had had the abortion. Her little child would have been a five-year-old by now, she thought – walking, talking, going to school. Or maybe even like that cheeky little boy in Dr Gorgoyne's surgery, she smiled to herself.

'Wakey, wakey,' said the assistant. 'That will be two seventy-five.'

Caroline nodded and handed over a five-pound note. It had always felt terrible having the abortion on Valentine's Day, a day of love, but it had been the only date available unless she had wanted to wait another two weeks – which would have been unbearable. At the time, she had told herself not to be ridiculous. How could it matter what day it was? What difference did it make?

But it had made a difference, thought Caroline, as she waited at the bus stop for a nineteen or a four to take her up to Highbury Hill. Now, every Valentine's Day she was reminded of this grim anniversary. She wondered now whether she would pay the price of that abortion for the rest of her life.

Caroline waited at the bus stop for over ten minutes but now she was on her way home from Sasha's and was waiting for a bus to take her in the opposite direction. It was five o'clock and already starting to get dark and Caroline felt exhausted.

It was not that she felt physically tired but she was emotionally drained.

Toby might throw tantrums for his mum but when Caroline was with him he was totally angelic.

'That's because you play with him all the time,' Sasha had said when she arrived home with the usual collection of designer bags. 'You spoil him rotten.'

Caroline had taken her nephew to the park and pushed him on the swings. There had been some men pruning the trees and Toby had been fascinated to watch them climb high up into the branches. His face lit up with excitement and he waved his fat little arms at Caroline and shouted 'Higher, higher!' He wanted to be up in the trees too.

They had then gone on the slide. Caroline was anxious that it was too big for her small but highly adventurous nephew and so she decided that she had better get on too and go down with Toby wedged between her legs. It was rather undignified but fortunately they did not get stuck halfway and there was no one around who knew her – only the usual mums.

Eventually, Caroline and Toby had a rest in the sandpit where they dug holes and built mountains and, even though it was February, they had had so much fun and were so busy that neither of them had felt cold.

Caroline only felt cold now, as she waited for the bus, alone.

On the way home from the park, Toby had asked for 'fweets' and so Caroline stopped at the newsagent to buy dolly mixtures and white chocolate buttons.

By the time they got back to Sasha's house, Toby had nearly fallen asleep in his buggy. Caroline gently undid his straps and took off the little boy's coat and hat. He grumbled a bit at this disruption but soon settled back to sleep in his aunt's arms.

For over an hour Caroline sat on the sofa with Toby lying on her tummy like a huge pregnant belly. She could do nothing while the sleeping child was pinned against her but she felt quite happy there with him, listening to his soft breathing and feeling his warm breath upon her neck. She thought of the article she had read earlier and wondered whether borrowing Sasha's baby in this way might do the trick.

It was Day Twelve and so it was really important to have sex every night that week, thought Caroline, but Richard would probably be so tired that she would have to pester him to do it.

The bus was taking an age to arrive and Caroline was freezing so she decided to start walking. In any event, it was not a long walk and she had plenty of time – she had called Richard from Sasha's and there was nothing to rush home for. As she had expected, her husband would be home late.

She walked on and reached the big church at the top of Highbury Park. As she passed, she looked up at the imposing building and noticed a light was on inside.

'Religion!' She heard her mother's laugh inside her head. 'It's all a load of baloney. And hypocritical too.'

Despite descending from a strong Irish Catholic line, her mother was fiercely anti-Church and Caroline was one of the few children who had never been dragged to a service, not even at Christmastime.

There was a billboard in the grounds of the church. *'Come inside all those who are heavy laden and I will give you rest.'* Caroline smiled at the irony. She was sadly not heavy laden, she thought, but somehow she felt the church almost pulling her in. She had hardly ever been inside one in her life before. Sometimes, on holiday, her father had taken her round the odd cathedral but even that had irritated her mother.

It could not hurt just to look inside, she thought, as she opened the gate and walked up the path. It was dark in the churchyard and the church walls were darker still but Caroline had made up her mind.

She would go in and she might even say a prayer, she thought defiantly. After all, she was prepared to try almost anything else to get pregnant. She knew her mother would laugh at her but no one needed to know. And, if it didn't work, then what the hell? She would not have lost anything either.

She pushed against the thick oak door but it was locked.

'Damn,' she exclaimed, and turned to go. Perhaps it had been a stupid idea, after all, she began to tell herself, but then she saw the window.

It was a big window and it was standing wide open. The bottom ledge was only a short distance off the ground and there was a stone conveniently lying against the wall that seemed to be inviting her to stand on it.

Caroline stood on the stone and peered in at the window. She could see a big, modern kitchen, with cupboards neatly labelled – Cups, Plates, Candles – she could just about read the words in the dim light. Caroline stood very still and waited, her heart pounding. There was no one around and it would be the work of a moment to climb over the ledge and into the sink below. Slowly she lifted her leg.

Chapter Nine

But the timing could not have been worse. When Caroline had called Richard from Sasha's, the Peruvians had just faxed Tazz to say that Centro's Application to Bid was technically non-compliant and, therefore, invalid. Apparently, there had been some cock-up and some of the credentials documentation had been put together in a mess.

'Who the fuck did the credentials?' bellowed Tazz as he stormed up to Richard's desk, brandishing the fax in his hand. He was so angry that the loose pink flesh on his face was quivering as he spoke.

'I'll call you back,' Richard muttered into the phone.

'I just wanted to know what time you'll be home,' said Caroline. 'I was thinking of cooking something special . . . after all, it is Valentine's Day.'

'Is it? I'm sorry, I forgot,' said Richard, covering the mouthpiece. 'I shan't be long,' he said to his boss, who had spread the offending fax out in the centre of Richard's desk for him to read.

'That's good,' said Caroline.

'No. Sorry, it's not good,' said Richard. He could feel Tazz's angry breath on the back of his neck as the man swayed back and forth on his heels behind Richard's chair. 'I don't know what time I'll be home . . .'

'I do,' Caroline heard a voice bellow. 'He'll be home late, very late. We're going to do the whole damned credentials thing again.'

'Did you hear that?' asked Richard.

'So, for Christ's sake, get off the goddamn phone and let's get it right this time. I've just called Hernandez and he says that we must get our act together immediately. I think it's just that some of the pages got into the wrong order but I want you to go through every word and check that it's absolutely perfect this time, OK? We've got another twelve hours. Hernandez says that it's really breaking the rules to let us have another chance and I had to beg him – so you'd better shift your goddamn arse, OK?' Tazz stormed off. Richard prayed that he would not return with his trumpet.

'Did you hear that?' repeated Richard.

'Yes,' said Caroline, buttoning up her coat. 'Poor you. It sounds bad.'

'An understatement,' replied Richard. 'Of course, Jeremiah was responsible for the Credentials.'

'Typical,' said Caroline. 'Jeremiah seems more trouble than he's worth. But why didn't you tell Tazz that? Why isn't the Tasmanian Devil yelling at him?'

'Well, first, needless to say, Jeremiah's already pissed off home – something about a hot date,' said Richard. 'And, secondly, Tazz is right. It is my fault. It was my job to check that everything went off to Peru OK. I should have come into the office after Christmas and gone through all the documents before Jeremiah sent them down the line to Julio in the Lima office. It was just that I so wanted to spend that time with Mum . . . and you.'

'You needed a proper holiday,' said Caroline.

'Yes, but this deal is a really big one and Tazz has set his heart on it. If we win this one, I'll take you to the Gavroche on Valentine's Day next year, I promise.'

'Thanks,' said Caroline. 'In the meantime, it's home alone, with an M&S ready meal for one.' She could hear a faint tap-tap-tapping sound that meant that Richard was already back to work on his computer.

There was a pause and then he realised she was still there. 'Sorry, darling,' he said.

It was not trumpet music that she could hear but the saxophone, perhaps, and maracas. As Caroline climbed out of the sink, there was a distinct but faint throb of Latin American music: a samba or a bossa nova or some such thing.

Caroline crept across the dark kitchen and peered through a glass door. There was a lobby on the other side of the door and it was even darker in there than the kitchen.

Slowly Caroline pushed open the kitchen door and crept into the lobby. She could no longer hear the music and wondered whether she had imagined it. There was another door from the lobby, also with a glass panel in it. Caroline peered through the window and saw, at last, the body of the church itself. She saw the rows and rows of chairs, aisles, flowers, candles and, of course, the altar. She studied the scene carefully. It was not so dark in the church as a few lights were on and also light was streaming through the stained glass windows from the street lamps outside.

But all was deathly still.

Caroline felt like a trespasser and almost turned to go back but she stopped herself. What did it matter? she thought. After all, if someone did find her in the church, she had only come in to pray, not to steal the silver candlesticks. So where was the harm in that?

She walked softly down the centre aisle and, to her amazement, she sensed her spirits lift immediately. It was wonderful to be alone in this place, this big holy place.

It surely could not hurt to pray, she said again to herself as she sat down in a chair in the second row from the front and put her head in her hands.

Caroline must have stayed there for some time, thinking about Toby, dear Toby, and that photo of Johnny's little baby. Then she thought about Johnny's other kids. Six children. Fancy having six children, she thought, and then she checked herself. She had no idea who or what she might be praying to, but she suddenly felt anxious that this sounded greedy. Of course, one would be enough. If it's a choice between one or none then, oh please, just one. One would be fantastic.

The words had only just passed through her mind when there was an almighty crash and all the lights went out.

'Good God,' cried Caroline aloud. Perhaps this praying thing *was* a bad idea after all.

She got up and made her way back down the dark aisle as quickly as she could, keen to make her escape. Just as she was about to open the door to the lobby another door opened on her right and a man appeared.

'I must have blown a fuse when I was trying to fix your lousy stereo,' he said loudly.

Caroline might, in other circumstances, have made a dash for it but she was so stunned at the appearance of the man that she was frozen to the spot.

It was not the suddenness of his arrival that stunned her, although that was alarming enough. It was the fact that he was, as Johnny would have put it, stark bollock naked.

'Sorry,' said the man. 'I thought the church was locked.'

'Er, it was,' replied Caroline.

And then another figure emerged from the shadows. It was another man but this time, fortunately, he was fully clothed.

The second man carried a candle which lit up his face in the gloom.

He was young – mid thirties at most, noticed Caroline, and he was smiling. He had deep laughter lines scored into both cheeks, as though he were a man who laughed a lot, a man who enjoyed life.

'Put some clothes on for heaven's sake, Steve,' said the second man to the first. 'I can see to the fuse box later.' He then moved closer to Caroline and she got a better look at his face. In the warm candlelight his eyes looked a deep blue and there was gold in his hair.

'I'm sorry,' said Caroline, moving again towards the lobby door. 'I don't know why I came in – it was just a mad impulse.' She pulled the door towards her.

'Hang on a second,' said the second man. The naked man called Steve had now disappeared, presumably to put his clothes on. 'That door only leads to the kitchen.'

'Sorry, that's the way I came in,' said Caroline.

The second man looked confused. 'But how?' he

asked and, to Caroline's horror, she realised that she would have to explain about the window.

'You must have been pretty desperate to get into the church,' laughed the man and suddenly Caroline noticed that he was wearing one of the those white collar things around his neck.

'Are you the vicar?' she asked.

'No,' laughed the man, putting out his hand. 'I'm Alex Howard and I'm the new curate here.'

Caroline looked blank. 'Curate?'

'It's a bit like being a trainee vicar,' Alex explained.

Caroline shook hands with the curate. His hands were strong and she felt a strange kind of energy from his touch. Something almost sensuous, she thought, as the curate continued to look at her and smiled warmly.

Caroline took her hand away quickly and the strange connection was cut but the curate's clear blue eyes still penetrated.

'I usually have to drag people into this place,' he laughed. 'Begging and bribery are the tools I often have to resort to – and yet you seem to have been so keen that you broke in through the kitchen window. Is that correct?'

Caroline nodded her head. There was no way that she could lie to those eyes.

'As I said, you must be a desperate woman.' The eyes were smiling but there was genuine concern there too. Alex seemed to be trying to look inside her head, to search out her problem and find some way to help.

Caroline felt exposed and looked away. 'It's nothing,' she said. 'Really, I don't know what came over me.'

'Come on Alex, let's call it a day,' a voice called out of the darkness. It was the man called Steve who reappeared now looking quite different in a dark suit and tie. He had strange hair that stuck up almost vertically from his head and wore heavy black-rimmed glasses.

'Sorry about that,' he said to Caroline, adjusting his spectacles. 'I must have given you rather a shock.'

Caroline smiled and Alex Howard, the curate, introduced his friend properly. 'This is Steve Barnes,' he said. 'Professional lunatic.' Then he paused.

'Caroline,' said Caroline. 'Caroline Roth. Another professional lunatic, I'm afraid.'

They all laughed.

'Let me introduce you to the door,' said Alex, leading Caroline towards a pair of wide double doors directly to the rear of the main aisle. 'OK,' he said to Steve. 'We'll be off in five minutes, mate. Just tidy things up a bit in the vestry would you, please?'

Steve disappeared muttering and Alex and Caroline passed through the double doors and into another lobby. There was an oak door ahead of them, the same oak door that Caroline had heaved against on the other side, barely thirty minutes earlier. This time it opened easily and the street lights shone inside.

'I'd like to help,' said Alex.

Caroline looked into his face again and it still radiated warmth and concern. She had a sudden extraordinary urge to throw herself into this stranger's arms and pour her heart out to him.

'What is it?' asked Alex.

Caroline looked away. Get a grip, she told herself, fighting back tears. She looked down at the ground.

'I'm sorry,' she said. 'It really is nothing. Nothing at all.'

This time, she managed to turn away and start her walk back through the churchyard. Although she heard nothing behind her suddenly he was there beside her again. She gasped in surprise.

'Sorry,' said Alex. 'I didn't mean to frighten you – but can't I give you my phone number? After all, the church is here to help and if you ever—'

Caroline shook her head but Alex's warm smile was irresistible. After all, how could it hurt – taking a vicar's telephone number? she asked herself.

There was some faffing about as Alex realised that he had neither pen nor paper on him and then Caroline started rummaging in her bag.

It was hard to see but eventually she found a piece of white card and her soft pink lipstick.

Not until she got home, of course, did she realise that Alex Howard had inscribed his name and number on the back of the Valentine card she had bought for Richard.

Chapter Ten

There were thirteen of them at dinner, counted Sasha. An unlucky number. Her grandmother, despite being a devout Catholic, had been very superstitious. Sasha could remember a Christmas from her childhood when there had been thirteen people for Christmas lunch and her grandmother had insisted on laying an extra place and had then sent Sasha to find a teddy bear to sit on the fourteenth chair.

Brown and Max sat at the other end of the table, deep in conversation. Sasha realised that they were both, of course, bisexual but they were discreet about their own relationship. Only once had Max suggested a threesome but Sasha had said no and the issue had never been raised again. She knew that, whatever the feelings between Max and Brown, they both loved her and cared about their children.

She sipped her wine and yawned. George, the man on her right who was Max's business partner, had disappeared to the lavatory or somewhere. The woman on her left, Rita, was very drunk and was expounding about her recent experience of genital warts. Not surprisingly, it was putting Sasha off her food.

'Disgusting,' she said, pushing the organic chocolate ice cream to the side of her plate.

'Is everything satisfactory, madam?' asked a waiter appearing at her elbow.

Sasha looked around the table at all her friends, her old friends, and suddenly felt very bored. There were eight men there and she realised that, at some stage or other, she had slept with them all.

'Everything's fine,' she said to the waiter.

But was everything fine? she wondered to herself. She was glad that she was not like Caroline, so bound up in what was right and what was wrong, so responsible. Why should she not have sex with whomever she chose? She looked around the table again and wondered how many of the people there Max had slept with – and Brown.

It did not matter, of course. She would not feel angry or jealous if they had slept with any or all of them. She just wondered where it would all end.

She was happy now and she reasoned, taking another slug of wine, if she ever got *un*happy, she could always change things.

'I wish I'd been more sensible,' moaned Rita on her left.

'It could have been worse,' said Sasha. Well, at least she had not slept with Rita.

The red roses appeared at the end of the week. Caroline recognised, at once, that they had been purchased from one of those roadside sales people you saw so often when you stopped at the traffic lights but, nonetheless, she was delighted to receive them.

'Thank you, darling,' she said and went into the

kitchen to put the flowers in water. They were already beginning to droop.

'God, I feel like shit,' said Richard, flopping into a chair and picking up the *Evening Standard*. He had been home late every night that week and had been leaving for work before Caroline was even awake.

'Do you want to talk about it?' asked Caroline.

Richard grunted and shook his head.

Caroline opened a bottle of wine and put a glass in front of her husband. 'I read this really interesting article in a magazine today.'

Richard said nothing.

'It said that having sex in a warm bath can more than double your chances of conceiving,' Caroline continued.

Richard grunted and turned a page of his paper.

'Richard, this is important,' said Caroline. 'Do you think we should give it a try?'

Richard looked up. 'What?'

'Never mind,' said Caroline.

Richard went back to reading his paper.

'Sometimes I don't think having a baby is important to you at all,' said Caroline.

Richard looked up again and put down his paper. 'Sorry, darling.'

'Oh never mind,' said Caroline, as Richard stood up and tried to take her in his arms.

'No, go on, darling,' said Richard. 'I'm listening. What was it you wanted to tell me?'

'It's all right for you,' said Caroline petulantly. 'You may be busy with your work but it's a lot better than having nothing to do all day except study the calendar and work out what time of the month it is.'

'Is it that time of the month?' asked Richard, pulling Caroline towards him again.

'Well,' said Caroline. 'It is Day Fifteen. We should have done it yesterday as well but you were too tired.'

'I'm sorry,' said Richard, turning away. 'I suppose you think I *enjoy* working all day and all night.'

'Yes, sometimes I think you do,' said Caroline. She knew she was probably being too hard on Richard but having almost to beg him to make love to her at the right time of the month was really getting to her.

'You don't think I'm slogging my guts out,' said Richard, 'so that we can afford a bigger house and so that when we *do* have children then you won't have to go out to work and you can stay at home and look after them?'

'Supposing I don't *want* to stay at home and look after them? Supposing I want to carry on working?'

'What do you mean?' said Richard. 'I thought you wanted kids.'

'I do. But we've never talked about whether I should stop working or not.'

'I always assumed you would,' said Richard. 'My mother—'

Caroline sat down and started to cry.

'I'm sorry,' said Richard. 'I didn't mean to upset you, Caroline.'

'I know,' she sobbed.

Richard put his arm around his wife's shoulder and Caroline was glad to feel his touch.

'I just want you to know that you don't *need* to go on working if you don't want to.'

'The way *my* mother did all the time that Sasha and I were growing up,' said Caroline, looking up with a tear-stained face.

'I didn't mean that,' said Richard.

Caroline continued to cry.

'Look,' said Richard. 'This is not getting us any-where and I really am exhausted. Let's go to bed.'

'OK, I'll come down in a minute,' said Caroline, putting her head in her arms on the table.

It was the first time that she and Richard had had anything approaching a row for a long time and it made Caroline feel very miserable.

She heard Richard getting ready for bed in the bathroom. He was listening to the radio as he brushed his teeth and washed. How could he, thought Caroline. How could he just forget all that had been said and coolly start listening to the radio? Did he have any idea how upset she felt?

Eventually Caroline pulled herself together and made a cup of tea. Day Fifteen was a critical day and so she knew that she would have to make things up with Richard. However, all hope of sex in the bath, she thought to herself, had now gone entirely down the plughole.

As soon as he saw her, he jumped into her arms.

'Toby simply adores you,' laughed Sasha.

'I simply adore him,' said Caroline. 'Where shall we go?'

'Donalds,' suggested Toby immediately.

'Certainly not,' said Sasha. 'McDonald's anywhere is hell but in Oxford Street – forget it, baby.'

Caroline saw at once Toby's disappointment and

hugged him close. 'There's a really good pizza place round the corner,' she said. 'Do you like pizza?'

Toby nodded his head.

'Good,' said Caroline. 'So do I and I'm starving.'

'You're looking well today,' noticed Sasha. 'How's Richard?'

'Oh, fine. Much the same as ever. Working like a lunatic and trying to turn me into his mum.'

'She's not a bad-looking old bird, is she?' laughed Sasha. 'I remember meeting her once.'

'No,' said Caroline. 'She's quite stunning in fact. And, if I keep in with my cosmetic surgeon friend, perhaps I can afford to look that good too when I'm sixty.'

'Oh that reminds me,' said Sasha. 'I got this for you in Fenwicks while I was waiting for you to turn up.' Sasha scrabbled around in one of her bags and produced a small pink aerosol.

Caroline examined the can. It was called Bust Lift but everything else written on the can was in French.

'Look,' said Sasha. 'It says it can improve the *fermeté* – that must be firmness – and prevent *relachement*. What's that? Relatching? Relaxing?'

'Droopiness, I think,' said Caroline.

'Oh yes,' said Sasha continuing to squint at the can. 'And it also promises *tonicité* – toning, I suppose. You just spray it on.' She looked up and smiled.

Caroline took the can and stuffed it into her bag. 'Thanks,' she said. 'I didn't know my boobs were in such an obviously bad way.'

'Don't be silly,' laughed Sasha. 'I bought some for myself as well. I mean any woman can always do with a bit of Bust Lift.'

'You don't need to worry,' said Caroline. 'You're still in your twenties and have a brilliant figure.'

Sasha glanced in a shop window they were passing and pulled a face. 'I don't know. Ever since I had you,' she said, looking accusingly at her son, 'I've had this blubbery layer round the middle that was never there before. It's really annoying.'

'I would be happy to have any amount of blubber if it meant having a child as gorgeous as you,' said Caroline, kissing Toby and strapping him into his buggy.

'Sorry Caroline,' said Sasha. 'How's all that stuff going?'

'Well, no progress, I'm afraid. It's two months since I stopped working for Johnny and zilch to show for it.'

'What about more sex?' suggested Sasha. 'Or is that too obvious?'

'That's what my doctor suggested,' said Caroline, weaving Toby's buggy through the crowds. 'But even that's beginning to be a problem. Richard is just working so hard these days.'

'Perhaps you should take a holiday?'

'Some chance,' said Caroline. 'Richard came home the other night beaming. "Guess what?" he said. "Tazz has agreed to roll this year's holiday entitlement over into next year." I think that was supposed to be good news.'

'Poor you,' said Sasha.

'No, poor Richard really. I get cross with him sometimes but I know he's trying his best and also he hasn't got over his father's death yet either. I think throwing himself into his work is helping him to cope.'

'I didn't realise that he had been that close to his father,' said Sasha.

'I didn't either,' said Caroline. 'That's the funny thing. I can hardly remember them even having a conversation together, other than discussing Scottish football at great length.' Caroline heaved the buggy up the steps into the restaurant. 'But today Richard took the first day off work that he's had in ages,' she went on.

'So what are you doing out with me?' asked Sasha. 'You should have him chained to the bed.'

Caroline laughed. 'It's the only way I would have kept him there. He was up at the crack of dawn to catch a flight to Scotland. He wanted to visit his father's grave – it's exactly a year since Archie died.'

Was it Janis Joplin or Joni Mitchell, Caroline wondered to herself, as the music from the next-door flat wafted through the wall. She made a mental note to go and check on poor Pearl the following day but, in the meantime, she turned up the TV.

There was nothing on as usual and so, after a while, Caroline went downstairs to bed. She had just settled herself and picked up a magazine when the phone began to ring. It was an unusual muffled tone and it took Caroline a while to trace the ringing to Richard's briefcase, which he had left in the hall. By the time she had answered, the caller had given up and Caroline was about to fling the instrument back in the case when she noticed the breasts.

They were huge and pendulous. There were two well-thumbed magazines and she flicked through them quickly. They featured breasts everywhere, all gigantic with enormous blood-red nipples. She threw the magazines back in the case and slammed the lid shut, her heart beating furiously as though she had just encountered a poisonous snake.

She could hardly believe it. She had never known Richard to buy pornographic magazines. Of course, it was only soft porn – nothing perverted – but still Caroline was shocked. And hurt. She went back downstairs and looked at her profile in the bedroom mirror. It was true that her breasts were small but they were still firm and a good shape. Richard had never complained.

Clearly, however, he preferred the more generously endowed figure, she thought, as she climbed back into bed and wondered whether Richard fantasized about the women in the magazines when they were making love.

She thought of Laurence Percival's brochure, still in the drawer of her desk. 'I can change anything,' he had said. But no, that would be ridiculous. She was not going to pump herself full of silicone, whether Richard would like it or not.

Caroline switched out the light and put her pillow over her head but it was only a matter of minutes before she was up again and spraying on her Bust Lift.

Chapter Eleven

Belinda Roth was a fortunate woman.

She reflected on this fact as she worked. She had chosen a deliberately limited palette of blues and greys for the cityscapes she was currently working on. She was saving the bright earth colours for the South American tour that was fast approaching.

Belinda and Graham had bought their place in Clerkenwell over fifteen years ago, just before the area had been invaded by property speculators and prices had gone sky high. They had not paid much for the run-down nineteenth-century printing factory but had now sold off three-quarters of the building and, on the proceeds, had converted the top floor into a spectacular penthouse with a view of St Paul's.

Belinda stood back from her work and screwed up her eyes. She used the pastels very heavily and the dust made her eyes and throat sore. It was time to stop, she thought, looking at her watch and spraying fixative over her painting.

Caroline was coming over to see her and she had just enough time to pop out and buy chocolate croissants, which she knew her daughter still loved.

She ran her fingers through her bobbed brown hair.

Graham had gone off to the library to work on his genealogy thing so she anticipated a nice girlie chat with Caroline. She clipped on a pair of huge dangly pearl earrings that matched her chunky pearl necklace, not real of course, and repainted her bright scarlet lips.

Dear Graham, she thought. It was good that he had now fully retired. They had been trying to get rid of him for ten years and eventually, at the end of the last school year and just before his seventieth birthday, Graham had given in to the pressure and stepped down. But now, of course, he seemed at a loose end, not knowing what to do with himself any more.

Belinda wondered whether he missed the chalky, stuffy classroom, the roughness and rudeness of all those scruffy but bright-eyed kids.

She, herself, had been happy to pack it all in years ago and would have done so earlier. That was the price, she realised, she had paid for having an affair with a married man. There had always been Graham's maintenance payments to consider.

But she had no regrets. She had joined Bulimer Comprehensive as a newly qualified art teacher in September 1964 when she was younger even than Sasha, just twenty-one years old. Graham was thirty-five, thirteen years older, and, although he had been at Bulimer for many years, it was his first term as head of history. He was an ambitious young man and had already set his sights on winning the headship of the school, when the current headmaster retired a few years later.

At first it had just been a close working relationship. There had been nothing wrong about staying late after work to discuss curriculum changes and even retiring to the pub sometimes, where it was more comfortable to chat.

Of course, over time the sessions became more frequent and fairly soon Belinda and Graham did not bother inventing excuses for their meetings. But still, there was no harm in a friendship between two colleagues, was there?

Graham said that he had felt so safe about the relationship that it had quite taken his breath away when Belinda had first kissed him.

And then, of course, there was no turning back.

She had meant no harm even then, she said. It had only been a friendly peck one evening – when she had probably had one gin and tonic too many for such a young woman – and they were saying goodnight.

But for Graham, it had meant everything. He suddenly realised how much he really wanted this woman, how much he had come to depend on her. Graham had returned Belinda's kiss passionately and they had embraced in a shop doorway, like teenagers, for hours – desperate to go further but without anywhere to go.

Belinda had shared her flat in South Bulwood with another colleague, a PE teacher, and so her place was out of the question.

The idea of a weekend school conference had been Graham's idea and they had spent two whole days making love in a Brighton B.&B. In the mid 1960s, London might have been swinging but, in South Bulwood, it would have caused a scandal if anyone had found out.

At first, they were very careful but soon they were so desperate for each other that they would sometimes make love anywhere they could, in the toilets, in the art supplies cupboard, in the air-raid shelters.

Graham knew things were getting out of control but he could not give Belinda up; she was like a drug he had become hooked on.

He had two sons whom he adored and his wife was good and loved him and Graham could not bear the thought of hurting them all. Justin and Sam were just four and two years old when his affair with Belinda started.

But when Belinda became pregnant with Caroline, things changed and Graham realised that he would have to make a choice. He would have to leave his wife.

It took quite a time, in those days, for a divorce to go through its full process. By the time that Belinda and Graham were free to marry, a church wedding was, of course, out of the question. Not only was Graham a divorced man but he then had two illegitimate daughters. The couple was quite beyond the pale of both the Catholic Church and the Church of England.

Of course, Belinda had not minded a jot about getting married in a register office. She had no religious beliefs at all. But it saddened and troubled Belinda's mother.

Belinda had been her mother's only child and not only the source of great joy to her, but also the source of great sorrow.

She had been born in 1943, the product of an illicit affair. Belinda never met her father. Her mother, Rose Hawkins, had always refused to discuss him but her aunt had told her a thing or two. She knew that he was an American, nicknamed Buzz, and had been very handsome. Rose's young husband, Tom, had been away for the best part of three years and it was not unusual for women in Rose's position to be seduced by the glamorous and generous Yankee soldiers.

It was just unfortunate that Rose had fallen pregnant with Belinda. Unlike Graham, Buzz had disappeared in a puff of smoke as soon as he found out about the pregnancy. Probably he too had a wife and children back in the States, thought Belinda.

Of course, Rose was a good Catholic girl and could not bring herself to have an abortion, although the back-street abortion clinics were doing a roaring trade in those days.

And when Tom found out, there was no way he could be a man and stand by her. He had no option but to hold his head high and leave the silly woman to it and so Rose had brought up her daughter single-handed. Not only Tom, but most of Rose's own family had turned their backs on her. It was a dreadful thing to be a single mother in those days and even Rose's beloved Church cast her out.

'It's only understandable,' Belinda remembered her mother saying to her when they talked about the Church. 'After all, they can't be for setting the wrong example, can they?'

But the sadness in her mother's eyes broke Belinda's heart. Day after day, as Rose walked her daughter to school and neighbours turned their faces away or young boys openly smirked at them, Belinda became more and more bitter. The so-called Christians were the worst, she would say, for at least they should know better, at least they should show compassion.

And so, Belinda had vowed she would never set foot in a church again and she had kept her vow.

Caroline was late, thought Belinda. She had returned with the croissants and was now desperate for a cup of coffee. She filled up the kettle and put it on and, as soon as it had boiled, there was a buzz on the intercom.

Caroline pushed open the heavy front door and ran up the stairs to her mother's flat.

'Great minds,' said Belinda as Caroline presented her mother with a large bag of chocolate croissants. 'Never mind, I'm sure I can force-feed some of them to your father when he gets home.'

'Where is he?' asked Caroline.

'Oh, off on some genealogy jaunt,' said Belinda, pushing down the plunger of the cafetière.

Caroline pulled off her coat and gratefully took the mug of hot coffee from her mother. The weather had taken a turn for the worse and she was frozen through.

'So where's Richard today?' asked Belinda. It was unusual for her daughter to come over to see her on a Saturday morning.

'Oh, he's still working on this bloody sewerage project.'

'Sounds glamorous,' said her mother.

Caroline laughed. 'How's the painting coming along?' she asked.

'Oh, I'm saving all my energy for the tour,' said Belinda. 'It's only a couple of weeks before we're off. Margaret told the doctor we were going to Libya not Lima and so she has had all the wrong injections.'

'Poor Margaret,' said Caroline. 'You know, I think

113

Richard is going out to Lima exactly at the same time that you and your group will be there.'

'Really?' said Belinda. 'I suppose he'll be too busy to meet up. Why don't you come on the course? There are still a couple of spare places.'

'Don't be ridiculous, Mum,' laughed Caroline. 'You know that I've inherited none of your creative genius. I'm even a qualified chartered accountant – you can't become an artist after that, can you?'

Belinda smiled and passed her daughter a croissant. 'You're a beautiful, intelligent *and* creative young woman,' she said. 'And, if Richard isn't careful, some-one else is going to tell you that and sweep you off your feet.'

'No chance of that,' said Caroline, taking a big bite of croissant.

'Why not?'

'Oh Mum, please! Mothers are not supposed to try to lead their daughters astray.'

'I've always believed in living dangerously,' said Belinda.

'I know,' said Caroline.

'Just as well for you, or you might never have been born.'

'Thanks,' said Caroline.

'I know that your father always felt bad about leaving Deborah when his sons were so small,' said Belinda. 'But she *neglected* him. I would never have stood a chance, if she had not neglected him so much.'

Caroline finished her croissant and looked out of her mother's panoramic glass terrace doors at the wet grey concrete and steel.

'But it *would* be good to get away from this place

for a while,' she said. 'It would be good to take a break.'

As Belinda and Caroline ate their croissants and chatted, a grey-haired man in his fifties ate his fourth Mars bar of the morning and watched TV. His clothes were crumpled and his expression blank but this man was no deadbeat. His house was in one of the smartest streets in north-west London and had been fashionably decorated and furnished by a trendy interior designer.

The man knew that he should go and pick up his wife. Her friend had called hours ago to say that she had passed out drunk on her sofa the night before and needed collecting. He had paid a fortune for Anabel to dry out at all the most expensive clinics but it was no good. The truth was, if Laurence was brave enough to admit it, that Anabel had never got over Johnny leaving her for Gaby and there was nothing anyone could do about it.

He slowly got to his feet and picked up his car keys. Sadly, the life of Laurence Percival was not as perfect as many people thought it was.

Chapter Twelve

'You'd hardly believe it was the same person,' said Steve, pulling open a bag of crisps and shovelling a large handful into his mouth. 'God, I'm starving.'

'Hard day on the floor?' asked Alex, as he sipped his pint. It was good to have his ecumenical collar off for a few hours and relax with his friend in the anonymity of a City bar.

'Oh, you know, the usual shit,' said Steve. 'Old bollocks-brain Firbrook was down two bar at one point.'

Alex winced. It was now six years since he had worked alongside Steve on the trading floor at Wallbanks but he remembered it well.

'Nothing changes,' said Alex.

'No,' said Steve. 'But I repeat, *you* have.'

Alex laughed. 'For the better, I hope.' He moved his chair a bit closer to Steve, as two other men joined them at the table in the crowded bar.

'You could hardly have got *worse*,' said Steve. 'The stories about some of the things you used to get up to, though, are now legendary.'

'Don't,' said Alex, picking up his pint. 'I shudder to think.'

116

'Like the time you got so pissed off that you threw Tanner's computer through the window and that brilliant occasion when Burton caught you shagging his wife at the Christmas party and then, a couple of hours later, he found you at it with his secretary.' Steve shook his head and wiped the beer that had trickled down his chin with the back of his hand.

'I can't bear to think about it,' said Alex. 'Those years are a complete blur. I was always pissed or high on something – I guess you have to be, to cope with the pressure, at least that was my excuse . . .'

'You must miss the Ferrari though,' said Steve wistfully. 'I mean, the girls I could do without – they're all the same these days. They want to have dicks like the rest of us. But I don't think I could chuck in the car.'

Alex laughed.

'What made you do it, Alex? I don't think I've ever really understood,' said Steve, draining his glass.

'Well, I'd been getting a bit fed up with things for a while.'

'Yeah, I know the feeling,' muttered Steve. He knew that he was getting too old for the floor. Most traders retired before they got anywhere near forty and Steve was already thirty-six.

'Then one morning,' continued Alex, 'I woke up in bed with that Sudanese girl – you know, the graduate that we used to send out for pizzas and stuff?' Alex played with his pint. He could no longer keep pace with Steve these days.

'Anna or Amber, wasn't it?' said Steve.

'Something like that. Anyway, she started telling me how she sent most of her salary home to her family in Africa every month. She told me about

117

their life in the Sudan and it, well, made me feel very small.'

'You were trading Third World debt at the time, weren't you?' asked Steve, rooting around in the crisp packet for the last few crumbs.

'Yes,' said Alex. 'I thought of all the money I was making and Wallbanks was making out of buying and selling these countries' debts, debts they had no hope of ever paying back, and I knew I no longer wanted to be a part of it. It was a small step from there to theological college.'

'But a giant leap for mankind,' laughed Steve. 'How's the flock?'

'Oh, they all seem fine. I'm lucky – St John's must be one of the few churches in the country where it's hard to get a seat some Sunday mornings.'

'Must be your sermons. Do you put in some of those dreadful jokes you used to tell on the floor?'

'Please. Don't start on those,' said Alex, pushing his half-empty glass around the table.

'OK,' said Steve. 'Look, am I going to have to wait all bloody night for you to finish that pint and buy another round?'

Alex got to his feet and put his hand in his pocket.

'Don't worry, vicar,' teased Steve. 'Save your pennies for the needy. Anyway, I've got the car with me today so I'd better go easy. Let's get out of here and pick up a few cans on the way home, OK?'

'Fine,' said Alex and so the two men jostled their way through the seething bar and into the street.

'But I really need to get pissed,' said Caroline. 'And Richard won't be home for hours.'

118

'Well, it's no fun getting pissed on your own,' said Sasha. 'Jump in a cab and come up here.'

So Caroline was in the cab and on her way to her sister's house in Highbury. She was feeling very low. It was Day One and she had really been hopeful this month but, once again, it was not to be.

Caroline sighed. It seemed that she would never get pregnant. Richard had still not gone in to see the Gorgon to have his sperm tested but Caroline felt sure that the problem was all hers anyway. There was nothing for it, she thought miserably. She would have to have the salpingothingy and then, if it was confirmed that her tubes were all clogged up, what would she do?

There was a copy of the *Evening Standard* on the seat beside her. Someone must have left it in the cab and, to take her mind off things, Caroline switched on the cab light and started to flick through it.

The first article that caught her eye was yet another one of those life pieces, this time about a woman who had had a baby for her infertile sister. Caroline read the article avidly and found it deeply moving.

'Up or down?' asked the driver, sliding back the little glass dividing window with a thud.

'Sorry?' said Caroline.

'Which end of the hill do you want, love? The top or the bottom?'

'Oh, the top, please,' mumbled Caroline. She could not think of a more beautiful, selfless thing one could do for one's sister. And then she thought of Sasha and immediately told herself to forget it.

'Here we are,' said the driver as the cab lurched to a halt.

Caroline folded up the paper, stuffed it into her coat pocket, and got out into the street.

Sasha was in the bathroom waxing her legs and yelled to Caroline to come straight up. 'Oh and there's a bottle of white wine in the fridge. Get two glasses and bring those up too,' she added.

When Caroline appeared, her eyes were red and her face pale.

'Oh, you poor dear,' said Sasha. 'Sit down and have a drink.'

Caroline sat on the loo seat and poured the wine. At least at this time of the month, she could have a drink without feeling guilty, she thought.

Sasha took a deep breath and ripped off a strip of wax. 'Aaargh!' she screamed. 'I can't believe that the salon was fully booked.'

'Bad luck,' said Caroline. 'Can I help?'

'Oh thanks,' said Sasha. 'It's murder trying to do it yourself.' She wrapped a towel over her face and signalled to her sister to get on with it.

Caroline swiftly ripped off the strips of wax from Sasha's long skinny legs.

'Aaaahh,' cried Sasha. 'Is it all done now?' She peeped out from her towel and Caroline smiled for the first time.

'You are such a baby,' she said.

'Too right. Pass me my bottle please.'

Caroline passed Sasha the wine and started to tidy up.

'Max is taking us to the West Indies tomorrow – so I could hardly arrive with legs hairier than a spider's,' said Sasha, as she watched Caroline chuck the strips of wax in the bin and fold up the bath towel. 'Don't worry about all that. Olga will be in in the morning. She won't know what to do if the place is all spotless.'

The two women wandered downstairs. Caroline stopped and looked in at Toby's room. The little boy was softly breathing in his cot, his chubby hand at his mouth and an arm around his teddy. Caroline stroked his curls and pulled up the blanket that he had kicked into a heap in one corner.

'Come on,' said Sasha at the door. 'I'm going on down – I thought you wanted to get pissed.'

'I won't be a second,' said Caroline, feeling suddenly that she could quite happily kneel down beside Toby's cot in the darkness and sit there all night, just watching him sleep.

Once she was settled downstairs, however, Caroline felt different. It was not difficult, she found, to drink one glass and then another and another and slowly the pain began to ease.

'It's so unfair,' said Sasha after she had listened to her sister say the same things she said every month about her fear that she would never have children. 'I feel so useless. Is there anything I can do to help?'

Caroline looked up at her sister, surprised that she seemed able to read her thoughts, but then she looked down again at her glass and shook her head. 'Johnny sent me a tube of something in the post this morning,' she said. 'It's called Love Oil and one of our clients is promoting it.'

'Love Oil,' cried Sasha. 'What do you do with it?'

'Well, you're supposed to massage it on the tip of the man's penis before you have sex. It's supposed to lubricate the path of the sperm – so that they shoot up inside you like greased lightning.'

They both laughed.

'There must be more hopeful strategies than that,' said Sasha.

Caroline sighed. She could not bear to raise the subject of surrogacy but, nonetheless, on her way down from Toby's room, she had stopped at Sasha's bedroom and left the copy of the *Evening Standard* on her sister's bed. It was still folded open at the article Caroline had been reading in the cab.

By the time they had finished their second bottle, Caroline and Sasha were starving hungry.

'I can't believe that there is *never* any food in your house,' said Caroline, squatting down in front of Sasha's fridge in disbelief.

'You know I *love* shopping,' said Sasha. 'But *food* shopping – that's quite something else.'

'Hi gorgeous,' said Max, coming into the kitchen. 'George and I have just had dinner with the boss of Tryons. I think they're going to sign up to develop a new model of the birthing chair.'

'That's brilliant,' cried Sasha, immediately equating this news with its potential cashflow.

'I think I'll leave you two to it and have an early night,' said Max, smiling at Caroline, who had sat back down again at the table, looking very red in the face and clasping her empty wine glass.

'OK,' said Sasha. 'But, since you're in, Caroline and I might pop out for a while and get some supper. The kids are both fast asleep.'

So Max babysat, while Sasha and Caroline went to

a Turkish restaurant in Highbury Barn and had something to eat together with another bottle of wine.

'I thought eating was supposed to sober you up,' said Caroline as she slumped across the table.

'Well, only if you stop drinking as well, I think,' said Sasha. 'Come on, let's get you a cab.'

It was unusual for Sasha to be playing the more responsible role out of the two of them and she could not remember a time when she had literally had to help her sister to her feet.

'Don't worry,' said Caroline as she staggered out into the cold night air. 'I can get the bus home.' The bus stop was on the other side of the road and she tottered towards it.

'Wait!' cried Sasha. She had stopped to exchange a few words with the waiter, who had cheekily asked for Sasha's telephone number when he had returned with her credit card.

But Sasha's warning came too late. There was a screech of brakes and a flash of headlights as a car spun in circles in the middle of the road.

Caroline's small crumpled body lay still in front of the wheels.

Within seconds, a small crowd had appeared but Caroline was already on her knees and brushing herself down. 'It's OK, I'm OK,' she said. 'The car didn't even touch me – I just fell over.'

'Christ, you frightened the fucking life out of me,' cried the driver, jumping out of the car and running up to Caroline and Sasha. He was a young man in his thirties with hair that stuck out vertically from his head, and black glasses.

'The naked man!' cried Caroline.

'She's in shock,' said Sasha, taking her sister by the arm. 'She doesn't know what she's saying. I'd better get her home.'

'But it *is* the naked man. You are the naked man, aren't you?' insisted Caroline.

The crowd that had gathered in the road all stared at Caroline as though she were mad and then a tall slim man stepped forward and said, 'Yes, you're quite right, Caroline. And I'm Alex, remember? The naked man's friend.' It was the good-looking curate whom Caroline had met the afternoon she had broken into the church.

'Shall I call an ambulance or the police?' asked the waiter from the Turkish restaurant, suddenly appearing at Sasha's side. Sasha looked at Caroline who shook her head – she just wanted to get home as quickly as she could. Alex looked at Steve who looked at his beloved car, which was mercifully unscathed, and he also shook his head.

'No, we're fine,' said Alex to the waiter, in a commanding voice. 'This young woman is a friend of mine,' he added to the crowd in general. 'I'll make sure that she and her friend get home safely.'

The words sounded patronising but they had the effect of dispersing the crowd.

Steve parked the car and then Caroline and Sasha, Steve and Alex all stood on the pavement for a while just staring at each other.

'I'm sorry about that,' said Caroline at last. She knew it was ridiculous but it was starting to rain and she could not help thinking what a mess she must look. She wondered if her nose was shiny and red and hoped that, if it was, then it would be too dark in the street to see.

'No,' said Alex. 'Steve is always driving too fast.'
Steve opened his mouth to defend himself but Alex
continued. 'Where do you live?' he asked.

'Well, she lives down in Barnsbury but I only live
round the corner so I can easily walk home,' answered
Sasha.

'So, perhaps, you will allow me to drive you home?'
said Alex to Caroline.

Steve opened his mouth again, wider this time. Alex
was insured to drive his car – it was sometimes useful
when they had been to a big bash and Steve had had
too much to drink – but he had never known Alex ask
to drive the car otherwise.

Caroline looked confused. 'Are you sure? Can't we
all squeeze in?' She looked at Steve's car and noticed
for the first time that it was a gleaming white convert-
ible Mercedes.

'Only room for two, I'm afraid,' said Alex as Steve's
jaw almost dropped to the ground. There had been
times when he and Alex had squeezed as many as six
into that car. 'Legally,' he added, reading Steve's mind
and holding out his hand for the car keys. 'Anyway,
Steve and I only live down the hill by the stadium and
five minutes' walk will do you some good, mate,' He
took the keys and gave Steve a friendly jab in the belly.

Alex helped Caroline into the car. He opened the
door and held her arm as she lowered herself awkwardly inside.

'Are you sure you're OK? Is there anything you
want?' he said as he closed her door.

Caroline shook her head. The eyes and smile were
the same as she remembered them, full of light and
warmth. She felt very safe and relaxed with this man.

'Just take me home, please,' she said.

Alex went round to the other side of the car and cheerfully waved at Steve before he got in and drove away.

Steve and Sasha stood side by side on the pavement and watched the car disappear.

'Wow. Smooth operator,' said Sasha. 'Who is he, James Bond?'

'Not quite,' laughed Steve. 'But you could say that he's a man with a mission.'

Chapter Thirteen

'So, have you broken into any good churches lately?' asked Alex, as they pulled up at the traffic lights opposite the Alwyne Castle.

'I'm sorry,' laughed Caroline. 'You must think I am a complete nutcase.'

'There's nothing wrong with praying,' said Alex.

Caroline studied her driver's profile as he watched for the lights to change. He had good strong features but, in his shabby tweed jacket and jeans, there seemed no scrap of vanity about the man.

'I don't believe in all that stuff,' said Caroline.

'There's probably a surprising amount of stuff *you* don't believe in that I don't believe in either,' he said, shifting into first gear and steering the car round the corner.

'My grandmother was a Catholic,' said Caroline. 'And, with her, it seemed nothing but rules and regulations. Perhaps the Church of England is a bit more easy-going?'

'Oh, there's still enough of the usual stuff to put most people off,' laughed Alex.

'But not you.'

'I may enjoy playing the role of Good Samaritan tonight but, believe me, I'm no saint.'

'Really?' said Caroline, realising how little she knew about this man. As they drove through the bright buzz of Upper Street, she noticed that he had streaks of green face paint on his cheeks. 'Isn't the, er, situation with you and Steve a bit of a problem – with the Church and everything?' she found herself asking.

Alex seemed a little taken aback by the question but suddenly burst into laughter.

Caroline felt embarrassed. 'I'm sorry,' she said. 'I wasn't trying to pry into your relationship. Forget I asked that question.'

'Certainly not. I should have explained before. I can hardly blame you for leaping to conclusions when you find me holed up in a church with a naked man.'

'It's none of my business,' said Caroline.

'No, it's not,' said Alex. 'But, just for the record, Steve and I are just friends. I am an amateur artist and Steve is the only person prepared to sit for me.'

'You were painting him?'

'Well, just doing a few sketches. Life drawing is a really useful exercise,' said Alex. 'Steve shares a house with me and we usually work there but the light at home is really dreadful at this time of year, so the vicar said I could use the vestry.'

'And what or who have you been painting today?' asked Caroline.

'How do you know I've been painting today?'

Caroline leant over and touched Alex's cheek. 'Green paint,' she said.

Alex seemed startled by her touch. He quickly glanced in the rear-view mirror and began rubbing his face. 'What a mess,' he said. 'I'm always frightening my elderly parishioners by going about the place as though I'm about to embark on a tribal war dance.'

Caroline laughed. 'My mother is an artist. Belinda Roth.'

'Belinda Roth,' said Alex thoughtfully. 'I've heard of the name.'

'Please,' protested Caroline. 'You don't have to pretend to have heard of her.'

'No, I think I saw something in John Jones about some painting course she ran in Tuscany last year – I almost went on it.'

'Yes,' said Caroline. 'That sounds like Mum. But, this year, she's decided that painting in Europe is becoming too boring. She's arranged to take her group to South America.'

'How exciting,' said Alex.

'Yes.' Caroline paused and then added, 'Actually, I think she's still got a place or two free. Perhaps you would like to go?'

'Are you going?' asked Alex.

'Oh no,' said Caroline. 'I can't draw to save my life.'

'That's what Steve says,' said Alex. 'I've tried teaching him but he's too impatient. He doesn't like to look properly and drawing is all about looking properly.' They had stopped at more lights and Alex took the opportunity to look properly at Caroline.

'Have you known Steve long?' she asked.

'We used to work together and we've lived together for six years,' said Alex. 'Of course, Steve could well afford to live somewhere a good deal smarter than Highbury but he's an Arsenal fan and quite enjoys living in the shadow of the stadium. And, besides, I suppose we've got used to each other now. In some ways, we're like an old married couple.'

'Like me and Richard,' said Caroline, fiddling with her wedding ring. 'We've been married for just over six years.'

Alex slowed down and looked at her again. It was as though she could see him taking in the information she had just imparted.

'Where do we go now?' he asked.

'Oh, it's the next right,' said Caroline. 'Number forty-three – about halfway down on the left.'

Alex said nothing until the car pulled up outside Caroline's house. 'Don't forget to drink a couple of pints of water before you go to bed,' he advised as he helped her out of the car. 'I've had enough hangovers in my time to remember what the morning after is like.'

'I don't know why I got so drunk tonight,' said Caroline. 'I'm not usually like this,' she found herself adding.

'I used to drink to blank things out,' said Alex. 'It was very effective.'

Caroline said nothing.

'Is there anything else I can do to help?' he asked.

Caroline shook her head and started rummaging in her bag for her keys. Like the time she had first met Alex, she was fighting an almost overwhelming desire to burst into tears. Why did this man have such a weird effect on her, she wondered.

'No, please don't worry,' she said. 'It's nothing – I'm fine.'

Alex touched her arm and smiled. 'OK. But, thank God, we met up again – Steve hasn't let me drive his car in months.'

Caroline smiled back. 'So much for the Good Samaritan,' she said, as Alex drove away.

'I thought you might enjoy a break,' said Richard, squinting at his laptop as Caroline poured herself a large glass of water.

'I would,' said Caroline. 'Thanks, it would be great.'

'Of course, I'll be working a lot of the time we're there,' said Richard. 'Tazz wants this deal at any price, he says, but there must be lots for you to see and do in Lima while I'm not around.'

'Yes, and Mum will be out there then too, so I could meet up with her for a bit,' said Caroline, taking a sip from her glass. Her period had finished and so she was back on the wagon again.

'Good.' Richard continued to tap at his machine.

'Thank you,' she said, leaning towards her husband with the intention of kissing his cheek but slipping and kissing his shoulder. 'I'm going to bed.'

'Careful,' said Richard, as the kiss jogged his hand and he pressed the wrong key.

'Sorry,' said Caroline.

'Don't worry. I've had enough of this anyway – I think I'll join you.'

'Come on then,' said Caroline, getting to her feet.

They went downstairs and got ready for bed. Richard was still in the bathroom when Caroline went into the bedroom and got undressed. It was as she was getting into bed that she noticed the tube of Love Oil lying on her desk. It was probably a bit early in the month, she thought, but, perhaps, it was worth a try. It might be quite fun.

Richard came into the room and quickly switched

out the light. Caroline slipped out of bed again to get the tube from her desk.

'What are you doing?' he asked, as Caroline returned and immediately started to stroke his buttocks. 'Good grief, is it that time again already?'

'Not really,' said Caroline. 'But I thought a bit of extra practice might not do any harm.'

Richard smiled and turned over. He took Caroline in his arms and kissed her neck.

'Hang on a second,' said Caroline. 'Johnny gave me this Love Oil stuff – we're supposed to put it on you first.'

'What?'

'It's a herbal thing or was it homoeopathic? Anyway, it's supposed to increase our chances,' said Caroline, holding up the tube in the dark

'Ridiculous,' said Richard, as Caroline took the top off the tube and smelt it.

'It's got a funny smell,' she said, struggling to think what it reminded her of. 'But it's got to be worth a try.'

'OK, then,' said Richard. 'If you insist.'

'I'll do it,' said Caroline, disappearing under the bedclothes.

'Not too much,' cried Richard, as Caroline squeezed out most of the tube. 'It's cold and it tickles.'

They laughed and made love and Richard came quite quickly after Caroline's very thorough massaging of the Love Oil. But as Richard tried to pull out of his wife, Caroline screamed. 'Careful!' she cried.

It seemed that they had somehow got literally stuck together.

Eventually, after wrestling painfully for a few minutes, they hobbled to the bathroom together, like Siamese twins, to find the nail scissors. Then, using half a jar of very expensive hand cream, they managed – with excruciating discomfort – to tear themselves apart.

Richard said that the makers of Love Oil should be sued but Caroline said nothing. She would wait a while, she thought, before she told her husband that she had picked up a tube of glue by mistake.

The following morning, Caroline sat at Richard's desk and folded up the details of the art course that her mother had given her. She put them in an envelope and then hesitated before sealing it.

It surely could not hurt to add a little personal note? In fact, it would be rather rude to write nothing, she thought.

She took the papers out and sat for some time thinking about what she should say.

Eventually she wrote:

Here is the stuff on my mother's art course. It's probably too late notice but I thought I'd send it anyway. Best wishes, Caroline.

She folded the papers up but then stopped again. After more thought, she picked up her pen once more and added:

P.S. I shall be in Lima myself from 28th March to 4th April so, if you do go, maybe we shall meet again!

This time she managed to get the letter folded up, into its envelope and sealed.

Her heart was beating fast as though she was doing something scary or wrong. But there was surely no

133

harm in telling Alex that she would be there? It would be odd not to, she told herself.

And, after all, he was only a vicar.

Chapter Fourteen

'Sorry,' said Dr Gorgoyne, sweeping biscuit crumbs from her desk and gesturing at Caroline to sit down. 'He's still not come in to see me.'

'He's working like a lunatic on some Peruvian sewerage project,' said Caroline. 'Actually, I'm going out to Lima with him on Monday night.'

'Well, it will be good for the two of you to get away for a few days,' said the Gorgon, settling herself across the desk.

'I thought I'd come in and fix a date for the salpingo-thing anyway,' said Caroline. 'I mean, it's ridiculous not to have my tubes checked. I feel as though, every month that goes by, my eggs are getting older and older and it will soon be too late.'

'Good,' said the Gorgon. 'I mean it's a good decision to have the salpingogram done but there's no need to panic,' she added, curling her scarlet lips into a hideous grin. 'I have women in their forties coming in here every day telling me that they are pregnant – women who are old enough to be grandmothers and some of them are!'

'Don't,' said Caroline. 'It just makes me feel worse.'

'You go away and enjoy your holiday,' said the

Gorgon, scratching her wiry old head. 'With a bit of luck and Latin magic, perhaps you won't need anything more.'

'Most unlikely,' said Caroline later, as Sasha put on the kettle to make her sister a cup of tea. 'My doctor thinks a few days in the sun will sort Richard and me out but it's not that simple. I really think something must be wrong with me.'

'Why don't you see someone else?' said Sasha.

'What?' said Caroline.

'Another doctor. This gargoyle woman is obviously useless and positively objectionable, from what you tell me.'

'Yes, I've talked about it with Richard,' said Caroline. 'But he says it's too early. He still thinks I'm panicking.'

Toby was asleep in his buggy and Siena was watching a *Friends* video on TV.

'There is more to life than kids,' whispered Sasha.

'I heard that,' said Siena, turning up the volume on the TV.

'Sorry, darling,' said Sasha. 'Only joking.'

She stood up and took Caroline's hand. 'Come on,' she said. 'Let's go into the drawing room for a few minutes, I've got something to tell you.'

'Something you don't want me to hear?' said Siena.

'Could be.'

'How sad,' said Siena. 'The thought that you could say or do anything that would shock me. You really are pathetic, Mum.'

'And you want kids,' said Sasha as she led Caroline away.

When they sat down in the big untidy room, Caroline

noticed for the first time how excited her sister was. She was grinning from ear to ear and was clearly dying to tell Caroline some news.

'What is it?' Caroline asked. 'I've been so tied up in my own thoughts, I haven't asked you how things are with you?'

'Well, since you ask,' beamed Sasha, 'things are fantastic.'

'Why? What is it?' repeated Caroline. 'Or should I say *who* is it, this time? Some beautiful West Indian you met on your holiday?'

'Caroline, please. I'm not going to tell you, if you're going to be horrid to me,' Sasha added petulantly, tossing her long golden curls over her shoulder and striking a pose by the window.

'OK, I promise not to be horrid. Now tell me.'

'Well,' said Sasha, turning back towards her sister and obviously desperate to reveal all. 'When I got home from the holiday there were two messages on the answerphone.'

'From whom?' asked Caroline.

'The naked man.'

'The naked man?'

'Yes, you know,' said Sasha. '*Your* naked man – the one who nearly ran you over.'

'Really?' said Caroline. 'But why?'

'Well, duh,' said Sasha impatiently. 'You *know* – him and me.'

'What?' cried Caroline in surprise. 'You don't mean to say that you're seeing him?'

'Well, it just sort of happened. After you and that flash vicar had shot off in Steve's car, we went for a drink together . . .'

'You didn't tell me,' said Caroline.

'So?' said Sasha defensively. 'You may be hanging out with a vicar – but you're not a priest, darling, and I'm not in the bloody confessional when I talk to you yet, OK?'

'OK,' laughed Caroline. 'But I'm not hanging out with a vicar.'

Sasha pulled a face.

'Anyway,' said Caroline, sipping her tea. 'He's a curate.'

'Same thing,' said Sasha, crossing her legs away from Caroline. 'So do you want me to tell you about Steve or not?'

'Of course I do.'

'Well.' Sasha turned back to face her sister with enchanting enthusiasm. 'He's divine. He is so charming and funny and strong and quite the most gorgeous man I have ever known.'

Caroline laughed. Sasha never changed. She was such a child, constantly falling in and out of love. It was quite endearing.

'How much have you been seeing each other?' she asked.

'We've only met three times,' Sasha said with a sigh.

'And been to bed together how many times?'

'Please!' said Sasha with mock alarm.

'Come on,' said Caroline. 'As your daughter says, there's nothing you could tell me that would make me fall off my chair.'

'Well, if you must know, we have *not* had sex yet.'

Caroline nearly fell off her chair.

'In fact, we have only kissed once – when he dropped me home last night,' continued Sasha.

Caroline put down her mug of tea. 'What on earth has happened to you?'

'I don't know,' said Sasha, trying to look wistful and getting up to look out of the window again.

A good effort, thought Caroline to herself, but she was not convinced.

'I just want things to be different this time. This man makes me feel very special – the way he looks at me, the things he says, the touch of his hand . . .'

As Sasha spoke, Caroline suddenly found herself thinking about Alex. But she quickly checked herself. After all, she was married and happily married. She did not want to have a relationship with Alex or anyone other than her husband.

'Have you told him about Max and Brown?' asked Caroline, bringing her sister back to earth sharply.

Sasha looked round and frowned. 'Well, yes and no.'

'What do you mean?'

'Well, I couldn't tell him the truth obviously,' said Sasha. 'So I, well, invented this sister. Er, Meggie, she's called.'

'Meggie?' asked Caroline. 'Why?'

'Well, you see, Meggie has these two children, a girl aged twelve and a boy aged two and, well, Meggie's not very well at the moment – a suspected brain tumour or something – and so I'm looking after them.'

Caroline stood up. 'Sasha – that's appalling,' she said.

'I'm sorry,' said Sasha. 'I know. But, I didn't know what else to say. Please don't tell him the truth, will you?'

'I don't suppose I'm likely to see him,' said Caroline. 'But if you continue seeing him, he's bound to find out some time.'

'Yes,' said Sasha. 'But I hope he will like me for who I really am by then instead of judging me by my past.'

'You poor thing,' said Caroline as she saw her sister's eyes brim with tears. 'You know, you're really not as bad as all that.'

'Please don't tell him the truth,' said Sasha. 'I'm so afraid I'll lose him if he finds out I've got two children and live with two men.'

'Hmm,' said Caroline but Sasha looked unusually pathetic.

'Please,' she implored. 'There was a time when I didn't care what other people thought or said but now things are different. You know, Max and Brown and me – I used to be so happy. I used to have it all but now it is starting to feel, well, wrong.'

'OK,' said Caroline, sitting down beside her sister and putting an arm around her shoulder. 'But you'd better fill me in fully on our new sister, poor thing. Where does she live and when did she get ill?'

Caroline and Sasha spent the next half-hour building Meggie into a real person. It was quite fun, like one of the games that they had played as kids together when they made up plays and acted them out for their parents.

Caroline could not help feeling that the whole Meggie thing was likely to end in tears but, as usual, she indulged her little sister.

'Thanks Caroline,' said Sasha, when it was nearly time for Caroline to go. 'I just want to do things differently this time. I want to try, you know, being faithful and sticking to one man. What do you think? What's it like?' Sasha looked up into Caroline's face, her eyes childlike and searching for comfort.

'It's good,' said Caroline. 'It's the way things should be.'

'So, you see, she had a very narrow escape,' said Graham. He was treating his daughter to lunch at Henry's, a small fish restaurant in Clerkenwell. Richard was working again that Saturday and poor Caroline was at a loose end.

Caroline nodded with interest as she listened to her father's story. 'And you and Sash and me – we're all descended from this woman?' she asked.

'All of us,' said Graham. 'Fascinating isn't it? If it had not been for that greedy sexton, none of us would be here.'

Graham had been telling Caroline a story he had discovered about one of their direct ancestors in the sixteenth century. This ancient relative, a woman called Flora Walford, had fallen into a 'mystical fit' and died. She had been pregnant at the time and, with great sadness, her husband had laid her to rest in the family vault in the local church. She was left with her rings still on her hands and later the sexton attempted to hack off Flora's fingers in order to steal the rings. The first finger he cut bled profusely and the sexton fled in horror, leaving the door of the vault open. Flora slowly recovered consciousness and managed somehow to get up and stagger home, frightening the life out of her husband who assumed she was a ghost. He would not let her into the house, at first.

'One wonders what guilty secrets the husband had – for him to be so scared,' said Graham.

'And Flora went on to have a healthy baby boy from whom we are all descended. It's an amazing story, Dad.'

'Yes,' said Graham, taking a large bite out of a chicken wing. 'This genealogy stuff is very interesting.'

'Mum says you're getting obsessed with it.'

'Well, she enjoyed that story anyway,' said Graham.

'Yes, I expect she did,' laughed Caroline. 'Particularly the bit about the thieving sexton – that would fit in with all her preconceptions about clergymen.'

Graham sipped his wine and poured Caroline some fizzy water.

'She never could stand anything to do with religion,' said Graham. 'I still rather miss going to church on Christmas Day, you know.'

'Do you?' asked Caroline, genuinely surprised. Her father had never said this before.

'When Justin and Sam were little, we used to make them wait until after church to open their presents,' he said. 'They got to have their stockings first thing, of course. But Deborah thought it was good to do the religious, the meaningful bit, first, before we spent the rest of the day indulging ourselves.'

'I suppose so,' said Caroline. She had never been to church on Christmas Day in her life but she thought she understood what her dad was trying to say.

There was silence for a while as the waiter cleared their plates. Caroline took the opportunity to study her father's face. He was getting older, of course, and his white hair had receded but his eyes were still full of warmth and love.

'It must be a terrible thing to be buried alive,' he said.

'Horrific,' said Caroline. 'It's hard to think of anything worse.'

'Make sure that I'm really dead before you bury me, won't you?' Graham laughed.

'Oh, Dad, please,' said Caroline but, although her father continued to smile, she knew that he was serious.

'I *know* it was here,' said Caroline, searching through her underwear for her passport. Somehow at work she had always been considered super-efficient and organised but her personal life was chaotic.

She got down to the bottom of the drawer and started tossing out suspender belts and G-strings – things that had somehow found their way into the drawer but which, of course, she never wore.

Tangled up in a knot of tights was a newspaper article. Caroline straightened it out and looked at it. 'Oh, I saved this,' she said to Richard. 'It's about adoption. Apparently, there are more lottery millionaires each year than adoptions of children under twelve months.'

'Really?' said Richard, propped up in bed reading the *Telegraph*. 'We could always adopt an older child.'

'But I want a baby,' cried Caroline, slinging a scarlet lace corset across the bed.

'Well, we don't need to think about adoption yet,' said Richard. 'Let's see what the salpingogram comes up with.'

'Yes, I suppose so,' said Caroline. Her underwear drawer was now completely empty.

'Perhaps it's slipped down the back. Try pulling the drawer right out.'

Caroline did as her husband suggested and, as usual, he was right. The passport had slipped into the drawer below.

'Thanks,' said Caroline, retrieving the document and looking at the passport photo of herself, taken several years before.

'So, when are you doing the test?' asked Richard.

Caroline continued to look at the photo. Where was the young, self-confident woman she had once been, she wondered. She hardly recognised herself.

'As soon as we get back from Lima. But, you know, you really should have had your sperm checked first. Just in case.'

'I know,' said Richard. 'But given, well, we got pregnant once before—' The words were the last thing Caroline wanted to hear; she was already beginning to worry about the salpingogram.

'I know! Don't say it,' she cried, jumping up from the bed. 'I know it's all *my* fault.'

'I didn't say that,' said Richard, trying not to raise his voice.

'You might as well, though,' she continued. 'You think I've messed myself up and we'll never have a baby now.'

'Don't.' Richard put out his hand and signalled for her to come back to the bed.

'Oh, it's so depressing,' said Caroline, slumping back onto the bed. 'And you don't seem really bothered one way or the other. All you seem to care about is your stupid work.'

'That's nonsense, darling. You're being irrational,'

said Richard, patting her head with maddening calmness.

Caroline did not wish to hear her feelings written off. Whether they were irrational or not was hardly the point, she thought. She needed to tell Richard how she felt, how worried she was. All she needed was for him to listen and understand.

But Richard had already picked up his paper again. 'Let's talk about it later,' he said. 'When you're feeling better.'

Caroline got up and flounced out of the room, slamming the door. Stuffed down the side of the medicine box, from which she took two capsules of paracetamol, she found the Valentine card that she had bought for Richard and on which she had written Alex's number. She sat looking at the number for some time and then picked up the phone.

'Sorry it's so late,' she said. 'I just needed to talk.'

Chapter Fifteen

'No problem, baby,' said Belinda. 'It's always a pleasure to hear from you and anyway I'm just sitting here waiting for your father to come to bed. He's still in his study compiling grisly tales about his ancestors so you weren't interrupting anything important, if you know what I mean.'

'Good,' said Caroline.

'Well,' continued Belinda. 'I'm off on the big tour tomorrow and shall be away for nearly a month, so I want to make sure your father remembers what he's missing while I'm away. Margaret says I should leave him a supply of bromide tablets, like they used to give the soldiers in the war – not that they did any good, of course.'

'Mum!' laughed Caroline. 'How *is* Dad?' she added, trying to change the subject.

'Oh, same as usual,' said Belinda. 'He's getting as bad as Richard. Tap-tap-tapping away at his computer all night – it's like being married to a bloody woodpecker.'

'Poor Dad. He did seem a bit morbid when I saw him for lunch.'

'Mm, I've asked Sasha to keep an eye on him while

we're away but she's so wrapped up in this new man she's seeing that I don't suppose she will be much help.'

'Don't worry,' said Caroline. 'Richard and I are only away for a week, so I'll go and see Dad as soon as I get back.'

'Thanks,' said Belinda. 'He's going to stay up in Cambridgeshire for a few days – but he should be back by then.'

'Is he going to see Justin?'

'Yes. He seemed to think it was a good thing to do while I was out of the way. Deborah lives with Justin now, you see.'

'Right,' said Caroline.

'I always thought that, in time, he'd feel less responsible for that woman,' said Belinda. 'After all, it is over thirty-five years since he left her and I've been his wife for over three times the time he was married to *her*.'

'Yes. It's a very long time. But I do think he still feels a bit guilty.'

'Well, he never talks about it to me. Whenever I try to probe, he tells me not to worry. I've sometimes suggested that he regrets leaving her but he just laughs at me and tells me I'm being irrational.'

Caroline could not help thinking of her own husband's similar comment a few minutes earlier.

'But he's right, of course,' she said. 'Dad adores you and I don't think, for a moment, that he has ever had regrets about leaving Deborah.'

'I don't know,' sighed Belinda. 'He's still in his study working – I'm afraid I don't turn him on any more.'

* * *

147

'You are big and buxom. Your breasts are full and large.'

There was a creak on the stairs but Caroline did not hear it. She stared at her semi-naked reflection in the mirror and continued in a louder voice.

'You have the biggest, firmest breasts I've ever seen.'

'Er, excuse me?' called a voice and Caroline almost leapt out of her skin. She grabbed a towel and bolted the door.

'Who is it?' she cried.

'Oh sorry, love, the front door was open. Is it a bad time?'

Caroline recognised, with horror, the voice of her neighbour, Pearl.

'Oh no, sorry,' said Caroline. 'Thanks. I'll be up in a second.' She must have forgotten to close the door properly when she got back from the newsagent. How embarrassing.

She had got home and become immediately absorbed in an article that claimed you could increase your breast size just by talking to your breasts and giving them some positive feedback. If Pearl had heard what she had been saying, thought Caroline, she would think that she was either mad or some kind of pervert.

'Don't worry, I'll close the door for you,' said Pearl. 'I was just on my way out and noticed it was open.'

Caroline heard the front door slam as she pulled her T-shirt over her head and ran up the stairs. She was just in time to see Pearl get into a powder-blue Jag. The silhouette of the driver looked male but Caroline could not see him clearly and the car sped away as soon as Pearl closed her door. It was good to see Pearl going out, thought Caroline, but she wondered who her neighbour's friend might be and how she had come to meet him.

She closed the door and felt bored and lonely. She had lost interest in talking to her breasts and wondered how much longer she should stay at home before giving up and going back to work. She missed Johnny and the rest of the gang at GLP. She felt she was turning into a mad housewife with nothing better to do than read silly articles in magazines while she waited for her husband to come home.

But, as she passed the study door, she could not help thinking about those other magazines she had found inside Richard's briefcase. She had asked him about them, of course, and Richard had looked embarrassed but he had been unable to give a convincing answer. He said that Jeremiah must have put them in there or something. It did not sound very likely, thought Caroline, but she had let it go.

'Are you sure you're all right?' asked Graham.

'Yes, fine,' said Belinda. She had just arrived in Lima and felt exhausted after the long journey. She wanted to collapse onto her bed but knew Graham would worry if she did not call to say she was there safely.

'Did all your students turn up?'

'Yes,' said Belinda. 'Most of them in a complete muddle, as usual, with enormous easels and cases full of materials. I gave them a list and told them to bring only the essentials but they never pay any attention, of course. Margaret had a handbag with her budgie in it. She said that she didn't like to leave him behind but they caught him when he went through the scanning machine. She'd forgotten to take off the little bell round his neck.'

'It sounds chaos,' laughed Graham.

'It was. Then that young man – you know, that one who signed on for the course at the very last minute, was also in a dreadful state. He had a huge suitcase which he could barely lift off the ground. God alone knows what he had in that.'

'Well, at least, you are all there safely and can relax now,' said Graham. 'Caroline will be with you tomorrow, won't she? I tried to call her this morning to say goodbye but the answerphone was on.'

'She's probably busy getting ready,' said Belinda, glancing around the room. The furnishings were clean but shabby and there was an ancient fridge humming in the corner. She had, of course, had to book modest accommodation for her class and the Pension Ibarra had been well recommended although she had not expected to find it located on the fifteenth floor of a tower block.

'Dear Caroline,' said Graham. 'She is so conscientious. Sometimes I can't help thinking she's too responsible for her own good.'

'Well, she doesn't get her responsibility genes from me,' laughed Belinda, digging in her bag and producing a bottle of vodka. 'I'm going to have a stiff drink and get some sleep.'

'OK, sweetheart. Take care,' said Graham. 'I love you.'

'I love you too,' replied Belinda. She lay back on the bed and could not help laughing to herself as she recalled the scene at Heathrow. The young man had arrived late, staggering under the weight of his bag, with paintbrushes sticking out of his pockets and a portfolio case strung over his shoulder like a huge satchel. But most ridiculous of all, he had been wearing a clergyman's collar.

Belinda had a word with him at once. He was clearly the most attractive man on her course, at least thirty years younger than any of her other 'students', but she was not going to go touring the sexiest continent on the planet with a bloody vicar in tow.

'Now look here,' she had said, plucking a paint-brush from his pocket and pointing with it at the offending collar. 'You can take that thing off at once. We're having no preaching on my course, except from me, OK?'

The young man had gone bright red and muttered something about having to get ready in a hurry and being unable to find a clean *normal* shirt. So Belinda had given him a tenner and told him to go and buy a T-shirt, for God's sake. He had come back a few minutes later proudly sporting the message *Up Yours!*

'Is that better?' he asked with a cheeky grin. Belinda was already enchanted.

'Much better,' she had said and made sure that she sat next to him on the plane.

'Good,' said Tazz. 'And remember to take care of Hernandez.'

Richard looked at his watch and checked that he had his passport, the tickets and his money.

'I mean, really take care of Hernandez – you know what I mean?'

Richard cradled the phone on his shoulder and put his wallet back in his pocket. 'Yes,' he said.

'I've sent round a bike. Don't leave before it comes – I've sent over what you need,' continued Tazz.

'What do you mean?' asked Richard. 'I'm sure I took everything I needed when I left the office.'

Tazz laughed. 'Not quite everything. I can see you're still wet behind the ears when it comes to doing business in some parts of the world.'

Richard said nothing.

'Good luck then,' said his boss.

'Thanks,' said Richard and put down the phone.

'Are you ready?' he said to Caroline, who was stuffing things into a very large bag. She could not get her brain to focus on what she really needed to pack and so she had just decided to take everything.

'Nearly,' she said, going up to the kitchen to look for her diary.

'I'll just call the cab service,' said Richard, 'and check the taxi is on its way.'

Seconds later, there was a loud blast on the doorbell.

'That must be the cab now. I'll get it,' called Caroline from upstairs.

She opened the front door and was surprised to find that it was not the cab but a despatch rider with an urgent parcel that she had to sign for.

'It's from Tazz,' said Richard, appearing at Caroline's side as she closed the door. Richard opened the envelope and stared at his wife. Caroline watched in amazement as he pulled out a thick wodge of cash. Then he pulled out another and another until there were four fat bundles in his hands.

'I can't believe it,' said Richard. 'US fifty-dollar notes.'

'What's it for?' asked Caroline.

'I don't know. I presume Tazz wants me to bribe the Peruvians with it.'

As he said this, there was another ring on the bell. Caroline jumped and gasped. 'It's the police,' she cried. But it was not the police, it was their cab.

'Come on,' said Richard. 'There's nothing we can do about it now.' He stuffed the money back in the envelope and went downstairs to collect their things. There was no way that he could leave such a huge amount of cash just lying about in the house, so he quickly tucked the large brown envelope into Caroline's bag.

It was disgusting, thought Richard, that Tazz should expect him to bribe their customers but he also knew that, if he refused to and then Centro lost the deal, he might end up losing his job.

He carried the heavy bags upstairs and got into the cab with Caroline. He no longer felt so sure that the trip would turn out the way he had hoped.

Chapter Sixteen

It was a seven-hour flight to New York and she breastfed all the way.

'It's very unusual to see babies flying business class,' said Richard as he offered Caroline a paper to read. His wife had been sitting staring at the mother and child since they took off.

'It's the only way to keep her quiet,' said the woman who sat just across the aisle from Caroline.

'She's beautiful,' said Caroline. The baby was only a few months old and she and her parents were relocating to New York where the father had been seconded by the management consultancy company that he worked for.

'It's a fantastic opportunity,' said the woman, stroking her daughter's fuzzy blonde hair. 'By the time we come back she will be running around and speaking with an American accent. It will be a much harder journey when we return.'

Caroline smiled.

'Do you have children?' asked the woman. It was the question that Caroline hated most.

'No,' she said quietly.

'I used to work full-time,' said the woman. 'I was

really crazy about my job and never thought I'd give up working. But having Lucy has changed everything. She may look like a real handful but she's worth it, believe me.' The woman seemed to think that Caroline needed convincing of the merits of motherhood.

Caroline smiled but Richard grunted. 'Let's watch the film,' he said.

They watched the film but ironically it was all about a couple who could not have a baby. They flew around the world having sex on top of various phallic monuments. Eventually they tried doing it in a hot air balloon which, for some reason, did the trick – except the husband, having fulfilled his purpose, lost his balance and toppled out of the basket to his death.

Caroline looked at Richard.

'Don't even think about it,' he said.

At JFK, they changed planes onto a LanChile flight that would take them overnight to Lima. Santiago was the end of the line in South America and the Chilean planes always stopped at Lima en route. The travel agent had suggested the Chilean service was better than Aeroperu and Tazz had said this was code for saying that a Chilean pilot was less likely to be stoned than a Peruvian one. The LanChile plane was half empty and Caroline started to unwind. It felt good to be getting so many miles between her and the cares that dogged her in London. She closed her eyes and tried to sleep.

Several hours later, Richard lifted a blind and the sun streamed in through the windows. They had just crossed the Andes and were descending towards Lima. The stewardess pointed out some large adobe pyramids in the middle of Lima's urban sprawl.

'They are five thousand years old,' she said. 'And were built in the U-shaped style that is characteristic of the temples on this part of the Peruvian coast – the shape was thought to promote fertility.'

Caroline sighed. There seemed no escaping the subject: first, the baby, then the film and now ancient fertility symbols. Perhaps they were good omens, however, she thought to herself and she determined to take Dr Gorgoyne's advice and enjoy the break.

Lima was big and hot and busy, as Caroline had expected, and extremely smoggy. They had arrived in the middle of the morning rush hour; the streets were noisy and dirty and it seemed to take forever for the *taxista* to get them to the centre of the city and the huge, colonial Gran Hotel Bolivar.

The hotel had a beautiful lobby but Richard was worried that they had been unable to get a room at the Lima Sheraton.

'Tazz will be furious. All our competitors will be at the Sheraton,' he said. 'Miraflores is much smarter than this part of town.'

They checked in quickly as Richard was running late for his first meeting. Caroline leant over the balcony while Richard had a shower. There was a spectacular view of the busy Plaza San Martin and the brooding ancient mountains camped close behind the city. Caroline took a deep breath as Richard kissed her briefly, grabbed his bag and rushed out of the room. Poor Richard, thought Caroline, as she closed the blinds and curtains and slid between the cool crisp sheets of her bed. He must be exhausted and yet she knew he had a full schedule of meetings ahead.

After several hours' sleep, Caroline woke refreshed. She drank some fizzy water from the mini bar, then phoned her mother's hotel and left a message for Belinda to call her. It was early afternoon and Belinda and her class would almost certainly be out sketching or painting. It was unlikely that either Belinda or Richard would call her for hours. So she took a shower and changed her clothes and set off to explore on her own.

One of the first things that struck Caroline about Lima was how young everyone looked. There were children everywhere, even tiny tots, without an adult in sight. Clusters of them hung round the traffic lights, in their bright but ragged clothes, selling huge plastic bags full of peaches and melons. Many ran alongside her as she walked down the street, begging for money. Richard had, of course, given her plenty of local money but it was all in large notes. She had no change to give to these big-eyed little children.

After a while she found a café in the main square, the Plaza de Armas, and sat down at a table in the shadow of the Government Palace that took up the whole of one side of the Plaza and drank *cusquena*, the local beer. She had a guide book to read but it did not interest her. She was only interested in the children who seemed to buzz around her like flies. Fortunately she now had some change from her coffee and was ready to give her money away.

Word soon spread about the generous *gringa* in the cafe and a huge swarm of children gathered around Caroline that the waiter angrily dispersed.

Caroline finished her beer and left and, as she walked

on, she noticed that a small chain of three little girls was following her. The eldest could not have been more than eight, the youngest looked scarcely two. They were all barefoot and very dirty. Their hair was black and hung in tangly pigtails but their huge brown eyes were clear and beautiful.

'*Señorita*,' said the eldest. 'You very pretty.'

Caroline smiled. 'You speak English,' she cried. 'How clever.' But the child looked blank now.

'What's your name?' asked Caroline, crouching down beside the girl.

The girl shook her head. 'You very pretty,' she said, holding out her small, grubby hand while the other hand held tight to her baby sister.

Caroline smiled and gently touched the little girl's thin shoulder.

'You very pretty,' repeated the girl for the third time. It seemed that this was just a phrase that someone had taught the child to say but still it touched Caroline's heart.

'Do you have a mother? *Mamá?*' asked Caroline.

The little girl nodded and pointed up to the hills behind the city.

Caroline rummaged in her pocket and produced a fifty-soles note. The little girl's eyes widened and her mouth fell open. She had never seen a fifty-soles note in her life before.

'We must give this to your mummy. To *Mamá*,' she said. '*Por dar a tu mamá*,' she added, wishing she could remember more of her schoolgirl Spanish.

The little girl nodded and took Caroline by the hand. It was an odd procession and Caroline began to wonder what she was getting herself into as the girls led her though streets that became shabbier and shabbier at each turn. They crossed the river and it was a long hot climb up into the *barriadas* where the little girls lived. Caroline was shocked at the poverty she saw. But children everywhere stared at her and then smiled. She did not feel threatened.

After a long time, they arrived at *la casa* and Caroline saw a young girl sitting outside with a middle-aged man in a grey suit. She was wearing a shabby white panama hat to keep off the sun and had a baby at her breast. But she looked far too young to be the mother of the three little girls.

'*¿Tu mamá?*' asked Caroline.

The little girl shook her head as her sisters went running up to the young woman and kissed her and pointed excitedly at the *gringa*.

'*Nuestra hermana,*' she said. 'Dolores.'

Caroline went over to Dolores and smiled at the young mother feeding her child. The baby was about the same age as the baby she had sat next to on the plane and was just as beautiful, but what a difference there was in the destinies of these two children. The baby on the plane would be afforded all she needed in life, whereas who knew what the future held for this poor little thing.

The man in the grey suit stood up and smiled at Caroline. Despite the smile, Caroline saw no warmth in his face.

'A beautiful baby,' he said in surprisingly good English.

'You are a lucky man,' said Caroline.

'Ah no,' said the man. 'I am not the father. The father, he—' He shrugged his shoulders and looked down at Dolores. 'It happens all the time here. Who knows where the father is now and this poor girl – her mother already is a widow and has six mouths to feed.'

Caroline put her hand in her pocket and took out three fifty-soles notes. She still did not like the look of the man in the grey suit, so she folded them and gave them to Dolores.

Dolores started and got to her feet. '*Gracias, mil gracias,*' she said.

For the first time, Caroline saw little Diego properly. He was, she thought, the sweetest baby she had ever seen.

Dolores noticed the tenderness in Caroline's face and held up her baby son for her to see.

'Would you like to hold him?' asked the man in the grey suit. '*¿Le deja agarrar a la gringa el bebe?*' he said to Dolores.

Dolores smiled and nodded and so Caroline held the little bundle in her arms and rocked him. The baby did not scream, as she had feared he would, but he looked up into Caroline's eyes and waved his tiny hands at her.

'This baby is looking for the adoption,' said the man in the grey suit, his English deteriorating a little as he tried to explain.

Caroline gasped and looked at Dolores. It seemed inconceivable that, even in such poverty, a mother would give up her son.

Dolores shook her head and glared at the man in the grey suit. She put out her arms to take Diego back and Caroline reluctantly handed the warm little thing back to his mother.

'My name is José,' said the man in the grey suit. 'Ten thousand American dollars,' he whispered into Caroline's ear. She recoiled instantly but she had heard what he said.

'I have all the papers proper. It is a legal thing,' said José.

Caroline backed away. Dolores had sat down and, as she fed her baby again, Caroline could see tears trickling down her cheeks.

José bent over Dolores and whispered something in her ear. Dolores looked up startled and then looked at her baby and at her sisters who were playing now inside the shack behind her. She burst into a new wave of sobbing and shook her head.

José smiled and returned to Caroline.

'Think on it,' he said. 'Only ten thousand American dollars for such a beautiful child.' He fished in his pocket and extracted a dog-eared business card which he pressed into Caroline's hand.

As Caroline ran back down into the city, she could not help but repeat over and over the words Don José had said. Ten thousand American dollars. It was less than the cash that sat in those four fat bundles in the large, brown envelope that was now locked in the hotel's safe.

She could take the cash to José the next day and return to London with that beautiful baby. 'Perhaps it might be as simple as that?' she wondered but her eyes filled with tears as the image of Dolores' sad face returned to her.

Caroline was almost blind with tears and her feet were sore with running, as she turned a corner into

161

the Plaza San Martín and bumped straight into a tall blond man.

'Ah, the desperate woman,' he cried, as he caught hold of Caroline and prevented her from stumbling into the road. 'What mischief have you been up to now?'

Caroline was fighting for breath and saw, to her amazement, that she was in the grasp of Alex Howard. 'The vicar!' she cried, fighting for breath – she had been running so fast.

Alex laughed. He was wearing a white T-shirt and blue jeans. He looked so young and vital that it was hard to believe he was a clergyman.

'Please,' he said. 'Not so loud. If your mother hears you referring to me as "the vicar", she will have a fit. She thinks my "calling", as she puts it, lowers the tone of her group.'

Caroline laughed. 'Of course,' she said. 'You're here with Mum. I thought bumping into you again was a coincidence too far.'

'That's a pity,' smiled Alex still holding Caroline's arm although she was now steady on her feet. 'I was hoping you might think it was the forces of destiny thrusting us together.'

Caroline blushed and looked away.

'I have to admit I was doing a tour of all the big hotels here to find out where you were staying,' said Alex. 'So, not much of a coincidence seeing you at all, I'm afraid.'

Caroline should, perhaps, have moved away but the firm touch of Alex's hand on her arm, courteously guiding her across the street, was extremely pleasant.

'How's the course going?' she asked.

'Oh, it's only the first day,' said Alex. 'But already I'm driving your poor mother crazy. She can't understand why I carry this great bag around with me.' Alex adjusted the strap of the bag on his shoulder. 'It weighs a ton.'

'What's in it, your art stuff?' asked Caroline.

'Well, yes. But don't tell your mother – I also carry around a stack of Spanish bibles. We've been sketching all over the city today and you wouldn't believe how much these poor people appreciate having their own copy.'

'I'm surprised the people here have any faith at all,' said Caroline, shivering at the strong grip of Alex's hand as he moved it up to the top of her arm and then steered her through the doors of her hotel. 'The poverty is unbelievable.'

'It's the other reason I'm here,' said Alex.

'You mean you didn't come just to see—' Caroline blushed again. 'I mean, you didn't come just for the course.'

'No. There's a church project going on here, called Latin Link. We're trying to build a new school and medical centre in one of the *barriadas*. I offered to see how things are going, do some drawings and take some photos. It will help the church with its fund-raising at home.'

Caroline nodded. It was ridiculous for her to presume that Alex had come to see her. She told herself to stop being stupid and turned towards the concierge.

'I'll just check whether my husband is back yet,' she said.

Alex backed off and leant against a chair in the lobby.

Caroline spoke to the small wiry man behind the desk and he shook his head. 'No, *señora*,' he said, holding up her room key. 'Your husband was back for some time this afternoon but I fear he has gone again.'

She asked whether there were any messages for her. The man went off to a wall of little pigeonholes and returned with a folded slip of white paper.

It was from Richard. *Sorry I missed you. Big problems with Hernandez and so must do dinner with him. Very boring – catch up with you later.*

Caroline put the paper in her bag and walked back to Alex. She should, of course, be disappointed that Richard would not be back for dinner but her heart fluttered with anticipation at the prospect of dinner with Alex. It would be interesting to get to know him better, she thought to herself.

Alex stood up as she approached him. 'Any news?' he asked.

Caroline shrugged. 'Richard is busy.'

'That's a pity,' said Alex but his eyes showed no great disappointment at the news at all. 'Do you think he would mind if I took you out to dinner?' he added.

'No, I think he would be pleased to have someone keep me company.'

'Good,' said Alex.

'I'll have to get changed,' said Caroline, for the first time thinking what a mess she must look.

'OK,' said Alex. 'But you look fine, as you are.'

Caroline laughed and blushed again. It was maddening, she thought. They were just a couple of friends having dinner together and yet she kept behaving like an infatuated little schoolgirl.

'I'll wait for you here,' said Alex.

He looked at her with such warmth that Caroline did not want him to take his eyes off her for a moment but somehow she backed into the lift, stumbling into a woman who was coming out of it with a baby buggy.

Alex ignored her embarrassment and Caroline urgently pressed the button inside the lift to close the doors. Her face was red and her heart beating fast. Was this really the way she behaved when she was just having dinner with a friend, she asked herself.

Eventually the cold steel doors mercifully slid closed and she was alone. As the lift juddered into action Caroline leant her head against the wall and cried aloud, 'Oh my God, Caroline Roth, what the *hell* are you doing?'

Chapter Seventeen

Caroline got into the shower. It was nearly midnight, London time, and she had not slept much in the last twenty-four hours but she did not feel tired. In fact, she was excited and full of energy.

She brushed her teeth and rinsed with mouthwash – something she wondered whether she would have bothered with, had she only been having supper with Richard. She even grabbed one of Richard's razors and quickly gave her legs a shave. Ridiculous, she thought to herself, since no one was going anywhere near her legs.

She spent a long time on her make-up. She put on the new black 'Maximiser' bra that she had bought recently and a dress that she knew she looked sexy in. Her heart was beating fast as she popped in some earrings, took a last look at herself in the mirror and picked up her key.

One of the room-service boys stared hard at her and made her feel that, perhaps, she was overdressed. She nearly rushed back to her room to change but told herself not to be so stupid. After all, she was having dinner with a friend, a *vicar*, who knew that she was married and was just keeping her company. So where was the harm in that?

Alex stood up to meet her when Caroline reappeared from the lift. He did not need to say anything – Caroline could tell that he thought she looked good – but Alex lifted his hands and said, 'Wow. You look stunning.'

Caroline blushed and smiled. She could not help thinking how seldom Richard bothered to pay her a compliment.

'I've been talking to the concierge,' said Alex, 'and there's a place he recommends down in Miraflores. It's only a short walk from here, is that OK?'

'That sounds great.'

'Oh, and you'll be glad to know that I persuaded the concierge to look after my bag for me, so I shan't embarrass you by handing out Bibles to our fellow diners.'

'Good,' said Caroline. 'Mum would approve.' They laughed and stepped out into the street.

The restaurant was surprisingly bright and trendy. Alex's Spanish was good so they managed to interpret the menu and order their food without too much difficulty.

At Caroline's suggestion, they stuck to drinking the local beer.

'I feel we should be drinking champagne,' said Alex, as he picked up his bottle.

'Why? What are we celebrating?'

'Oh, just being here.'

'You're very romantic,' laughed Caroline.

'Am I?' asked Alex, seeming genuinely surprised. 'I just try to enjoy life as I find it.'

'You sound like my sister,' said Caroline. 'And yet

you could hardly be more different. She is a hopeless case.'

'Come on. No one is a hopeless case,' said Alex.

'I'm not so sure.' Caroline laughed again.

Ceviche, the classic national dish of raw fish marinaded in lime juice, arrived for both of them and they ate.

Alex asked about Caroline's job and, before long, she had explained to him that she was taking a break from work and hoping to have a baby.

Alex listened quietly and looked concerned. He did not offer any advice but it was such a relief, thought Caroline, to be able to talk about it with someone who would really listen. She began to feel a great weight lifting from her.

'It's so good to talk to you about it,' she said. 'It's a great release – in fact, every time I see you I feel like bursting into tears.'

'Thanks,' laughed Alex.

'No. I just mean you listen so well, it's like being with a – a therapist or something.'

'I was hoping you would say it was like being with a friend – a good friend,' said Alex, reaching across the table and touching her hand.

'It is,' said Caroline, looking up and smiling. 'That's exactly what it's like. Being with a good friend.'

On the way back to Caroline's hotel, they stopped at a café. There was a small jazz band playing in the corner and some people were dancing.

'This music is called *criolla*,' said Alex as he watched the dancers and Caroline watched him, her stomach churning with anticipation. But, when Alex looked back at her and smiled, she had no hesitation and got to her feet. What could be wrong with having a dance?

Alex held her in his arms gently but with such control that she felt as light as a feather, as though her feet were hardly touching the ground. They moved slowly around the small space that was the dance floor and Caroline realised how long it had been since she had danced and what a wonderful thing it was to do.

'I love Latin music,' said Alex.

'Yes,' said Caroline, suddenly remembering the music she had heard playing the night she had broken into Alex's church. 'Weren't you playing this music the evening we first met – in the church with Steve?'

'I don't remember,' said Alex.

Caroline blushed but fortunately it was dark enough to be imperceptible. 'I was in a terrible state that night. I don't know what you must have thought of me.'

Alex tightened his grip on Caroline as a woman in a short red dress nearly crashed into them.

'I was very impressed,' said Alex. 'I've never encountered such an attractive intruder before.' His face was very close and his eyes looked directly into hers.

'I don't know why I did it,' said Caroline.

'I do.'

'Why?'

'You wanted to pray about the baby,' said Alex. 'You were deeply troubled and wanted to pray about it.'

Caroline stumbled slightly as the dance floor became more crowded and they were penned into one small corner of the room. 'Yes, I suppose so. But it's ridiculous. I mean, I don't even believe in God.'

'Everyone prays whether they believe in God or not.'

Alex paused and then added, 'When there's nothing else left to do.'

'But there is,' said Caroline. 'At least, I hope there is,' she added, the tears coming at last.

'Let's sit down,' said Alex as the woman in red crashed into them again. He took Caroline's hand and led her back to the table. He moved his chair beside hers and sat down. Then he put his arm around her and held her close while Caroline buried her face in his shoulder.

'We've been trying for over a year and nothing's happened,' said Caroline. She could not bear to tell Alex about the abortion; she was afraid he would be horrified. 'My doctor is going to do some tests but I can't help feeling that there is a serious problem.'

'Poor you,' said Alex softly.

'That evening I broke into the church, I'd been at my sister's house. Sash— I mean, Meggie,' stammered Caroline, cursing her sister. 'My sister has two lovely children. I'd been babysitting her two-year-old. I had held him in my arms while he slept and I just felt I would never have the pleasure of holding my own child.'

'Poor you,' said Alex again. 'That sounds terrible – children are so wonderful.'

Caroline looked up at Alex through her tears. 'Do you want children?' she asked.

'Oh, very much,' said Alex. 'As many as possible, if I can find a wife who's prepared to have them for me.'

Caroline looked down again but Alex hugged her closer and stroked some hair out of her eyes. She felt almost childlike in his arms.

'Richard says that having babies is not the most

important thing in the world. I think sometimes he doesn't care whether we have children or not,' said Caroline.

'I'm sure he does care. But he's right in a way. I think he is trying to help when he says these things – he probably doesn't want you to feel that if you *can't* have children then there is no purpose in your life at all.'

'I suppose. But I'm not ready for that yet. I'm not ready to give up hope.'

'Of course not,' said Alex as he paid the waiter and told him to keep the change. 'Shall we go?'

Alex and Caroline walked slowly back up the Paseo de la Republica towards the Gran Bolivar. They both seemed to realise what a short distance it was to the hotel and wanted to make the walk last as long as possible. There was a stone seat on the corner of the square and Alex suggested they sat for a moment. Caroline was calm now and so there was no excuse for Alex to put his arm around her again. They sat side by side on the stone seat a short distance apart.

'I was almost offered a baby today,' said Caroline. 'When we bumped into each other, I had just come down from the *barriadas*.'

Alex looked surprised. 'What were you doing up there? It's not safe, you know – you could easily have been mugged.'

'I don't know,' said Caroline. 'I met three little girls, three sisters and they took me up there to see their mother.'

'Did you see her?'

Caroline shook her head. 'No. Only another sister, an older sister with a tiny baby. There was a man with her who offered to sell me her baby.'

'It's so sad,' said Alex shaking his head.

'He was a beautiful baby,' said Caroline. 'She even let me hold him. And I have the money – I could easily take it up there tomorrow. This is the man,' Caroline fumbled in her bag and produced Don José's card. 'He says he can fix it all.'

'Is that what you're going to do?' asked Alex.

'No,' said Caroline quietly.

Alex said nothing but reached across and touched her hand.

Caroline bit her lip. She really did not want to start crying again so she looked away.

'No,' she repeated. 'It would be the wrong thing to take the baby. I'll just have to take my chances and hope that my doctor can sort me out.'

Alex squeezed her hand.

Caroline looked back at Alex and suddenly felt out of her depth. 'I'm sorry to go on,' she said, extracting her hand. 'But it's been a big help talking to you tonight. I feel so much better.'

'Good,' said Alex as they got up to leave.

'Thank you so much for dinner,' said Caroline rather awkwardly.

Alex shook his head. 'It has been one of the most enjoyable evenings of my life.'

'I can't believe that for a moment,' laughed Caroline. 'I've spent most of the time blubbing and pouring my heart out to you. I don't know why I should choose *you* to bore to death with all my problems.'

Alex kissed her gently on the cheek. 'I know it sounds corny,' he said. 'But that's what friends are for.'

Chapter Eighteen

'How's it going?' asked Caroline. She was still half asleep but conscious of her husband moving about the room collecting his things together.

'Well, Hernandez is seriously considering a rival bid so I'll have my work cut out trying to change his mind,' said Richard. 'Particularly if I'm not going to use Tazz's money.'

'Poor you,' said Caroline, propping herself up on one elbow. 'I'd hoped we might do some sightseeing together.'

'No chance,' said Richard taking a slug of orange juice from his breakfast tray. 'Have you seen your mother yet?'

'No,' said Caroline, slumping back on the pillows and thinking back to the night before and her dinner with Alex. She really should tell Richard all about it. There was, of course, no reason not to. Richard would not have been upset to hear that she had bumped into a friend and had dinner with him.

'I suppose you were too tired to do much yesterday,' said Richard. 'Do you feel better today?'

Caroline smiled and nodded. 'I'll call Mum this

morning. She's flying down to Santiago tomorrow evening – so, perhaps, we could all do dinner tonight?'

Richard shook his head. 'No chance. I need to have dinner with the Minister of Utilities and the Finance Minister. Tell your mum I'm sorry.'

But Caroline did not tell her mother that Richard was sorry. In fact, she did not call her at all. Knowing that Richard was busy for dinner that evening, she could not help hoping that Alex would call and invite her out again. It would be much more fun having dinner with Alex than with her mother.

She spent the whole morning mooching around in her hotel room, reading the papers, then reading a paperback novel, watching TV and, not least, watching the phone.

It was ridiculous, she told herself. She should just pick up the phone and call her mother. But she knew that Alex, of course, would also be flying down to Santiago the following night and so this was the only night that she might see him again.

When the phone eventually rang, Caroline almost leapt out of her skin. Her heart was beating so fast and her hands were so hot and clammy that she almost dropped the receiver as she picked it up.

'Hello,' she stammered, like an awkward teenager.

'Caroline, is that you?' her mother's strident tones blasted over the line.

Caroline sighed. 'Hi Mum.'

'Hello baby. Are you all right? Why haven't you called me?'

'Oh sorry. I don't know – I was a bit tired after the journey . . .'

'Listen darling,' interrupted Belinda. 'We're going down to the Barranco today to paint the ocean. It's a lovely part of the city – very romantic. Why don't you come with us?'

Caroline hesitated. It would be fun to go and she had nothing else to do but what would Alex think? She was a dreadful painter and he might get the wrong impression if she went. He might decide she was running after him and that would be just *too* embarrassing.

'I'd love you to come with us,' said Belinda.

'No, thanks,' said Caroline. If Alex had wanted to see her again, he had had plenty of time to call. 'Let's do dinner this evening.'

'OK,' said her mother. 'There's a good little *chifa* near our hotel. Very ethnic – I had something called *antecucho* there yesterday which was delicious until I was told it was beef heart kebabs. Margaret ordered some *jalea*, thinking it must be jelly, but it turned out to be whitebait which did not go down well with her ice cream at all.'

'I'll make sure I have a good lunch,' laughed Caroline, 'so that I'm not too hungry.'

'Pick me up at the hotel at eight thirty,' said Belinda. 'I must dash – the troops are getting a bit twitchy. They have their brushes at the ready and can't wait to get started.'

Caroline put down the phone. The thought of Alex getting twitchy about his painting was oddly irritating. But that was absurd, she told herself. After all, Alex had come to paint not to see her. She told herself to grow up and got dressed and wandered downstairs. The hotel had a pool and she suddenly felt very tired.

She would have a quiet day by the pool resting and reading in the sun. It would also mean that she would not miss any messages if, of course, someone should decide to call her.

'So how was your day?' asked Belinda as she emerged from the apartment block lifts in a flowing orange dress. She was wearing a colourful beaded necklace and huge matching earrings. 'You really missed some sensational scenery,' she added before Caroline had a chance to say a word. Caroline felt self-conscious in her pale purple T-shirt and white capris. She felt out of place in the dull grey room which served as a lobby for her mother's *pension* which was crowded with surly locals who sat silently or talked in whispers. This was not a hotel frequented by foreigners, by *los gringos*, and there were no signs of Belinda's students, no sign of Alex.

'Where's your tribe?' asked Caroline.

'Oh, the poor dears. They're all out for the count,' laughed Belinda. 'All that sea air and then the passion of seeing the sun set over the Pacific was too much for them. Margaret took off her stockings on the beach and some little urchin picked them up five minutes later, thinking they were some kind of seaweed – I hope his mother doesn't cook them for their supper. It was such a pity that you did not come.'

Caroline smiled. She could not bring herself to ask specifically about Alex but she could not help wondering where he was and what he was doing.

These thoughts persisted and dogged Caroline throughout the whole evening with Belinda. She could hardly concentrate on what her mother was saying.

'You seem a bit low,' said Belinda at last. 'A pity that Richard has to work so hard. It seems hardly worth inviting you, if he can't spend any time with you.'

'Oh, it's fantastic just to get away for a few days,' said Caroline pushing her food around her plate. 'I needed to have a break from London and I've had a very peaceful day at the hotel pool.'

'You sound as worn out as one of the poor old girls on my course,' said Belinda. 'What you need is some excitement in your life or you'll be old before your time.'

Caroline forced a smile. She was in no mood for a lecture from her mother but she could see one coming with the momentum of a juggernaut and there was nothing she could do but to let it roll over her.

'You should stand up for yourself more,' her mother went on. 'Tell Richard what you need, before he finds it's too late.'

Caroline said nothing so Belinda continued. 'You remind me of Mum. You're too self-sacrificing, too willing to take the blame for things.'

'Gran had a difficult life,' said Caroline.

'Life is what you make of it,' said Belinda emphatically. 'Mum always blamed herself for the affair she had during the war with my father but it wasn't really her fault. She was young and any number of young women in those days were being swept up in the arms of Yankee soldiers. She was no different.'

'She was a married woman. Just because everyone is doing something doesn't necessarily make it right.'

'She was unlucky,' continued Belinda. 'She got pregnant and, in those days, there was nothing you could do about it. She had to have me – and thank goodness for both of us that she did – and her husband, when he came home and found out I was on the way – well, he had no choice. It was a question of honour, he said. He had to leave her.'

'It must have been very hard for her,' said Caroline. 'And you.'

'We were outcasts. Social outcasts. It didn't bother *me* much – I got used to the teasing at school. But it broke poor Mum's heart.'

Caroline nodded.

'I'll never forgive those hypocrites, those oh-so-God-fearing hypocrites, for what they did to Mum,' said Belinda, angrily stuffing a big forkful of rice into her mouth as she finished speaking.

'I'm not sure you should be so hard on them. They were just trying to stand up for what they thought was right.'

Belinda shook her head but her mouth was too full for her to be able to reply.

'Perhaps today it's too easy to do just what you want, regardless of how it hurts others,' continued Caroline. 'Gran must have hurt her husband and her family a lot.'

Belinda swallowed hard and stared at her daughter. 'Take my advice,' she said, waving her fork. 'There's little enough pleasure to be had in this world, as it is. You should take whatever you can get.'

Caroline looked at her watch. It was not yet ten o'clock and she had done virtually nothing all day but she now felt exhausted. 'I'd better get back to the hotel,' she said. 'Richard will be waiting for me.'

But Richard was not waiting for Caroline when she

got back to the hotel. Another man was waiting and Caroline felt her heart leap into her mouth as she recognised the back of his head.

'Alex,' she cried as the man turned and got to his feet. 'What are you doing here?'

Alex smiled. 'What does it look like? I just decided to come to this hotel for a drink.'

'Did you?' asked Caroline, noting a row of empty glasses on the table where Alex had been sitting.

'No, of course not,' said Alex. 'I've been waiting for you.'

'Have you been waiting long?'

'Either that or I'm a very fast drinker,' said Alex.

'I'm sorry,' said Caroline. 'I've been out with my mum.'

'Don't worry. I should have called. Do you have time for a drink now?'

'Yes. Richard won't be back for a while.'

'Let's go to a bar outside the hotel,' he said. 'It's a bit too "five star" in here for a humble curate.'

So Alex took Caroline by the arm and she felt the same rush of excitement that she had felt before when he touched her.

They walked all the way down to the Barranco where Alex had been painting with her mother that day.

'Your mother was right,' said Alex. 'You should have come – the sunset was beautiful but not as beautiful as it would have been if I had had someone to share it with.'

'You had your fellow students,' said Caroline as they stopped to buy *picarones* – small doughnuts laced with honey – at a stall in the street.

Alex laughed. 'They're all very sweet. But it's a bit like being on holiday with your grandmother – multiplied by about ten.'

Caroline and Alex sat on the Puente de los Suspiros, the Bridge of Sighs, to eat the doughnuts. There was the gentle sound of someone playing the guitar, probably in one of the cafés there, and Caroline could resist the temptation no longer. 'So it's off to Chile tomorrow?' she said.

Caroline had, of course, already studied her mother's programme closely but she still felt the need to confirm that Alex was really about to leave.

'Yes,' said Alex. 'Your mother's tour moves at a terrifying pace – I'm worried that some of the older people will find it too much . . .'

Caroline smiled. 'So, what time do you leave?'

'Well, they leave in the evening some time.'

'They?' asked Caroline, sitting up straight, her heart pounding with anticipation. 'Aren't *you* going with them?'

Alex shook his head. 'I've decided to stay on here for a few more days. Perhaps I'll rejoin them later – when they fly over to Argentina.'

Caroline looked down as she felt Alex's full gaze upon her.

'Well, it's the Latin Link thing,' he said. 'I'd like to get a better idea of what's going on with the project in the *barriadas*, when they will start building the school and medical centre.'

'Ah yes,' said Caroline. 'Of course.' She picked up another doughnut and took a bite. It was crazy to think that Alex might have stayed on to see her, she told herself.

Suddenly, however, she felt his hand touch her shoulder. 'But you're right,' he said.

Caroline looked up into his face. 'Right?'

'Yes,' he said, smiling. 'I can't say that the hope of spending more time with you was not a factor in my decision to stay on here. I thought we might do some sight-seeing together – that is, if your husband is going to be busy working?'

Caroline smiled broadly. His words were exactly what she had been hoping to hear all evening. She felt elated. 'I'd love that. Richard is frantic with work and I've had a very boring day on my own today.'

'We'll do something exciting tomorrow,' said Alex. 'I have everything planned.'

Chapter Nineteen

Caroline and Alex were inseparable and did everything there was to do in Lima over the next two days. They went to the beautiful baroque Church of San Francisco and inspected the huge piles of bones in the monastery's catacombs. They went to the Torre Tagle, an eighteenth-century mansion occupied by the Foreign Ministry, and Alex was amused to discover a sixteenth-century carriage in its courtyard complete with built-in lavatory. They spent hours in the Barranco wandering among the musicians and artists there. They danced and drank in the Miraflores bars and there were still two more days before Caroline was due to fly back to London.

'I'll have to ask Richard,' said Caroline as they strolled around the Parque de las Leyendes, late on the Friday afternoon.

'Perhaps he can come too,' said Alex.

Caroline pulled a face. 'I doubt it. He's *far* too busy to take a whole day off.'

'We should really go for longer than one day. I'm told the classic Inca trail takes at least four days to do properly.'

Caroline blushed at the thought of spending a night

away with Alex. It was, of course, impossible. 'Will we have time to get up to Machu Picchu?' she asked.

'I hope so,' laughed Alex. '"Getting up to Machu Picchu" sounds very naughty indeed.'

Caroline smiled and blushed even deeper. Being with Alex was such fun.

Being with Richard, on the other hand, was getting to be quite a rare experience. Richard had been rushed off his feet all week and had been feeling guilty about leaving Caroline to her own devices for so long. It was a stroke of luck, he thought, that Caroline had met up with this vicar friend and had someone to do some sight-seeing with.

When Caroline told him that she and Alex were planning a trip to Cuzco and Machu Picchu, he was relieved.

'It sounds fantastic,' he said, as he gobbled down his 'Americano' breakfast at the Gran Bolivar. 'What time will you be back?'

'Well, late, I think,' said Caroline. 'The flight is about an hour and there's a lot to pack into one day.'

'OK. Well, have fun. But don't forget that tomorrow is our last night and I insist on taking you to the best restaurant in town. Would you like that?'

'That would be great,' said Caroline, smiling and feeling guilty that she did not sound as enthusiastic as she should. She knew that poor Richard had been working dreadfully hard and she felt sorry for him.

'Good,' said Richard, patting her on the arm and pecking her lightly on the cheek as he got up to leave. 'I'll catch up with you later.'

*　　　*　　　*

The trip to Cuzco was more magical than either Alex or Caroline could possibly have dreamt.

When they arrived, they were surprised to find how thin the air was. They were over three thousand metres above sea level and the atmosphere went straight to their heads. They sat at a café in the main square and drank corn beer, or *chicha* as it was called, and wondered at the imposing mansions that surrounded them on all sides.

'It seems an outrage,' said Caroline, 'that the Spaniards tore down all the Inca temples.'

'Sheer brutality,' agreed Alex. 'The churches that they grafted onto them are splendid enough but the old Inca city must have been magnificent with its gold-sheathed walls and monuments. And now it has been lost forever.'

After three days together, it was quite customary for Alex to slip his arm around Caroline's shoulder or to take her hand as they walked along. It was quite customary but, nonetheless, Caroline was still not accustomed to it – her heart still leapt when he touched her.

They took a train up to Machu Picchu. It was very hot and crowded and exciting.

But Machu Picchu was not quite the Indiana Jones experience that Caroline had expected – a lost Inca city swathed in the green creepers of an encroaching jungle. It was rather shabby and commercialised with busy crowds and rubbish and hot dog stalls.

Nonetheless, as they made their way to the ruins and stood in the centre of the great polished rocks, there was a feeling of both magic and sanctity. Caroline felt infinitely small and was glad that Alex was standing close beside her or, she thought, she might easily disappear entirely.

The rest of the day passed quickly, very quickly.

In what seemed like hardly any time at all, they were walking back down to the train station at Aguas Calientes in the long shadows of the late afternoon and both knowing that this was the end of their time together in Peru and that this strange, stolen encounter would never be repeated.

Suddenly, when they reached the platform, Alex stopped and turned to Caroline. He stood before her, took her face firmly in his hands and stared deeply into her eyes. 'We get on a train here that takes us back to Cuzco, back to Lima . . .' he said. His lips were inches from her own and Caroline's heart had almost stopped as she realised he was about to kiss her. But Alex did not kiss her, he continued speaking. 'Or,' he smiled. 'We could jump on another train and head away from Cuzco into the jungle. We could escape – legend has it that there are other cities, still completely undiscovered, out there in the wild.'

'You are the most romantic man in the world,' said Caroline, feeling she would die if he did not kiss her soon. 'I think I could follow you anywhere.'

Alex continued to hold her tight and stare into her eyes but suddenly he released her and shook his head sadly as he put his hands back down by his sides. 'I'm sorry,' he said, turning away. 'You are so beautiful and this place is so enchanting.'

'No, Alex,' said Caroline but Alex moved away.

'I'm sorry,' he repeated.

Caroline's eyes filled with tears. She wanted to catch hold of him and tell him how much she had wanted him to kiss her. There was a big part of her that wanted to jump on that other train and escape with him into the jungle but the moment had gone. The Lima train was pulling into the station and Alex shook his head.

'It's been a beautiful day,' he said smiling and Caroline wiped her eyes. She loved being with Alex but he was right, of course. It could only ever be a good friendship and she did not want to do or say anything that might mean they could not go on seeing each other.

They got on the train and sat silently side by side. About halfway through the journey back to Lima there was an earth tremor, what the locals called a *temblor*. It was nothing to worry about, said the Peruvian passengers, although the carriage lurched dramatically from side to side for a minute or two. Alex held Caroline close and, although it was frightening, Caroline could not help relishing the opportunity of being pressed hard against Alex's breast. For a moment, she had a wild thought that they might die together in that rickety train, far away on the other side of the world, but the rocking was already beginning to slow. Eventually it ceased altogether. Alex released her and the Peruvians laughed at the *gringos*, saying again and again that it was only a *temblor* – nothing like the real thing.

The final day of Caroline's stay in Lima was Mother's Day. 'They call it *El día de la Madre*,' Belinda told Caroline when she called from her hostel in Punta Arenas in the southern part of Chile. 'I thought you might have tried to get in touch,' she said. 'What have you been doing for the past few days? I've called several times.'

'I've been to one or two places. You know, sight-seeing,' said Caroline, wanting to tell her mother all about her time with Alex but worrying that Belinda might jump to the wrong conclusions. So she decided to change the subject. 'How's the art course going?' she asked.

'Oh, not so much fun – now that our young man has deserted us. I was quite put off to start with when I found out he was a vicar or something but he was such fun, so charming. Margaret fell in love with him, of course, and was beginning to become embarrassing. I heard her tell him that she was once in the Salvation Army which was a bare-faced lie. I've known her since the day she bought her first girdle and she's always drunk like a fish. That dear, sweet clergyman believed every word she said, of course.'

They were back to talking about Alex and so Caroline, glancing briefly at Richard who was still half asleep in the bed beside her, quickly changed the subject again. 'Richard has finally finished his work but, poor thing, he is too exhausted to do anything. He is sleeping this afternoon and then we're going to the Brujas this evening.'

'Oh, the Brujas de Cachiche?' said Belinda. 'I heard about that place while I was in Lima. Apparently it means something about witches and they can do some kind of magical healing there while you eat, if you want it.'

'Really?' said Caroline. If her mother had told her this when she had arrived in Lima, she might have seen it as an opportunity, perhaps, to seek a cure for her infertility. But now the idea just seemed absurd. 'I've had a wonderful time here – I feel so well, Mum. I don't think I need any healing.'

'You seemed stressed out when I last saw you,' said Belinda, thinking back to the evening she had spent with Caroline over dinner at the *chifa* and how preoccupied her daughter had appeared.

'I was. But this time in Peru has been very special. I feel much happier and more confident. In fact, I feel on top of the world,' laughed Caroline.

'You sound like Margaret. Perhaps you have fallen in love too.'

Caroline was taken aback by her mother's remark. 'Mum,' she cried. 'When will you *ever* grow up?'

'Sorry baby,' said Belinda. 'It was just a joke.'

Chapter Twenty

But Caroline's euphoria did not last long.

She had half expected Alex to get in touch soon after she got back to London but ten days had already passed and there had been no word.

Of course, there was no reason why he *should* call her, thought Caroline, and as time passed the days they had spent together in Lima seemed more and more like a dream. Her life slipped back to normal. It was almost as though she had never been away, that Machu Picchu had never happened.

It was pouring with rain and the streets were covered with sodden blossom that had fallen from the trees. Caroline's period had just started which was hardly surprising, she thought, since she and Richard had not made love on the Peru trip at all.

Caroline turned away from the cold window. The days were long with little to fill the hours, she thought, except hanging around hoping vaguely that the phone would ring.

But that was ridiculous. Caroline shook her head at the idea. If she had told herself that it was ridiculous once, then she had said it a thousand times. Why *should* Alex call her? It had been a casual meeting of friends in a far-flung place. They had had good times together but that was all. They would now go back to their lives as though nothing had happened. And indeed nothing *had* happened, Caroline reminded herself again. And again.

Meanwhile, Alex sat in his sister's kitchen in Yorkshire and sipped a big mug of hot chocolate. He was two hundred miles away from Caroline but it was raining there too and Caroline had once again crept into his thoughts.

Alex shifted his chair closer to the Aga and shivered.

'Are you warm enough now?' asked Nona. 'I can't believe you let Millie keep you out, playing football in the pouring rain for so long.'

Tim, Nona's husband, was bathing the two children upstairs and so it was a good opportunity for brother and sister to chat. Alex and Nona had always been close and Nona could tell that something was on her brother's mind.

'Do you want to talk about it?' she asked.

Alex looked up, rather startled and laughed. 'Stop reading my mind,' he said. 'You might get a terrible shock one of these days.'

Nona smiled and perched on the Aga rail. 'I'm so glad you decided to come up for the weekend. That's always been the biggest drawback of a career in the Church, to my mind – having Sunday as the busiest working day of the week.'

'Yes, it was good to get away. David was very good about letting me go at short notice. Being the rural dean means he's very busy these days and depends on me a lot.'

'I expect he realised how much you needed a break.'

'Hardly,' laughed Alex. 'After all, I've only recently come back from two weeks in Peru.'

'But that was Church business, wasn't it?'

'Partly.' Alex, buried his face in his mug as he took another mouthful of hot chocolate.

'Well, the kids really love having you to stay,' said Nona. 'You're so good with them.'

'Thanks. But it's not difficult. They're great kids, Nona.' Nona smiled but Alex looked sad. 'I only wish I had kids of my own,' he went on.

'Good grief,' laughed Nona. 'You're hardly past your sell-by date, old man. There's plenty of time yet.'

'But it's so difficult,' said Alex. 'I used to have loads of girlfriends but now I never meet the sort of woman I would want to marry – well, not one that's eligible anyway.'

'Mm,' said Nona. 'I suppose you are a bit more demanding these days. I mean just how many sassy-looking Christian virgins *are* there in the world?'

'Exactly,' said Alex rather glumly. 'I keep telling myself to leave it up to God, to leave it to destiny, but then I seem to find myself being led in totally the wrong direction.'

'Ah,' said Nona. 'Who is she?'

'Oh no one. It's nothing. I'm just a sad frustrated old sod – in need of a good shag, as Steve would say.'

Just then, Millie and George burst into the room, shiny clean and clad in their pyjamas. They both climbed onto their uncle's lap and Alex spent the next hour reading them stories and drawing pictures for them.

* * *

Next door to Caroline's house. Pearl Gardner put on a CD.

'That din is getting impossible,' moaned Richard. It was Friday evening and, for once, Richard had got home in time for supper.

'At least she's playing something a bit more cheerful. I think it might even be Joan Armatrading,' said Caroline, as she cleared the table.

'I don't care – it's too loud, whatever it is,' said Richard, switching on the TV to drown out the sound.

'How are things at work?' asked Caroline.

Richard shook his head. 'Fine,' he said, staring at the screen.

It was the first evening they had spent together in ages and it seemed that all Richard wanted was to immerse himself in television.

'Talk to me, Richard. I'd really like to hear about your day,' persisted Caroline.

'Not now,' grunted Richard. The news was doing a special report about the US elections, not a subject that Richard had previously shown much interest in, but now he seemed fascinated by it. 'Let's watch the news.'

Caroline sighed and agreed. When it was finished she got up and switched off the TV but still Richard was not in a receptive mood.

'I'm sorry. I just feel so tired. I don't want to do anything at all, even talk.'

Caroline tried to be sympathetic. 'Come and sit next to me on the sofa,' she said. But Richard had already got to his feet.

'Sorry, love,' he said. 'I've simply *got* to go to bed.'

'But it's only nine thirty,' said Caroline, who was not tired at all and felt in dire need of a hug.

'Sorry,' repeated Richard, as he stumbled out of the room. He felt guilty at upsetting Caroline but he had had a really bad day at work and could not bear to talk about it. Tazz had been furious when Richard had returned from Peru and handed back the brown envelope with all the cash still in it.

Later in the day, Richard heard from Tazz's secretary that Tazz was planning to get him moved back to the Engineering Division. It would mean a big drop in pay and Richard did not want to worry Caroline about it at the moment. She had enough on her plate what with the salpingogram and everything. And he still hoped that, if – by some miracle – the Lima project did come through, then Tazz might change his mind.

In the meantime, Caroline switched back on the TV, flicked through the channels and settled down to watch a programme about sex.

'Sex, sex, sex. Is that all you ever think about?' laughed Alex. It was Sunday night and he had just arrived back from Tim and Nona's to find Steve lying on his bed reading a copy of *Tits and Bums*, or some such thing. 'And can't you read that stuff in your own room?' he added as he started to unpack his things.

'Sorry,' said Steve. 'But my TV's on the blink so I thought I'd come in here.'

'Look,' said Alex with unusual sarcasm. 'One, you're not watching TV – you're "reading" a magazine. Two, there's a perfectly good TV in the sitting room down-stairs. And three, this is *MY* room.'

'Sorry. Sor-ry,' said Steve with exaggerated senti-ment. 'I didn't realise you were feeling so touchy.'

'I'm not feeling touchy,' said Alex sinking into a chair and flinging his feet up onto the bed.

'Want to have a look?' asked Steve tossing the magazine into his friend's lap.

Alex flicked through a few pages and threw it back at Steve.

'What you need mate—' began Steve but Alex inter-rupted him.

'Don't tell me. I know exactly what you think I need but you're wrong. Not all men want to go around shagging everything in sight, you know.'

'Don't they?' asked Steve in mock surprise.

Alex could not help but laugh. 'Oh Steve,' he said. 'You are such a bastard.'

'Now, now, vicar – language!' exclaimed Steve in the shrill tone he used to imitate the sort of middle-aged ladies he presumed went to Alex's church.

The two men laughed and decided to walk down the road for a pint.

The pub was drab and dingy and empty. The tables at the Inn of Friendship were grubby with beer spills and crisp crumbs.

Steve plonked the drinks down and sat opposite his friend. 'Get that down you lad,' he said.

'Thanks,' said Alex. 'I'm sorry I was in such a foul mood.'

'No need to apologise. And, in any event, I am in an extremely good mood so there's nothing you could do or say to upset me anyway.'

'Oh really? So what's new? Have Wallbanks announced an even more obscene bonus than usual this year?'

'No, I wasn't thinking about money for once,' said Steve, sipping his beer.

'Oh right,' smiled Alex. 'So, if it isn't money, it must be shagging. Who is she this time?'

'It is *not* shagging,' said Steve with feigned indignation.

'So what is it?' asked Alex. 'If it's neither money nor sex, I have to admit being at my wits' end.'

Steve leant across the table and whispered something in his friend's ear. The communication had the effect of making Alex choke on his beer and splutter froth all over his friend's face.

'Steady on old chap,' said Steve, wiping his face with the back of his hand.

'You steady on,' said Alex, wiping his own face. 'You *must* be joking.'

'I am not joking. I am deadly serious – this is the one. It is true *lurve* this time.'

Alex laughed. 'But she's a good shag too, OK?'

'What is this with you vicars and all this shagging?' said Steve in a deliberately loud voice. Alex went slightly red and glanced around him but no one was paying attention to their conversation. In fact, there were only a couple of sad old men sitting together but apart at the bar, staring into space in a catatonic sort of way.

'As a matter of fact,' said Steve, leaning over the table again in a conspiratorial way. 'We haven't actually done it yet.'

'What?' said Alex. 'And how long have you been seeing her?'

'A few weeks,' said Steve, balancing a pyramid of beer mats. 'I don't know why, but I don't want to rush it this time. I mean, it feels special.'

Alex saw, at last, that his friend was serious. 'That's great,' he said.

'Sad, you mean,' laughed Steve, unable to resist joking for long. 'We're turning into two miserable celibate old gits.'

Alex smiled. 'Why is it different?'

'Oh, I don't know,' said Steve. 'Maybe I'm getting older, but I'm getting fed up with the tarts I usually hang out with. This woman is really nice.'

Caroline is really nice too, Alex could not help himself from thinking, and he wished he could see her again.

'When I kissed her for the first time,' said Steve, 'it was like I was fifteen years old, I was so excited.'

Alex knew exactly what Steve meant. Well, he didn't, of course, as he had never kissed Caroline but he had thought of kissing her, dreamt of kissing her, many times.

'It was such a knock-out, that first kiss,' continued Steve. 'I thought my bollocks were going to hit the ground.'

'Steve,' laughed Alex. 'You have such a poetic way of putting things.'

'Thanks mate,' said Steve, as his pyramid of mats came tumbling down. 'Your turn.'

Alex looked confused for a moment. He wondered whether Steve was inviting him to confess his innermost feelings or play with the beer mats. But then he realised that Steve was just suggesting another round.

'Right,' he said, getting to his feet. 'Same again?'

Steve nodded and Alex made his way to the bar. He recognised one of the old boys sitting there, who he was pretty sure came into the church sometimes. But Alex made an effort not to catch the man's eye; the last thing he wanted to do was to talk to one of his parishioners. In fact, he realised there was only one thing he wanted to do, only one person he wanted to speak to.

He glanced across at the pay phone in the corner of the room, then rummaged in his pocket and pulled out a matchbox, a five-pound note and a handful of change which he spread out on the counter. The matchbox was rather grubby and had the name Masai Simbara embossed on one side and a picture of a lion on the other. Under the lion there was a telephone number. It was Caroline's. She had written it on the box and given it to him when they had said goodbye in Lima.

'Thanks mate,' said the barman, ignoring Alex's offer of the five-pound note and picking out the sum he wanted from the coins on the counter. Alex started to say something about needing the change but there was a loud ting and a clatter as the coins fell into the till.

'Don't worry – it's good to have the change,' the barman assured him, plonking two fresh pints in front of his customer with a big, red-nosed grin.

'Thanks,' said Alex, picking up the drinks and heading back to Steve. It was, perhaps, a sign, he thought to himself. It would have been quite the wrong thing to have called Caroline. Quite the wrong thing.

Chapter Twenty-One

It was Easter week and Woolworth's was full of great towering Inca-style pyramids of chocolate Easter eggs.

Caroline was meeting her sister for lunch and it was the last time she would see Sasha before Easter Day. She had gone to Woollies to buy chocolate eggs for Siena and Toby so that she could give them to their mother.

The shop was swarming with noisy and jostling mums and kids, their arms piled high with wobbling towers of bright coloured boxes. If there were ever a sight likely to put people off having children then that was it – all those greedy kids, grabbing and pointing and whining and tugging at their mothers' sleeves.

Nonetheless Caroline was blind to all this. She processed up and down the aisles in a daze wondering at the glittering piles of confection, selecting her eggs and wishing that she had her own children to buy for.

She had read somewhere that surrounding oneself with fertility symbols could be an aid to conception and so, somewhat sceptically, she bought a large bag of tiny eggs which she planned to scatter about her bedroom.

*   *   *

'You really shouldn't bother,' said Sasha when the two sisters met for lunch at the Dome café and Caroline gave her the eggs for Siena and Toby. 'Their fathers buy far too much chocolate for them as it is.'

'I like to do it,' said Caroline. 'If I didn't buy for them, I'd have no children to buy for.'

'Don't Richard's brothers have any kids yet?' asked Sasha.

'Well, Freddie's only twenty-one and he's still at Leeds reading Japanese or something, and Mark is too busy making lots of money divorcing people – he's probably far too disillusioned to think about settling down himself.'

Sasha slid out of a pink fifties-style jacket and hung it on a peg. Caroline was already seated at the table.

'Ah yes,' said Sasha. 'Wasn't it Mark who acted for Jemima Howell when she split up with that rock star?'

'Yes,' said Caroline. 'He's been very successful and is making a fortune. We hardly ever see him or Freddie these days – they're so busy with their own lives.'

'Nothing wrong with that,' said Sasha picking up the menu card.

'No. But they could do more for their mother. Richard seems to have taken on all the load himself, particularly since his father died. He wants us to go up and stay with his mother for a few days on her birthday next month.'

'Is that a problem?' asked Sasha, passing the menu to her sister.

'No,' said Caroline. 'She's a really nice woman, just too perfect really. I think Richard would like me to be a carbon copy of her.'

'Well, he should be thankful that at least you're not a carbon copy of your own mother.'

'Absolutely,' laughed Caroline. 'I haven't seen Mum since Lima. Is she back yet?'

'Next week I think,' said Sasha. 'That's if she hasn't shacked up with some Argentinian gaucho by then.'

'Don't,' said Caroline. 'I wouldn't put it past her – Dad would be devastated.'

'I'll have the ciabatta au Brie,' said Sasha as the waitress appeared. 'With an extra plate of chips.'

Caroline ordered some salad and smiled at her sister who was looking even more beautiful and radiant than ever that day. 'I don't know how you don't put on any weight – you eat like a horse,'

'I need to refuel – after all the energy I expended last night,' whispered Sasha, putting out her cigarette.

'What happened last night?'

Sasha laughed. 'Guess.'

'I wouldn't dare.'

'It was the best time ever,' said Sasha, a big smile spreading across her face.

'With the naked man?' asked Caroline.

'Yes – the first time and it was fantastic.' Sasha sighed gently and leant back in her chair.

'Great,' said Caroline. 'Tell me more.'

'What can I say? He's simply divine. We see each other all the time. In fact, we can't get enough of each other. It's wonderful. I feel amazing.'

'Have you come clean about Max and Brown and Meggie yet?' asked Caroline.

'No,' said Sasha, looking down at her plate. 'That's the problem, of course. I've told so many lies now, I don't know how to start undoing them.'

'You'll have to take a deep breath and tell him the truth. And just hope he understands.'

'I know, but not yet. Please, not yet.'

'So, have you never taken him home?' asked Caroline.

'No,' said Sasha. 'We always go to his place.'

'What? The place he shares with Al—, I mean, the vicar?'

'Yes. The vic is quite a sweetie actually. He's always very charming and didn't turn a hair about me and Steve sloping off upstairs for hours yesterday evening, while he was preparing his sermon or whatever.'

Caroline shifted uncomfortably in her chair. She could not help feeling strangely jealous that her sister had been spending time with Alex, *her* Alex.

'I suppose the vicar is very busy with Easter and stuff,' she said.

'I suppose so,' said Sasha. 'But he's very friendly. He's always got time for a chat.'

Caroline picked up her fork and vigorously tossed the salad that had just arrived. She hardly dared to look at her sister as she asked the next question. 'Did he say anything about Peru?'

'Peru? Why should he say anything about Peru?'

'Oh nothing,' said Caroline, going red and continuing to stare at her plate. But, as usual, Sasha was too self-absorbed to notice her sister's discomposure.

There was silence and then Sasha asked, 'Did you have a good time there?'

'In Peru? Yes, it was magical. It seems like a dream now.'

Sasha gobbled down her chips, huge forkfuls at a time, but her thoughts had drifted back to Steve. 'I don't want to lose him,' she said suddenly. 'But I really can't tell him about Max and Brown – he would be so, so disappointed.'

'Maybe you will have to make a choice then,' said Caroline.

'But Max and Brown are the children's fathers – they would miss them, if they moved out.' Sasha put down her fork.

'Oh Sash, do you think this thing with you and Max and Brown will last forever? Even if it does, is that what you want for the rest of your life?'

'Oh darling,' laughed Sasha. 'You're so dramatic. You know I never think about "the rest of my life" and stuff like that. That's for grown-ups, like you.'

'Maybe,' said Caroline rather testily. It was annoying how Sasha always made her feel like a priggish old maid. 'I was just thinking of your own happiness in the long term.'

'I know, I know,' said Sasha, smiling and patting her sister's hand. 'And you're right. Max and Brown would be happier living together without me but I don't think they want to upset me by suggesting it.'

'Why don't *you* suggest it?' asked Caroline.

'I don't know. I suppose I'm a bit afraid – supposing this Steve thing doesn't work out?'

'So? You'd manage on your own and I'd be more than happy to help with the children.'

'You are a saint,' said Sasha. 'I think you must have got all the good genes from Mum and Dad and I got the rest. You always do the right thing.'

Caroline sipped her fizzy water and shook her head. She was tired of being good, of doing the right thing all the time.

If only you knew, she thought to herself, looking

across at her sister who was still filling her face with food like a greedy child. If only Alex had called her, if only he had given her the slightest encouragement, she might so easily have melted into his arms.

As usual, Richard and Jeremiah went for a quick drink after work. They still called it a 'quick' drink but, in fact, it often developed into quite a lengthy session. That evening, they were at The Mitre, a particularly dingy pub just off Moorgate.

They were on their fourth pint when Jeremiah took a call from his girlfriend on his mobile and told her he would be home in half an hour.

'Women!' laughed Jeremiah. 'Kate's getting worse than your wife.'

Richard laughed. It had always been a source of amusement to his colleagues how many times Caroline would ring up and ask him when he was coming home, sometimes even summoning him home in the middle of the day. He had, of course, never been able to explain why once a month he might have to drop everything and dash off – it would have been far too embarrassing.

'I suppose we'd better make a move,' said Jeremiah, draining his glass and getting to his feet. 'Are you going away for the weekend?' he asked as he watched Richard slowly stub out his cigarette. They had spent all the time in the pub discussing office politics and the Peruvian deal; they were still waiting to hear whether they had won it.

Richard shook his head. 'Caroline's dad is coming over on Easter Day but, otherwise, we have nothing planned.' Perhaps he should have arranged something, he thought, but he had been so busy at Centro that there had been no time for anything else.

'That sounds good,' said Jeremiah. 'Kate and I are doing nothing too. We're staying in bed for three whole days and then we might just get up by Monday and make it to Kempton. That money I won on Golden Boy in the National is really burning a hole in my pocket.'

Richard smiled but he was not really listening. He mumbled good luck to his colleague and flagged down a taxi.

Caroline had surrounded their bed with a circle of tiny Easter eggs – Richard kept slipping on them when he got out of bed in the middle of the night. She had said something earlier in the day about making love that night with his shoes on. It was just another of Caroline's crazy theories, of course, thought Richard, but it was becoming exhausting, being asked to preform all these bizarre rituals. He felt that Caroline no longer wanted to make love to him for the sake of it but just wanted to tap him for his sperm at the optimal moment of the month. It made him feel rather sterile, like a machine or something.

The cab swung round in a huge U-turn and started puttering up the City Road. Richard took out his copy of the *Evening Standard* from his briefcase and began flicking through the pages to the TV listings.

Alex flicked through the service sheet for Easter Day. He had spent many hours in church that week checking the music and the flowers and the polishing the candlesticks and now, at last, the big day had come.

The organ started to play at full volume and he followed David up the aisle carrying the Easter banner high above his head. He knew he should look straight ahead but he could not help occasionally turning his head from left to right as he scanned the rows and rows of the congregation. But she was nowhere to be seen.

Hail thee Festival Day, Blessed Day that art Hallowed Forever.

He had not realised how much he had hoped to see her. As he vainly searched every face and figure, he felt his heart sink. There was no great stigma about going to church on Easter Day, he had told himself. Easter Day was one of the two days in the Christian calendar that thousands and thousands of people were happy to turn out for, even if they never set foot in a church for the whole of the rest of the year.

Day wherein Christ arose, Claiming the Kingdom of Heaven.

The congregation belted out the hymn as Alex arrived at the altar and dejectedly resigned himself to the fact that she had not come. But why *should* she have come, he asked himself. What had happened between them in Peru? It had been nothing, nothing at all – he had not even kissed her.

And that was just as well, he thought, as he slipped out towards the end of the service to hide Easter eggs in the church grounds for the children. From inside the church he heard the congregation echo his thoughts. *Thanks be to God*, they all said.

Chapter Twenty-Two

Graham was really annoyed. Belinda should have been back at the weekend and then she could have delivered the stuff herself, he thought. As it was, she had called on Saturday, just when Graham had been about to set off to the airport to meet her, to say that she was staying on in Buenos Aires for a few more days.

'Sorry darling,' she said. 'But I'm getting such good things done that I really need to stay on a bit longer.'

Graham was greatly disappointed. He had missed his wife enormously but he knew how much her work meant to her. 'Don't worry darling,' he said. 'But come home soon – I miss you.'

They had had a nice conversation following that and Graham had felt reassured of Belinda's love for him.

Then, just before she said goodbye, Belinda dropped her bombshell. 'Oh sweetheart,' she said. 'You wouldn't be an angel and deliver my paintings to the Royal Academy for me? They simply have to be delivered on either Tuesday or Wednesday of next week or they won't be considered for the Summer Exhibition this year.'

'Of course,' said Graham willingly. It was only later that he discovered that the pieces Belinda wanted delivered were huge works that he was quite unable to fit in a taxi. He had had to hire a van and had almost done his back in helping the driver to heave the paintings into it. Belinda had also omitted to tell him that he was supposed to deliver the works to the Burlington Gardens entrance. This information would have saved him unloading in the middle of Piccadilly and holding up the traffic while the precious exhibits were lugged across the road only to be lugged straight back again.

'Poor you,' laughed Caroline as she passed her father a large glass of whisky. 'Mum just *totally* takes you for granted.'

Graham accepted the drink gratefully and took a big slug.

Richard was out to dinner with clients and so Caroline had suggested her father came round and had supper with her. They would be two sad abandoned spouses together, she had joked.

Graham poured Caroline a glass of wine and then they went out into the garden. It was getting cooler but the small garden was west-facing and it was still warm enough for them to have their drinks outside.

Caroline perched on the low stone wall around the little pond that Richard had renovated when they had moved in. He had been so enthusiastic about their home in those days, she thought. Now the jobs that needed to be done were mounting up but Richard was always too busy or too tired when Caroline mentioned them.

'So how are things going with you, sweetheart?' asked Graham. The whisky was very restorative and he could not feel unhappy for long when he was in the company of his lovely daughter.

'Oh much the same as ever,' said Caroline. 'I'm very bored most of the time but I'm doing a lot of reading and I help Sash out with Toby sometimes.'

'Hm,' said Graham. 'I think Sasha takes you for granted too.'

'Perhaps. But I enjoy being with Toby. I don't know what I would do without his chubby little arms squeezed around my neck and the way he says "Big cud!" when he cuddles me is just adorable.'

'He is a sweet child,' said Graham. 'But I wish Sasha would sort herself out. I know Max and Brown are very good to her and the kids, but it doesn't seem – you know – *right*.'

Caroline shrugged. 'Mum seems to think it's OK. You know how she always says "Follow your heart" and that's what *you* did too, isn't it? And you and Mum are happy.'

Graham nodded and took another sip of his whisky. 'Yes we are,' he said. 'I felt bad about leaving Deborah and the boys – I still do sometimes, if I'm honest – but I've no regrets. After all, if I'd stayed with Deborah I'd never have had you.'

Graham smiled fondly at Caroline and she returned the smile warmly. She loved her father very much. He was always so kind, so accepting and there were no demands attached to his love.

'I went up to stay with Justin and his family last month,' he said. 'Sam came over for the weekend with his wife and kids. There were twelve of us altogether and we had a wonderful time.'

'Good,' said Caroline. 'I would love to see them all sometime.'

'No, we've been through all that before. Deborah wouldn't mind but your mum would be very upset. She's never met Justin and Sam's children herself.'

'It is sad.'

'Yes. I've got six beautiful grandchildren whom my wife refuses to meet. She will hardly even look at their photographs. It's an important part of my life and yet I can't share it with Belinda at all.'

'Mum's a strange person,' said Caroline.

'She's a wonderful and very warm person, that's the funny thing,' said Graham.

'I suppose it goes back to her own experiences. She had a tough time when she was growing up.'

'Very tough, in fact it's probably what's made her the way she is – a woman who knows what she wants and goes all out to get it.'

'I wish I were a bit more like her,' said Caroline.

Graham put down his empty glass and went over to sit beside Caroline on the wall. They stared at a speckled goldfish that seemed to have got itself trapped in the back leg of a huge frog.

'Marriage,' he said, putting his hand in the water and disentangling the pond life. 'It's a difficult thing. But I knew I had to take my chance with your mother. It was as though destiny had pulled us together and we felt so strongly for each other that it had to be right. Of course, having Justin and Sam so small made it hell for me to decide and I'll always know that I did a bad thing as far as they were concerned. I think they resent me for it still.'

Graham paused and shook the water from his wet

hand. The frog was a bright, almost fluorescent, green and, now free of the goldfish, it was struggling to clamber up the steep side of the pond.

'Of course, if there are no kids it's an entirely different matter,' continued Graham.

'Is it?' asked Caroline, jumping as the frog lost its grip and plopped back down into the dark water.

'Of course. It's a much easier decision. You can take your mother's advice and follow your heart more easily if there are no children to suffer.'

Caroline shivered. 'Let's go in,' she said. 'It's getting cold out here.'

Nearly a month had passed since that evening Caroline had spent with her father. Her mother returned, flushed and excited from her South American adventures, and still there was no word from Alex.

Caroline tried to accept that he did not want to see her again and that was probably for the best. She tried to put him out of her head.

It was Richard's mother's birthday the next weekend and Caroline was determined to make it an enjoyable time. Nonetheless, things started to go wrong from the outset.

Caroline had bought her mother-in-law a novel about fox-hunting. She knew that Jane loved both hunting and reading but when she showed it to Richard, he dismissed it as highly inappropriate.

'Why?' Caroline had asked, feeling rather hurt.

'I don't think I told you what Dad spent the last twenty years of his life doing,' said Richard.

Caroline shook her head. Archie had never appeared to do much at all besides whatever it was he did in his wife's whisky business, but he had been a charming man and had always made her feel welcome and comfortable.

'Well, what was it? What was he doing?' asked Caroline putting the book back into its black plastic bag.

'He was writing a novel,' said Richard. 'About fox-hunting.'

'Really?' said Caroline, astonished. 'I had no idea.'

'No.' Richard gave a sad smile. 'Mum only found out after he died. She had never thought to quiz him about what he was up to when he retired to his study for hours on end in the evenings. But she found this huge manuscript in the bottom drawer of his desk. He had written over a hundred thousand words – all by hand.'

'How amazing,' said Caroline. 'Is it publishable?'

Richard shook his head. 'Mum won't let anyone read it. I think she may even have burnt it. Nona thinks it contained a number of unsuitable passages.'

'What do you mean?'

'Oh, you know,' said Richard. 'Apparently Dad seemed to enjoy writing about rather bizarre sexual practices. You would never have thought it likely, would you?'

'I don't know,' said Caroline. 'I never really knew your father that well.'

Richard turned and walked out of the room. 'Neither did I.'

It was a quiet weekend. Jane had two aged chocolate labradors and, although Caroline was not fond of dogs, she took them for walks every day. It was good to get out of the house and breathe in some fresh Scottish air. It helped her to clear her mind. She had a good, responsible husband, she told herself, whom she loved. She would soon forget all about Alex. But, in the desolation of the Scottish countryside and with only the companionship of the dogs, she found herself saying his name out loud.

'Oh Alex, Alex, Alex,' she called. There was nothing to say, nothing she could hope for. She just called his name again and again. She was not expecting him to appear out of the mist like a character in a romantic novel and, of course, he didn't. But it somehow helped just to speak his name. Perhaps, she thought, it might help exorcise him from her heart.

On the final evening of their stay with Jane, there was a special supper to celebrate Jane's sixtieth birthday. Richard was more than usually attentive to his mother's every need and Caroline felt very much in her mother-in-law's shadow.

'She's just lost without him,' said Richard when they went to bed later that night.

'She seems to be coping really well,' said Caroline. 'Despite the way you treat her as though she were a frail old geriatric. She's a good-looking woman and she's only just turned sixty. She could make a whole new life for herself. She might even remarry.'

Richard looked shocked at these words and Caroline realised that she had said too much.

'I'm sorry,' she began but it was too late. Richard had his back towards her as he sat on the side of the bed doing up his pyjama jacket.

'I suppose you would think that,' he said.

'What?' asked Caroline.

'Well, marriage doesn't count for much in your family does it?'

Caroline had never heard Richard sound so cold. 'What do you mean?'

'Well, look at your mum and dad. Your mum broke up your dad's marriage when his sons were little more than toddlers. And then there's your sister—'

'What about my sister?' cried Caroline defensively.

'Well, it's hard to know where to start,' said Richard as he rolled inside the blankets and picked up a book. 'I mean she's shacked up with two men and they're all shagging each other stupid and she's got two little children living in the house too. It's disgusting.'

Caroline was shocked. Richard had never spoken like this before and his words made her feel physically sick. 'I'm sorry you think so badly of us,' she said, getting into bed but keeping her distance from her husband as though there was an electric fence running down the centre of the bed. Richard said nothing but continued to read. Caroline lay down and stared at the ceiling.

Richard had said horrible things but the most horrible thing of all was that they were true. Absolutely true.

'Oh, Alex, Alex, Alex,' she wanted to cry aloud – the way she had cried during her walk. If only she had someone to talk to, someone who would understand.

Back home in Islington later that week, things returned to normal again.

Sasha had started a fashion design course at the local technical college. It was three mornings a week and Caroline was happy to babysit Toby while Sasha did her thing. 'It's just for fun, of course,' Sasha had said. She did not need to work – both Max and Brown were earning good money – but, since she had been seeing Steve, she had had a strong urge to be more independent, to try to do something on her own for the first time.

It was easy looking after Toby, thought Caroline. He was a very sweet child and was talking well. He loved being read to and singing songs and Caroline was happy to go along with whatever he wanted.

'You very pretty,' he said one day when Caroline sat beside him at the kitchen table, rolling out playdough and letting him cut out shapes with pastry cutters.

Caroline laughed. But the words made her think of the girl, the young mother, she had met in Peru and she wondered what had become of her and her beautiful child. The child that Caroline might have bought, who might have been her own, sitting on her lap that very moment.

'You're very pretty too,' said Caroline. 'My very pretty baby.'

She popped Toby onto her lap and hugged him and Toby looked up at her. 'You my pretty baby too,' he said laughing and the love in his eyes almost broke her heart.

Later that day, Caroline walked slowly down from Highbury to Barnsbury. It was hot and she paused to take off her cardigan as she passed the big church on the hill, Alex's church.

As usual, the church was quiet and its doors were closed. There was the same billboard in the churchyard that she had seen the afternoon she had had that mad impulse to break in. But now it just carried a notice about the times of the various services. She stopped and read it.

The name of Rev. Alex Howard was written beside the eleven o'clock service for the following Sunday morning. Caroline stood there for a few moments, her eyes fixed on Alex's name. It seemed something of a relief to confirm that he still existed and had not been a dream.

All she had to do, if she wanted to see him again, was to turn up at church. And what was wrong with turning up at church? asked a niggling voice inside her head.

She would just see Alex one more time and then she would be happy. Then, of course, that would be that. She did not even need to speak to him and he might not even notice her, if she sat right at the back of the church.

Although it was midday and the sun was at its highest, Caroline felt a shiver as the plan began to form in her brain.

Chapter Twenty-Three

Belinda was in a state of high excitement. One of her paintings had been accepted for the Summer Exhibition and on Varnishing Day, the day that artists get to see the exhibition once it has been hung, she was amazed to see that her painting had been given pride of place in the first room.

'I've been submitting stuff for years and was almost on the point of giving up,' she said to Caroline. 'It just goes to show that if you really want something, it is worth persevering.'

It was Saturday morning and Belinda had got Caroline a ticket for one of the Friends' Preview Days.

They wandered from room to room and Belinda pontificated loudly on what she liked and did not like. There was some brilliant stuff, thought Caroline, but also much that might easily have been the work of Toby – on a bad day.

There was quite a cluster of people around one particular exhibit. Belinda and Caroline squeezed among them to see what they were looking at. It was a small red square box with a glass disc in the centre. Written across it were the words *In Emergency – Break Glass*.

'Brilliantly executed,' said one man.

'Quite inspirational,' gasped a woman at his side.

'Are you sure it's not the fire alarm?' Caroline could not resist asking. The small cluster turned and they all stared at Caroline and then sighed and murmured to themselves. But they soon drifted away, leaving Belinda and Caroline to collapse into giggles on their own.

'Come on,' said Belinda. 'You'll get us chucked out.'

They walked on and then went down to the restaurant for some lunch.

'Dad must be pleased to have you home,' said Caroline when they had sat down.

'Yes. It was a great trip but it's good to be back.'

Caroline toyed with her salad, took a deep breath, and asked, 'How did the vicar get on during the rest of the course?'

'Oh, didn't I tell you?' said Belinda. 'I could hardly believe it. After paying for the full course, he only did a day and a half's painting. He stayed in Lima and never caught us up. He said something had come up with some missionary project, I think. Apparently, it was very important.'

Caroline said nothing.

'Well, it was probably that he was just desperate to get away from Margaret,' continued Belinda. 'Poor chap must have been terrified she might come and pounce on him in the middle of the night. I wouldn't put it past her – I saw her bolting down handfuls of vitamins when I made the mistake of sitting her next to him at breakfast the first morning.'

Caroline laughed.

'I rang him up and offered to give him some of his money back,' said Belinda. 'Not something I would normally do but he did seem such a nice person and I felt sorry for him.'

'What did he say?' asked Caroline.

'Oh, he insisted I kept the money. He said the trip had been more than worthwhile – he had enjoyed it immensely. Then he said something odd. Something about it being a very special and precious experience that he would never forget. A strange thing to say, don't you think?'

'Very,' said Caroline, her heart leaping at her mother's words.

'With all the goodwill in the world, I can't think for a moment that he was referring to Margaret,' added Belinda.

But Caroline was hardly listening.

So her time with Alex had been special for him too, she thought, and Caroline could not help wondering whether he had said these things to her mother in the hope that Belinda might pass them on.

Caroline was still thinking about what her mother had told her when she got up the following morning. This was the day, she thought, as she slowly got out of bed. She was going to do it. She would go to church and she would see Alex again.

Even though she told herself it was stupid, Caroline could not help but spend extra time getting herself ready and attending to her make-up. As usual on a Sunday morning, Richard was propped up in bed reading the papers.

When, at last, Caroline appeared at the bedroom

door in a pale blue summer dress and her freshly washed red hair gleaming in the sunlight, her husband was surprised.

'Where are *you* off to?' he asked.

'I thought I might go to church,' said Caroline, her heart beating fast and feeling absurdly guilty.

'What?' cried Richard astonished. He had forgotten how beautiful his wife was. 'Why?'

'Why not? I thought it might do some good.' Richard looked puzzled and Caroline came and sat next to him on the bed. 'I went into a church a few months ago and prayed about the baby and I think it gave me some kind of strength,' she said.

Richard nodded and smiled and kissed Caroline's head. He knew how much Caroline wanted a baby and, of course, he wanted her to have a baby too. He only wished he could be more supportive without putting further pressure on her.

'Good,' he said. It was strange though, he thought. He had never known Caroline to be at all religious.

'I'll pick up some lunch from the deli on the way home, OK?' said Caroline getting to her feet again. 'And we'll have a really nice lunch.'

'OK.' Richard went back to his reading.

Caroline left the room and went upstairs to the hall. Her heart was still pounding as she picked up her bag and opened the front door. She felt as though she was about to commit some heinous crime, like a murder. How could she be so ridiculously melodramatic, she thought to herself. It was not as though she was going to do anything wrong.

When she got to the church, however, Caroline felt

almost sick with apprehension. She could not bring herself to go inside with the rest of the congregation who were arriving and so she stayed in the churchyard, lurking behind a tree like some kind of fugitive.

She waited until the service had begun and she could hear people singing the first hymn and then she made a dash for the door and slipped inside.

The church was, thank heavens, quite full. Caroline found a seat in one of the back rows where she was largely obscured by a pillar.

She was already regretting coming. What on earth would Alex think if he saw her? He would presume that she had come solely to see him. That she was running after him when he had made it clear that he did not want to see her again.

The service progressed and eventually there was a hum and a shuffle as people seated themselves for the sermon.

It was then for the first time that Caroline heard his voice. Those strong warm tones that she had missed hearing all these weeks. She peeped around the pillar and there he was. The same pale gentle face, the ready smile and kind eyes. But, as Alex turned to her side of the church, Caroline quickly darted back out of sight.

She sat and listened to Alex's voice, not really hearing what he said, but just basking in the sound. For many people, a sermon cannot be over fast enough but Caroline felt she could have happily listened for hours. Before she knew what was happening, however, she was back on her feet and singing the next hymn.

The rest of the service progressed rapidly and Caroline knew that she would soon need to make her escape. She had seen him and heard him and now she would have to go. The thought of him actually spotting her filled her with panic.

It was not, therefore, until she was almost running through the park and back towards Highbury Corner that Caroline regretted not waiting. Why had she been so afraid to say hello to him? After all, why should she *not* say hello? They were just friends. There was no reason why Alex should read more than that into her presence at the church.

By the time she had reached the deli on Upper Street, Caroline had decided that there could be no harm in saying hello. She would go back to church the following week and do just that.

The following week, however, Caroline felt almost as anxious as before. She waited in the grounds until the service had started and then slipped inside. But, this time, she did not hide behind a pillar, she found a seat nearer to the front and in full view of the clergy.

It was some time before Alex noticed her but, after he had done so, he hardly took his eyes off her for a moment.

There was a bit in the service when the minister invited the congregation to 'share a sign of peace' with their neighbours and, at this point, Alex made straight for Caroline.

He seemed to devour her with those blue penetrating eyes and he took her hand firmly in both of his and smiled. 'Peace be with you,' he said and Caroline returned his smile.

·· Eventually he had to let her hand go and she watched him turn to her neighbours and hold their hands in the same way and smile the same smile. But he did not hold their hands for quite so long or speak with such feeling as he had with her. Or was she just being ridiculous again, thought Caroline, as she rummaged in her bag for some change for the collection.

After the service, the congregation was invited to stay on for a cup of coffee in the Fellowship Room. It was crowded and everyone was very friendly. Many people introduced themselves and said they had not seen Caroline before and they hoped she had enjoyed the service and would come again. Caroline smiled and made polite conversation but all the time she was scanning the room for Alex.

After a while, the crowd was beginning to thin as people went off for their Sunday lunches and Caroline was left with an earnest young woman who was trying to persuade her to help with the mothers and toddlers group.

'I don't have any children,' said Caroline.

'Oh, that's not a problem,' continued the woman, a toddler clinging to each of her legs.

But it is. It is, thought Caroline to herself. There was still no sign of Alex and she could not bear to speak to this insensitive mother for a moment longer.

'I'm sorry,' she said. 'Do you know where Alex Howard is? I wanted to have a word with him before I go . . .'

The woman glanced around her. 'He usually stays

for coffee,' she said. 'I'll just ask David.' She prised her children off her legs and hoisted them up, one on each hip, then waddled over to the Reverend Homer· to introduce Caroline.

The vicar had a soft pink friendly face but studied Caroline carefully as she spoke. 'Alex?' he said. 'Oh, I'm afraid you've missed him. He said he had some problem at home and had to dash straight off. Can I give him a message?'

Caroline was stunned. How could he have dashed straight off? How could *anything* at home have been more important to him than speaking to her?

'No, sorry,' said Caroline, her face reddening under the vicar's scrutiny. 'It wasn't important.'

Caroline walked down through Highbury Fields again. It was a brilliantly sunny day and there were children running and playing all over the park, but the hot tears streamed down her face. How could she have been so stupid? What on earth had she expected?

By the time she got to the deli in Upper Street, this time, Caroline had decided that she would never set foot in that church, or any other, again.

Nonetheless, the following Sunday morning Caroline was yet again skulking behind her tree outside the church. This time it was dark and spitting with rain and Caroline shivered as she slipped inside the building.

As usual, the church was quite full and Caroline took a seat at the back but not behind a pillar.

This time Alex was clearly looking out for her and when, at last, he spotted her he again kept her almost permanently in his sights. Caroline had already started to make excuses for him. Perhaps there had been a flood at his home or someone in his family was sick? There had to be an explanation for his odd behaviour the week before.

When it was time for the 'Peace', although Caroline was sitting right at the back, Alex almost ran down the aisle and greeted her first. There was warmth and relief in his face but also pain and Caroline felt desperate to speak to him, to know what was wrong.

'I'm sorry I dashed off last week,' he whispered. 'I'm afraid I must this week as well.'

Caroline froze. The obvious conclusion to draw was that Alex was giving her the brush-off but the warmth, the affection, in his eyes as he continued to hold her hand seemed to convey an altogether different message. Eventually the Reverend Homer came across the aisle and appeared at Alex's side. He gave his colleague a slight nudge and a scrutinising glance.

'Peace be with you, my child,' said Homer to Caroline as Alex eventually let go his grasp and turned to the little old lady on Caroline's right.

The service continued and Caroline felt horribly confused. As things drew to a close, however, she decided to slip outside and wait for Alex. Even if they only had time for a few words, it would be better than nothing, she thought.

By this time the rain was coming down in sheets. Caroline tried to shelter under her tree but, after a flash of lightning and a huge thunderclap, she decided it might be safer to stand out in the open, on one of the gravestones.

Within a few minutes, she saw a hunched figure

come running out of a small door. He had his coat held up over his head as a makeshift hood and crashed straight into Caroline as he made for the gate.

Caroline and Alex both stumbled to the ground and found themselves sitting in a muddy puddle staring at each other.

'I'm so sorry,' said Alex putting out his hand to help Caroline to her feet. But Caroline shrank back.

'It's all right,' she said perching herself on the gravestone. 'I can't get any wetter now.'

Alex sat down beside her and put his coat around her shoulders.

'There was a time,' said Caroline, 'when it seemed I couldn't go anywhere on the planet without bumping into you. Now I have to risk catching pneumonia just for the pleasure of a few words.'

'I'm sorry,' said Alex.

'What is it?' asked Caroline. 'Why have you got to dash off without speaking to me?'

Alex looked at Caroline and then put his head in his hands. 'I don't have to dash off,' he said. 'I've got nothing and nobody to dash home to – I only wish I did.'

'So why?' continued Caroline.

'You know why,' said Alex, sweeping the rain from his face.

'I do not.'

Alex opened his mouth to say something but then thought again. He got to his feet and held out his hand. 'Come on,' he said. 'I'd like to buy you a drink. Some brandy I think might be appropriate.'

Caroline and Alex sat in the corner of the warm

pub and the windows steamed up as they began to dry off.

'I'm sorry I didn't phone,' said Alex.

'Did you lose my number?' asked Caroline.

'No,' said Alex, producing the Mombasa matchbox. 'I carry this with me everywhere I go, just in case I get the courage to call you.'

Caroline laughed.

'I know,' said Alex. 'Ridiculous isn't it? I was just scared you might misinterpret things.'

Caroline said nothing but stared at her drink. She really did not drink at lunchtimes but the brandy had brought a glow to her cheeks and she was beginning to feel relaxed.

'I've thought about you every day since we said goodbye in Lima,' said Alex. 'I hope things are sorting themselves out for you.'

'Oh they are,' said Caroline. 'Richard is still working like a lunatic but I don't feel quite so stressed about the baby problem any more.'

'That's good.'

'How about you?' asked Caroline. 'Mum was very pissed off that you dumped her after only one day of her course.'

'If she knew the reason why, she'd understand,' said Alex smiling at Caroline just the way he had smiled at her when they had been together in Peru.

They chatted for a long time and Alex bought a second round.

By the time Caroline got to the deli in Upper Street she felt a bit woozy but she was glowing with happiness. It was, perhaps, as well that when she got home, she was greeted by a note on the kitchen table. Tazz had summoned Richard into the office for a couple of hours. *Sorry darling*, the note said, *I'll be back as soon as I can.*

Caroline threw the note in the bin and sighed. It felt good to be alone. She ran a hot bath, took off her damp clothes and got in. She lay there in the warm soapy water for a long time going over and over the conversation she had just had with Alex, analysing and reanalysing every word and every gesture. There was still nothing in their relationship, nothing that even made it a relationship at all.

But she knew that she would see Alex again.

Chapter Twenty-Four

'What day did you say?' boomed the Gorgon.

'Day Eight,' said Caroline.

'Good, perfect,' said the doctor. 'Whip off your bottom half then, jump on the couch and open your legs.'

Caroline jumped but, otherwise, stayed exactly where she was. 'I've already had the salpingogram,' she said.

'No, no,' said the Gorgon, scrunching her features into a frown. 'Didn't Miranda tell you? You're due for your next smear test.'

Caroline's heart sank as she got up to remove her clothes. The salpingogram had been extremely uncomfortable and undignified and now, it seemed, there was more of the same to come.

She lay on her back and stared up at the dingy grey ceiling as the Gorgon screwed a cold metal instrument up inside her which felt and looked like a giant bottle opener. Once the instrument was in place, the Gorgon stood back to admire her handiwork and took a sip of coffee.

Get on with it, for Christ's sake, thought Caroline, grimacing. Doesn't she realise how uncomfortable this is?

When the Gorgon eventually started fishing about inside her with a huge spatula thing, she told Caroline how pleased she was that the salpingogram had given her tubes a clean bill of health. Caroline writhed in discomfort and grunted.

'So it's just sex, sex and more sex – that's what I suggest,' said the Gorgon, throwing back her wild wiry head and laughing, which jolted the metal instrument that she was just removing. Caroline winced and sat up.

'The egg is only fertile for a few hours a month,' the doctor continued, smearing a glass slide with the spatula. 'Most people underestimate just how much sex is required to make a baby.'

Caroline nodded grimly. It was becoming more and more of an effort to have sex with Richard. He was sometimes too exhausted even when she told him the traffic light thing was bright green.

'Look, don't worry yet. I think we should give it a few months more,' said the Gorgon, almost reading her patient's mind and smiling sympathetically. 'And then if you want to bring Richard in to talk about IVF . . .'

Caroline nodded and got to her feet. She was just about to pull on her pants when the Gorgon tripped on one of her shoelaces and dropped the slide which smashed on the floor.

Caroline stared at the broken glass in horror. The Gorgon turned and could hardly suppress a giggle.

'I'm sorry, I'm so sorry,' she cried. 'I'm afraid we'll have to do it all over again.'

Caroline groaned, lay back down on the couch and opened her legs.

*　　*　　*

As usual, in the summer, the underground was a hellhole of sweaty angry bodies. After going through her agonising ordeal with the Gorgon a second time, Caroline was over twenty minutes late when she hobbled into the restaurant, still uncomfortable from her doctor's incompetent fumbling.

Caroline threaded her way through the close-set tables to find her lunch date patiently waiting and, as soon as she caught sight of Johnny, her spirits lifted. She realised how much she had been missing GLP and her old job. All the deadlines and panics, the office bust-ups and the drinks after work – they had seemed such a nightmare at the time but they had been a real support to her, they had given her an energy that she now missed.

'Great to see you,' said Johnny, standing up and kissing her on both cheeks.

Johnny had already ordered some fizzy water and a bottle of white wine and he poured Caroline a glass of each.

'So how are things going at GLP?' asked Caroline.

'Good, good,' said Johnny. 'But we're all missing you – which is why, in case you hadn't guessed, I suggested this lunch.'

'Do you want me to come back?' asked Caroline.

'Yes, desperately,' smiled Johnny. His hair was beginning to regrow. It was a bit spiky and patchy and gave him a rather punkish look. 'But it would have to be full time. You know what our clients are like. They require servicing around the clock – most of them are worse than babies!'

'How is *your* baby?' asked Caroline.

'Well, the little rugrat is now nearly six months old

and crawling about chewing table legs and sticking his head down the john. A delightful stage,' laughed Johnny.

'I'm sure he is delightful,' said Caroline quite seriously.

'I'm sorry,' said Johnny. 'I presume no joy in that department as yet?'

Caroline shook her head.

'Well, I can't say I'm that unhappy,' grinned Johnny. 'I'm so keen to get you back to GLP, the last thing we want is for you to get preggers now.'

Johnny realised his insensitivity as soon as he saw Caroline's face go red.

'I'm sorry,' he said. 'Only joking.'

Caroline smiled and said, 'Tell me about work.'

'Well, there's a new job to do for Merciful Percival – you know, my friend the boob job man. He wants to promote his new breast enlargement treatment.'

'Yes,' said Caroline. 'He gave me a draft brochure about it a couple of months ago.'

'It's a new type of operation apparently,' said Johnny. 'Totally safe. He said he'd give you free treatment, if you come up with a good idea to promote it.'

'Thanks,' said Caroline. 'He obviously thinks I need it.'

'I think it's a very generous offer,' said Johnny. 'Christ, if Gaby was given the chance, she'd have the full works.'

Caroline laughed. 'She hardly needs it.'

'I know,' said Johnny. 'I keep telling her she's got fantastic boobs. I mean, some women really *do* need a bit of a boost, but not Gaby.'

Caroline picked up her menu and held it up in

front of her chest. Now, she felt that even Johnny was making insinuations about the size of her breasts.

They ordered their food and got back to talking about business. Johnny explained some of the other new deals that were in the pipeline, many of which were projects starting up in the autumn. Then there would be, as usual, the mad build-up to Christmas.

'If you started back at, say, the end of September, would that be good?' asked Johnny.

'Yes,' said Caroline. 'God knows what will happen to me if I stay off work much longer.'

'You are an angel,' said Sasha. She had asked Caroline at short notice to babysit Toby and, as usual, Caroline had agreed to help her sister out.

Sasha was going to a party with Steve and anyone would have thought it was her first date. When Caroline came into Sasha's bedroom with her little nephew on her hip, there were clothes scattered all over the bed and the floor and Sasha was rooting around in her wardrobe in her bra and pants.

'I've got simply nothing to wear,' she wailed and Caroline had to laugh as Toby draped a piece of black chiffon around his face and made scary noises.

'It's a black-tie dinner with Steve's boss at Mansion House. I think the Chancellor of the Exchequer is going to be there,' said Sasha. 'I've got nothing suitable.'

Caroline picked up a dark red velvet evening gown. 'What about this?' she asked.

'Too gothic,' said Sasha.

Caroline tried something short and black.

'Too tarty,' said her sister.

Toby picked up something long and orange.

'Yes, yes, Toby,' shrieked Sasha. 'That will be perfect.' But, by the time she had wrested the dress from her two-year-old's grasp, Toby had already smeared peanut butter down the front of it.

'Sorry,' said Caroline, grabbing a tissue. 'I should have cleaned his hands.'

'Don't worry,' said Sasha, collapsing onto the bed. Caroline could not help noticing and envying her sister's figure. She wore a tight black underwired bra and her breasts swelled impressively over the cups. She appeared to have put on a little bit of weight and the effect was to make her look even more gorgeous than ever.

'I don't know why I feel so nervous. I suppose I want to make a good impression for Steve,' said Sasha.

'Now *you* sound the sad old bag tonight,' laughed Caroline.

'Oh but I'm not really,' said Sasha, rolling onto her tummy and inspecting her long coral-coloured fingernails. 'I couldn't be happier.'

Caroline lay down on the bed next to her sister with Toby astride her tummy.

Sasha looked at Caroline and Toby and put her hand on Caroline's arm. 'Well, of course, I *could* be happier,' she said. 'How are things going with the Gargoyle's relaxation therapy?'

'Nothing,' said Caroline. 'I'm beginning to feel like it's just not meant to be.'

'Rubbish,' said Sasha, squashing a pillow under her breasts. 'You've just got to keep at it.'

'That's what the doctor says,' said Caroline. 'But she's also started talking about IVF.'

'Brilliant,' said Sasha.

'Well, not really. For a start, I'm told it's absolute hell and there's still only about one chance in four of being successful.'

'Worth a try though,' said Sasha, stroking her son's blond curls as he bounced up and down on his aunt.

'Not according to Richard,' said Caroline. 'He says he wants to wait a bit longer before we try IVF.'

'I guess you've still got plenty of time,' said Sasha.

'Not really,' said Caroline. 'In just over five years I'll be forty.'

'That's still plenty of time. And if IVF doesn't work, I suppose there's always adoption left to consider,' said Sasha.

'Or surrogacy,' said Caroline staring fixedly at the ceiling. The word just popped out before Caroline had time to think about it. She hardly dared to look at her sister's face.

'Surrogacy?' cried Sasha. 'You wouldn't.'

'Why not?' asked Caroline.

'Well, yes. But who with?'

Caroline leant her head on one side, glanced at her sister and smiled.

Sasha sat bolt upright and almost leapt off the bed. 'You mean me and Richard?' she screamed.

'Well, you don't have to actually *do* it, you know,' said Caroline. 'There are ways.'

'Caroline, darling,' said Sasha, propping herself up on her elbows again at her sister's side. 'You know that I love you to bits and I'd do *anything* for you—'

'Don't worry. Forget I even mentioned it. I know that it's a ridiculous thing to ask.'

'Ridiculous?' said Sasha. 'Not ridiculous at all. In

fact it's a very beautiful and flattering thing for you to ask and I would love to do it for you . . .'

'But?' prompted Caroline.

Sasha turned onto her back and stared at the ceiling. She had dreaded telling her sister her news but now she could keep it a secret no longer. 'I'm pregnant,' she said.

The news was shattering and Caroline felt that she had no one she could really talk to about it. She had tried talking to Richard but it was impossible. He told her that it was only natural, given their own problems, that she would feel upset about Sasha's pregnancy and it would just take a while for the news to register.

But this only made Caroline feel worse. She moped about the house all day and could think of nothing but her beautiful, fecund sister. She knew it was a mean thing to think but did Sasha really deserve to have another child?

'Tell me all about it,' he said, the following Sunday, as soon as they sat down at the little table.

Caroline felt miserable but it was such a relief to see Alex again, to have lunch with him. He seemed to have noticed at once how upset she was.

'It's selfish really,' said Caroline, once she had poured out her heart for over an hour and Alex had sat quietly, merely nodding occasionally and listening. 'When I think of those poor people we saw in Peru,' she continued. 'It seems pathetic of me to be going on about my trivial problems. So self-indulgent.'

'I don't think so,' said Alex, taking her hand and squeezing it.

They had finished their meal and were sipping sweet Turkish coffee.

'You know, you are a very beautiful woman,' he said. Caroline had been aware of Alex's eyes exploring her face all the time that she had been talking. It had been quite sensual.

'Not at all,' she said, blushing slightly. 'In fact, I've even been considering having cosmetic surgery.'

'What?' cried Alex. 'You must be joking.'

'No,' laughed Caroline. 'Everyone seems to think I need a boob job.'

But Alex did not laugh, he lowered his eyes from Caroline's face to her breasts and Caroline blushed even more. She was wearing a light pink cardigan and, self-consciously, she pulled it tight around her.

'You are beautiful,' repeated Alex. 'It would be a sin to make any changes to such perfection.'

Caroline looked up and met Alex's eyes. He was smiling warmly and sincerely and looked deep into her eyes.

'In fact,' he said, 'I should love to paint you.'

'Oh no,' said Caroline, looking away.

'Please. I can't keep using Steve – he is not at all beautiful and, anyway, Steve is very caught up with his new girlfriend these days.'

'My sister,' said Caroline.

'Yes, I know,' said Alex. 'She's very nice.'

'Sasha would be a far better model – she's far better-looking than me,' said Caroline.

'Impossible,' smiled Alex. He continued to look at her with great warmth and longing for several minutes and Caroline was happy to bask in his affection. They said nothing and might have sat there longer if the waitress had not suddenly appeared and asked whether they wanted anything else.

'No, nothing,' said Alex, extracting a credit card and giving it to the waitress.

Then he took Caroline's hand and said, 'Would Thursday afternoons be OK?'

Caroline smiled. 'Thursday afternoons would be fine,' she heard herself answer.

Chapter Twenty-Five

It was Caroline's first visit to an antenatal clinic. The waiting room was filled with huge-bellied women who sat with legs gaping apart under their voluminous cotton dresses. They looked hot and tired and surprisingly miserable.

'What a depressing place,' whispered Caroline to Sasha.

'I'm sorry,' said Sasha. Toby was threading his way around the room in and out of the legs of the furniture and of the waiting women. 'You shouldn't have come with me.'

'Oh, I've nothing else to do,' said Caroline. 'And I don't mean it's *depressing* depressing. I just mean,' she added in a whisper, 'it's sad how downhearted all these women look – when there are people like me who would be overjoyed to be in their condition.'

Caroline got up and retrieved Toby who was now trying to climb through the straps of one woman's handbag and had got his foot stuck inside it.

'How many weeks do you think you are?' asked Caroline, when she sat back down again next to Sasha.

'I'm not sure. I never was one for making discreet little annotations on the calendar.'

'You should see *my* calendar,' laughed Caroline, as she struggled to hold her adventurous nephew on her knee.

'Sorry,' said Sasha. 'I guess it must be about eight or nine weeks – hardly there at all.'

Caroline looked at Sasha's impressively flat stomach. It was incredible to think there was another little life, a new person, starting out inside her sister's body.

'Have you told anyone other than me yet?' asked Caroline.

'No,' said Sasha, leaning forward and putting her head in her hands.

'You haven't told Max and Brown yet?'

Sasha shook her head. 'I haven't even told Steve.'

'Why not?' asked Caroline, putting a hand on Sasha's arm.

'I don't know,' said Sasha.

'Are you absolutely sure the baby is Steve's?'

'Yes, of course. I haven't had sex with either Max or Brown for months. Well, not since I started seeing Steve. I told you before – Steve has changed everything.'

'So why don't you tell him?

'I don't know,' said Sasha. 'But I can't bring myself to tell him. I'm afraid it will change things.'

'Have you told him about Max and Brown yet?'

'No,' said Sasha. 'I still haven't told him – it's getting to be a huge strain keeping up the lies.'

'It must be,' said Caroline, looking across at Toby who had wriggled free and was on the loose again.

'Yes. Sometimes something just pops out and I have to make up more lies to cover it up but I just can't bring myself to tell him the truth.'

'I think you must,' said Caroline.

'Things have changed with me, Max and Brown,' said Sasha. 'We're still all getting on as well as ever. We still love each other but, well, Max and Brown are really a separate item now. They sleep together most nights.'

'Do you mind?' asked Caroline.

'Not at all,' said Sasha. 'It's a relief really. But I can't bring myself to ask Max and Brown to move out of the house. I really should do but, I mean, they are the children's fathers and the kids would miss them.'

'Yes,' said Caroline. 'But, on the other hand, Steve is bound to find out sooner or later. It's better that you tell him before he does.'

'Yes, I know,' said Sasha, idly watching Toby, who had climbed on top of a sleeping baby in his buggy. The mother was a thin but heavily pregnant girl who was too much engrossed in *Teen* magazine to notice.

Caroline got up to retrieve Toby.

'It's just that Steve has this idea that I'm a really nice person,' continued Sasha. 'He thinks I'm wonderful because I've been looking after my sister's kids for so long. He would be appalled if he found out they were mine and I lived with both of their fathers.'

'I can see it's difficult,' said Caroline, apologising to the young girl when the sleeping baby awoke as soon as Caroline removed Toby and the baby started to bawl.

'Very difficult,' said Sasha. 'And Steve is such a good man, a nice man. I don't want to lose him when he finds out what I really am.'

'Sasha Roth,' announced a crisp white-coated nurse, suddenly appearing in the room with a large clipboard and scowling at the waiting women. Sasha jumped to her feet like a naughty schoolgirl.

'You're not that bad,' said Caroline as her sister was led away and Toby toddled along behind her.

'Look, I hate to disillusion you,' said Alex, as he put on the kettle in the tiny but reasonably tidy kitchen. 'But I'm really no saint.'

Caroline smiled. It was the first time that she had been to Alex's house and she had not realised how jealous she had felt of her sister, who had been there so many times before. It was wonderful to see where Alex lived, where he drank his coffee in the mornings, the sofa where he watched TV, the little garden where, perhaps, he meditated on his sermons.

'I mean it,' insisted Alex. 'I don't want Steve to get hold of you one day and tell you the story of my life and then you would be horrified.'

'You tell me then,' said Caroline going over to the fridge to look for milk. But Alex quickly anticipated her and got to the door first.

'Here, for a start,' said Alex, barring Caroline from opening the fridge door, 'is a fine example of the squalor in which Steve and I usually live.'

'I was just thinking how impressively clean and tidy things are,' said Caroline.

'Yet another deception, I'm afraid,' said Alex. 'I stayed up for hours and hours last night tackling about a six-month backlog of cleaning – just because you were visiting today.'

Caroline smiled and blushed and, at last, Alex turned and opened the fridge door. 'Here you have a fine display of some thirty or forty different vintages of pasteurised, semi-skimmed and gold top milk,' he said. 'Some have probably been here since the day we moved into the house – but only *I* know which one was delivered this morning.'

Caroline laughed as Alex extracted the appropriate bottle and made the tea.

They took the tea into the small sitting room and Caroline sat on the sofa while Alex fiddled about arranging his drawing things.

'I'd just like to do a few sketches, if that's OK?' he said.

Caroline nodded. She felt oddly exposed and vulnerable but, at the same time, excited.

'Am I all right like this?' she asked, crossing her legs and hugging a cushion to her chest.

Alex went over to her and took the cushion away. He swept a lock of hair off her forehead and moved her arm onto the back of the sofa so that she was slightly reclined. He stared warmly into her eyes as he did this. He was wearing a black T-shirt and jeans and Caroline could not help noticing his strong muscular arms. She had this crazy thought that he might grab hold of her and make passionate love to her on the sofa but she knew, of course, that she was being ridiculous.

And, within moments, Alex was safely back over the other side of the room sorting his pencils and paper again.

Caroline told herself to stop being so silly. They were not lovers. They were just two friends and she was helping him out by posing for a few sketches and that was all.

Alex got quickly to work and Caroline began to relax and enjoy being drawn.

'So tell me the full story of your life,' she prompted.

'Well,' said Alex. 'I had a very middle-class upbringing in Hampstead. My dad worked for Shell all his life and my mum was his secretary until they got married and they've been together for nearly forty years. Very suburban, don't you think?'

'Very nice,' said Caroline.

'Dad had a good job and sent me and my sister, Fiona, to private schools,' said Alex. 'Of course, I didn't realise how privileged we were then but we had good educations.'

Caroline smiled. It was wonderful to relax and listen to Alex talk. She felt that she could listen to his voice for the rest of her life.

'I went to school at Winchester and was a real pointy head. I won a scholarship to read Maths at Cambridge when I was sixteen and came down with a first, three years later.'

'Wow,' said Caroline.

'Precisely,' laughed Alex. 'But it was all downhill from then on. I got a big job in the City – trading and arbitrage of Third World debt. I was working with Steve and we were paid obscene amounts of money but it was never enough. We spent almost everything we got paid on fast cars and booze and, of course, women. Until I decided to leave and then I saved a bit so that I wouldn't be too impoverished as a clergyman.'

Caroline listened and said nothing.

'I'm ashamed now when I think of some of the things we got up to,' said Alex. 'But then again, sometimes I'm even more ashamed when I *miss* the things we got up to.'

'Do you?' asked Caroline, a little surprised.

'Well, not really. But I do feel lonely sometimes. I hate sleeping alone every night.'

'So, why did you decide to go into the Church? Couldn't you have changed your lifestyle without going to that extreme?' asked Caroline.

'I suppose so,' said Alex. 'But I was so sick of myself and the low-grade life I had been leading, I wanted to swing the pendulum right back the other way. To see whether I could cope with self-denial and self-control and concentrate on giving something back to others, rather than taking all the time.'

Caroline said nothing and Alex continued with his drawing.

'I'm sorry,' he said. 'That sounded horribly serious.'

'It sounded fine,' said Caroline. She paused and then added, 'I'm afraid you're doing a terrible job of convincing me that you're not a saint.'

Alex laughed, put down his pencil and paper. He stood up and walked across to the sofa where he knelt before her, their faces just inches apart, and his eyes, as ever, fixed on hers. Caroline felt certain that he was going to kiss her.

But the phone rang suddenly and broke the moment.

It was Steve, Caroline guessed, and clearly he wanted to talk to Alex about something important.

'I'm sorry mate,' said Alex. 'But I've, er, got someone with me . . . Yes, yes, OK, if you insist – I'll meet you for a drink.'

There was a pause as Alex listened to Steve.

'Don't worry,' he said. 'I said I'll be there, OK?'

Alex put back the phone and found that Caroline was already on her feet and standing near the door.

'I suppose I'd better go,' she said.

Alex smiled. 'Please come again next week,' he said, touching her arm but allowing her to slip away and into the hall.

Within a few minutes Caroline was out of the house, striding up past the Arsenal stadium to the main road and muttering insistently to herself under her breath. People passing gave her odd stares but she paid no attention to them. She just kept repeating over and over to herself, 'It is just an innocent friendship. It is just an innocent friendship.' He had still not even kissed her.

Chapter Twenty-Six

Alex had arranged to meet Steve in their usual pub, close to Steve's office. Steve was late and Alex was both irritated and relieved about the timing of his friend's phone call. He had so nearly kissed Caroline and he knew that, if he did, there would be no stopping things. He shook his head and sighed. It was probably just as well that Steve had called when he did.

'Thanks mate,' said Steve as he arrived at Alex's table. He dug his mobile phone out of his pocket, switched it off and sat down.

'It must be important,' said Alex.

'What?'

'For Steve Barnes to turn off his mobile phone.'

Steve laughed. 'It is important, But not more important than getting a good strong pint inside me. I'll get the first round.'

Steve disappeared to the bar which was already beginning to get crowded even though it was barely six o'clock.

Alex looked around at the groups of giggling young women at the tables near him. Their skirts were too short, their thighs too plump and their voices too loud and yet he would have happily chatted them up in the old days. He would have been confident of getting one or more of them into his bed.

Now they almost filled him with disgust. He was no longer interested in a one-night stand, he wanted a serious and committed relationship with a woman he truly loved. He longed to marry and he knew he had found precisely the right, yet equally the wrong, partner.

'She's definitely the one,' announced Steve as he placed Alex's glass on the table and took a drink from his own.

'Who?' asked Alex, rather startled at Steve's remark.

'Sasha. I know I've said I would never do it but, you know, I'm thinking of proposing to her.'

'What?' asked Alex, nearly choking on his beer.

'I'm serious,' he said. 'I think it's time I settled down and she's so nice – I don't think I'll find another woman whose both fun and so kind-hearted too. They're becoming a rare breed.'

Alex wiped his chin. 'You think you'd be faithful to her?' he asked. Alex knew his friend well. Steve's sexual appetite was voracious.

'She's sensational in bed,' said Steve. 'I'll never need anyone else.'

Alex smiled. 'Tell me what you think,' persisted Steve. 'We've been together so long now – I really needed to tell you first.'

'Well, I can't help being surprised – but I'm delighted. Congratulations,' said Alex.

'Thanks, mate.' Steve beamed at his friend. 'But I haven't asked her yet. I'm a bit worried she'll turn me down.'

'Why?'

'Well,' said Steve. 'Unlike most women, whenever I steer the conversation round to marriage she changes the subject. She's always saying how happy she is the way things are and hopes they will never change.'

'Perhaps I could have a word with her sister?' suggested Alex.

'Which one?'

'Caroline, of course. I didn't know she had another.'

'Oh yes,' said Steve. 'They're very close. Her name's Meggie and she has two kids.'

Alex nodded and drank his beer. He vaguely remembered Caroline mentioning her sister Meggie once but never again. It was odd that she had never said anything more.

'The other thing, of course, is that Sasha knows very little about my past,' said Steve.

'Just as well,' laughed Alex. 'Or you wouldn't have a cat's chance in hell.'

'Yes. But I'm worried she'll find out. I can't avoid introducing her to my friends forever and there are some terrible stories lurking around out there.'

'But they're all history,' said Alex. 'You've not cheated on her while you've been seeing her, have you?'

'Not at all,' said Steve indignantly.

'Then I wouldn't worry,' said Alex. 'Most women are prepared to draw a line under the sins of the past.'

'I hope so,' said Steve. 'I remember my last serious girlfriend giving me the push and it really hurt.'

Alex laughed. 'Oh come on. Julia came home to find you in bed with her best friend. Don't you think you were asking for it?'

'I tell you, as I told Julia at the time – we weren't

doing anything. We were just old friends having a chat in bed.'

'Yes and stark naked at the time too,' said Alex.

'It was a hot day,' said his friend.

'OK,' laughed Alex. 'But we're not talking about that sort of thing here. She's a nice girl and you get on well. I think you're right. I think you should pop the question before she finds out what a bastard you really are.'

'Thanks,' said Steve.

'My pleasure,' said Alex. 'Another drink?'

'No thanks,' said Richard.

Caroline had opened a bottle of lager and taken it into the study where he was working. Centro had won the Peruvian contract and Richard's job was safe for the moment. But now there seemed even more work to do in getting the project up and running, thought Richard. He had been working flat out for weeks.

'Sorry,' he said, still staring at his screen. 'But it's only another a couple of months and then it will all be over.'

'Good,' said Caroline, sitting in an armchair and sipping the lager herself.

'At least we got the Lima deal,' continued Richard. 'It should mean I'll get that promotion in September. My salary will go up and we will probably be offered options in the US parent company.'

'Great.'

'You don't sound that excited,' said Richard.

'There's more to life than making money,' said Caroline.

Richard stopped working for a second and swivelled round in his chair to look at his wife. 'I know,' he said.

'And I'm disappointed that taking all this time off work hasn't done the trick. But we can move to a new house and have a really good holiday in October—'

'I'll be back at GLP then,' said Caroline.

'Right. But you've had a really good rest this year. Sometimes I think I've never seen you looking so well. I don't know what it is but the break has definitely been good for you.'

'Has it?' asked Caroline, taking another sip of lager as her husband got up and came over to her. He took her in her arms and kissed her.

'What was that theory you had about doing it in the bath?' he asked.

Caroline let him take her down to the bathroom and make love to her but she could not help feeling guilty that her thoughts were, all the time, with Alex.

It was the end of July and the sixth Thursday that Caroline had sat for Alex. They had settled into a routine but Caroline was always full of both guilt and anticipation when she arrived for the sessions. She adored being in Alex's company. She adored watching him while he drew but she knew she was becoming too fond of him.

She sat for hours, admiring his strong arms and his quick delicate fingers as he worked. The drawings he produced were really very good.

When she arrived that particular Thursday, she went straight to the kitchen and made the tea while Alex got his drawing things ready as usual. She took the tea into the sitting room expecting to find Alex there waiting for her, but the room was empty.

After a moment or two, Alex appeared in the doorway and smiled. 'I thought we might do something different this week,' he said.

Caroline returned the smile and gave Alex his tea. 'OK,' she agreed.

'I've set up my things upstairs,' he said.

Caroline's heart leapt into her mouth.

'The light is so much better in my room,' explained Alex. 'Do you mind?'

'No,' said Caroline. 'I don't mind at all,' she added, as she followed Alex up the stairs.

Alex was right. The room was bright and sunny and Caroline felt a new fondness for Alex when she saw the simplicity of his room, the stack of books and newspapers by his bed, the pile of loose change on the table.

'I thought you might lie on the bed for me?' said Alex.

Caroline blushed but took off her shoes and climbed onto the bed. She was wearing a shirt and trousers and Alex sat on the bed beside her just looking at her.

'You know,' he said. 'I'm bored of drawing your clothes.'

Caroline propped herself up on one elbow. 'What do you mean?' she asked, her heart now beating so loudly that she was sure Alex must be able to hear it.

'Maybe if we just undo your shirt?'

'OK,' said Caroline.

'Let me do it,' said Alex as she started fiddling with the first button.

Alex gently undid the buttons and held the shirt open. Caroline was wearing a very ordinary white bra and she could not help but wish she had worn her black 'Maximiser'.

'Can we take this off so that I can see your breasts?' asked Alex.

Caroline let him slip the shirt off her shoulders and undo her bra. She sat before him naked to the waist and felt his eyes upon her.

'You are so beautiful,' he said.

Caroline wanted him to take her in his arms and press her hard against him, the way he had done in that train in Machu Picchu, but he just put her shirt back on, leaving it open so that he could see her breasts.

'That's perfect,' he said, getting up and standing back to look. 'Perfect.'

He got a chair and sat beside the bed and started to draw.

Caroline lay back on the bed, on Alex's bed, and basked in the warm sunlight. She could feel Alex's eyes gently exploring her breasts as though his hands were touching them. It felt very sensual, very erotic, and yet they talked of all the usual things: his work, Richard and the baby.

'How is your sister?' asked Alex suddenly.

'Er, fine,' said Caroline.

'I mean the one who is ill. I don't think you've ever said much about her but, I'm afraid, Steve told me all about the brain tumour the other day and how Sasha is taking care of her kids.'

Caroline froze and cursed Sasha. The last thing she wanted was to lie to Alex. But what could she do? Sasha had still not come clean with Steve about her domestic set-up and she could not blow it for her.

'Ah, Meggie,' said Caroline. 'Yes, I don't like to talk about it too much – it's so upsetting.'

Caroline felt such an idiot. The words seemed so out of character. She was worried that Alex would think she was cold and hard-hearted or hiding something from him. Would he wonder why she herself had not offered to take care of her sister's children?

'Would you like me to pray for her?' he asked.

'No,' said Caroline sharply. 'No, please don't.' Oh my God, she thought to herself in panic. What am I saying? He must think I'm a complete bitch. 'No, sorry, Alex,' she went on. 'Do. Please do pray for my sister – she needs all the prayers she can get.' But not Meggie, thought Caroline. Pray for my other sister because I think I shall kill her when I next see her for getting me caught up in this mess.

Alex dropped the subject and continued with his work. It was getting late and the sun had moved round so that it was now much cooler in the room.

'Perhaps we should leave it there,' he said, putting down his things and coming over to the bed. Alex sat down beside Caroline and gently picked up one side of her shirt to cover her breasts. As he did this, the palm of his hand brushed briefly, accidentally, against one nipple.

It was almost too much to bear, thought Caroline, as she made her way home alone. It was, of course, crazy to think that Alex might make love to her. He was a curate and she was a married woman. There was no way that they could have a sexual relationship and, yet strangely, she felt as though they already did. He had still not kissed her. He had asked to see

253

her breasts just so that he could draw them – it was only a professional interest, she told herself – just the opportunity to improve his life drawing skills.

But she shivered as she recalled how the experience had felt. It was as though Alex's eyes, his lips, his hands had been all over her face and breasts, that she had been totally his, lying in his bed, for him alone, all of that long summer's afternoon. She could not help feeling guilty but she realised too that she had enjoyed it immensely.

Chapter Twenty-Seven

And it was not long, of course, before Alex wanted to paint her naked.

'I'd really like to do a proper painting,' he said. 'Oils or, perhaps, pastels. It would take several sittings to do it.'

They were having lunch at an Italian restaurant in Highbury. It was a Thursday in the middle of August and they had slipped into the habit of having lunch before the afternoon's sitting.

Alex topped up Caroline's glass of wine and waited for her reply.

Caroline knew, at once, that she would do it. In fact, a part of her had been yearning for him to ask her to do it. She wanted Alex to have as much of her as he could. Nonetheless, she hesitated at first.

'I'm going back to my job at GLP at the end of next month,' she said.

'Really?' said Alex, looking surprised and a little disappointed. He thought for a moment and then continued. 'That would give us about six sittings. I'm sure I could do it in that time.'

Caroline smiled. 'OK. In fact, I should like you to do it.'

Alex reached across the table and took her hand. 'Thank you.'

They went back to Alex's house and, this time, Caroline let Alex take off all her clothes. As he did so, his hand slid from her shoulder very gently down her arm and she longed for him to take her in his arms. He looked at her intensely and his eyes seemed to consume every inch of her flesh.

'You really are the most beautiful woman I have ever seen,' he said. Caroline moved a step towards him but Alex quickly turned away and busied himself with his painting materials.

Caroline got onto the bed and, after a few moments, Alex returned and arranged her body the way he wanted it.

'That looks great,' he said, standing back and smiling.

Alex had decided to do the painting in pastels on a huge sheet of sandpaper.

'I'm afraid I'm not going to let you to see the painting until it is finished,' he said.

'Why not?' asked Caroline. It was the first time that Alex had appeared to show any modesty about his work.

'I want it to be special. It would spoil things, if you saw it before I've finished.'

Caroline pulled a face.

'Trust me,' said Alex. And so she did.

Alex made a start on the painting and they talked, as usual, about many things. Alex told Caroline that he had been invited back to Lima to help with the Latin Link project in the *barriadas*.

'The school?' asked Caroline, thinking of the beautiful

young Peruvian mother she had met and wondering whether she had kept or sold her little son.

'Yes. We've got the funding together but there are some legal problems with the site – disputed ownership or something. Someone needs to go and sort it out. And then they will need someone out there full time for a while to check that the building works are carried out properly and the whole thing gets up and running OK.'

Caroline's heart sank. The thought of Alex going away to the other side of the world for weeks or months seemed unbearable.

'Will you go?' she asked.

'I don't know,' said Alex. 'It would mean going away for quite a while, but I'd like to help.'

'Yes,' said Caroline. 'It sounds an enormously worthwhile thing to do.'

She stared up at the ceiling and fought hard to stop the tears that had filled her eyes. It was preposterous, and always had been, to think that Alex cared for her more than as a friend. They would never be closer than they were; they never could be.

'Of course, I hate the thought of going,' said Alex suddenly.

'Do you?' asked Caroline. 'Why?'

'Well, you know,' smiled Alex. 'I'd miss you.'

The words were too much for Caroline and the tears poured down her face. She sat up and put her head in her hands. 'I'm sorry, I'm sorry,' she said. 'Now you'll never get me back in the right position.'

'It doesn't matter,' said Alex, coming over to the bed and wrapping his dressing gown around her shoulders. He held her in his arms and stroked her hair.

After a while, Caroline's sobbing stopped and she looked up into his face but Alex pressed her tear-stained face back down into his shoulder and just held her tight.

'I'll go downstairs and make some tea,' he said, 'while you get dressed.'

It was Belinda's birthday and Richard and Caroline were taking her and Graham to the Granita for supper. Richard had come home early for once and tried to make love to his wife before they went out but Caroline was not in the mood. The incident with Alex had upset her and she still felt confused about it.

In her heart, she was sure that Alex was in love with her, that he wanted her as much as she wanted him. But it was clear that he could resist the temptation to give in to his desires, that he would never attempt to kiss her, let alone make love to her. Which was as well, she kept telling herself, because she felt sure that she could no longer resist the temptation herself.

'I thought we were supposed to do it as often as possible. Doctor's orders,' said Richard.

'Sorry,' said Caroline rather guiltily. 'I just don't feel like it right now.'

She got up from the bed and, as she straightened her clothes, there was a sudden blast of classical music from the flat next door – probably Mahler, thought Caroline. It was interesting and encouraging that Pearl's musical taste seemed to be developing from morose folk singing towards something more positive.

'That woman drives me crazy,' moaned Richard.

'I haven't seen Pearl in ages,' said Caroline. 'It's a relief to know she's still alive.'

'I'm going to have a word with social services,' muttered Richard as he watched Caroline take off her shirt to change.

There was a strange new confidence in the way that Caroline removed her clothes, he thought to himself, as he watched his wife undress. A greater confidence in her body than she used to have. He suddenly realised how sexy she was.

'I think you should come back to bed,' said Richard but Caroline, totally naked, walked out of the room.

'I'll just take a quick shower,' she said.

It was unusual for Caroline even to go from the bedroom to the bathroom without putting on her dressing gown. There was definitely a change in her, thought Richard.

He stayed in bed and waited for her to return. There was no way that he was going to ignore Dr Gorgoyne's advice.

Caroline and Richard arrived late at the restaurant.

'Sorry,' said Richard. 'Something important came up at the last minute.'

Caroline blushed bright red and sat down next to her father.

'Have you been waiting long?' she asked.

'No, not at all,' said Belinda. 'We went up to see Sasha before we came and had a drink there. She may come down and join us later when one of her men turns up and can hold the fort for her.'

'Good,' said Caroline, taking a sip of fizzy water and wishing her face would cool down. She could feel her mother staring at her, perhaps rather smuttily putting two and two together. 'How is she?'

'Well, much the same as ever,' said Belinda. 'Poor thing.'

'Is everything OK with Steve?' asked Caroline.

'Yes. But it's driving her crazy. He's even proposed to her but she still can't bear to ask Max and Brown to leave.'

'I can understand in a way,' said Caroline. 'She's been with them both for a long time and they've looked after her and the kids fantastically well.'

'But she does seems besotted with Steve,' said Belinda. 'And I have to admit, he's very attractive.'

'Have you met him?' asked Caroline, surprised. Sasha was at great pains to guard her Meggie story and it seemed unlikely that she would risk exposing Steve to her mother, who might easily blurt out the wrong thing.

'Well, ages ago,' said Belinda. 'He came round to see me with that strange vicar chap – the one that Margaret had a crush on. You know, she sent some of her poetry to him but he wrote back saying it wasn't suitable for the parish magazine. I hadn't read it myself, of course, but I'd bet my life it wasn't suitable, knowing Margaret.'

'Why did they come round to see you?' asked Caroline.

'Oh, they came to return a drawing board I'd lent the vicar on the course. What *was* his name?' Belinda added, almost to herself.

'Alex,' said Caroline before she could stop herself.

Richard looked up, remembering the name. Alex was the chap that Caroline had run into in Lima, the one who had taken her sight-seeing.

'Do you know him?' asked Belinda.

Caroline was, for once, grateful that her face was already flushed. She picked up her menu. 'Not really,' she said. In fact, it sometimes seemed as though she hardly knew him at all, she thought, even though she had been lying on his bed totally naked that very afternoon.

'According to Sasha,' continued Belinda, 'Steve is getting suspicious that she never takes him home.'

'She's dug herself into a huge hole,' said Caroline. 'And the longer it goes on, the worse it will get.'

'Oh, I don't know,' laughed Richard. 'Sasha has a knack of always landing on her feet. I expect she'll get what she wants in the end – she's that sort of person.'

Graham laughed and looked warmly across the table at his wife. 'She's like her mother then,' he said.

Alex continued with his painting but insisted that Caroline could not look at it. He was always careful to cover it quickly when the sitting was over.

'Let's go downstairs and have a drink,' he suggested. It was past six o'clock and they had had a very long session.

The picture was really beginning to take shape, thought Alex. He was tired but pleased with his work and looked forward to having a drink with Caroline.

'I'm sorry,' said Caroline, hooking up her bra, as Alex watched her dress. She was now more relaxed about being naked in his presence. 'I've got to get back early tonight. Richard is taking me out to dinner.'

Alex started. 'Oh, how nice,' he said but Caroline could see a pang of jealousy in his face.

261

'It's our wedding anniversary,' said Caroline. 'Our seventh.'

Caroline thought back to the day of her wedding. She had been so happy and so in love – it would have seemed impossible to her then that she could ever love anyone else but Richard.

Alex came over to the bed and stood before her, wondering what thoughts were passing through her head. Caroline must be able to hear the blood pumping through his veins, he thought. He wanted to take hold of her more than he had ever wanted to before. He wanted to tear off those clothes and kiss and touch every inch of her. He could not bear the thought of another man making love to her.

'Richard is a very lucky man,' he said as Caroline silently stood before him.

It was another opportunity, he realised. She was just staring into his eyes, her lips very slightly parted, very delicately inviting him to press his mouth against them. She wanted him and she would yield to him. He could have her, he knew, but it was impossible.

He turned away and retreated across the room in despair.

'I'll have to finish the painting soon,' he said.

'You know, I love coming here, being with you,' said Caroline coming up behind him and putting her arms around his waist.

Alex held her hands tightly but did not turn to face her. He did not want her to see the tears that choked his throat.

'I'll see you next week,' he said and Caroline slipped away.

She had married him, thought Alex, in the same

year, the same month, that he had entered the Church. Perhaps, seven years ago, she had been in a church for her wedding at precisely the time he had been in another church for his ordination.

If only he had known that he would meet this woman, he thought angrily to himself, as he wandered downstairs to the kitchen. If only he had met her before, he would have had no hesitation.

Alex unscrewed a bottle and poured himself a large glassful of Steve's best malt. He drank the whisky straight, glass after glass, until he had completely anaesthetised his wretched feelings. Then he sank down miserably on the sofa and hoped that Steve would be back soon. He knew that he had gone too far.

'That's one thing I won't miss if I ever find a woman to marry me and I move out of this pisshole,' said Steve, storming into the room and picking up the empty bottle of whisky. 'To think that I *choose* to live with an arsehole like you, just because I like you – because I feel sorry for you, you sad old bastard.'

Alex shrugged his shoulders and continued to stare blankly at the TV.

'I don't know how you'll survive if you ever have to buy your own booze,' continued Steve, rooting around in the fridge and, with much relief, finding a cold beer. 'You'll be stealing the bloody communion wine.'

Alex said nothing.

'To think I earn enough to be living in Kensington or poncey Notting Hill,' Steve ranted on, as he levered off the bottle top. 'I must be crazy.'

Alex still said nothing.

At last, Steve swigged back the cold beer. 'God, I'm sweating like a pig. The tube is a fucking nightmare.'

Alex had now stopped staring blankly at the TV and was staring blankly at Steve.

'Are you all right, mate?' asked Steve, collapsing into an armchair, and suddenly realising that his friend was looking odd.

But Alex just grinned and said, 'Jsh-aver-nother-jshrink?'

'He was totally pissed,' said Sasha, filling up her glass. 'I just rang for a chat. It was only eight o'clock but he could hardly speak.'

'It's not like you to be so easily shocked,' said Richard, shuffling along the sofa to make room for his sister-in-law. He and Caroline had arrived home to find Belinda and Graham waiting for them with a bottle of champagne they had brought round to celebrate Richard and Caroline's wedding anniversary. Then Sasha had called feeling rather low and Caroline had suggested that she should join them.

'But it's unlike Steve,' said Sasha. 'You know, he likes a drink or two as well as the rest of us but it's unlike him to get pissed at home and so early in the evening.'

'Perhaps he's not quite as perfect as you'd have us all believe,' said Graham.

Sasha glared sulkily, then laughed. 'He said the bloke he shares his house with had led him astray.'

'Is that funny?' asked Graham.

'Well, he shares his house with that vicar. I mean, it's hardly credible is it?'

Caroline almost choked on her champagne. 'So, what did he say happened?' she stammered, as Graham patted her on the back. She did not wish to show too much interest in her sister's story but she had to find out more.

'Christ, can't a couple of blokes get pissed in their own bloody home without a full-blown Spanish Inquisition?' asked Richard.

Sasha ignored him. 'He said he got home to find Alex pissed out of his brains and begging him to go out and buy another bottle of whisky. How *can* he lie to me like that?'

Caroline shook her head. 'That's a bit rich, Sash,' she said. 'Given the scale of lies you are telling him.' Sasha shrugged and finished her drink.

The conversation moved on to other things. Graham was asking Richard about the contract in Peru and Belinda and Sasha were whispering together about the new baby.

Caroline sat silently and played with her glass. So Alex had got pissed after she had left him, she thought. She could not help feeling pleased.

It had been quite hurtful when he had turned away after Caroline had told him how much she enjoyed seeing him on Thursday afternoons. She had put her arms around him, almost blatantly asking him to turn and hold her but he had not done a thing.

Now she knew that he must have some feelings for her. Perhaps he wanted her as much as she wanted him. Why else would he have got himself drunk? It was so out of character, thought Caroline. Her heart beat faster as she watched her family chatter and laugh around her. She had no interest in joining the conversation but sat back in her chair and immersed herself in her own private thoughts.

If only he would just kiss her, she thought to herself. Just one kiss and then she would be happy. Then that would be that.

Chapter Twenty-Eight

'What a bitch!' exploded Steve, as he stormed into the house and threw his briefcase across the room so that it exploded onto the sofa, disgorging papers and various pieces of peripheral electronic equipment.

'Good day?' asked Alex, nodding as Steve offered him a beer.

'No, a real bitch of a day. I thought that my promotion was in the bag but I fouled up a really big trade today – dropped half a bar, in fact. And the Warthog went ballistic. It's a total disaster – what with it being so close to the year end and everything.'

'Bad luck,' said Alex, sipping the beer. It was still very hot and, although he had done little all day, he felt exhausted.

Steve rifled through his papers and extracted a magazine. He took off his shoes and socks, collapsed amid the papers and put his feet up on the coffee table to read.

'Aren't you going out with Sasha tonight?' asked Alex, pushing Steve's feet off the table. They were making a dreadful stench.

'Sorry,' said Steve, repositioning his feet on the arm

of the sofa. 'I don't know, maybe,' he added in answer to Alex's question.

'What?' cried Alex. 'I thought you two were inseparable.'

'Yeah. But something's wrong, Alex. You know, we've been seeing each other for months now and she still won't take me back to her place.'

'She has her sister's kids staying there, doesn't she?'

'Yes, but so what?' said Steve irritably. 'I'm not quite the Hunchback of Notre Dame or Frankenstein's monster am I? What does she think I'm going to do – scare the living daylights out of them?'

'I suppose they must be feeling a bit sensitive, with their mother so ill and everything,' said Alex. He thought again how strange it was that Caroline never talked about her sister Meggie.

'I told her I thought she was hiding something from me,' said Steve.

'And what did she say?' asked Alex.

'Oh, she got into a most frightful tizz. And flounced off saying that, if I didn't trust her, then she never wanted to see me again.'

'Ah,' said Alex. 'When was that?'

'About half an hour ago,' said Steve, glancing at the phone. He threw down his magazine, got to his feet and started pacing the room. 'I'm not calling *her*, that's for sure.'

Alex watched his friend prowl back and forth like an angry beast and tried to ease the tension. 'I shouldn't tell you this – but her sister Caroline says that Sasha adores you.'

Steve stopped pacing and, most uncharacteristically, went rather red. 'Really?'

'Really,' said Alex. 'Caroline says that, whenever she sees Sasha, she can't stop talking about you.'

Steve smiled. 'She *is* a really sweet girl,' he said, moving towards the phone but suddenly stopping himself. 'Nonetheless, it is strange and, anyway, I think that *she* should call me.'

Alex said nothing more and Steve resumed his pacing.

'So, are you still painting Caroline?' asked Steve.

'Yes, we do a sitting every Thursday afternoon.'

'I must say it's a great relief,' said Steve. 'I was getting fed up being your only model. I know David said it was OK for you to paint in the vestry but I'm not sure he'd have been too happy if he'd found out that you were painting me naked.'

'It was purely for my art,' said Alex.

'Is that what you tell Caroline?' laughed Steve.

Alex jumped to his feet angrily. 'What do you mean?' he demanded.

'Sorry,' said Steve. 'I didn't realise it was such a sensitive matter.'

'It is not a sensitive matter,' said Alex, trying to calm down. He was embarrassed at having reacted so violently. 'In fact, it's our last sitting tomorrow. She's going back to work next week and so that will be that.'

'Can I see the painting?' asked Steve.

'No,' said Alex defensively and, much to Alex's relief, the phone started to ring.

Steve pounced on the phone like a wild animal and Alex could tell immediately from the smile on his friend's face that it must be Sasha.

Alex took another beer from the fridge and escaped

into the tiny back garden. The sun was much lower in the sky now and there was only a small patch of sunlight in a far corner. Alex made his way towards it and sat down on the ground.

He had counted up the days in his diary that afternoon and knew that he and Caroline had now spent fourteen Thursday afternoons together. Fourteen hot summer afternoons, he thought, with a beautiful woman – whom he adored – and still he had not even summoned the courage to kiss her.

Well, of course, it was not courage he lacked or was it? He had kissed her a thousand times in his dreams but he knew that, if he kissed her in real life, things could never stop at a kiss. He did not want to kiss Caroline, he wanted to make love to her, to possess her, to make her his forever. And yet she was married, she was forbidden fruit. He had prayed again and again for guidance, for the strength to walk away from this relationship, but he knew that he could not. He had tried to do so at the beginning but, when he had seen her in the churchyard, sodden beside that tree, just waiting for him in the pouring rain, he knew then that it was meant to be. He had needed to see her again, he had needed to let his relationship with her develop. He did not regret it and could not regret it as he loved Caroline more than he had ever loved any other woman. Alex took another swig of beer and closed his eyes. There was just one more sitting, he thought, just one more chance for him to make his move and then the opportunity would have gone forever.

Alex was so absorbed in his own thoughts that he

did not notice Steve had joined him in the garden and had been watching him for some minutes.

'You look in bad shape,' said Steve. 'Do you want to come out to dinner with me and Sash?'

Alex looked up and shook his head. 'No. You and Sasha need time on your own to sort your own problems out. You don't need to be worrying about mine.'

'And what are yours?'

'Oh nothing really,' said Alex, getting to his feet and dusting off the earth and grass from his jeans.

There was silence for a moment and then Steve said abruptly, 'I think you should do it.'

'Do what?'

'Oh come off it,' said Steve. 'Do you think I'm completely fucking stupid? It's quite clear that you are absolutely arse over tit about Caroline and I think you should go for it.'

'That's easy for you to say, Steve,' said Alex. 'But she's *married*. It may not mean much to you but it does mean something to me.'

'It means something to me too,' said Steve. 'I'm planning to marry Sasha and, if she's ever unfaithful to me, I'll kill her.'

'Exactly,' said Alex.

'Yes, but with Caroline, it's different,' continued Steve.

'Oh yes. And why is that?'

'Well, her husband totally neglects her.'

'What do you mean?' asked Alex. 'What do *you* know about their marriage?'

'Oh, Sasha and I talk about these things. Sasha says that this guy, Richard, is a complete workaholic. He spends his whole life at the office and doesn't even

271

really care whether or not they have kids. As far as I can make out, he takes Caroline totally for granted. She's very unhappy.'

'Is she?' said Alex.

'Sasha says she should have left him ages ago,' said Steve. 'They've been trying to have a baby for years and Richard won't even go for a sperm count.'

'That does sound a bit unkind,' said Alex.

'It seems to me that the bastard has it coming to him. If you won't be the knight in shining armour to whisk her off her feet then, sure as hell, some other bloke is going to come along soon and do the job for you.'

'Thanks. You have such a romantic way of putting things.' Alex picked up his empty beer bottle and made to go inside.

Steve followed him. 'I'm sorry,' he said, touching Alex's arm. 'But I'm serious Alex. I've never seen you so strung up about a bird before.'

Alex said nothing.

'I think it's really right between you and Caroline,' said Steve. 'I think it's one of those things that are just meant to be – and you should let destiny take its course.'

'Thanks Steve,' said Alex, turning back to his friend and smiling. 'I didn't want to talk about it but I'm glad you know. It's been quite a burden trying to keep it a secret.'

'I guessed some time ago. And Sasha says Caroline is crazy about you too.'

'Does she?' Alex's eyes lit up with irrepressible enthusiasm. 'Did Caroline actually say that to Sasha?'

'Well no,' said Steve. 'I think, like you, she's in total self-denial about the relationship – but Sasha says she can tell. Caroline talks about you a lot and is always interested when Sasha tells her something about you.'

'That hardly means she's crazy about me,' said Alex, going back into the house.

'Look, Alex – she would leave that useless husband of hers tomorrow, if you were to ask her to. Sasha would bet her life on it.'

'Perhaps,' said Alex, turning and watching the final square of sunlight recede up the garden wall and disappear. Perhaps if Caroline had already decided to leave Richard, he thought, if she had decided to leave her husband irrespective of himself – perhaps then, it would be all right. Surely then, he would not be stealing another man's wife, would he?

'Yes,' said Sasha. 'But surely you suspected.'

Steve propped himself up on one elbow and stared at Sasha's stomach. 'Real men never notice these things,' he said, now marvelling at the small bump that meant so much.

'I don't know why we women worry so much about diets and stuff,' laughed Sasha. 'I mean I'm five months pregnant and you see me naked nearly every day and yet you didn't notice.'

'I just thought you were putting on a bit of weight,' said Steve. 'I didn't want to upset you by mentioning it – I didn't want you to come over all bulimic or something, if I said the wrong thing.'

Sasha laughed and kissed Steve's shoulder. 'You are funny,' she said.

'You are fantastic,' said Steve. He stroked Sasha's stomach.

'Are you pleased?' asked Sasha.

'What do *you* think?' smiled Steve. 'I'm ecstatic. Now you'll *have* to marry me.'

Sasha climbed on top of Steve and kissed him. 'Are you sure you want to marry me?' she asked.

'Yes, absolutely certain.'

'But you don't know that much about me. Suppose you found out terrible things about my past?'

'They can't be worse than the terrible things in my past,' laughed Steve.

'I never thought I was the marrying sort,' said Sasha, channelling her fingers through Steve's thick dark hair. 'But I should love to be your wife and I am so happy to be having your baby.'

Steve held Sasha tight and gently rolled her over so that he was on top. He smiled and looked deep into her eyes. 'I love you,' he said. 'I'll never want anyone else.'

'I love you too,' said Sasha and she pulled Steve close towards her so that he would not see the fear in her eyes.

In the room below, Alex was sipping his coffee in the dark. It had been one of the hottest days of the year and the garden doors were still wide open.

Alex was ready to go to bed but he knew he would not sleep. It was still too hot and the vigorous creaking of Steve's bed was an unbearable sound. He was pleased, of course, that Steve and Sasha were happy together and he hoped that their relationship would last. But he could not help feeling jealous as well. He needed a wife desperately but sadly there was only one woman he wanted.

Chapter Twenty-Nine

Caroline woke feeling exhausted. It had been a hot night and she had slept fitfully. Richard had already left for work and, looking at her watch, she realised that Sasha would be arriving in half an hour.

She took a shower and washed her hair. The air was still very thick and muggy as she dried herself and dressed, with an overcast and heavy purple sky creating a somewhat ominous atmosphere for the day ahead.

Sasha, however, breezed through the door in the lightest of spirits.

'He loves me,' she announced, a huge self-satisfied smile spread right across her face.

Caroline made coffee for her sister and the two women sat at the kitchen table together.

'Have you told him yet?' asked Caroline.

'I told him last night,' said Sasha, sipping her coffee.

'What did he say?'

'He was really pleased. He said he loved me,' said Sasha dreamily.

'But did you tell him everything – I mean, about the Meggie thing?'

Sasha put down her cup and looked at her sister

pathetically. 'I couldn't. It would have spoilt every-thing – and he was being so sweet. He is absolutely delighted about the baby.'

'Sash, the longer you leave it, the worse it will be,' said Caroline.

'God, Caroline,' exploded Sasha. 'Sometimes you sound like a bloody Sunday School teacher. You're spending too much time with that vicar bloke.'

Caroline got to her feet and started stacking things into the dishwasher. 'I don't know what you mean.' It was getting really hot and Caroline thought, perhaps, she should change her jeans for a skirt.

'Of course you do,' said Sasha. 'Steve and I are not total idiots, you know.'

'I don't know what you mean,' repeated Caroline.

'Look, you've been spending every Thursday after-noon with him, alone in his house,' said Sasha. 'It doesn't take a rocket scientist to work out what you've been getting up to.'

'Sasha!' exclaimed Caroline, stopping stacking and turning to glare at her sister. She went back to the table and sat down so that Sasha could see her face. 'Look, Sasha,' she said. 'I swear that not a thing has happened between us. He just does his drawing and painting and we talk about this and that but he's never *done* anything, if you know what I mean. He has never even tried to kiss me.'

Sasha looked at Caroline and knew she was tell-ing the truth but the tears in her sister's eyes told another story.

'But you wish that he had?' she asked.

Caroline looked away and wiped her eyes. 'Oh no. I don't know,' she said. 'I do find him fantastically attractive and he's so kind and understanding and listens so well to all my problems. I think he is the nicest man I've ever met.'

'Why don't *you* make the move then?' suggested Sasha.

'Don't be ridiculous, Sasha,' said Caroline. 'Anyway I'm married and it would be impossible. I couldn't deceive Richard.'

'Oh really. Married people have affairs every day of the week, let alone just Thursday afternoons.'

'But not me,' said Caroline. 'I'm worried that if I let things develop with Alex, there would be no way we could just keep it as something on the side. It would mean leaving Richard.'

'Is that so unfeasible?' asked Sasha, taking her cup over to the sink, emptying the remains and leaving it on the side.

'Yes. No. I don't know. Richard's a good husband and I do still love him. It's just that he's become so absorbed in his work lately – and then Alex came along and—'

'Exactly,' said Sasha. 'And the blessing is that you haven't any kids yet either, which makes it much easier.'

'Oh, Sasha, it's not easy,' said Caroline, putting Sasha's cup into the dishwasher. 'I'll just go and find a skirt to wear and then we'll be off.'

Toby was now at nursery three days a week so Sasha and Caroline had a few hours on their own and had decided to treat themselves to a full body massage at the Sanctuary.

It had been Sasha's idea, of course, but Caroline had

suggested doing it that particular Thursday morning. Had she wanted to make her body as soft and yielding as possible for that last afternoon sitting? Of course not, she told herself. But as she closed her eyes and let the masseuse knead her calves and thighs, she knew that there was only one person's hands she wanted touching her and she could not help hoping, dreaming, even praying, that Alex would just kiss her that afternoon.

After the massage, Caroline and Sasha went to Belinda's for lunch.

Belinda, as usual, was so absorbed in her work that she had not only forgotten the time but also that her two daughters were coming to see her.

'Darlings, what a wonderful surprise,' she cried, waving her brush at them theatrically and ushering them into her studio.

'Don't worry Mum,' said Caroline. 'If you're busy we can get lunch out somewhere.'

'No, not at all,' said Belinda, stripping off her painting overall and standing before them in nothing but a large lacy white bra and pants. 'Sorry! But I get so hot working in this weather that I can hardly bear to wear a thing.'

Graham came into the room and kissed the three women in turn then went off to find Belinda a dressing gown.

'Shall we have a drink on the terrace?' asked Belinda.

'Yes please,' Caroline heard herself reply somewhat eagerly. It would be good to have a drink before she left for the final sitting. She needed something to ease her nerves.

Graham had a bottle of cold Chardonnay in the fridge which he brought out with some glasses. They sat and looked out over the blue-grey Cityscape that surrounded them. The sky was darker now and, although it was unbearably hot, it looked as though the relief of rain would come soon.

Despite the humidity, Belinda invited Graham to squeeze in next to her on the bench seat. Sasha reposed on the sunlounger and Caroline sat upright in a hard white cast-iron chair.

'You're looking fantastic,' said Belinda, looking fondly at Sasha. 'Can you feel it moving yet?'

'Just the odd flutter,' said Sasha. 'I can still hardly believe that I'm pregnant again.'

Caroline looked away and Sasha immediately apologised.

'It's all right,' said Caroline. She was, in fact, feeling much more relaxed about Sasha's pregnancy. A few months ago, she had been seething with jealousy but now she was pleased for Sasha and Steve.

They talked more about the new baby and Toby and Siena. Sasha told how she and Siena had had a dreadful row about whether she could give up studying Latin at school.

'I don't want her to grow up to be a total airhead like me,' said Sasha.

Belinda smiled and shook her head. She had been worried, of course, when Sasha had first announced she was leaving school at sixteen and was signing up with Johnny Lord's model agency but things had turned out for the best. Sasha had done well for herself and was as happy and beautiful as ever.

'And how are *you*, sweetheart?' asked Graham, changing the subject and smiling warmly at Caroline.

'I'm fine,' said Caroline. She looked at her watch.

There was only an hour and a half to go before she had to leave for her sitting with Alex and she was beginning to feel absurdly apprehensive.

'And Richard?' asked Belinda.

Caroline started at the sound of her husband's name. 'He's fine,' she said.

'Oh that reminds me, darling,' said Graham, sitting up suddenly. 'Richard called this morning and asked whether you would ring him when you arrived. I'm sorry, I forgot to tell you.'

'That's OK,' said Caroline, getting to her feet. 'I'll try him now.'

The heat and apprehension were beginning to get to Caroline and she undid another button on her shirt.

'Richard is at lunch,' said a familiar voice.

'Is that Jeremiah?' asked Caroline.

'Yes. I'm holding the fort for a couple of hours. Do you think I've time to slip out and get a bet on the one thirty at Newmarket?'

Caroline laughed. 'What would Tazz say?'

'Oh, he would probably stuff that goddamn trumpet of his up my arse, if he found out,' said Jeremiah. 'He's in a really foul temper today.'

'What's new?' said Caroline.

'Exactly, I think that's why Richard was trying to get hold of you – I'm afraid it's going to be another late one tonight.'

'We're supposed to be having dinner with friends in West London,' said Caroline.

'Well, I doubt if he'll be away from here before eleven,' said Jeremiah. 'There's a new Indian project just come in – and Tazz wants Richard to run the bid again, after he did so well in Peru.'

'Tell Richard I'll cancel the dinner.'

'OK,' said Jeremiah. 'But I really don't know how you cope being married to him – he's always letting you down.'

'It's not so bad. When you've been married as long as we have, these things are not so important.'

'Don't tell my girlfriend,' laughed Jeremiah. 'She's threatening to pack me in, if I keep on standing her up. She's not at all understanding like you.'

Caroline laughed and said goodbye. Was she understanding, she wondered, as she put down the phone. Was it really not important that, when you had been married so long, your husband started taking you for granted? Jeremiah's words had hurt and Caroline could not help wondering whether she would have fallen in love with Alex so easily, if Richard had been more attentive.

There was a rumble of distant thunder and Caroline went back to join her sister and parents who had now come back into the flat to prepare lunch.

'Everything OK?' asked Graham, putting an arm gently around Caroline's shoulder.

'Fine,' said Caroline, stealing a sliver of Parma ham from the table. But as soon as the meat touched her lips, she realised that she was not hungry. 'I think I'll be off,' she said to her mother. 'I've got to get up to Highbury by two thirty and, if I go now, I can get home and change first.'

Caroline noticed her mother and sister exchange a glance.

'It's so muggy,' said Caroline, blushing slightly. 'I feel really sticky.'

Sasha saw her sister to the door and kissed her

goodbye. 'Good luck,' she said, squeezing her arm, but Caroline frowned in return.

'Don't be ridiculous,' she said.

There was more thunder as Caroline showered again and changed her clothes but it was too hot to take a coat. She walked up through the park to Alex's house, her heart beating fiercely as she went, and a few spots of rain fell on her burning face. As she passed the big old church where she and Alex had first met, she felt that her fate was now in the lap of the gods.

Chapter Thirty

There was a crack of lightning as Alex opened the front door and the sudden flash seemed to release some of Caroline's tension.

'Crikey,' she laughed. 'Someone certainly sounds angry up there.'

Alex smiled and let her inside. It was beginning to rain and Caroline's hair was slightly damp. She ran her fingers through it to loosen it up and Alex thought that he had never seen her look more beautiful.

Caroline smiled as Alex stood still and silent, just looking at her.

'Shall we go upstairs?' she asked.

Alex jumped slightly but nodded. 'OK, yes, let's go up.'

As soon as they got into the room Caroline, as usual, started to get undressed but Alex made no effort to get his painting things set out. Caroline had unbuttoned her shirt and was about to slip it off when Alex came over to her and touched her shoulder.

'No,' he said, pulling the shirt together across Caroline's chest. 'There's no need.'

Caroline looked surprised. 'Don't you want to paint?' she asked.

'The painting's finished,' said Alex. 'It's been finished really for a couple of weeks but I didn't like to tell you. I didn't want to stop the sittings.'

'But now?'

Alex turned and walked to the bedroom window where the rain was flooding down the pane. 'That's it, I suppose,' he said.

Caroline felt shaken and confused. What was he saying? Did he want her to leave?

'Can I see the painting?' she asked.

'Oh no,' said Alex defensively. 'It's not very good. I've put it away. I'm sorry but I really can't show it to you.'

Caroline felt quite giddy and sat down on the side of the bed. Crazy thoughts poured into her head. Perhaps Alex had never cared for her? Perhaps he wasn't even serious about his painting? He might have been pretending to paint, while all along it had only been an excuse to get her to undress so that he could ogle her naked body like some revolting voyeur.

Alex had turned to face her and walked back to the bed. His face was white and drawn and, looking into his eyes, Caroline saw once again into his heart. She knew immediately that he was sincere and cared for her greatly.

'Alex, please,' she said, standing up and putting her arms around his neck, but Alex backed away.

'I think you should go now,' he said abruptly and Caroline's arms dropped to her sides.

She waited for a moment or two but Alex said nothing more.

Eventually Caroline turned and stumbled numbly to the door. At the same time, Alex also turned and watched her go. Then he stared bleakly at the bed, the bed where she had posed for him all those sunny afternoons, and heard her slam the front door.

The rain was coming down in sheets but Caroline barely noticed it as she fled up the street and on towards Highbury Hill. She felt betrayed and embarrassed. She had exposed not only her body but her heart and soul to this man and, in the end, he had coolly rejected her. How could he have been so cruel?

As soon as Caroline had gone, Alex dropped into a chair and held his head in his hands. He had thought through those minutes so carefully and he had executed them perfectly. He had rehearsed the scene over and over again and had known it would be agony for him but it was best to say nothing, best to just let her go without ever telling her how he really felt.

He had not, however, taken into account how *she* would feel. He had not been prepared to see that Caroline seemed to suffer as much pain as he did. How could he have been so heartless? Whether or not it was the right thing to do, he had badly hurt the woman he loved and she would never know how much he really did care for her. Perhaps if she had not said those simple words – Alex, please – so tenderly as she had put her arms around his neck, he would not have been so certain. But it was clear, it was absolutely indisputable that Caroline had wanted him just as much as he wanted her.

There was a huge clap of thunder and Alex jumped up from his chair. He raced down the stairs and ran out into the rain. She only had a few minutes' head start. If he ran really fast, perhaps he could catch her? Perhaps he could just tell her that he really did care.

Alex was fighting for breath as he reached the church on the top of Highbury Hill. He glanced around him in all directions but there was no one in sight. Everyone was sheltering from the rain which continued to fall in sheets. It was dark, the clouds a livid angry purple, as he pressed his forehead against the cold black railings of the churchyard.

And it was there, between the bars, that he saw her. She was standing in the exact same spot that she had stood when she had waited for him outside the church that morning and it had been raining then too.

Alex's heart leapt as he raced around to the gate and ran towards her. The noise of the rain was so loud that Caroline did not hear him approach and she jumped with fright as he snatched her into his arms.

Her face, her hair were drenched with rain but Alex said nothing. He just kissed her as hard and fiercely as he could. The release as their lips, their mouths, touched at last was so intense that they both stumbled and almost fell. Alex could not bear to let her go and they kissed passionately without pausing for breath. Alex held her so tight that Caroline felt almost subsumed into his body and the sensation was incredible. It was as though her lips, her body had never been touched before and she could not get enough of this man, this man that she waited so long for.

'I love you,' said Alex at last. He held her face in his hands and looked longingly into her eyes. 'I had to come and tell you. I love you with all my heart, my body and soul, Caroline,' he said and kissed her again.

Caroline was weeping with joy but the tears were

indistinguishable from the rain that streaked down her cheeks. 'I love you too,' she said. 'I've wanted this for so long.'

Alex kissed her again and crushed her close against him. His mouth was all over her face and his strong arms were tense with passion.

'Shall we go back to your house?' Caroline asked.

'No,' said Alex. 'I can't wait that long.'

Caroline laughed. 'But we can't carry on here,' she said. 'You'll be arrested outside your own church.'

'Come with me,' said Alex, leading Caroline around the back of the church to a small outbuilding. 'This is the Sunday School – I've got a key.'

Caroline could not help feeling anxious about using the Sunday School to consummate their passion but Alex was already unlocking the door. The room inside was big and sparsely furnished with a few tables and tall piles of plastic chairs. There were no curtains at the windows and Caroline still felt exposed.

Alex locked the door from the inside and led her across the room to a door in the corner. 'In here,' he said. It was the Sunday School materials cupboard and was shelved out with bottles of paint, tubes of glue and baskets of pencils. There was a small window at the far end of the cupboard so that when Alex closed the door there was still some light.

It was warm in the cupboard and as Alex took her again in his arms, Caroline began to relax. He kissed her hard and with purpose and began to take off her clothes. It was not long before they were both completely naked and they held each other close, still standing, and explored each others' bodies with their hands and mouths.

A pile of *Children's Songs of Praise* toppled onto Caroline's head as they sank to the floor and Alex climbed on top of her.

'I want to make love to you,' said Alex. 'I want so much to make love to you.' He sucked at her nipple and Caroline's only thought was to get him inside her as quickly as she could. Her desire was intense, almost too painful to bear.

'I want you too,' she cried but Alex had moved to one side. He rubbed the palm of his hand hard against her and kissed her. Eventually she could not help herself from reaching a climax.

'Do it please,' said Caroline, trying to pull Alex back on top of her. 'I want you to, I really do.'

But Alex just led her hand to him and she did what he wanted her to do.

When they had finished, Alex lay holding her close beside him. The storm had passed over and, although it was hot in the cupboard, the air seemed suddenly more clear.

'Why didn't you let me feel you inside me?' asked Caroline.

'I couldn't,' said Alex, stroking Caroline's face. 'I have to leave that to your husband.'

'Supposing I didn't have a husband any more?'

'Well, that might be different,' smiled Alex. 'But you do,' he added sadly, as he sat up.

They started to get dressed and Caroline immediately began to straighten out the Sunday School equipment. 'What a mess,' she said. 'They will wonder what has gone on in here.'

'They will never begin to imagine what a beautiful

thing has gone on in here,' said Alex, pulling Caroline back into his arms. They kissed again and again all the time they were getting dressed so that it was a long time before they were fully clothed.

The sun was shining when they re-emerged into the churchyard and Caroline pointed out a rainbow that made a huge arc over the church.

'A more positive sign than all that thunder,' she said and Alex smiled as they walked slowly to the bus stop. They must have looked an odd pair to anyone passing by. Their clothes were dreadfully crumpled and their hair looked completely wild but Alex and Caroline did not notice these things. They said goodbye and went back to their homes, with hearts rejoicing at what had happened but with heads already agonising over what was now to come.

When Caroline opened the front door, she was shocked to see Richard's briefcase in the hall. She rushed downstairs to the bathroom without finding her husband and saying hello first. She quickly bolted the door as she heard Richard call her name.

'Caroline? Is that you?'

Caroline looked in the mirror and was shocked at her reflection. She looked as though she'd just been fucked stupid. Hardly surprising, she thought, since that was more or less what had happened.

She washed her face in cold water and realised, with horror, that her hairbrush was in her bedroom. She could not possibly let Richard see her in such a state.

Richard tried opening the door but was surprised to find it locked.

'Are you all right in there?' he asked.

'Fine. Sorry,' said Caroline. 'I won't be a second.'

'I'll make some tea,' said Richard and Caroline was relieved to hear his footsteps retreat upstairs. She made a dash for her bedroom and quickly changed and tidied herself up but her heart was still beating fast and guiltily when she appeared in the kitchen a few minutes later.

'I thought you had to stay late at the office,' she said. 'I've already called Karen and told her we're not coming.'

'Good,' said Richard, smiling warmly at his wife. She looked quite flushed and radiant and very sexy. 'I'd much prefer a quiet evening at home. I thought I'd surprise you by coming home early for once – I told Tazz I'd get to work early tomorrow and go through the stuff he wants me to do then.'

'And he agreed?' said Caroline, taking the mug of tea that Richard held out for her.

'Well, no, of course not,' said Richard. 'But I put my foot down for once.'

'Really?' Caroline turned away as Richard went to take her in his arms. 'I'm sorry, darling,' she said. 'I'm feeling very tired. I think I'll take my tea and read in bed for a while.'

'OK, good idea,' said Richard. 'I'll join you.'

The last thing Caroline wanted to do was to make love to her husband but it seemed impossible to avoid it. When they were finished, Richard got up and said something about checking his e-mails on the computer.

Caroline stayed in bed and stared up at the ceiling. She could hear a soft moaning filtering through from the flat next door. It was not exactly an unhappy kind of moaning but, nonetheless, Caroline pulled the sheet over her head to muffle the noise and also to hide her own tears that now streamed across her cheeks.

Caroline and Richard had not made love for some time. Richard had stroked her hair and kissed her breasts but Caroline had encouraged him to skip the foreplay and just get on with it. Richard came within a minute or two and Caroline felt guilty but relieved.

Normally she would have been disappointed with such quick sex but making love with Alex had changed things. They had spent nearly an hour in the Sunday School cupboard exploring each other's bodies with insatiable passion. Caroline could not remember ever having had such a powerful orgasm – and he hadn't even come inside her. She could not help but wonder what it would be like to be Alex Howard's wife.

Chapter Thirty-One

It was the Saturday before Caroline was due back at work and Johnny, Gaby and young Felix were coming round for supper.

'Are you sure you want to go back to work quite yet?' asked Richard as Caroline sprinkled the potatoes with extra-virgin olive oil and shoved them in the oven. She looked at her watch and made a rough calculation as to when they should be ready.

'It's been nine months now,' said Caroline. 'Time to have conceived and had a baby. I suppose we've given the Gorgon's relaxation strategy long enough.'

'I suppose so,' said Richard. 'It seems so unfair. Some women, like your sister Sasha, seem to get pregnant just *looking* at a bloke . . .'

'I'm very pleased for Sasha,' said Caroline defensively. 'But, perhaps, you were right about us in the first place. Perhaps we're just not meant to have a baby and we should accept it.'

'What?' asked Richard. 'What do you mean? I thought you wanted to have a baby?'

'Yes, I did. I mean, I do,' said Caroline, pouring herself a glass of wine. 'And there was a time when I would have tried anything to conceive.'

'But?' Richard topped up his own glass and sat down beside his wife.

'I suppose I'm beginning to give up hope.'

'Don't say that,' said Richard, taking his wife's hand. 'You know, darling, I've always wanted a baby very much too. I'm sure we will get there in the end, if we keep on trying.'

Caroline looked up at Richard, somewhat surprised. There was genuine care and concern in his face and it was the first time in a long time that he had been so open on the subject.

'I suppose I've avoided talking about it because I was just scared of putting too much pressure on you,' he continued. 'But we mustn't give up hope.'

Caroline sipped her drink.

'Perhaps we should go and see the Gorgon and get on with that IVF stuff, after all?' he continued.

'Really?' Caroline put down her drink and spilt some on her shirt. 'I thought you wanted to wait a bit longer.'

'I know. But I was just saying that. I thought if you stopped worrying so much, something might just happen,' said Richard. 'I wanted you to know that I love you and that's the most important thing, of course – but I think I've always wanted a baby too – perhaps, as much as you do.'

Caroline got to her feet and walked to the other side of the kitchen to wipe her shirt with a cloth. Why did he have to do this now, she said to herself. Just when she was beginning to get things sorted in her mind, just when she was beginning to accept what she had to do, Richard had to start being so nice to her.

'I don't know,' she said, as she turned and went into the hall to answer the door. The Lords had arrived.

'Johnny,' cried Richard, shaking Johnny's hand and looking Gaby up and down. 'How brilliant to see you. And Gaby – you look fantastic. No one would believe you've just had a baby. Come in and have a drink.'

Caroline helped Gaby park Felix in the drawing room – he was already sound asleep in his portable car seat – and then she took her guest's jacket. Gaby was wearing a short skirt and a tight, low-cut top which showed off her ample bosom. Caroline could not help staring at Gaby's breasts as they wobbled precariously over the edge of her top while the young mother bent down over her son to rearrange his blankets.

'I hope you don't mind if I pop them out later,' said Gaby standing up and pushing her breasts back down inside her top. 'I'm still breastfeeding the little beast and he's as hungry as hell.'

Caroline smiled and shook her head.

The dinner went well. Johnny was full of news about Good Lord Productions. He said that everyone wanted to do the Mile High Fashion Show again but, perhaps, Caroline could come up with something a bit different this year.

Caroline was genuinely excited about the prospect of returning to her job and realised, as she chatted to Johnny, just how much she had missed it. But, by the time the Lords had left, she felt exhausted again.

'Sweet baby,' said Richard.

'Yes,' said Caroline, slowly beginning to clear things off the table. Felix had been awake for most of the meal but had been firmly clamped to his mother's nipple. There had been an awkward moment when Gaby had dribbled the vichyssoise all over her breast and into poor Felix's ear. Richard and Johnny had both looked away and Caroline had had to help mop her up.

'Let's leave this stuff until the morning,' said Richard, taking a plate from Caroline's hand.

'I'd rather get it done now,' said Caroline. 'I have to get to church in the morning.'

'Again? I have to work in the afternoon – I thought we might have a nice, relaxing lie-in.'

'I really get something out of going to church,' said Caroline. 'I have to go.' The thought of missing church and not seeing Alex again was unbearable. What would he think if she just didn't show up? He might presume that she had regretted the whole business in the Sunday School cupboard. And yet, although she felt guilty, she did not regret it – it had been more wonderful than she had ever imagined it might be and she knew that she wanted Alex to hold her in his arms again.

'Don't worry, I'll do it,' said Richard, putting his arms around Caroline's waist. 'I'll clean up in the morning while you're off saying your prayers.'

'Thanks,' said Caroline, wishing Richard would stop being so kind, and so they switched off the lights and went downstairs to bed.

It was a relief that Richard had had quite a lot to drink. As they got into bed, he touched her breast in a perfunctory way but, when Caroline said that she was too tired, Richard did not try to change her mind.

'OK sweetheart,' he said, turning his back towards

her. 'But don't forget to fix that appointment with the Gorgon.'

'OK.' Caroline curled up behind Richard and silently cried herself to sleep.

The following morning Caroline went to church, as usual, but was surprised to find that Alex was not there. She looked around all through the service and her heart beat fast at the thought that she might not see him, that he might have regretted what had happened the Thursday before.

At last the service came to an end and Caroline made her way to the Fellowship Room for coffee. She was now fairly well known among the congregation and there was no shortage of friendly people who came up to her to make conversation.

But Caroline had no interest in talking to anyone but Alex. She continued to glance urgently around the room until she could bear it no longer. She went over to David, who had taken the service, and asked where Alex was.

The old vicar looked intrusively into Caroline's eyes and sadly shook his head. 'He left yesterday,' he said.

'What do you mean?' asked Caroline. 'Where has he gone?'

'The Latin Link project in Lima,' said David. 'Did he not tell you about it?'

'Yes, yes, he did mention it,' said Caroline, somewhat dazed. 'But I didn't realise that he had decided to go. And so soon.'

'He made up his mind suddenly,' said David, pausing and pondering for a moment. 'It must have been only

Thursday night when he rang me and said he wanted to get on with it as soon as possible – if I could spare him.'

If *he* could spare him, thought Caroline. Alex had been concerned about leaving the old vicar in the lurch but what about *her*? The colour had drained from Caroline's face and she was afraid that she was going to faint. It suddenly felt very hot in the room and she hardly felt David's hand on her arm as he helped her to sit down.

'I'm sorry,' he said, resting his hand gently on her shoulder.

Caroline looked up at the vicar. 'What?' she said. 'I don't understand.' But the vicar just smiled and shook his head. There was no need for him to say anything. Caroline could see that the old man knew everything, although she was sure that Alex would not have breathed a word to him.

'I'm sorry,' he said again.

Caroline walked home through the park. It was the first day of October and there was a slight chill after the weeks and weeks of intense heat. She shivered and tried to come to terms with the news she had just received.

How could Alex just take off to Peru without even saying goodbye? She had been so looking forward to seeing him again. In fact, she had been *dying* to see him again. It seemed clear, however, that Alex did not feel for her quite so intensely. There was no way that she could have disappeared to the other side of the world for weeks, or even months, without so much as a word. But, of course, Caroline also suspected the truth. Alex knew very well that if they met again, their passion would be irresistible and it was inevitable that their relationship would continue. An impossible situation, he would have thought, while Caroline remained married to Richard.

When Caroline arrived home she was surprised to find her father there. Belinda was busy finishing some paintings and did not want to break for lunch so he had called Richard and asked to come over.

'Where *is* Richard?' asked Caroline, putting down her bag on the table and pouring herself a glass of water. She still felt quite faint.

'Oh, he said he was glad that I was coming over as he had to go over early to his boss's house. And I could keep you company for lunch.'

'Thanks,' said Caroline. 'Yes, I think he did mention something about having to prep Tazz for his trip to Delhi tomorrow.'

'Well, it's always a pleasure for me to keep my beautiful daughter company,' said Graham.

'Oh Dad,' said Caroline, fighting hard not to cry. 'You are much too nice to me.'

'No more than you deserve,' said Graham warmly.

They made drinks and sat in the garden quite silently, Caroline staring down into her glass and Graham picking at the cobwebs that laced the ivy-covered fence.

After a while, Graham got up to refill his glass and when he returned, he sat down closer to Caroline. 'It was a difficult decision,' he said.

'What?' asked Caroline, looking rather startled.

'I've given it a lot of thought since I stopped working,' said Graham. 'In fact, for some strange reason, I've found it hard to think of much else.'

'What?'

'Oh, you know – running off with your mother, the way I did. I suppose I never really came to terms with it in my conscience. While I was working, it was easier to push thoughts to one side but your conscience is a funny thing. It's very patient. It doesn't mind waiting and coming back a long time later to ask the same old questions.'

Caroline nodded. 'So you still worry about it after all these years?'

'Of course,' said Graham. 'Perhaps it was the *right* decision but it was very difficult nonetheless.'

'Tell me about it.'

And, for the first time, Graham opened up and told her the whole story. He told her how terrible it had been. Deborah had begged him to stay – she had pleaded with him to think of the boys. She had pursued him for years trying to make him change his mind, even after Caroline and Sasha had been born. Belinda had become very jealous and it had been difficult keeping in touch with Justin and Sam. The worst part was when Justin was ten years old and asked his dad to stop coming to see them so much; Justin said that it was too upsetting for everyone.

'Of course, if we had not had the children, it would have been much easier,' said Graham.

'I don't know how you did it,' said Caroline.

'Oh, in that sense, it was easy. It may not have been the right decision but it was a *good* decision, I know that.'

'How do you know that?'

'You see,' said Graham. 'I loved your mother – and still do – with all my heart and soul. I had never felt that way about any other woman. I had never really loved Deborah and I knew I could never be happy again without your mother. So I had to follow my heart, no matter how hard it was at the time.'

Caroline put her head in her hands. 'I'm sorry Dad, I don't feel too well,' she said. 'Do you mind if I go to bed?'

By the time Richard got home, it was early evening and Caroline had been in bed most of the afternoon. She could not sleep but, on the other hand, she did not have the energy to be up doing anything. When Richard came into the room, she had her eyes open.

'Sorry about that,' he said, throwing himself onto the bed beside her. 'Are you feeling OK?'

'Fine,' said Caroline. 'Just having a bit of a rest.' She could not help noticing how ebullient her husband seemed and hoped that he would not want to make love to her.

Richard was smiling and looking at her expectantly, waiting for her to ask him his news.

'So, what is it?' she asked. 'You look very pleased with yourself.'

'I've got it,' said Richard.

'Got what?'

'My promotion, of course. Director of Centro Utilities International, Projects Division.'

'Fantastic,' said Caroline, trying to sound genuinely enthused. She knew how much it meant to Richard.

'Yes, it is,' said Richard proudly. 'It means that my

salary will double, that we'll get options in the US company on the Big Board – you know, the New York Stock Exchange.'

'Well done.'

'I know it has been difficult, darling. With me working so hard and everything but now we'll be able to move to a bigger house and—'

'It's great news,' said Caroline.

Richard stroked her hair and Caroline could not help thinking how much she enjoyed him doing that. Then he kissed her gently on the cheek and got up.

'You stay there and have a snooze,' he said. 'And I'll make some supper for us.'

Richard left the room and, as she listened to him clanking noisily about in the kitchen above, Caroline realised that she did still love her husband.

Chapter Thirty-Two

It was about seven o'clock the following morning when Steve took his usual short walk to Highbury and Islington tube station. It was a small detour on his way to work to go past Sasha's house but he liked to do it.

That morning, he stood silently before the huge imposing Victorian property and put his head on one side.

He had to admit that Sasha's life just did not add up. How could she afford to live in this enormous house on her own? Presumably that was how things were before her nephew and niece moved in, he thought.

Although Sasha did not talk about her parents much and had avoided introducing him to them, he knew through Alex that the Roths were not loaded.

He had pressed her over and over again to tell him more about herself and to take him home. He had promised to be on his best behaviour and be very sensitive with the kids but she flatly refused.

And now she was expecting his baby, thought Steve, as he took a deep breath and opened the cast-iron gate. He needed to find out what was going on, what she was trying to hide.

*　　*　　*

Inside the house, Siena had been up for a while. She had a friend who lived in the Barbican close to her school and she liked to go to her friend's house for breakfast, since her mother could never be bothered to get up and see her off.

This was not entirely true, Siena had to admit to herself, but she was still feeling sore about the Latin row. It was unforgivable that her mother should think she had a right to make important decisions for her daughter, who was nearly a *teenager*, she grumbled to herself, as she got up to answer the front door. Particularly given the way her mother ran her own life, thought Siena, as she opened the door and came face to face with a man she had never seen before.

'Is Sasha in?' asked Steve.

Siena nodded and waved Steve into the hall.

She opened her mouth and was about to yell up the stairs when she suddenly changed her mind. 'I think she's asleep,' she said to Steve. 'Do you think she would mind if you went up and disturbed her?'

Steve looked up the dark stairs and thought of his beautiful lover asleep in her bed with their precious child in her womb.

'I'm a close friend,' he said.

'OK,' said Siena. 'Go upstairs. It's the first door on your left.'

Steve crept up the silent stairs, his heart beating fast, and wishing that he had stopped to buy flowers. It would have been romantic to have surprised Sasha with roses.

He tapped gently on the door and turned the handle at the same time. The door swung open to give Steve the shock of his life.

*   *   *

303

'I don't know how she could have been so cruel,' wept Sasha inconsolably. Caroline put her arm around her sister and stroked her head.

'You can't blame Siena,' she said. 'How was she to know what was going on in your bedroom?'

'I know,' sobbed Sasha. 'You're right. I've been so stupid.'

Caroline stood up to make another cup of tea. There was no denying it – her sister had been very stupid indeed.

'The irony is,' continued Sasha, 'that I hardly ever sleep with Max and Brown these days. We'd just stayed up late watching a video on my TV and couldn't be bothered to move.'

'But you were all naked,' said Caroline. 'Which didn't help.'

'I know,' said Sasha. 'But it was a hot night – and, with the baby and everything, I feel much hotter these days. And Max and Brown always sleep naked.'

'What did he say?'

'I can hardly bear to think of it.' Sasha covered her face with her hands. 'He called me all the names under the sun, a whore and a bitch, and he picked up Max's precious birthing chain – you know, the new prototype that he is working on, and I thought for a moment he was going to smash it over my head.'

Caroline felt an embarrassing compulsion to giggle. She turned away from Sasha and looked out of the window at the yard outside.

'He just managed to stop himself and let Max take the chair from him,' continued Sasha. 'He said that, if it were not for the baby, he would have torn my limbs off.'

'Poor you,' said Caroline, going back to her sister and putting her hand on her shoulder.

'It's not as though I've let either of them make love to me, or even get anywhere near me in that sense, for months,' cried Sasha. 'I've never actually been unfaithful to Steve but he'll never believe me.'

'I'm afraid not,' said Caroline.

Sasha looked up pathetically at her older sister. Her tear-stained face was pale, almost grey, and her eyes seemed to appeal to Caroline to do something.

'I'm sorry,' said Caroline. 'I can't think of anything to say or do.'

'If only I'd taken your advice and asked Max and Brown to go. I'm sure they would have done. They might even have been relieved,' moaned Sasha. 'I knew that Steve was the only man I wanted. I really love him and now I've lost him for good.'

'Did you explain about the Meggie business?' asked Caroline.

'There wasn't time. It all happened so quickly. And, well, it wasn't easy to talk – with two naked bystanders looking on.'

'I can imagine,' said Caroline, stifling a most inopportune laugh.

'He slammed the door so hard that one of Mum's huge pictures fell off the wall and I thought the whole house was going to fall down.' Sasha took the mug of tea from Caroline and sipped at it.

Then she stood up suddenly, rushed out of the room and Caroline heard the unmistakable sound of her sister throwing up in the bathroom next door.

Later that afternoon, Caroline picked up Toby from

Sasha's and pushed him around the park in his buggy. Poor Sasha needed a rest and the least Caroline could do was to leave work early and look after Toby for an hour or so.

The park was busy as usual with lots of mums and their kids and a few teenage couples smooching about. Probably bunking off school, Caroline decided.

She had gone over to see Sasha in her lunch break to talk about Alex, to ask her sister's advice, but when she arrived, Caroline had found Sasha in a terrible state. It had been impossible to turn the conversation to Alex and Caroline wondered how her own problems compared with those of her sister. After all, Sasha was pregnant and that made a difference – it was more serious for her to lose Steve than for Caroline to lose Alex. Or so everyone would presume, thought Caroline miserably. Toby had caught sight of the swings and the sandpit and was struggling to get out of his buggy.

'OK, sweetheart,' said Caroline stopping to undo Toby's straps and letting the little boy trot along beside her. Toby was happily oblivious of the cares of both his mother and his aunt. It was a sunny morning and all he wanted to do was to play.

'That's all I want to do,' said Steve as he slid the heavy canvas into the hall. 'Deliver the painting and go.'

Caroline grabbed his arm. 'No, don't rush off. I'd like to talk, Steve, please. Not about Sasha,' she added as Steve jerked himself free of her grasp.

'About Alex?' he asked.

Caroline's eyes filled with tears as she nodded

her head and Steve could not help feeling sorry for her.

'OK,' he said. 'But I'm not sure I can tell you much.'

It was early evening and Richard was unlikely to be home for an hour or two but Caroline did not feel comfortable talking in the house so they walked over to Upper Street and found a bar.

Caroline sipped her beer but Steve upended his and almost downed it in one go.

When he had bought another and they were seated again at a small table in the window, Caroline realised that she did not know what she wanted to talk about, where to begin.

Steve seemed to read her mind and smiled gently. 'You don't have to say anything. I'll tell you all I know.'

Caroline listened silently while Steve explained the agonies that Alex had endured in making his decision to go to Peru.

'He adores you,' said Steve. 'But he feels he can't see you again while you are still with Richard.'

'I wish he'd spoken to me,' said Caroline.

'He wanted to, desperately, but he thought that would only put more pressure on you. He doesn't want you to leave Richard unless that's what you really want to do – quite independently of him.'

Caroline played with her beer bottle. She did want Alex more than anything in the world but, on the other hand, she did still love her husband.

'It's difficult,' said Caroline.

'That's what your sister said,' said Steve. 'But I don't see it that way. I think you know your heart and you

307

have to make a choice, a firm choice. Or else, everyone ends up getting hurt.'

'I suppose so.' Caroline pulled her cardigan close around her shoulders. The bar was filling up but she still felt rather cold.

'Alex called me yesterday from Lima,' said Steve. 'He asked me to bring over the painting for you.'

'He would never show it to me while he was doing it,' said Caroline. Those illicit yet innocent hot summer afternoons seemed an eternity away now, as she stared out into the darkening street.

'He said that it's finished but he hasn't signed it yet,' said Steve. 'He wants you to have it. I think he regrets not letting you see it.'

'Can you give me an address or a telephone number where I can contact him?' asked Caroline.

'Yes,' said Steve. 'But I've promised not to. He doesn't want you to call him – he says that won't help.'

'Please,' pleaded Caroline. 'I need to speak to him – I must.'

'I think that if you really want him, Caroline, you will have to leave Richard and go and find him,' said Steve.

'What? Go to Peru?'

'I'd go to the ends of the earth, if it was that important to me,' said Steve, his face furrowing under the weight of his own thoughts.

'I'm sorry,' said Caroline. 'You must be feeling like shit too.'

'Yeah, the last two days have been really bad,' he said, draining his second bottle of beer.

'She's really sorry,' said Caroline very quietly.

'Don't even talk about it. It's over. I don't even want to hear the excuses. There are no excuses.'

'It may have looked worse than it really was,' said Caroline.

Steve gripped the empty beer bottle so tightly that Caroline was afraid that it might shatter in his hand. 'I've been such a fool – such a deliberately blind fool. I suppose I just wanted her to be different from the other bitches I've seen.' He stared bleakly out of the window and then suddenly turned to look back at Caroline.

'Sorry,' he said. 'I don't mean that *all* women are bitches – it's probably just the ones that I'm attracted to.' He managed a rather grim smile and Caroline finished her beer.

'Thanks,' she said. 'I'd better get home.'

Steve walked her to the corner of Barnsbury Street. 'Take my advice,' he told her as they said goodbye. 'Don't fuck up with Alex. He's the nicest guy on the planet and he worships you.'

Caroline smiled and kissed Steve on the cheek. There were tears in her eyes as she ran down the street.

'What's this? Competition?' asked Belinda as Caroline came into the hall.

'Oh hi, mum,' said Caroline. 'I didn't know you were coming over.'

'I just popped over for a chat, about Sasha and everything. She's in such a state – I've never known her to be so upset about a man before. She usually takes everything in her stride.'

Caroline took off her jacket and squeezed past her mother. 'Come on through to the kitchen,' she said. 'And I'll find you a drink.'

'Aren't you going to show me this first?' asked Belinda, pointing to the huge canvas that stood against the wall wrapped in thick bubble wrap and brown paper. 'It looks a big one. Expensive.'

'It's a gift,' said Caroline. 'From a friend. I haven't even seen it myself yet.'

'Well come on then,' enthused her mother. 'Let's have a look.'

It had not been Caroline's plan to open the painting in front of her mother. In fact, she had been keen to get home quickly so that she could try to hide it away somewhere before Richard got to see it.

'I'd rather not,' said Caroline, blushing a deep scarlet.

'What is it?' asked Belinda, more curious than ever as she noticed Caroline's reaction. 'Who is the artist?'

Caroline shuffled her feet awkwardly and looked down at the floor like a guilty schoolgirl. 'Do you remember the vicar who went on your course?'

'Yes, of course I remember him,' said Belinda. 'Margaret spent a fortune having her bunions done before turning up to some foot-washing ceremony at his church around Easter time. But he wasn't there and she ended up doing the foot washing herself, for some old boy whose feet smelt so much that she was on her inhaler for a month after that.'

Caroline could not help but smile. 'I've been sitting for him,' she said. 'It's a portrait.'

'What?' cried Belinda. 'How wonderful, I love portraits.'

Caroline continued to stare at the floor.

'So why have you come over so coy about it?' asked her mother.

'It's a nude.'

'You sat for the vicar naked?' cried Belinda.

'There's no need to shout about it,' said Caroline defensively.

'But that's fantastic. Margaret would boil you in oil, of course, if she knew. I would never have thought that you, Caroline, would have done such a thing. Well done.'

Caroline blushed deeper still. It felt as though she had just confided to her mother that she had lost her virginity or something. Her mother could be so incredibly patronising and insensitive at times.

'Oh come on,' persisted Belinda. 'Just a teeny-weeny peek.' She was already tearing at the corner of the paper.

'All right,' said Caroline. 'If you must.' Her heart was beating fast as she let her mother strip away the wrappings covering the picture. When it was laid bare, the two women gasped in amazement.

'I have to admit – it's spectacularly good,' said Belinda. 'I'd like to be able to do something as good as that.'

Caroline was speechless. She could not believe that Alex could have painted her like that. Like that.

Before she had time to recover herself, there was a familiar scrabbling at the lock and Richard appeared on the threshold.

At the sight of her husband, Caroline felt near to collapse. Oh my God, she thought, what on earth would Richard say when he saw the picture? He would guess at once what she had been up to. In fact, he would guess at once what she had *not* been up to at all those sittings.

311

'Isn't it fantastic?' cried Belinda.

Richard stood beside the two women and stared at the painting. Then he turned to Caroline and stared at his wife and finally opened his mouth to ask the inevitable question.

'It's the best thing I've ever done,' said Belinda. 'Don't you think, Richard?'

Richard wheeled around and stared at his mother-in-law. 'Y-you did this, Belinda?' he stammered.

'Yes,' said Belinda. 'It's not my usual style, of course. But I wanted to try something different and Caroline kindly agreed to be my model.'

Caroline could hardly believe her ears. Her mother was not patronising and insensitive, she cried to herself, she was brilliant. A genius, a fairy godmother. Caroline resolved never to let a bad word about her mother pass her lips again.

'It's very beautiful,' said Richard, examining the portrait in more detail now. He crouched down to get a better look. 'And an amazingly sweet idea to paint her as though she is about nine months' pregnant.'

'Just wishful thinking on the part of the artist,' said Belinda, darting a look at Caroline.

'And very romantic. The window behind the couch looking out over the domes and spires of Venice, I think,' said Richard, looking more closely.

'A bit of romance always helps,' agreed Belinda.

Caroline sat down on the foot of the stairs and watched her husband and mother admire Alex's painting. She wanted to look again herself but later, on her own, would be better, she thought. She felt numb at the narrow escape she had had from Richard discovering

312

about her and Alex. But why should she care so much, if she really loved Alex more?

'Thank you, Belinda. I take back all the rude comments I've ever made about your work,' said Richard, kissing his mother-in-law warmly. 'We'll put it up in the bedroom and hope it does the trick.'

Caroline smiled weakly back and then, at last, they went off to find a drink.

Chapter Thirty-Three

'She's up in her room,' said Siena when she opened the door to Caroline the following evening. 'I've just put Toby to bed, so don't make too much noise.'

'That was very sweet of you,' said Caroline. 'Helping your mum.'

'Yes,' said Siena, turning away. 'I suppose it's the least I can do, after all the trouble I've caused.'

'It wasn't your fault,' said Caroline as Siena started to cry.

'I know,' sobbed Siena. 'And Mum says she doesn't blame me but she's just so unhappy. I've never seen her so upset – it's scary.'

'I know, I know,' said Caroline, hugging her little niece. 'But she'll be OK. It just takes time to get over these things.' Was that true, she wondered to herself. Would it just take time for her to get over Alex?

Caroline made Siena some hot chocolate and then crept quietly up the dark stairs to see Sasha. She had to weave her way through heaps of bags and boxes at the top of the stairs and stubbed her toe on Max's birthing chair before she got to Sasha's room.

Then she knocked and opened the door in the same

way that Steve had done on that fateful Monday morning.

But, this time, Sasha had no one in bed with her except her Barbie dolls. She had one perched on her knee and seemed to be deep in conversation with it.

'Hi,' said Caroline.

Sasha looked up rather startled as Caroline switched on her bedside light.

'How are you feeling?' she asked.

Sasha flopped back on her pillow and put her arms over her face. 'Worse than ever,' she moaned. 'I had a long talk with Max and Brown last night and they decided that the best thing was for them to move out – whatever happens with Steve. In fact, they were so keen about it that they've gone already, leaving their stuff all over the stairs and everywhere.'

'Well, I suppose that's for the best,' said Caroline. 'I mean, even if you and Steve don't get back together, it would be the same problem if you met some-one else.'

'I'm not going to meet someone else. There isn't another Steve,' said Sasha, rolling over onto her side and burying her face in the pillow. 'I'm going to spend the rest of my life on my own, just me and three children all with different fathers, none of whom live with us. It's too awful.'

Caroline stroked her sister's long tangly blonde curls. 'Have you spoken to Steve?'

'He won't return my calls,' said Sasha. 'I've tried writing a letter but can't find the right things to say.'

'How about – you're sorry and you love him?'

'It's not good enough,' moaned Sasha. 'He thought I was something I wasn't and now he will never love

315

me again. He knows now what I really am: a selfish stupid bitch.'

'Don't,' said Caroline softly. 'You're not as bad as all that. You've brought up two great kids who think the world of you.'

'*Do* they?'

'Yes,' replied Caroline. 'Siena is really sorry.'

'I know, poor darling, I've told her it wasn't her fault but she's still very upset. Do you think she would prefer to go and live with Max and Brown?'

'I doubt it,' said Caroline.

There was silence for a while as Caroline got up and began to tidy the room.

'Why don't you try to get some sleep?' she suggested. 'I'll stay for a bit until Siena is ready for bed. Richard's mum is having supper with us tonight but she likes to eat late.'

'Thanks, Caroline.' Sasha put the Barbies carefully into a box on her bedside table. 'I need a good rest – I haven't slept since Sunday night.'

Caroline got Sasha some water and helped to settle her in bed. It was hard to see Sasha suffer but it helped to distract Caroline from her own problems. She looked at her watch. It was eight o'clock London time and so it must be late afternoon in Lima. Caroline wondered what Alex would be doing. Would he be thinking of her or would he be already so absorbed in the Latin Link project that he had almost forgotten her?

'She's the most important person in your life,' said Jane, as she glanced around the huge and resplendent dining room. She had come down to London to visit an old friend who was ill and had stayed with Richard and Caroline the night before.

Over breakfast, Jane had asked Richard if he could have lunch with her.

'Well,' said Richard, consulting his diary. 'I'm supposed to be having a working lunch with Tazz and Jeremiah—'

'That will just have to wait,' said Jane with surprising authority. 'I'll book a table at the Savoy Grill for one o'clock. Don't be late.'

So Richard cancelled his lunch and met his mother at one o'clock on the dot.

'It's insane that you haven't had time for a holiday this year,' said Jane, when they had finished eating. 'I should have been furious with Archie if he had ever been so inconsiderate.'

It was unusual of Jane to be so critical of her son. As Richard lit a cigarette for himself and one for his mother, he could not help noticing how his mother's confidence seemed to have increased considerably since the death of his father.

'Absolutely Mother,' he said, laughing. 'I can't remember you and Dad arguing about anything. You were always happy to go along with whatever he wanted.'

'Yes,' said Jane. 'But only because he was always such a good man. He did what he wanted but what he *really* wanted was to make me happy. So there were rarely any problems.'

'It's hard sometimes,' said Richard. 'With such a perfect example as you and Dad. I love Caroline with all my heart but, now and then, I can't help wanting her to be exactly the same as you.'

Jane smiled and looked at least ten years younger

than her true age. She put down her cigarette and took a sip of claret. 'She *is* the same as me, Richard,' she said. 'She's a woman.'

Richard smiled at his beautiful mother with great pride but did not register the seriousness of her tone.

'It's funny how the people we love most are the ones we most easily take for granted,' said Jane.

At last, Richard saw what his mother was trying to tell him. He had taken his father for granted and had been filled with grief when he had lost him. Was he about to make a similar mistake with Caroline?

'It's not too late yet,' Jane reassured him. But, in her heart, she was less sure.

Jane Carnforth was a perceptive woman and just in the few hours she had spent with her son and daughter-in-law the evening before, she had noticed that something was dangerously wrong.

A few hours earlier, Caroline had been trying to get hold of Sasha. She had called her sister's number at least ten times but there was no answer. The phone would ring and ring and then switch over to the answerphone. Caroline had left messages, of course, but there had been no reply.

At around twelve thirty, Caroline was feeling nervous and decided to call Toby's nursery to check whether Sasha had dropped him off that morning.

'No,' said Marianne. 'We were expecting Toby in but he's not turned up and Sasha hasn't called.'

Caroline felt her stomach turn. She called Richard but he had already left his office to meet his mother and his mobile was switched off.

Caroline had a key to Sasha's house which she held

tightly in her hand all the way to Highbury in the back of the cab.

Perhaps she should have called the police or an ambulance at once, she thought to herself. But it was ridiculous to panic. There was bound to be a perfectly rational explanation. It was quite in character for Sasha to change her plans suddenly and why shouldn't she keep Toby off nursery for one day? She had probably decided to go shopping or take Toby out somewhere. Caroline tried to calm herself with these thoughts. But she found herself inching further and further to the edge of her seat as the traffic up the City Road crept forward at a snail's pace. It was maddeningly slow and terrifying images of what might have happened to Sasha and to poor dear little Toby flashed through her head like a trailer for a horror movie.

By the time Richard got back to his office, it was late and Tazz was prowling up and down beside his desk.

'Sorry,' said Richard. 'Were you looking for me?'

'What do you think?' grumbled Tazz irritably and stormed off towards his office, waving at Richard to follow him. Richard noticed an urgent message to call Caroline but he would have to deal with Tazz first.

Once they were inside Tazz's little glass capsule of an office, Richard's boss picked up his trumpet and started polishing the brass with his handkerchief.

'This Indian project is really hot,' he said. 'I need someone out there right away.'

'What?' cried Richard. Following his conversation with his mother, he had been hoping to ask Tazz for a couple of weeks' leave.

'I know you've been working hard,' said Tazz. 'But

we're really on a roll with these deals. This would be a great one to get and there's no one else I can send.'

'But—' began Richard.

'It's a real opportunity for you,' continued Tazz. 'Maybe I can even persuade the board to drop the "Projects Division" tag to your new title.'

To be a full main board Director of Centro Utilities International was more than Richard could have dreamt of but he hesitated for a moment.

'How long would I be out there?'

'A couple of weeks at first,' said Tazz. 'But then, if we get through the first round, you'd probably need to be out there for the best part of two months.'

Richard started to shake his head and Tazz peered down the trumpet of his instrument inspecting the effectiveness of his cleaning.

'Of course, you could take your wife out with you for some of the time – if that's what's worrying you.'

Richard thought back to the Lima trip. It had been nice to take Caroline and she seemed to have enjoyed herself but it was fairly pointless. They had hardly spent any time together at all.

'Can't Jeremiah go?' asked Richard.

'Jeremiah?' exploded Tazz. 'That imbecile?' He put his trumpet to his lips and gave it a powerful blast, as if to emphasize his disgust. 'The deal should be put to bed by February at the latest. I promise you – then you can take a good break. Make it up to the little woman in style,' he added laughing.

Richard winced at his boss's patronising tone. Caroline was not a 'little woman', she was his wife and the most important person in the world to him. He left the room as Tazz began to play some scales.

He stormed back to his desk, lit a cigarette and started to rethink what Tazz had said. In theory, of course, his boss was right. If he did just one more deal, his future at Centro would be secure and then he could really make things up to Caroline.

'It'll be too late,' said Jeremiah, as Richard sat down at his desk. 'Give me a tenner now if you want me to get it on the three thirty at Kempton.'

Richard dug around in his pocket and extracted a ten-pound note.

'Don't look so glum, old mate,' said Jeremiah, snatching the money and his jacket and making for the door. 'This one's a dead cert. You can't lose.'

But Richard shook his head as he picked up the phone to call Caroline. He was not so sure at all.

Meanwhile Caroline sat in the hospital waiting room nursing Toby on her knee. Belinda had gone to Sasha's to be at home when Siena got back from school and Graham was on his way to join Caroline at the hospital.

Toby was still sobbing but much more quietly now. He was very hot and rather sweaty. He had been absolutely frantic when Caroline had rescued him from his cot a few hours earlier.

There was another woman in the waiting room who talked to Caroline. Caroline knew that she was just trying to be friendly, just trying to take her mind off things, but Caroline wished she could be quiet and alone.

'Is there a chapel in the hospital?' Caroline asked.

'What?' cried the woman, surprised. 'Are you religious?' She asked the question in the same tone that

321

she might have used had she been asking Caroline whether she had just arrived from Mars.

Caroline shook her head. 'No, I just wanted to go somewhere quiet for a while.'

The woman shuffled in her chair and glared at Caroline. 'I see,' she said. 'I'll just mind my own business then.'

Caroline felt miserable. She had not wanted to offend the woman and the enforced silence that subsequently ensued was almost harder to bear than the incessant chatter.

'We go home now?' asked Toby.

'Soon, darling. Soon,' said Caroline, stroking her nephew's hot head and noticing a few small blisters on his neck. It seemed impossible that anything more could go wrong but she anxiously lifted his vest and discovered that the poor child's body was covered in blisters.

The woman in the room had turned her back on Caroline and was noisily leafing through a copy of *Woman's Own*.

Caroline picked up Toby and went to find a nurse to look at him but, as she opened the waiting-room door, she came face to face with her father.

'What is it?' he cried. 'You look terrible.'

'It's Toby,' said Caroline, suddenly realising that the boy had a raging temperature and trying to remember what the symptoms for meningitis were. 'Look at him.'

Graham inspected the rash. 'Chickenpox,' he said. 'Nothing to worry about there.'

'Are you sure?' asked Caroline.

'Absolutely. Both you and Sasha had it at the same

322

age, just after you'd started at nursery.' He took his grandson from Caroline and held him over his shoulder. 'So did Justin and Sam,' he added.

'Did you speak to the nurses on the way in about Sasha?' asked Caroline.

'Yes,' said Graham. 'No more news, I'm afraid. They still won't let us see her.'

'But they think she's going to be OK?'

'They said you got her here just in the nick of time.'

They sat down and spoke in whispers but Caroline could feel the woman reading the *Woman's Own* straining to catch what they were saying.

'Your poor mother is in a dreadful state,' said Graham. 'She blames herself for not staying with Sasha last night.'

'It was an accident,' said Caroline.

Graham shook his head. 'What happened exactly?' he asked.

Caroline shuddered. 'I can't bear to think of her lying there all that time in agony.'

'Thank God you got there when you did. How did it happen?'

'She said she got up feeling dizzy. She had hardly slept at all and still gets morning sickness. Then she just tripped over Max's birthing chair which he'd left on the landing and she fell down the stairs, impaling herself on one of the chair legs.'

Graham put his arm around Caroline.

'It was horrible,' she said. 'The paramedics had to take the whole chair with her in the ambulance as they were too scared to try pulling the leg out. Poor Sasha was in agony and very scared.'

'How is she now?' Graham asked.

'"Comfortable", they say. The baby is still alive but they're doing a detailed scan later to check whether there are any injuries.' Toby whimpered in Caroline's arms. 'I'd better take him to see a nurse,' she said.

Caroline got up and went to the door again but, this time, she came face to face with her husband.

'Why didn't you call me? Is she OK?' asked Richard, putting his arms around Caroline and Toby.

'Yes, yes,' said Caroline, greatly relieved to feel her husband's embrace. 'It's been a big shock but she's going to be fine.'

'Thank God,' said Richard. 'And the baby?'

'It's too soon to say, but it's still alive.'

'Why didn't you call me?' asked Richard.

'I did,' said Caroline. 'But you were out for lunch and then everything happened so quickly that there wasn't time.'

Richard hugged Caroline tight. 'Oh darling, poor you,' he said. 'It must have been terrifying.'

Graham took Toby from Caroline's arms. 'I'll take him and get something for his temperature.'

'Thanks, Dad,' said Caroline, sitting down.

'And try not to worry,' added Graham.

Richard watched his father-in-law bend over Caroline and whisper something in her ear, which brought a smile briefly to her pale face.

'What is it he whispers in your ear every time he says goodbye?' asked Richard, as Graham and Toby left the room.

'He just says "I love you".'

Richard nodded. Of course, he thought, it was obvious really and he could not help thinking how rarely he said those words to Caroline himself.

Chapter Thirty-Four

Sasha had begged Caroline not to call Steve but what could she do? The child was his too – didn't the man have a right to know about the accident?

The answerphone was on, of course, and although Caroline left a message asking Steve to call her urgently about Sasha, there was unsurprisingly no response. She called again from home that evening and thought about leaving a more detailed message on the answerphone but then decided it would be better to drive over to Steve's house, to Alex's house, and see him face to face.

It was just after nine when Caroline rang on the familiar door. There was no sign of life inside and Caroline was just about to leave when the door suddenly opened. A young girl dressed only in a man's shirt stared at Caroline and then burst into embarrassed giggles.

'Sorry,' she said. 'I thought you were the pizza man.'

'Is Steve in?' Caroline asked hesitantly.

The girl disappeared into the dark interior. Caroline heard her call up the stairs to him.

After a moment or two, she returned and asked who Caroline was, but Caroline was already inside the hall and had switched on the lights. She peered up the stairs and could see Steve's large dark head peering over the banister.

'Oh, it's you, is it?' he said.

'Sorry to disturb you,' said Caroline as the young girl flitted back upstairs.

'There's no point, Caroline. As you can see, there are plenty more fish in the sea.'

'Do you mind if I make a cup of tea while I wait?' asked Caroline. She suddenly felt exhausted.

'OK, go ahead,' sighed Steve. 'I'll be down in a minute.'

Caroline waited on the sofa where Alex had first drawn her. After a minute or two, the doorbell rang and Caroline answered it and paid off the pizza man. She put the pizza box on the only empty chair in the room. Caroline could not help noticing that the house looked distinctly shabbier and untidier since Alex had left.

'Thanks,' said Steve, shifting the pizza onto the floor as he entered the room. He reimbursed Caroline and then sat down. 'Do you want some pizza?' he asked but Caroline shook her head.

'Sasha's in hospital,' she said. 'She fell down the stairs and impaled herself on a chair leg, but they think she's going to be OK.'

Steve dropped the slice of pizza he had just put to his lips and the blood drained out of his face. He leant forward in his chair and stared at Caroline.

'What?' he cried. 'How? When did it happen?'

'This morning. I couldn't get hold of her and had this dreadful premonition that something was badly wrong. When I arrived at her house, she was lying at the bottom of the stairs, cold and almost blue with shock – I thought I was too late. I thought she was dead.' The tears began to pour down Caroline's face as she recalled the incident and Steve knelt beside her and put his arm around her.

'Siena had gone off to school before it happened,' continued Caroline. 'And poor Toby had been in his cot all morning, screaming with fear and hunger.'

'Oh my God,' said Steve. 'Are you sure she's going to be OK?'

Caroline nodded but started crying even harder.

'What about the baby?' Steve asked.

'It's OK,' sobbed Caroline. 'There was a scare this afternoon when she started to bleed. We all thought that she was going to have a miscarriage.'

'Oh my God.'

'But they've managed to stabilise the situation. She's going to have to stay in hospital for some time, but they think the baby will be OK.'

'Oh God,' cried Steve, clasping his hands over his face. 'Why didn't you call me? Why didn't you call me straight away?'

'I tried to,' said Caroline. 'The answerphone was on. I left messages but you never called me back.'

Steve stood up and roared in frustration. He did not notice that the girl in the shirt had entered the room, now fully clothed. She wore a short black skirt and stiletto heels.

'Oh my God, I should have been with her,' he cried. 'To think we nearly lost our baby and all the time I was sh—' He stared at the girl in the short black skirt.

'It wasn't your fault,' said Caroline.

'But I didn't even listen to her,' said Steve. 'I didn't even give her a chance to try to explain.'

The girl in the black skirt glared at Steve. 'What's going on?' she asked.

Steve ignored her. 'It is all my fault,' he said. 'If only I'd called her, agreed to speak with her . . .'

'It was an accident, Steve. It was nobody's fault,' said Caroline.

'Get your things,' said Steve to the girl in the black skirt. 'I'm running you home.' The girl looked confused.

'But, the pizza. I thought we—' she started, but Steve was already on top of her, pushing her towards the door.

'Sorry. Just get your things please. And hurry.'

Then Steve turned to Caroline and took down the details of Sasha's hospital. 'I'll get over there as quickly as I can,' he promised.

Caroline could see the fear and passion in Steve's eyes. 'Good,' she said. 'Thanks.'

When Caroline arrived back home, the house was dark and quiet. Richard had stayed at the hospital with Graham but he had just left a message on the phone to say that he was now on his way back.

Caroline had a short time to read the letter that Steve had stuffed into her hand as she had got into her car.

She switched on a table lamp and climbed into bed. The house was eerily quiet and Caroline realised that she had not heard a sound from her neighbour next door in days. She shivered and pulled up the blankets as she started to read.

The letter was addressed to Steve and was full of

practical instructions about household matters and payments due to people like the local newsagent. Caroline skimmed through all this and got, at last, to the part that Steve had intended her to read.

I have been here for five days now and cannot tell you how many times I have thought of jumping on the bus to the airport. I think about her night and day. I thought that going so far away would help but it only seems to make things worse. Please write and let me know if you have seen her and know how she is. Does she miss me, do you think? Was she upset when she heard that I had gone away – or was she relieved?

Please, please, don't let her get in touch with me. I yearn to hear her voice and see her beautiful face – but I know that, if I hold her in my arms just one more time, I shall never be able to let her go again.

The letter then continued to give more practical instructions, this time with respect to messages that Alex wanted Steve to pass on to his parents and his sister, and there was no further reference to herself.

Caroline read Alex's words over and over again until she knew them almost by heart. Then she quickly folded up the letter and stuffed it into a drawer as she heard her husband let himself into the house.

The following morning Caroline awoke with her mind made up. Richard was still asleep when she got out of bed and made some coffee but he was awake by the time she was ready to leave.

'I'm just going out to do a bit of shopping,' she

said, passing Richard the newspapers that had just been delivered.

'Thanks darling,' said Richard, propping his pillow up behind him in bed so that he could read comfortably. 'Are you sure you're all right?' he added but Caroline had already turned her back on him and run up the stairs.

Steve stood at the foot of Sasha's bed and waited for her to open her eyes. She looked so weak and vulnerable in the crisp white hospital sheets and Steve felt very large and awkward. He held a bunch of white roses – despite everything, he had been unable to buy red ones – and he put them down on the bed.

The movement disturbed Sasha and she opened her eyes and focused on her visitor. As she recognised his face, she opened her eyes wide but quickly turned her head.

Steve sat down heavily on the bed so that it lurched awkwardly to one side and made a terrible noise.

'I'm so sorry,' he said.

Sasha looked back at Steve, her eyes full of tears.

'I'm so sorry,' Steve repeated, taking Sasha's small white hand.

The tears poured down Sasha's face. 'Our baby,' she said. 'I nearly lost our baby.'

'I know,' said Steve, looking down.

Sasha put her hands over her face and sobbed. 'I was so scared.'

Steve glanced around. The ward was full of patients all watching them out of the corners of their eyes but he did not care. He climbed onto the bed beside Sasha and took her in his arms.

'Please don't be too nice to me,' said Sasha, and, at last, she told Steve all about the Meggie story and why she had invented it. 'I've been such an idiot,' she concluded.

'Me too,' said Steve.

'How did you get in?' she asked. 'I'm not supposed to have visitors after seven thirty p.m.'

Steve smiled. 'Partners are an exception.'

'Did you say that you were my partner?' asked Sasha.

'Actually, I said that I was your husband.' Steve glanced around again. 'Something I still hope to be.'

Sasha smiled and the tears flooded down her face.

Steve leaned forward and wiped her eyes. 'Can I kiss you?' he said.

'Yes,' said Caroline as she sat on a bench outside the travel agency. 'I'm sorry to call so early, but please get Johnny to call me as soon as he's up. It's urgent.' Gaby wanted to chat but Caroline could not pay attention to what she was saying. She even forgot to ask after young Felix.

Eventually Gaby said goodbye and Caroline put the phone back in her pocket and stared at the travel agency's door.

Steve's words in the bar the other night echoed in her head – *if you really want him . . . you will have to leave Richard and go and find him* – and also the words in Alex's letter – *if I hold her in my arms just one more time, I shall never be able to let her go.*

But then Richard had been so sweet to her recently. He had been so kind the night before, after Sasha's accident. When he had got home, he could not stop telling her how much he loved her, how sorry he was he had been so distracted at work these past few months. Perhaps Sasha's accident had made him realise how dangerous it is to take things for granted.

But her mind was made up. She needed to see Alex one more time and, at least, have the opportunity to talk things through. She took a deep breath and got to her feet. As she made for the travel agency's door, however, a man ran in front of her and nearly knocked her off her feet.

He turned and Caroline recognised him immediately. 'Richard!' she cried, astonished and embarrassed. What on earth was Richard up to?

'Caroline!' cried Richard in equal surprise. 'What on earth are you doing here?'

Caroline blushed and stammered and eventually made some excuse about 'just having a look at possible holidays for next year.'

'I don't believe it,' said Richard and Caroline felt her heart beating so loudly that she was not surprised her husband was suspicious. 'I had exactly the same thought,' he added. 'But I was thinking of something sooner.'

'What do you mean?' asked Caroline. 'I thought Tazz wants you to do the Indian deal.'

'I've been thinking about it,' said Richard. 'I rang Tazz last night on the way home from the hospital. I told him that you really need a break and that next February will be too late. You need a break now.'

I do, thought Caroline. I do.

'What did he say?' she asked.

'He went ballistic, of course,' said Richard. 'He said that he could not let me take any time off and he would sack me if I didn't do the India deal. But I told him where he and his Indian deal could go, if he would not agree.'

'Really?' said Caroline.

'It's taken a while for me to get my priorities sorted. But, well, I was starting to feel I might lose you – just for some godforsaken sewerage deal.'

Caroline smiled as Richard took her in his arms.

'What did Tazz say?' she asked.

'Well, first of all, he went crazy,' said Richard, looking rather proud of himself. 'But, when he realised I was serious, he backed down almost immediately. I guess I've been letting him bully me around for too long and just needed to stand up to him for once.'

'Well done,' said Caroline, her mind racing as she tried to take in what was happening, how her plans seemed to be collapsing around her.

'I got Tazz to agree a long weekend – this weekend coming. I was going to surprise you with tickets. Do you think Johnny will let you go?'

'I don't know,' said Caroline as her phone suddenly began to ring in her pocket. It was Johnny, of course, whom Caroline had asked to call back urgently.

'Is anything wrong?' asked her boss.

'No, no, nothing,' said Caroline. She hesitated. There was only one excuse she could make for disturbing Johnny on a Saturday morning.

'Richard wants to take me away for a long weekend – next weekend,' she said and Richard listened, smiling broadly. 'Is that OK with you?'

'Fine, fine,' said Johnny. 'So long as you make sure I know what I'm supposed to be doing in your absence.'

'I'll get everything sorted on Monday,' promised Caroline.

'Good,' said Johnny. 'I was worried at first. Gaby said you sounded a bit upset when you rang. I thought you were going to tell me you were eloping to deepest, darkest Peru or something.' Johnny laughed loudly and Caroline pressed her phone hard against her ear so that Richard could not hear his words.

'Come on,' said Richard. 'Let's see what they've got.'

Just a few minutes quicker, thought Caroline. If she had just been a few minutes quicker, she might have had her ticket and been on her way. Was it bad luck, she wondered to herself as she followed her husband into the shop. Or was it the way things were meant to be?

Chapter Thirty-Five

When Caroline arrived at work the following Monday, Johnny was rushing about like a headless chicken.

'Thank God you're here,' he cried, grabbing Caroline and giving her an affectionate hug. 'Vanilla Bernhardt is pulling out of the De Veres bash and the Platts won't come unless she's there and Ken Gilby won't come if the Platts aren't there—'

'OK, OK,' said Caroline. 'Don't panic.'

Johnny shook his head. 'I can't help panicking about it. The whole damn event is beginning to collapse like a row of bloody dominoes. I'm worried that that bastard at Oz has fixed up a spoiler for the same night.' Oz Communications was GLP's biggest competitor and they were bitter rivals. It would be totally in character for Jean Ozwald to try to spoil GLP's bash.

'Diamonds Are A Girl's Best Friend will be the best party of the year,' said Caroline confidently. 'Don't worry about it.'

She picked up the phone and set to work. Johnny, who was usually so laid back, was always twitchy about parties, ever since one occasion when he had booked Jennifer's restaurant in New Bond Street and suffered the ignominy of only eight people turning up.

It was a long time ago but it was the sort of gaffe in the PR business that no one ever forgot or was allowed to forget.

Caroline worked hard all day and went over to Psion House in the afternoon to check the final arrangements for the party the following night. When she got back to her office, there was a big pile of messages which she flicked through quickly. There were three from Richard. She called him back but he said that he had only called to check that she was OK.

'Let's have supper out tonight,' he suggested.

'OK, thanks,' said Caroline. Richard was being so attentive, she thought; she had forgotten how kind he could be. The rest of the week shot by and, before Caroline knew what had happened, it was Thursday night and she was in her room packing. It was six o'clock and Richard was already home and having a quick shower.

Caroline put things into her bag without paying much attention to what she was doing. Richard had wanted Florence but the travel agent had persuaded them to go for Venice.

'More romantic,' he had said with a creepy smile. 'And cheaper,' he had added – most unromantically, thought Caroline.

And so Venice it was. Their flight was early the following morning and they were staying for three nights in one of the city's best hotels, just off St Mark's Square. Caroline knew that she should feel excited but she was so confused that she almost felt numb.

After a while, she abandoned her packing and went to the kitchen in search of a drink. She poured herself a glass of fizzy water and sat drinking it on the sofa in the drawing room without switching on the lights. She stared up at the dark ceiling and occasionally a shaft of light would wind across the room as a car passed down the street outside but, otherwise there was complete silence. Caroline realised that she had not heard a sound from their noisy neighbour in nearly two weeks and she suddenly started to feel worried.

'We'll go and check on her in the morning,' said Richard who had been looking for Caroline and came into the room, switching on all the lights. He had stopped on the way home and bought a bottle of champagne and some smoked salmon.

'I thought I'd make some supper for us – to get the weekend started on the right note,' he said. Caroline got to her feet but Richard signalled to her to stay where she was.

'I'll do it,' he said. 'You just relax. This is your weekend and you deserve to be thoroughly spoilt.'

Caroline smiled. It was nice to have Richard make supper for a change and it reminded her of how things had been when they had first met. He had been so romantic in those days. It was hard to believe, but she had been totally besotted with him then. As besotted as she was with Alex? she found herself asking herself. It seemed such a long time ago that she hardly knew.

When Richard called Caroline for supper, Caroline still looked troubled.

'Don't worry,' Richard said, assuming Caroline was still fretting about the woman next door. 'I'm sure she's fine.'

'I hope so,' said Caroline. After the shock of finding Sasha, she now had a dreadful image of poor Pearl lying dead for days and days in her flat. It was too horrible to think about.

'Have some champagne,' said Richard, passing Caroline a glass.

Caroline smiled and sipped her drink. Richard was really trying so hard that she did not have the heart to argue. She was not very hungry but she put a forkful of scrambled eggs in her mouth and nibbled at her smoked salmon.

The following morning Caroline and Richard overslept. Although Caroline had been awake most of the night, she had finally fallen into a deep sleep in the early hours.

The cab they had booked had already arrived and they quickly dressed and threw their things together.

'If he puts his foot down,' said Richard, bundling his wife out of the door. 'We should just get there in time.'

It was pouring with rain and he could hardly make himself heard with the wind blowing so hard in his face.

Caroline struggled with, as usual, a very large and overfull bag.

'Just get in the cab,' yelled Richard, giving her a hand. 'Heathrow,' he added to the driver. 'As fast as you can.'

Caroline closed her eyes, as they pulled away. She could still do it, she thought. She could make some excuse at the airport and just disappear. By the time Richard realised what had happened, she would be on her way to Peru. It was possible, she thought, looking across at her husband, who was sweeping the rain from his coat and closing the cab window. But could she do it? she wondered, as the thunder rumbled through the dark street outside. Could she really do that to Richard?

She was so absorbed in her thoughts that not until they arrived at Terminal One did Caroline remember they had forgotten to check on Pearl.

Chapter Thirty-Six

Alex sat on the steps of the mission house in the hot Sunday sun. He held in his hand the dog-eared business card that Caroline had once given him. It was the card that Don José had given her months ago when he had approached her in the *barriadas* about buying a young girl's baby.

Caroline had been much affected by her meeting with the young girl and her sisters and baby and Alex had promised to seek them out if he ever went back to Lima.

He sipped his mineral water and watched the busy street. An old woman in a battered trilby was squatting down beside a small child and plaiting the girl's long black hair. The woman, who might have been either her mother or her grandmother, had very dark skin and heavy lines carved around her eyes and mouth. The climate here was unkind to one's skin, thought Alex, as he watched. Everyone looked old and downcast after the age of about twenty-five. He thought about the cosmetic surgeon Caroline had told him about, who had wanted to 'enhance' her breasts. He shook his head. Cosmetic surgeons would have a field day here, he thought – if it were not for the fact that not one of these people had enough money for more than the next meal.

Alex had been working hard since he had arrived in Lima. He had hoped that, if he worked hard enough, he would stop thinking about Caroline. But it was impossible. Everywhere he went in Lima he was reminded of her and those wonderful days they had spent together there. He remembered how carefree and happy they had been, how innocent their relationship had seemed. They had just been friends meeting up in a strange place and exploring the city together. But Alex knew that he had been deceiving himself, even then. If he were honest, he knew that he had fallen in love with Caroline the first time he had met her, that night when she had broken into the church. He had gone to Lima, ostensibly on the painting course and to investigate the Latin Link project but really, of course, in the hope that he would meet up with her and, from that day at Machu Picchu when he had so nearly kissed her, he knew that there would be no turning back. Things had gone too far, even then.

Don José was reluctant at first to take Alex to Dolores but, after some persuasion – both verbal and financial – he led the way. Dolores was still living with her mother and brothers and sisters in the little shack in the *barriadas* and Alex was pleased to see that her son, Diego, was still with her. He was a small and thin baby but he crawled with agility around his mother's feet as she sat cross-legged in the road.

Alex told Dolores about the nursery school that his church was building in the area. It would mean that she would be able to go back to work, that the little ones would be cared for during the day.

Dolores smiled and nodded but her eyes were without hope. '*Gracias, señor,*' she said. She did not say any more but Alex felt he could read her mind.

He shook his head and offered the girl his bottle of mineral water. She was right; one could make things easier, more comfortable, for these people but there was no real solution. Dolores would never escape from the *barriadas*, there was no way out for her now.

Just then, however, Dolores' sisters came running up. They were shouting and laughing and raced to pick up little Diego. The baby shrieked with laughter as his tiny aunt held him high above her head and Alex had never seen a child look happier.

Dolores smiled as she watched the children play. She said something in Spanish to Alex and José translated.

'She say – it was hard for her at first,' he said. 'She see how the others live down in the city, in San Isidro.' The sisters took turns in nursing the precious baby and Dolores watched them with pride and love. 'But those rich people – like your friend who came up here looking for a baby – Dolores say that they are not happier than we are.' José laughed and looked contemptuously at Dolores but Alex smiled at her warmly.

'*Tiene razon,*' he said. She was right. Happiness was an elusive thing, Alex knew well, and had little to do with money.

'You have to make the most of whatever God gives you,' he said to José, who shrugged and translated for Dolores and then sloped away down towards the city.

Alex looked down at the red-brown ground. He had

342

prayed and prayed for strength but he knew he could not continue to hide from her. He would have to go back to London sooner or later and he could not help praying that, when he returned, Caroline would no longer be with Richard. That she might be free for him to have as his own, for him to marry her and to be his forever.

The sun was at his hottest and Dolores' sisters carried Diego up the hill to the chapel to play. It was cooler up there and their friends hung out there at this time of day. Sometimes people from the church brought toys for them to play with and one day someone had brought a big bottle of Coca-Cola.

The children skipped along the road and it was only when they were almost out of sight that Alex and Dolores felt the first *temblor* shudder under their feet.

The view from the window was beautiful. Caroline leant over the balcony and breathed deeply.

'It's like the scene from the window in your mum's picture,' said Richard from within the room.

Caroline straightened up at these words and looked at the view again. Richard was right. It was almost as though she were looking out of the window in Alex's painting. The thought brought a stab of pain and guilt as she saw, in her mind, Alex painting as she lay there for him, naked and happy.

Oh, if only Alex were here with me to share this, she thought to herself. Surely he *should* be here to share this view. Richard had been really sweet all weekend but Caroline still ached to see Alex.

It was six o'clock in the evening and Richard was

lying on the bed reading a book. There was a knock on the door and a waiter appeared carrying a tray.

'I ordered some wine,' said Richard. 'Come and have a drink.'

Caroline went over to the bed and found her own book. She lay down on the bed beside her husband as he poured her a glass of wine.

'It's been a lovely weekend,' said Richard, raising his glass to Caroline and smiling. 'Thank you.'

Caroline had seemed to enjoy herself, he thought, but she had been oddly distant at times. Perhaps, he thought, she was still worrying about Sasha.

'You know, I had myself tested,' he said suddenly, putting down his glass.

'What? What do you mean?' asked Caroline, looking up from her book, somewhat confused.

'I had a sperm count,' explained Richard.

'Really?' said Caroline. 'When?'

'Oh, months ago. I did it privately – I couldn't bear to place myself in the hands of that dreadful Gorgon woman.'

Caroline laughed. She put down her book and picked up her glass. 'I don't blame you. But why didn't you tell me?' She sat up straight and took a sip of wine.

'Well, I was worried about it, at first. There was the mumps thing, of course. I was scared that my sperm weren't up to the job. And then, I hated the thought of doing it – you know, wanking into a bottle in some sordid little hospital room,' said Richard. 'I had to buy one of those porno magazines to help me get going.'

Caroline stared at her husband. 'I can't believe you didn't tell me,' she said.

'I was going to afterwards. But then the test came back good. Apparently my sperm count is fine, and I thought that if I told you that, then you would feel under terrible pressure. That it was all your fault that we couldn't have a baby.'

'Richard,' said Caroline, putting down her glass and propping herself on one elbow beside her husband. 'You are an idiot.'

'Sorry,' said Richard.

'By the way,' continued Caroline, pulling a disapproving face. 'I found that porno mag – in fact, there were two – and they gave me quite a complex. I nearly let Percival give me a boob job.'

'What?' cried Richard, pulling his wife towards him. 'You must be joking. Your breasts are perfect.'

Caroline laughed as Richard stroked her hair. She loved him to stroke her hair and only wished he would do it more often.

Richard was aware that he and Caroline had only made love once over the weekend, on the night they had arrived and in the dark. He had hoped that it would be a romantic weekend but Caroline had seemed preoccupied.

Now Richard pulled her towards him with great desire and kissed her mouth hard. Caroline felt confused and distracted but she let Richard lift her T-shirt over her head and pull down her bra.

Then he climbed on top of her and began to make love to her with a passion and intensity that she had long forgotten.

'*Madre Santissima, protegenos,*' screamed Dolores.

The quake had started with a few mild *temblores*

345

but had built up to a terrifying strength. Women and children were screaming and planks of wood and sheets of corrugated iron crashed to the ground.

'Get down and cover your head,' cried Alex, throwing himself on top of Dolores.

'*Mi bebe, mi pobre bebe*,' cried Dolores as rubble and earth rained down on top of them. Alex spotted a sheet of corrugated iron and dragged himself and Dolores under it.

The earthquake could only have lasted a few minutes but it seemed to go on forever. Dolores was praying and sobbing in Alex's arms and the noise of the whole world shaking itself to the ground around them was deafening.

'I love you,' said Richard as he and Caroline made love. His hands held her body tight and Caroline was gasping for breath as she dug her fingers into Richard's strong hard shoulders. He kissed her everywhere. It was as though he wanted to reclaim every inch of her as his own, to repossess her.

And, suddenly, Caroline realised that she really wanted Richard too. She wanted him very much. As Richard drove deeper and deeper inside her, Caroline felt that she wanted him to make love to her with all his heart and soul. She wanted him to fill her up with his love, fill her so much that there would be no more room for anyone else, even Alex. That he would take away her pain.

She screamed as the earthquake reached its peak and Alex held Dolores' head in his hands. When it was all over, they continued to lie there under the corrugated iron for some time, panting for breath and unable to speak.

'That was fantastic,' said Richard, collapsing to one side of Caroline and smiling at her warmly.

Caroline quickly wriggled under the sheets. She felt strangely exposed, exhausted but elated.

Alex took his hands from Dolores' face. Then he heaved himself and Dolores out from under their shield. They lay together side by side on the ground for a moment, their hearts beating fast, as they recovered from the shock.

'*Gracias*,' said Dolores, sitting up as she watched Alex get slowly to his knees.

They both looked up the hill and saw, to their relief, that the chapel was still standing.

'*Gracias a Dios*,' cried Dolores, getting weakly to her feet and taking a few unsteady steps forward.

'*No. Te quedas aquí*,' said Alex. He told her to stay where she was and to take cover again, if there were any after-shocks. He would go up to the chapel and find the children.

Alex set off up the hill. He was wringing wet with sweat and panting and he took off his jacket and tied it around his waist. People were beginning to emerge from makeshift shelters on all sides. They were weeping and moaning and giving thanks to God that their lives had been spared. Alex could not but admire the faith and dignity of these simple, unprivileged people.

As he reached the top of the hill, Alex saw the children huddled together in a corner of the chapel doorway. The girls crouched like a group of terrified rabbits and the baby howled between one child's legs. They stared at Alex wide-eyed as he approached and then darted inside the chapel and up the main aisle.

'No. Afuera. Afuera,' yelled Alex, chasing after them and calling for them to get outside of the building quickly.

But it was too late. He was hardly more than a few steps from them when the second quake came. It was nothing like as strong as the first had been but it came fast and the chapel had already been shaken to its foundations. With this further onslaught, it only took seconds for the roof to come crashing down.

Dolores watched from the bottom of the hill. The chapel seemed to sway back and forth in slow motion and then crumpled into a huge cloud of rubble. It would have been almost beautiful to watch, she thought, if she had not known that the children were inside.

'Madre Santissima,' Dolores cried and ran screaming up the hill. The earth was still shaking and she stumbled as she went but she ran on. Her feet were cut to shreds by the time she arrived at the great burial site. There were others at her side as Dolores began to pull the rubble apart, piece by piece. There was a horrible dirge of wailing and groaning as many lay trapped, buried alive. And her little son and sisters too, thought Dolores, as she and the others tore at the rubble with their bare, bleeding hands.

Richard ran a bath for Caroline and gently massaged her neck as she lay in the soapy water and closed her eyes. The soft pummelling movement of Richàrd's fingers was helping her relax, at last, and Caroline felt all the tension of the last few days slowly release itself. For once, she was not thinking about Alex but about her father. She was thinking back to the time she had had lunch with him and he had told her about her ancestor who had almost been buried alive. That was exactly how she had been feeling, she thought. It had been as though someone had buried her alive, since Alex had left, and now, at last, she felt that she was coming up for air. She scarcely noticed the tears that poured down her face.

But Richard noticed, of course. He knew that something had happened to Caroline, something serious, and he did not want to ask what it was. He continued to massage her gently and watch her cry. Whatever it was, he hoped that she was through it now, that the crisis had passed. He knew that he had come close to losing her but now he felt she was back and he might just have a chance.

The rescue work at the chapel continued all through the afternoon. Dolores was exhausted but she refused to take a break. She felt that she could hear her baby crying for her beneath the bricks and stones and she would not rest until she held him again in her arms, dead or alive.

Caroline and Richard had a good dinner and Caroline was feeling almost happy when she got into bed. After Richard switched out the light she began to collect her thoughts. She lay still in the darkness, feeling torn and confused. She needed to decide what to do and could think of nothing better than to pray for help. She prayed that God would give her a sign, that something would happen that would show her clearly what was the right thing to do.

Chapter Thirty-Seven

The following morning Caroline could hardly believe her eyes. She stared, in horror, at the front page of *Il Mondo*.

40,000 MORTI – TERREMOTO A LIMA – Migliaia sepolti mentre i morte raggiungono 40,000

Her Italian was not good but there was no mistaking what had happened in Lima the previous day. Caroline put down her coffee and struggled to interpret the report. She had prayed for a sign but surely not this, she thought to herself.

Much of the city, it seemed, was in ruins and the poorer districts had been hit the hardest.

'Bad news for Tazz's water project,' said Richard, glancing over her shoulder, and then he looked up sharply as a waiter crossed the breakfast room and whispered something in his ear.

It was Tazz, of course, and Caroline was relieved that Richard was forced to get up and take the call in the lobby outside. She was almost shaking with shock at the news.

She wondered who she might call, who would know whether Alex was safe. The waiter returned with a basket of fresh bread but Caroline was not hungry. She got to her feet and ran up to her room.

Lines to London were busy but eventually she got through to Steve at his office.

'I've called the mission,' said Steve. 'I'm afraid they don't know what's happened to him. No one has seen him since yesterday morning, three hours before the quake started.'

'Oh my God,' cried Caroline, collapsing onto the bed. 'But he's missing?' she whispered. 'He's not confirmed dead?'

'No, I don't think so,' said Steve. 'It's very hard to get information. Everyone seems in such a state out there.'

'Do you think we should go out there? I mean, I could easily take some time off work?' Caroline was suddenly angry with herself for having been so pathetic. Alex had virtually asked her to go out and join him and she had wanted to follow him but somehow things seemed to have conspired to hold her back.

'I spoke to his parents last night,' said Steve. 'They're flying out to Lima this morning. With a bit of luck, we'll get better information through them.'

'Oh Steve,' said Caroline bursting into tears. 'Why didn't I go? If only I'd gone out there, I'm sure this would never have happened.'

'Try not to think the worst yet,' said Steve.

But Caroline was cold with fear as she put down the phone.

She had been torn as to whether she should go out to see Alex and now, through her indecisiveness, this terrible thing had happened and taken the decision out of her hands. Absurd though it undoubtedly was, she could not help feeling in some way culpable.

Caroline thought back over the last few days and how she had wrestled with her conscience. She knew that she had begun to wonder whether Alex's departure might have been for the best. Richard had become so much more attentive and was clearly trying very hard. He was a good husband and she did still love him. If he had not been working so hard all the time, perhaps she might never have fallen in love with Alex in the first place.

If she was honest, Caroline had to admit she had almost persuaded herself that she would get over Alex in time. But now she hardly knew what to think.

Richard took a cab from the airport straight into work and Caroline took the tube up to King's Cross and a cab home from there.

When she arrived, she was surprised to see a man standing on Pearl's doorstep. Caroline paid off her cab driver and was in a hurry to get inside and be alone to think for a while.

Nonetheless, she could not help recognising the man who stood at her neighbour's front door. Caroline was then amazed to see the door open and Pearl greet the eminent cosmetic surgeon with a very familiar hug and kiss.

'Laurence,' cried Caroline. 'What on earth—'

Laurence turned around and his face went blood-red when he saw Caroline.

'Do you two know each other?' asked Pearl.

Caroline nodded. 'We've worked together for years. I've known Laurence and Ana—' Caroline checked herself quickly. 'I mean, yes, Laurence and I go back a long way.'

'Pearl and I have been seeing each other for some time now,' said Laurence. 'It started when I was treating her face.'

'You've done a fantastic job,' said Caroline looking at her neighbour who smiled confidently and looked happier than Caroline had ever seen her.

'The surgery was great,' said Pearl. 'But, I think, it was finding Laurence after so many months of solitude and loneliness that really made the difference.'

'For me too,' said Laurence. 'I'm afraid things between me and Anabel had broken down some time ago.'

Caroline said nothing.

'She has a bad drinking problem, as you probably know. I tried sending her to all the best drying out clinics but nothing seemed to work. I don't think she really wanted to get better. I decided I had to make a break and take my chance for happiness when I met Pearl.'

Caroline nodded and smiled. 'I'm glad for both of you,' she said. 'Not least because it may mean a permanent end to all that dirge-like music Pearl used to play every night.'

Pearl laughed. 'I can't quite break with Leonard Cohen but I have chucked away my whole Grateful Dead collection.'

'Richard will be delighted,' said Caroline.

Pearl slipped her hand through Laurence's arm and pulled him inside her house.

Caroline went inside her own house and called Steve. But there was no news.

Caroline rang Steve every few hours for the following two days but still no one could confirm whether

Alex was dead or alive. It was agony waiting and Caroline was only glad that things were busy at work.

That Wednesday she was working on a big party for the London Contemporary Dance Company to be held in the evening at the Tower of London. Caroline had to go over and check that all was well.

There was, of course, the usual last-minute chaos. The party organisers had misinterpreted a handwritten fax someone had sent.

'I couldn't work out whether it said "Don't forget the *drinks* or the *crisps*,"' said a painfully thin young girl in pink stilettos. 'I showed it to Celine and she said it couldn't possibly be either of those things. Of course, she said, we wouldn't forget the drinks and there was no way that any of Celine Dior's clients would ever ask for *crisps*. She said it just had to be *chimps*.'

Caroline disentangled a small primate from her leg. '*Clips*,' she said. 'Remember. We were going to show *clips* of some of the dance company's recent performances.'

'Oh, yes. Sorry,' said the girl in the pink stilettos, as she trotted behind Caroline, very ineffectively trying to help round up the chimps who were clambering, dribbling and worse in every direction.

It was a complete nightmare but Caroline could not help being charmed by the cuteness and cheekiness of the monkeys' antics. After all, they were only like little children, she said, and so they decided to let one chimpanzee stay and sit with the guests on the top table.

'If he behaves himself,' she said to the chimpanzee keeper who had agreed to stay on and supervise.

By five in the afternoon there was reasonable order at last but Caroline was exhausted.

'Can I buy you a drink?' asked her father, calling on her mobile.

'Lunch, maybe,' said Caroline. 'I haven't stopped all day.'

So they met in the basement cafe of a bookshop nearby.

'You look really tired, darling,' said Graham, who usually never failed to tell her how beautiful she looked.

Caroline slumped down into the red metal chair.

'You look as though you've been up all night at a party,' said her father.

'A chimpanzees' tea party,' said Caroline. 'Believe me, it's worse.'

After she had told her father about that afternoon's farcical events, they both laughed and then fell silent.

'I hope you're not still worrying about Sasha,' said Graham. 'She's really feeling much better now and this chap Steve has been very good to her.'

'He's a nice man,' said Caroline.

Graham got up and bought some sandwiches and fizzy water. When he got back to the table, Caroline was holding her head in her hands.

'I've finished my genealogy thing,' he said as he unloaded the tray and sat down again.

Caroline looked up with bleary but dry eyes.

'We can trace our family right back to William the Conqueror,' added Graham proudly.

'Great,' said Caroline. 'Well done.'

She picked up the sandwich, took a tiny nibble and then slumped back in her chair.

'Why don't you tell me what's wrong?' asked Graham, touching Caroline's hand.

'I can't,' said Caroline miserably. 'I can't really talk about it with anyone.'

'Is it Richard?' asked Graham.

Caroline shook her head. 'Sort of,' she said. 'He's such a good husband. He's being so nice to me at the moment and I do love him so much.'

'Is that a problem?'

'No. I don't know,' said Caroline. 'If I'd never met Alex . . .' Just saying his name out loud made Caroline feel guilty so she said nothing more.

'That's how it was with me when I met your mother,' said Graham. 'It took courage to do what I had to do.'

Caroline pushed the plate of sandwiches away from her.

'I've always felt guilty,' said Graham, 'as you know. But the scare over Sasha seemed to help me sort things out in my head and I feel much happier now. It made me realise how precious and precarious life is.'

Caroline nodded her head. She was too miserable to speak.

'I had a big talk with your mother last night,' said Graham. 'I think it was the first time I've ever put my foot down on anything important.'

Caroline listened and Graham continued.

'I told her that I was going to start seeing more of Justin and Sam and their families again. I said I hoped that she would support my decision but, if she didn't, that was just too bad – I was going to do it anyway.'

'What did Mum say?' asked Caroline, looking up rather surprised. 'She must have been livid.'

'She was taken aback, at first,' said Graham breaking open a packet of tuna and cucumber sandwiches. 'But she knew I meant it, that it was really important to me, and so she didn't argue. She was silent for a while and I thought she was going to explode but then she just smiled and gave me a hug. In fact, I think she was even a bit relieved. She said she was fed up with me looking so down in the mouth.'

'Good,' said Caroline. 'That's great news.' She glanced around the room. It was mostly full of rather worthy-looking fiftysomethings, sipping water and reading mind-improving books.

'You don't get many chances at happiness,' said Graham, taking his daughter's hand. 'You have to run to catch hold of them, sometimes.'

'That's what everyone keeps telling me,' said Caroline.

Caroline and Graham finished their lunch and walked to the tube station together. As they went down the stairs, a woman was struggling with a buggy. Graham helped her with it and then went back to his daughter.

'At least you don't have children to consider,' he said.

'I suppose so,' said Caroline, as Graham fumbled in his pockets for some change for the ticket machine. 'I know I would never be able to leave my children.'

Graham shook his head. 'It was hard but I didn't love Deborah any more,' he said. 'There was only room for your mother.'

Caroline smiled and kissed her father goodbye. I only wish it were that simple for me, she said to herself.

She loved Alex passionately, desperately, but she had never stopped loving her husband too. She loved

Richard in a deep, different way but, all the same, it was a love that could not easily be cast aside.

When Caroline got home that evening, she was surprised to find Sasha, Steve, Siena, Toby and Richard all waiting for her.

'Surprise!' said Sasha.

'What's going on?' asked Caroline, as Richard put a glass of champagne in her hand. 'Is it my birthday or something?'

'No, it's mine,' said Siena. 'I'm thirteen – an official teenager and I am about to disengage you as my godmother since you have clearly forgotten my birthday.'

'Oh Siena, I'm sorry,' said Caroline.

'Don't worry about her,' laughed Sasha. 'She's quite spoilt enough as it is.'

Siena pulled a face at her mother but Sasha continued. 'Richard suggested that we come round here to celebrate.'

'Yes, it's really a triple celebration, said Richard.

'Why? What else are we celebrating?' asked Caroline.

'Well, first, Sasha's release from hospital today with all now looking good for the baby.'

'Yes,' said Caroline, hugging her sister. 'That really is the best news.'

'And, secondly,' continued Richard, 'my boss, Tazz, was dismissed today. His boss in the US found out about the backhanders he'd been paying out to win contracts and sent him home. They're carrying out a full inquiry but I don't think we'll see Tazz and his dreaded trumpet again.'

'Well, that really is something to celebrate,' said Caroline.

'Yes,' said Richard. 'And, to top it all, it looks as though I may be given Tazz's job. Managing Director, Centro Utilities International.'

'That's fantastic, Richard,' said Caroline, feeling genuinely delighted for her husband who hugged her and kissed her. Richard had worked so hard, he really did deserve to be rewarded. She could not help feeling very proud of him.

It was true that Richard had become obsessed with his work and this had pulled them apart, thought Caroline, but she also wondered whether she was not equally to blame. Perhaps she had been so obsessed about getting pregnant that this too had created a barrier between them, a barrier that it had taken Alex to break down for them.

Pizza arrived at the door and they all sat down and ate. Then Steve produced a huge chocolate birthday cake for Siena and so it was not long before Toby was violently sick. Sasha, who was lying on the sofa, was still under orders to keep her feet up so Richard volunteered to take Toby downstairs to the bathroom and clean him up.

It was only then that Caroline got the chance to ask Steve about Alex.

'No,' said Steve. 'His parents are still out there but there's no news. He's still missing.'

Caroline sighed and said no more.

'We'd better be going,' said Steve, when Richard and Toby came back into the room. 'We didn't bring the car, so I'll just call for a cab.'

As Steve went over to the phone, Richard suddenly remembered something.

'Oh Caroline,' he said. 'I almost forgot to tell you

– there was an odd call for you, just before you got home.'

Caroline looked up. 'Who was it?' she asked.

'It was a Spanish woman,' said Richard. 'She could only speak Spanish but she had a woman with her who spoke a bit of English. She said they would call again.'

'What was her name?' asked Caroline.

'I didn't quite catch it, I'm afraid,' said Richard. 'But it began with a D.'

'Dolores,' said Caroline to herself. It had to be Dolores.

Steve glanced at Caroline but said nothing.

'I think we should get him home to bed,' he said to Sasha, as he picked up Toby and tucked him inside his jacket.

Caroline sat quietly while Richard called for a cab. Why was Dolores calling her all the way from Lima? What did she know about Alex and how on earth had she got Caroline's telephone number?

Chapter Thirty-Eight

LORD OF THE DANCE. Johnny was delighted with the headline on the media pages of the *Guardian*. The party at the Tower had been a tremendous success.

He passed the paper to Caroline who read it and smiled.

'Well done,' he said. 'GLP's got some really good press out of this one. And that chimp idea was sheer genius.'

'Thanks,' said Caroline.

Johnny beamed at his colleague. Caroline was brilliant, he thought to himself, the perfect combination of initiative and good sense.

'How's the fashion show coming along?' he asked, perching himself on the corner of her desk and leafing through a magazine.

'It's fine,' said Caroline. Johnny had decided to repeat the Mile High Fashion Show which had worked so well the year before. They were still chartering their own VC10 but this time, at Caroline's suggestion, they were doing the show on the ground in Nairobi rather than in the air. The event had been rechristened The Down to Earth Fashion Show and Caroline felt much happier about it.

'I'm so glad to have you back,' said Johnny. 'You really make things happen, Caroline.'

'Do I?' asked Caroline. She shook her head. 'There was a time when I thought I could make anything happen, if I really wanted it enough. I remember telling you once that I didn't believe in destiny, but I'm not so sure I was right.'

'Well,' laughed Johnny. 'There's no evidence here that you can't perform miracles. In fact, I *rely* on you performing miracles.'

Caroline smiled and pushed Johnny off her desk.

It was the end of the day and the end of the week. Caroline took the tube to the Angel and walked up Upper Street. She turned into Barnsbury Street and swooshed along through the thick layer of fallen leaves that covered the pavement. She had hardly noticed autumn arrive and now it was nearly over. There was a cool breeze and she hurried home.

It was over a week since Dolores had tried calling her but there had not been a word since. At first, Caroline had been frightened to leave the house in case she missed the call and her heart had leapt every time Richard picked up the phone.

But, as luck would have it, the call came one evening, just the moment she had stepped into the bath. Richard was still at work and Caroline ran, naked and dripping wet, into her bedroom to pick up the phone before it switched to the answer machine.

'*Doña Carolina?*' The line was good and Caroline could hear perfectly.

'*Si, si. Dolores?*' she replied.

She listened as Dolores said something in Spanish and passed the phone to someone else.

'Good afternoon,' said a woman's voice.

'Good afternoon,' said Caroline, grabbing the duvet off the bed to wrap around herself and sitting down.

'I call for Dolores.' The woman went on to identify herself as Sister Rosita, one of the nuns working on the Latin Link project. 'I have news of Señor Alex,' she continued.

Caroline moved to the edge of the bed. 'Yes, yes,' she said. 'What news?'

'First, I tell you that Señor Alex – he did not die in the *terremoto*.'

'He's not dead? Oh, good, good,' cried Caroline almost bursting into tears. 'Thank God.'

'*Si, Gracias a Dios*,' echoed Sister Rosita.

'But what happened? Where is he and why didn't he tell anyone he was safe?' asked Caroline.

'Señor Alex is a brave man,' said Rosita. 'He saved the life of Dolores' baby and her sisters.'

'What?' asked Caroline. She could hear Dolores saying something to Rosita in Spanish.

'Dolores wants me to tell you what happened,' said the nun.

'Yes. Tell me, please.'

'The children were in the chapel on the hill. The second big *temblor* came and Señor Alex managed to throw them all under the altar, before the roof fell in. It was a big marble altar and was the only thing that remained standing after the *temblor*. They were all trapped there in the dark for nearly twenty four hours before they were rescued.'

'How dreadful. But were they OK? Were they all all right?' asked Caroline.

'They were all all right, *Gracias a Dios*. Nothing more

than little cuts and – what's the word? – brūises but they were very scared,' said Rosita 'And very weak.'

'Oh, poor things, it must have been terrifying for them,' said Caroline.

'*Fue un milagro.*' Caroline heard Dolores' voice again.

'Dolores says it was a *milagro* that they were saved. How do you say that – a miracle?' asked Rosita.

'A miracle,' confirmed Caroline.

'Yes. Señor Alex – he crawled out from under the altar carrying the baby in his coat. He gave Dolores the baby wrapped in the coat and then he disappeared. She says that he refused to go to the hospital but he was hardly walking,' said Rosita.

'Oh my God,' said Caroline.

'Dolores found your number in the pocket of his coat. It was written on a little matchbox with a lion on it. It said Caroline and she brought it to me and begged me to call you.'

The matchbox she had given Alex all that time ago, thought Caroline. He still carried it with him.

'Señor Alex is your husband?' asked Rosita.

'No,' said Caroline. 'He's not my husband. Just a friend, a dear friend.'

'We have not seen Señor Alex since that day,' said Rosita. 'But Dolores wanted to say thank you.'

'Please, Sister Rosita, thank you for calling. And, please, if you find Alex, ask him to call home. Tell him to come home.'

'I will do that,' said Rosita. 'I will tell him La Carolina says come home.'

'Yes,' said Caroline. 'Thank you.'

'*Y gracias a usted,*' came Dolores' voice. '*Gracias a su amigo.*'

'Dolores says thank you and thank you to your friend,' said Rosita. 'We must say goodbye now. Goodbye and God bless you.'

Caroline said goodbye and put down the phone. The duvet was soaking wet and she was a shivering a bit but, in her heart, she was elated. Alex was not dead – he was alive, she told herself. Thank God. Almost to convince herself it was really true, she said the words out loud.

'Alex is alive. Alex is alive.' She cried the words over and over again, still trying to believe the good news, but quickly she checked herself as she heard Richard's key in the lock of the front door.

It was another week before there was any further news. Belinda and Graham were having supper at Sasha's house to celebrate Sasha and Steve's formal engagement when the call came.

'Mrs Howard?' said Steve and waved at the others to be quiet.

They all watched Steve as he strained to take in every word that Alex's mother said. He said little himself, just the occasional yes or no.

'What did she say? What did she say?' cried Sasha, as soon as Steve put down the phone.

For the first time Steve smiled and, when he smiled, the smile spread right across his big, warm face as he beamed with joy and relief. 'They've found him at last. He's coming home.'

'What? How, where?' asked Sasha.

'His mother says he took off to some remote part of

366

the jungle for a few days,' said Steve. 'He wanted to get right away to be on his own and think.'

'Why didn't he tell anyone where he was going?' asked Graham.

'Oh, that's just the way Alex is,' said Steve. 'He would never have dreamt that anyone might have been worried about his safety.'

'Children can be so thoughtless,' said Belinda.

'He had been back in Lima for a couple of days,' continued Steve, 'before the Howards found him. He was hanging out in some place called the Barranco or something, living like a tramp with a bunch of artist friends.'

'How romantic,' said Belinda.

'Yes, I remember Caroline telling me about that place,' said Sasha. 'She said it was beautiful – that she had spent a lot of time there.'

'Well,' said Steve. 'He's decided to come home. He's got a few things to tie up at the mission but he should be back within a week or two.'

'That's wonderful news,' said Sasha.

'Let's hope so,' said Graham quietly. He was thinking back to his recent conversation with Caroline and wondering what his daughter would do.

Caroline burst straight into the house, raced to the bathroom and was violently sick. It was the third time it had happened that week and, as she squatted on the cold white tiles, she was suddenly struck by a terrible thought.

It was ages since she had bothered counting the days on the calendar like a little child waiting for Christmas Day, but now she rushed to her desk and picked up her diary. Flicking through the pages, she remembered that her last period had started just after she got home from church that dreadful Sunday morning. The morning she had learnt that Alex had gone off to Peru.

Her heart beating fast, she counted up the days and then counted them again. She could hardly believe it. It was forty days. She had not had a period for forty days. She was over ten days late.

Caroline sat down on the bed and clasped the diary to her face. 'I can't believe it, I can't believe it,' she cried. 'Not now, surely not now.' She stood up and put her coat back on. As she did so, the coat brushed heavily against her breasts and she realised how sore and sensitive they felt. She looked at her watch. It was ten to six. The chemist would be closed in a few minutes and then she would have to wait until the morning to find out.

She ran down Barnsbury Street towards the chemist on the corner of Islington Park Street and Upper Street. Her mind was racing. Supposing she *was* pregnant, was that good news or bad? She so wanted a baby but this had to be Richard's baby and did that, as her father had said, make it more difficult to decide what to do? Or did it make it easier?

When she arrived panting at the chemist's door, the lights were switched off and there was a large CLOSED sign hanging up. Caroline threw herself at the door in despair and was surprised to find that it swung open.

She stumbled into the dark shop and was greeted by the same assistant as usual, the over-familiar woman who was once again wearing her discman headphones. 'Sorry, luvvie, we're closed,' she said cheerfully.

Caroline went further into the shop. 'Oh please,' she said. 'I'm desperate.'

The assistant looked at her and raised a well-tweezed eyebrow. 'What is it you want?' she said in her penetrating voice.

Although there was no one else in the shop this time, Caroline still felt embarrassed.

'I'm sorry,' she said. 'It's for my sister. I promised I'd pick up a pregnancy test for her. She'll be very disappointed if—'

'For your sister,' said the woman very loudly and raised her eyebrow even further. She clearly did not believe Caroline's story. 'Oh, for goodness' sake,' the assistant cried, glancing up at the door. 'Now we've got the whole world coming in.'

She stomped round to the front of the counter and Caroline turned to see the man who had just come in.

It was gloomy in the shop but there was still no mistaking his identity.

'Have I caught you breaking and entering again?' he smiled.

'Alex!' she cried.

Alex came up to her and stood in front of her, just looking at her without saying a word, the way he always did.

The assistant bolted the door behind Alex, sighed and went back to the counter.

'Here you are then,' she said slamming a pregnancy testing kit into Caroline's hand. 'That will be nine pounds ninety-nine,' she added. 'But I've closed the till, so I can't give you any change.'

Caroline fumbled in her pocket and produced a ten-pound note. 'Thanks,' she said.

'And, as for you,' said the assistant. 'You're too late. You're not having anything.'

Alex shook his head. 'Don't worry,' he said. 'I've got what I came in for.'

He took Caroline by the arm as the assistant let them out of the shop. Caroline was still clutching the pregnancy kit and tried to stuff it quickly into her pocket but Alex had already seen it.

'Congratulations,' he said.

'Oh Alex, Alex, why did you go?' asked Caroline.

Alex held Caroline's face in his hands and stared deep into her eyes. 'I had to. I'm sorry.'

'Oh Alex, I've missed you so much,' said Caroline. 'I was so worried—' But she said no more as Alex had her in his arms and was kissing her face with more love and tenderness than she could bear.

They stumbled across the street and into Canonbury Square and continued to kiss and hold each other there.

After a time, the woman from the chemist walked by. She sniffed and stared at them. 'Are you two still at it?' she cried loudly. 'Can't you wait until you get home?'

Alex and Caroline sprang apart for a moment and watched her march away.

'Steve's selling the house,' said Alex. 'I'm staying with my sister for a bit and then going back out to Peru.'

He took Caroline in his arms again and there were tears in his eyes as he spoke. 'I had to come back and see you one more time. I didn't want you to think that I had any regrets about the time we had together.'

'We still can spend time together,' said Caroline. 'Can't we?'

'No,' said Alex. 'I think we both know it would be impossible.'

'The painting is beautiful,' said Caroline.

'*You* are beautiful,' he said, holding her head close against his chest. 'I'm glad you like the painting. I didn't sign it. I didn't think I could or should – but it has a title. I called it "Madonna" and that seems appropriate now.'

'Madonna,' repeated Caroline. 'Oh Alex, Alex, it's not too late. I haven't even taken the test yet.'

Alex looked into Caroline's face again and smiled sadly. 'I think you have,' he said.

Caroline's eyes filled with tears and the two of them kissed again. When Alex, at last, took his lips away Caroline could not bear the thought that she might never feel their touch again. She watched him turn and walk across the square, through the heavy sea of leaves and out of the gate.

She wanted to run after him but her legs would not move. She just sank to the bench and wept.

It was some time before she felt a light touch on her shoulder. She looked up and a man was smiling down at her.

'Sorry, love,' he said. 'I've come to lock up the square.'

Caroline got to her feet and slowly made her way home. Her face was smudged with the kissing and crying and she knew she must look a mess but she did not care.

As soon as she got home, she went straight to the bathroom and did the test. It was simple to do and she had done similar tests before. It only took a couple of minutes for the little stick to show its result.

While she waited, Caroline took the stick into her bedroom and sat down in front of the picture that Alex had painted, the picture that now hung at the foot of her bed.

She looked at the painting of her big swollen belly and glanced down as the first thin blue line started to appear. The word Madonna, Alex's name for the painting, echoed in her head and she suddenly remembered the dream she had had, almost a year ago, that night in Mombasa.

It had been a powerful and erotic dream and she remembered that the man who had made love to her, who had caressed her great, pregnant belly, had said just that: Madonna. She closed her eyes and saw the man again. He kissed her again and held her as though she was the most precious thing in the world and suddenly she realised that he was Alex. Alex had made love to her in her dream, before she had even met him.

When she opened her eyes, a second thin blue line had appeared. She was pregnant.

Caroline got to her feet and, with tears in her eyes, picked up the phone and dialled a familiar number. 'Richard,' she sobbed. 'I have to tell you something.'

'You sound in a state, sweetheart,' he said. 'Are you OK?'

'No, really, I'm fine. It's just that I have some news.'

'What? What's happened? Good news or bad?'

Caroline looked at the little blue lines and smiled through her tears.

'Good,' she said. 'Very good.'

* * *

It was fifteen months later that Caroline and Richard found themselves once again on a flight down to Peru.

This time Caroline sat breastfeeding her son, Archie, almost all the way.

'It's the only way to keep him quiet,' said Richard, noticing a young woman across the aisle staring at Caroline.

Caroline looked up and smiled. She did not ask the young woman whether she had children herself. There was no need.

'He's very beautiful,' said the woman.

'Yes, thank you,' said Caroline. 'He is.' She detached Archie from her breast and put him across her shoulder to wind him after his feed. He was just old enough to clasp his chubby hands around her neck and stroke her hair.

'Do you want me to take him for a bit?' asked Richard.

Caroline shook her head. 'No,' she laughed. 'As you know, I could happily sit and cuddle him all day but, if you really want a turn, I don't mind sharing him.' She passed Archie across to Richard and watched as her husband proudly took his son in his arms and stroked the baby's head.

He really was a beautiful baby and Caroline could not quite believe how fortunate she was to have him, having waited so long and having almost convinced herself that she would never have a child. It still seemed a miracle.

She had been anxious throughout the whole of her pregnancy that something might go wrong and when eventually the nurse laid the wet wriggly little infant on her tummy, she had cried as though her heart would break.

Archie was perfect and Caroline was happier than she had ever dared imagine she might be. But, perhaps, the greatest joy of all in having dear Archie, thought Caroline as she watched Richard tickle the baby's tiny pink feet, was the difference it had made to her husband. Caroline felt that she must have been blind not to have seen how much Richard had wanted a child too and how difficult it must have been for him to hold back from saying so.

Having Archie had brought her and Richard back together again and they had never been more happy. The love that she had worried was growing old and tired had rekindled to the strength and warmth that she remembered from the days when they had first met. In fact, looking across at Richard as he phlegmatically mopped up the vomit that Archie had just spurted all over his new Hermes tie she knew that she loved her husband more than she had ever done before.

Nonetheless, as the seat belt sign ping-pinged the passengers to attention and the plane bounced jauntily down to earth, Caroline still felt a slight shiver of anticipation at the thought of seeing Alex again.

The church was packed. Caroline and Richard did not recognise a single face but then suddenly Caroline felt a touch on her shoulder and, when she turned, she came face to face with David Homer.

'I've come to take the service – it will be a mix of Common Prayer Book and Catholic Mass, I'm afraid,' said David, smiling warmly and kindly into Caroline's face. 'But I'll do most of it in Spanish and English, so you should be able to follow what's going on,' he added.

Caroline and Richard sat down at the back of the church. Archie had most opportunely fallen asleep in his buggy but Caroline wanted to be in a position to take him out quickly if he woke up and started making a noise. They were sitting behind a pillar, so she had to crane her neck to see to the front and it took a while for her to recognise him from behind. She could not help being reminded of the morning she had first gone to see him at the church in Highbury. She felt almost as sick with apprehension as she had done then.

Alex was standing in the front pew facing the altar. His figure still made the tall, slim silhouette that she remembered so well and then Caroline saw him turn and smile, that same deep, warm, beautiful smile. But this time he was not smiling at her, he was smiling at his beautiful bride who had just entered the church.

The organ started to play the opening hymn and Caroline and the rest of the congregation rose and turned to see Dolores glide ceremoniously down the aisle. She was accompanied by her proud tearful mother and followed by her three sisters, who smiled and skipped behind her, delighting in their beautiful white bridesmaid dresses and blue satin ribbons. A few steps behind toddled a little boy in navy shorts and a white shirt. He was about two, thought Caroline, and just had to be Dolores' son Diego, the baby she had cradled in her arms the afternoon she had first spent in Lima, all that time ago.

Of course, Alex had written to Caroline some time

before to tell her about him and Dolores. It had come as a bit of a shock, at first, but Alex told her how much Dolores had helped him and Rosita get the nursery school project up and running and how deep and inspiring her faith in God was. He felt that his relationship with Dolores had been strangely predestined.

Caroline was pleased that Alex had found happiness but she could not stop her eyes from filling with tears as she watched him take Dolores' arm and whisper something in her ear. Dolores smiled and the joy in the young girl's face was overwhelming.

There was a hush as the ceremony started.

'Dearly beloved,' began David and Caroline jumped as she felt Richard softly slip his hand around her waist. They listened as Alex made his vows first in Spanish and then in English and as Dolores made hers, just in Spanish, but in a surprisingly strong and confident voice. The couple exchanged rings. There was a moment's silence and then David looked out sternly across the congregation and, as he spoke the next words, his gaze perhaps rested for a fraction of a second longer than necessary on Caroline's face.

'Those whom God hath joined together,' he cried, 'let no man put asunder.'

The words echoed around the church and Caroline felt Richard squeeze her a little closer towards him. She swallowed back her tears and turned and smiled at her husband.

'Weddings always make me cry,' she said, smudging mascara from her eyes. 'Do I look a mess?'

'You look beautiful – more beautiful even than on your own wedding day,' said Richard.

'You may now kiss the bride,' announced David.

Richard held Caroline close.

'I love you,' said Caroline.

And, as the bride and groom kissed at the front of the church, a couple behind a pillar at the back of the church also kissed – as though it were also the happiest day of their lives.